Questions bombarded him.

Questions about the bank robbery and questions about his attraction to a woman with a baby.

He'd sworn off putting his heart on the line. He'd had his shot at a family and happily-ever-after and it had been snatched from him when his wife had died in childbirth.

So why couldn't he get the pretty mother out of his mind?

Tossing aside the covers, he padded to the window that overlooked the lake. Peering across, he could see Maggie's house lit up like a Christmas tree.

Realization hit him.

She was all alone and scared. And with the threat the robber had left ringing in the air, she would be jumping at every creak and moan of the house.

Without a second's hesitation, he picked up his phone and dialed her cell phone. She might be afraid of the phone ringing at this time of night, but his number and name were programmed in her phone. Once she saw it was him, she would be all right.

LYNETTE EASON

and

New York Times Bestselling Author

SHIRLEE McCOY

danger
in the
shadows

Previously published as *Danger on the Mountain* and
Stranger in the Shadows

LOVE INSPIRED
INSPIRATIONAL ROMANCE

LOVE INSPIRED®
INSPIRATIONAL ROMANCE

Recycling programs
for this product may
not exist in your area.

ISBN-13: 978-1-335-46776-8

Danger in the Shadows

Copyright © 2021 by Harlequin Books S.A.

Danger on the Mountain
First published in 2012. This edition published in 2021.
Copyright © 2012 by Lynette Eason

Stranger in the Shadows
First published in 2007. This edition published in 2021.
Copyright © 2007 by Shirlee McCoy

This edition published by arrangement with Harlequin Books S.A.

For questions and comments about the quality of this book, please contact us
at CustomerService@Harlequin.com.

Love Inspired
22 Adelaide St. West, 40th Floor
Toronto, Ontario M5H 4E3, Canada
www.Harlequin.com

Printed in U.S.A.

CONTENTS

DANGER ON THE MOUNTAIN

Lynette Eason

To my Lord and Savior, who lets me do what I do. I love You, Jesus!

You are my hiding place; you will protect me from trouble and surround me with songs of deliverance.
—*Psalms 32:7*

Chapter One

Deputy Reese Kirkpatrick stiffened when he felt something hard jam into his lower back. He started to turn when a voice whispered in his ear, "Get on the floor or the baby's mama gets a bullet."

Stiffening, his adrenaline in sudden overdrive, Reese looked around and saw a young woman with a baby in a carrier standing in front of the teller's window. As his adrenaline spiked, details came into focus. The teller's nameplate said Lori Anglero. The woman with the baby had soft blond hair that fell to her shoulders in pretty waves. The man behind him had bad breath and needed a shower.

Reese's time as a cop on the streets of Washington, D.C., now served him well. He didn't even blink. "You think this is going to work for you?"

"Yep. You're the only man in here. I don't need you having a hero complex because I'm trying to do this without killing anyone. But I will if I have to. On the floor. Now."

The door chimed one more time, and Reese caught sight

of two more masked men entering the First National Bank of Rose Mountain.

"Everybody down! Now!" The man behind Reese gave him a hard shove.

Reese dropped, grateful he wasn't wearing his uniform and that the gun hidden under his coat in the small of his back had gone undiscovered.

Screams echoed and Reese saw the woman in front of Lori's window drop down to become a human shield for the baby.

"Down! Down!" The man who'd taken Reese by surprise aimed his gun and pulled the trigger.

The bullet slammed into the wall above Maggie Bennett's head. With a scream, she tightened her protective stance over her eight-month-old daughter's carrier.

Terror spiraling through her, Maggie whipped her head to the left to see three gunmen in black masks. One stood by the door, his broad shoulders and tight grip on the pistol in his left hand saying he'd be a force to reckon with. Another, tall and lanky, hovered in a threatening stance over the man on the floor. The third held his weapon in a way that said he knew how to use it—and would. The tall, skinny one with his weapon trained on the man on the floor grunted, "Charlie, get the cash."

Charlie leaped over the counter. As he did, his foot caught the nearest silver pole holding the red velvet ropes used to separate customers into lines. The pole crashed to the tile floor with a loud clang, and Maggie cringed. Charlie cursed, regained his footing and pointed the gun in bank teller's terrified face. "You deaf? I said get down!"

The teller dropped.

So did Ashley O'Neal, the other teller who'd been so friendly to Maggie last Sunday at church.

At three o'clock on a Monday afternoon, Maggie and the man now on the floor were the only customers in the bank. She watched his hand angling under his heavy suede jacket.

What was he doing?

Her eyes darted from robber to robber, to the door then back to the man on the floor.

There was no security guard and no help in sight.

The broad-shouldered one who stood by the door appeared to be in charge. He jutted his chin toward the man on the floor. "Cover him, Slim. He looks like he might be thinking he wants to put up a fight."

Still hunched over Belle's carrier, Maggie felt strangled by her fear and she wasn't sure what to do. She was frozen in place, watching the incidents playing out before her as though they were on a big screen and she was in the audience.

But she wasn't. This was real. And it was happening to her.

Her first reaction was to look for a way to protect Isabella. Her second to silently screech out a desperate prayer as she slumped to the floor next to the fallen pole, keeping herself between the men and her baby. Her foot became entangled in the rope now snaking the floor, but she ignored it. Her only thought was to keep her cool and survive. Old instincts surfaced, and a chill that matched the November air outside the bank swept through her.

As her eyes jumped from one robber to the next, she let her gaze land on the other bank customer. He lay still, left hand away from his side, right still hidden by his jacket. His sharp green eyes took in the unfolding scene. Maggie could see the tension in his shoulders and face and prayed he didn't do something stupid, like try to be a hero.

He'd get them all killed.

"You!" Charlie yelled at the teller who'd been helping Maggie. "Stand up!"

The woman obeyed, tears tracking her cheeks, hands raised as she backed up away from her station. "D-don't shoot me. Take what you want."

Slim continued to hold his gun on the man on the floor while Charlie threw a large bag at Maggie's teller. "Load it up. Now."

The woman caught it, fumbled it, shot a terrified glance at the man, then went to work. Even from her spot at the last teller station next to the wall, Maggie could see the woman's hands shaking.

"Hurry up!" The lookout man next to the door shifted, the chink in his calm demeanor grabbing Maggie's attention. So he wasn't as cool about this as he'd first appeared.

Charlie shot him an aggravated look, his eyes piercing and hard behind his mask. "Just watch the street."

Then he turned back to jab the teller with his weapon. "Move! Move! This ain't a tea party!"

Lori's hands shook so hard Maggie was afraid she'd drop the cash and the man would shoot her. She almost offered to help but bit her tongue. As long as Lori was getting the money in the bag, Maggie would stay quiet and keep her body covering Belle's. She darted a glance in the direction of the offices. One door was closed. The bank manager in hiding?

She prayed that no one else would walk in and this would all be over in a few seconds. Dark spots danced before her eyes, and she realized that she was holding her breath. She gasped in air. The dancing spots disappeared, but Belle started to cry. Maggie froze.

The lookout lifted his gun and pointed it at her. "Shut the kid up."

Immediately, Maggie knelt and unbuckled Belle from her car seat. Picking her up, she settled the baby against her and turned her back to everything going on. Belle sniffed and lay her head on Maggie's shoulder, thankfully content to be out of the carrier and to suck on the pacifier Maggie shoved in her mouth.

Maggie glanced over her shoulder as Charlie hauled himself back on the other side of the counter and held up the bag. "Got it!" His gaze landed on Maggie and she stilled, not liking the look in his eyes.

Slim spoke. "Get the other drawer."

"We don't have time for that, Slim," the lookout protested. So maybe Slim was the one in charge?

Charlie ignored his partner and slung the bag back at the teller who moved to the next drawer.

Sirens sounded and the three masked men exchanged a glance. Slim growled, "Who tripped the alarm? Who?"

The robber nearest the door immediately turned and disappeared through it.

Maggie saw the well-built customer on the floor clench his jaw even as he slowly moved his hand back under his jacket.

The door burst back open. "The cops are almost here! I got the car! Let's get this done!"

Slim looked up and his gaze slammed into Maggie's. "Get over here."

She froze once again, arms gripping Isabella too tight. The baby hollered her displeasure, and Maggie shushed her even as her eyes met the narrowed brown ones of the man who'd ordered her to move.

"My name's Reese Kirkpatrick. I'm a cop. You've got what you want, you'd better leave while you can."

Maggie jerked her gaze to the man on the floor. He'd been silent throughout the whole ordeal. Silent and watchful. Slim raised his gun and brought it crashing down toward Reese's head. Reese rolled. Slim missed and stumbled, his finger jerking the trigger. The weapon bucked in his hand, the bullet shattered the tile floor beside Reese's left leg.

Reese now had a weapon pulled and aimed at Slim. Without a word, he pulled the trigger.

Slim screamed and jerked as his gun tumbled to the floor.

Charlie whirled and dropped the bag of money as he moved toward his wounded partner. He lifted his weapon, aiming toward Reese who was now moving across the floor toward Slim. Charlie's left leg stepped in the midst of the red velvet ropes.

Without thinking of the possible consequences, Maggie jerked on the rope.

Charlie went down hard, the back of his head cracking against the floor. Reese lunged for Slim and snagged the mask. It came off and Slim howled his outrage even as he landed a lucky blow with his good hand to Reese's solar plexis.

Reese grunted and stumbled back, gagging. Slim looked like he might go after Reese again, but the screaming sirens outside seemed to change his mind and with a final glance at the unconscious Charlie, and a hard glare at Reese, he backed toward the door, hand held tight against the wound in his shoulder. "I'll kill you for this!" His gaze landed on Maggie and she flinched when he said, "Her and the kid, too!"

Reese finally got his feet under him, snatched the weapon from the unconscious man on the floor, then stumbled after the wounded robber. But by the time he hit the door, the man was in the car. The door slammed shut halfway down the block.

Reese whirled back into the bank and checked to make sure Charlie was still out cold.

He was.

Next he checked on the woman with the baby. She sat on

the floor, eyes dry, jiggling her infant in her lap. He noticed the ringless left hand. And wondered why he would notice such a thing at a time like this.

"Are you all right?"

She lifted soul-deep dark brown eyes to his and the fear in them felt like a sucker punch to his midsection. Her low "Yes" vibrated through him. Then she drew in a deep breath and a tinge of color returned to her pale cheeks. "Yes, we're all right. Thank you." Then the baby turned her attention to him, spit out the pacifier, stuck a finger in her mouth and grinned around it.

This time it was a blow to his kidneys.

He nodded and turned, hoping his desperate need to get away from them didn't show on his face. He forced his mind to the matter at hand. Thank goodness she'd kept her cool over the last few minutes. If she'd been the hysterical type, they might all be dead. His ringing ears testified to just how close the gun had been to his head when it went off. He just hoped the ringing wasn't permanent.

"Is it over?" One of the bank tellers—the one named Lori—peered over the edge of the counter, mascara streaking her cheeks.

Grateful for the interruption—and the fact that he heard her, Reese nodded. "All except for the cleanup."

More tears leaked from her eyes and he saw her lips move in a grateful, whispered prayer.

Rose Mountain Police cruisers pulled in. Eli Brody, sheriff of Rose Mountain, bolted from the first one like he'd been shot from a cannon. The man strode toward him and Reese quickly filled him in. Eli snapped orders into his radio and two cruisers immediately headed out after the escaping getaway car. He then marched toward the other two officers, leaving Reese to question the tellers.

"Thank you."

The quiet words captured his attention and he turned to see the woman with the baby gazing up at him. Clearing his throat, Reese said, "You're welcome."

"I'm Maggie Bennett." She shifted and before Reese could gracefully slip away, she blurted out, "Was he serious? Do you think he'll come back and—" She bit off the last part of the sentence, but the fear lingered and he knew exactly what she was asking.

Reese shook his head. "I don't think you have anything to worry about. All those guys care about is getting away."

Doubt narrowed her eyes. "But we made him really mad. And you have one of his partners in custody because I interfered. We saw his face. You honestly don't think they'll be a tad upset about that?"

So she had spunk and she wasn't comforted because he told her what she wanted to hear. She wanted the truth, no matter what. He liked that.

He said, "All good points. The fact is, I don't know. We'll take precautions, get his picture from the bank camera and distribute it around the town. But as for whether he would really come back here…" He shrugged. "I'm sorry, I can't tell you."

"No, you can't." A sigh slipped out and she placed a kiss on the baby's forehead.

A baby girl with big brown eyes like her mama.

A knife through his heart wouldn't be any more painful. He had to get away. He'd come to Rose Mountain to escape memories of a wife and baby who were no more. Grief was sharp. Growing up in foster families, all he'd ever dreamed of was having a family of his own. And he'd had that for a while. Until they'd died.

"What's your baby's name?" He couldn't help asking.

"Isabella. But I call her Belle."

She said the name with such love that his heart spasmed once again. "That's a pretty name."

Her face softened as she looked at the baby in her arms. "Thanks. It was my mother's."

Was. Past tense. Her mother was dead. He recognized the pain in her eyes. The same pain he saw when he thought about his own mother who'd died when he was nine. Clearing his throat, he asked, "Do you need to call someone? A husband or...?"

"No, no one." A different sort of pain flashed in her eyes for a brief moment and Reese wondered what that story was. Then he blinked and told himself it wasn't his business.

A bank robbery was.

She was saying, "You said you were a cop. I don't remember seeing you around here before."

"It's my first week." He shook his head. "I just moved here from Washington, D.C. One of Eli's deputies quit, he needed another one and asked me if I'd take the job." He lifted his shoulders in a slight shrug. "Eli caught me at the right time. I was ready for a change." Eli said he'd seen something in Reese that had been familiar, something Eli had experienced only a few years before. Burnout.

A weariness of the soul. And grief.

And why was he sharing this with her? There was something about the way she looked at him. As though she really cared about what he had to say.

"Maggie, are you all right?"

Reese snapped his head around, and Maggie's gaze followed his to see Eli bearing down on them. The man's thunderous expression said the bank robbers had escaped.

Maggie nodded. She'd met Eli her first day in town. His wife, Holly, owned the Candy Caper shop on Main Street and when Maggie had stopped in for a bite to eat, Eli had been having lunch with Holly. They'd asked her what she was doing in town, and she'd told them she was looking for her grandfather's old cabin. They'd helped her move in, and they'd been friends ever since.

"I'm fine," she said. "Shaken, but fine."

"I see you've met Reese."

"Yes." She tried to smile. "He saved the day, I do believe."

Eli lifted a brow. "Oh?"

Reese shifted, the flush on his face revealing that he wasn't comfortable with the praise. "Just doing my job."

"Not even on the clock yet and already a hero, huh?"

"All right, that's enough," Reese said, his mild tone not hiding his embarrassment. "Maggie's the one who kept me from getting shot."

At Eli's raised brow, Maggie shook her head and refused to let Reese turn the attention back on her. However, she let him off the hook as she shifted Belle to her other hip. She couldn't help shivering as she remembered the look in the one robber's eyes. "He was going to make me go with him," she whispered.

"What?" Eli demanded.

She nodded. "If Reese hadn't intervened, the robber would have taken me and Belle with him."

Eli snapped a look at Reese. "That true?"

"It sure looked that way."

Eli's frown deepened. "Robbing a bank is serious business, but they were willing to add kidnapping, hostage taking, to it?"

"They were." Reese's nose flared. "And not only that, but one of them threatened Maggie and her baby—and me—as he escaped."

Now Eli's brow lifted and he reached up a hand to stroke his jaw. "Do you feel threatened?"

Reese looked at Maggie. "I'm not worried for myself, but I think you should make sure you have extra patrols around Maggie's place."

So he was worried about her.

Eli nodded. "I can do that, but she's pretty isolated out there on the lake."

"The lake?" Reese asked. "Which one?"

"Rose Petal Lake. Not too far from your place, I don't think."

Maggie spoke up. "I'm staying in my grandfather's old house. I'm trying to decide if I want to stay there permanently or get something here in town."

"Maggie teaches school," Eli said.

"Which one?" Reese asked.

"It's an online academy," Maggie said as Belle leaned over, trying to wriggle free of the arms that held her. Maggie expertly kept the baby from tumbling backward and said, "I teach fifth grade. It allows me to earn a living and keep Belle with me." And allowed her to try to figure out if she'd ever return home. She stiffened her spine. No, that house had never been home.

For the past six months, Rose Mountain had been home.

And she didn't see that changing in the near future.

Eli scratched the back of his head, and Maggie felt Reese's gaze on her and Belle. And it unnerved her that every time his eyes landed on Belle, he looked away. In fact, other than asking her name, he hadn't acknowledged her presence. Did he not like babies? Children? Disappointment shot through her.

Squelching the unexpected feeling, she hugged Belle closer and said, "I've got to get her home for a nap. She's going to start getting cranky if I don't."

Eli nodded, placed the strap attached to his camera around his neck and said, "I just finished a weeklong crime scene processing training class last month." His lips quirked. "Thought I should update my skills just in case, but the whole time I kept wondering why I was there." He looked around and shook his head. "Guess now I know."

Maggie had lived in Rose Mountain long enough to realize that small town law enforcement officials often had to take care of the forensics side of things. If the nature of the crime warranted a higher level of expertise than the local sheriff, he had to call someone from a bigger city. Eli said, "You'll need to see the psychologist about the shooting and file a report."

Reese grimaced. "I know."

Eli nodded. "Why don't you see the ladies home, and I'll finish up here."

"Uh...yeah, sure."

He looked caught, trapped with no way out. She frowned. What was his problem?

Then he smiled and she wondered if she'd imagined the whole expression. She settled Belle back into her car seat carrier and he led her to the door. Stepping outside, she breathed in the fresh fall air, grateful to be alive.

"Which one is your car?" he asked.

"The blue Ford pickup." He looked surprised, and she laughed. "Didn't expect me drive a truck, did you?"

"No, I was looking for a minivan or something."

Maggie clucked her tongue. "Shame on you. Stereotyping?"

He grinned, and she felt that tug of attraction she'd been hoping she wouldn't feel again. The last thing she or Belle needed—or wanted—was a man in their lives. His eyes held hers a bit longer than necessary. She looked away as he said, "Yes, I guess so. Sorry."

Maggie settled Belle into the back of the king cab and opened the driver's-side door. Climbing in, she noticed Reese watching. He gave her a nod and let her lead the way. Pulling out of the bank, she turned right onto Main Street. As she drove, she listened to Belle chattering in the backseat. At least she hadn't suffered as a result of their scary adventure this morning.

Soon, she'd have to feed the baby her afternoon bottle or her sweet chatter would turn to demanding howls.

Maggie headed up the mountain, the short mile to her home seemed to take forever. Pulling into the gravel drive, she cut the engine and waited for Reese to drive up beside her.

He climbed out and looked around. He pointed. "See that house just across the lake?"

"The one with the white wraparound porch?"

"Yeah. That one's mine."

"It's beautiful. I noticed it the day I moved in." Maggie pulled the carrier with the sleeping Belle from the backseat with a grunt. She slid the handle onto her arm up to the crook of her elbow. "She gets heavier every day, it seems like."

He shut the door for her and asked, "Where's Belle's father?"

"Dead." She heard the matter-of-fact tone in her voice.

When she turned, surprise glistened in his eyes. "I'm sorry," he said.

"I am, too. Sorry he's dead, not sorry he's out of my life."

Chapter Two

The woman just kept surprising him. The gentle, mommy demeanor hid a spine of steel. Also evidenced by her cool-under-fire reaction at the bank earlier.

Opening the door, she led the way inside, holding the carrier in front of her. "I'm surprised she's still sleeping." She set the baby carrier on the kitchen table and opened the refrigerator to pull out a bottle filled with milk.

"Why aren't you sorry he's out of your life?"

While Maggie placed the bottle in a pot of water she began heating on the stove, she kept her back to him. He wanted to turn her around so he could see her face. When she didn't answer, he leaned against the counter and crossed his arms, wondering why he was asking questions that were none of his business.

At first he thought she was going to pretend she hadn't heard him, but when she turned, she said, "I shouldn't have said that."

Reese lifted a brow at her.

She shrugged and grimaced. "He wasn't a very nice person."

He'd abused her. She didn't say so, but she didn't have to.

His gut tightened as visions of women he'd pulled out of domestic violence situations crowded his mind. Their bruises, their damaged faces, bodies…souls. The ones who had died. He blinked the images away and focused on Maggie.

"When did he die?"

"About a month after Belle was born."

"Car accident?"

Maggie sighed. "Not exactly."

She didn't want to tell him?

Belle woke suddenly and let out a howl. Reese flinched and watched Maggie calmly unbuckle her daughter from the car seat and pick her up. She then pulled the bottle from the heated water, tested the temperature of the milk on her wrist and stuck it in the squalling mouth.

The silence was sudden.

"You're good at that."

Maggie laughed. "I've had a lot of practice."

As the baby ate, Reese took in his surroundings. "Nice place."

She looked up from Belle's face to smile at him. "I like it. It's simple, functional and pretty much everything Belle and I need."

He nodded. "You said you were an online teacher."

"I am. I teach learning disabled students online. It's perfect for us. I get to make a living and Belle gets to stay home with me. So far so good."

"What about when you have to teach and Belle doesn't want to cooperate with your schedule?"

Maggie grinned. "I have a neighbor who comes over. Mrs. Adler. She's a retired nurse and lives twelve hours away from her grandchildren. She loves Belle and acts as if every moment she gets to spend with her is the highlight of her day."

A shadow moved across the window right in his line of sight. He straightened and narrowed his eyes. She caught his expression and frowned. "What is it?"

"Probably nothing," he said. "Just thought I saw something move outside of your window." He walked over to it and, out of habit, stood to the side, keeping himself from being a target should someone other than a friend be out there. The blinds were open, the sun high in the sky.

What had he seen?

Anything at all?

Or was he still jumpy from this morning? He saw Maggie settle into the rocking recliner next to the couch, Belle's small hands clasped firmly on the bottle she eagerly devoured. In his mind's eye, he replaced the scene with one containing Keira and his own baby girl. But that wasn't to be. Sorrow clamped hard on his heart, and he had to make a supreme effort to shut the feeling down.

He was in Rose Mountain, making a new start. There was no place for sorrow or sad memories. Two things he'd been desperate to get away from back in Washington. "I'm going to check outside around your property."

Her frown deepened. "You think someone is really out there?"

"I don't know, but it won't hurt to check."

Worry creased her forehead as her eyes followed him out the door.

Once outside, he stood still, taking in the sights and sounds he'd become familiar with in such a short time. Nothing seemed out of place. Nothing set off his internal alarm bells.

He made his way over to the window in the den. The open floor plan had allowed him to be standing in the kitchen, looking into the den. If he'd kept his eyes on Maggie and her daughter, he'd never have seen the shadow.

If that's what he'd seen.

Circling the perimeter of Maggie's house, he kept an eye on the area around him and on the ground in front of him.

With Thanksgiving just around the corner, the air had a bite to it. He shivered, wishing he'd grabbed his coat on the way out. The hard, cold ground held no trace of any footprints. No evidence at all that anyone had been in front of the window.

Then what had caught his attention? Anything? Or was he so on edge that he was now seeing things?

He frowned, shook his head and walked back into the house to find Maggie still holding Belle. The baby swiveled her gaze to him and he swallowed hard when she grinned. Two little white front teeth sparkled at him.

Maggie asked, "Did you find anything?"

"No. It was probably just nerves left over from this morning."

She shot him a doubting look. Fear flickered in her eyes before she turned back to Belle, who'd finished her bottle. Maggie settled the baby into a sitting position and started a rhythmic patting on the small back. Her actions were automatic, but her eyes said her thoughts were on their conversation. She asked, "You think it could be the man who said he'd kill us?"

Did he? "I think that guy's long gone."

Maggie bit her lip and he wondered if she believed him. And he couldn't blame her. He wasn't sure he believed it himself. She sighed. "So what's next?"

"We'll question the robber in custody, see if he'll talk for a deal."

Maggie shuddered. "Did you see his face? His eyes? They

were hard. Empty. I don't think he'll be talking any time soon."

"Don't be so sure." He glanced again at Belle who stood on Maggie's thighs, holding on to her mama's hands. Reese averted his gaze. "I'm going to head back to the station and see if he's said anything."

"All right." Maggie stood and shifted Belle to her hip. "She's got a nap to take, and I've got an afternoon class to teach." She paused. "Will you keep me updated on what happens? I'm still a little nervous about that threat."

He smiled, hoping to reassure her. "Sure thing."

Maggie walked him to the door and locked it behind him. Then she walked into Belle's room and placed the sleepy baby in the crib. Even though Belle had fallen asleep for a short time on the ride home from the bank, she needed a real nap or by the evening, she'd be so cranky Maggie wouldn't know what to do with her.

Belle protested for a while, but she finally fell quiet, her cries fading as she slipped into sleep.

Maggie smiled. It had been so hard to learn to let the baby cry, but once she'd tamped down her instinct to hold Belle every time it was naptime, they were both a lot happier. Belle slept better, and Maggie was able to get a few things done.

Like teach her online class. She still had about ten minutes before she had to sign in. Mrs. Adler should be arriving soon. The woman lived just a few houses up from Maggie and often walked over to be there in case Belle woke up while Maggie was in the middle of a class. Maggie paid her a weekly wage, and Mrs. Adler was thrilled to be making money and honing her grandmother skills.

With Reese's dominating presence gone, she now felt an absence she'd never noticed in the small house before. What shocked her was her lack of nervousness when he was around. She'd actually let him in the house. The fact that he was a cop helped. She felt safe with him in a way she didn't feel with other men who were not in law enforcement. Officers had helped her when she needed it most. Like Felicia Moss, the officer who'd listened to Maggie's story and then taught her how to hide once she escaped from Kent.

All that knowledge, and she hadn't needed it. Kent had been killed before she could put into practice everything she'd learned.

Gulping, she pushed aside the memories and booted up the computer. Signing in, she greeted the students already in the room and got started.

Forty-five minutes later, she signed off, thanked God once again for the ability to work from home and got up to check on Belle. Sleeping soundly.

Mrs. Adler had slipped in and was sitting in the recliner reading a book. "Hello there."

The woman set the book in her lap and looked up to smile at Maggie. "Hi. Belle's sleeping away, and I'm enjoying a good book. How'd your class go?"

"Great. I only had three show up today, and we had a fascinating discussion about right angles."

Mrs. Adler grimaced. "Please don't talk about math. I still get hives if I have to think about numbers without a calculator in front of me."

Maggie laughed. "I love math. I actually prefer it." A noise outside the door made her jump and turn. "Did you hear that?"

"Hear what?"

Shivers danced in her stomach, but she didn't want to alarm Mrs. Adler unnecessarily. "Um... I thought I heard Belle. Do you mind checking on her?"

"Sure, hon." Mrs. Adler walked down the hall and Maggie swiveled to stare at the front door.

She slowly walked over to it.

The knob jiggled and she stepped back, heart thumping. "Who is it?" She hated the tremble in her voice, but after this morning, the bank robber's threat loomed close to the front of her mind.

The knob stilled. Faint footsteps reached her ears, and she felt her pulse kick it up a notch.

Maggie went to the side window and looked out just I time to see a slim jean-clad figure race around the side of the house.

Slim, tall, ragged, loose-fitting jeans.

Slim? The man from the bank?

Her breath snagged in her throat and fear thumped through her.

Fingers fumbled for the phone. Finally, she wrapped her hand around it then punched in 911.

Reese slapped the pen down onto the desk. He'd prefer to work with a computer, but his hadn't been set up yet. Looking around, he smiled. Not that much different in this office than the one he'd come from. Washington, D.C., was just bigger and louder.

Eli shoved a ragged-looking man in front of him as he escorted him down the hall to the holding cell. The man let loose a string of curses that didn't stop even when the door clanked shut.

Reese's radio crackled on his shoulder.

Nope, not that much different. And maybe just as loud.

He looked at Eli and gestured toward the prisoner. "That Pete?"

"The one and only."

Pete Scoggins. The town drunk. Reese had heard about him five minutes after being in town.

Pete wilted to the floor of the cell and Eli slid into the desk opposite Reese. "Anything on the bank robbery?"

"No. Anything on the identity of the man who cracked his head on the floor?"

Eli shook his head. "He's awake and released from the hospital and into our custody, but he's not talking."

"She said he wouldn't," Reese murmured.

"What's that?"

"Maggie. She said the man wouldn't talk."

Eli blew out a sigh. "Well, she's got it right so far."

"Anything on a gunshot wound coming in at any of the hospitals?"

"Nothing." Eli pursed his lips and ran a hand over his chin. "I've gotten the word out to be on the lookout for the two other robbers, one with a gunshot wound in his shoulder. So far, we're batting zero."

"Hey, I can hear you back here real good," Pete hollered from his cell. "You talking about those boys who robbed the bank, ain't ya?"

Eli rolled his eyes. "Yeah, Pete. We are. We'll try to keep it down so you can sleep it off."

"I seen 'em, you know."

Reese lifted a brow and got up to follow Eli. Eli stood in front of Pete's cell. "Where? What do you know about them?"

Pete yawned and shrugged. "I'll tell you after I get me a good hot meal."

"Aw, you're just yanking my chain," Eli said and turned to go back down the hall. But Reese wasn't so sure.

"Give me something on those guys, and I'll see what I can do about the hot meal."

Pete eyed him. "You're new here."

Reese met his gaze. "I am."

"Don't know if I can trust you." He looked down the hall. "Hey, Eli! This new boy trustworthy?"

"Yep," Eli hollered back.

"Saw 'em in Miz Holly's café eating before the robbery. I was sitting at the counter drinking me a coffee and they were talking real low, but I could hear 'em. I inched over and heard one of 'em say he'd take care of the woman."

The woman. Maggie? Reese's gut clenched. How would they—

The dispatcher's voice came over his radio. "911 call, an intruder at six, seven, zero, Firebird Lane."

Eli frowned and stood, grabbing his keys. "That's Maggie's address."

Reese's heart thudded, his sudden adrenaline rush familiar, pushing his senses to the hyperalert range that had kept him alive more than once. "I know. I just dropped her off."

The two men raced for the door, Eli barking into his radio. "Let her know we're on the way."

"Hey!" Pete hollered. "Don't forget my food!"

The ten-minute drive up the mountain to the clearing that led to the lake seemed to take forever. Reese found himself imagining all sorts of awful things happening. "Do you think he came back?"

Eli didn't ask who he meant. "I don't know. I wouldn't have thought it, but weirder things have happened."

Worry surged through him. Would the bank robber, known only as Slim, have any compunction about hurting a baby? A wave of nausea swept through him at the thought.

"Is she still on the phone?"

Eli relayed the question to the dispatcher then nodded. He shot a glance at Reese. "She said the guy ran off into the woods. He had on baggy jeans and a black T-shirt with short cropped hair."

Reese's jaw tightened. "That's pretty close to how the robbers were dressed. They all had masks on, too."

They finally pulled into the driveway he'd just left about an hour earlier. Deputy Jason White swung in behind them.

On the outside, everything looked fine, peaceful. Undisturbed. But when Maggie opened the door, he could see the strain on her face, the tension in her shoulders.

Climbing out of the car, he and Eli walked up to the porch. She pointed to the back of the house. "He ran that way."

Eli nodded and glanced at Reese. "You stay with her. I'll check it out." He looked at Jason. "You go that way, make a search of the perimeter."

Jason took off.

Reese took her soft hand in his and led her back inside. "Why don't you sit down and tell me what happened."

She dropped onto the couch, leaned her head back and closed her eyes. "I do believe this has been the longest day of my life."

Reese could see her frustration, her fear.

"My husband called. I'm going to have to go." Reese looked up to see a woman standing in the doorway to the den.

Maggie made the introductions. He reached for his radio and said, "Just a minute. I'll get Deputy White to escort you home as soon as he's finished clearing the perimeter of the house. Until we find out the intentions of the person snooping around, I don't want you out there by yourself."

Mrs. Adler nodded, her frown furrowing, the lines in her forehead deep with worry. Five minutes later, in response to Reese's call, Deputy White appeared on the front porch and Reese waved him inside. "Anything?"

Deputy White shook his head. "Nothing that I can see. If someone was here, he's gone now."

"Thanks. Mrs. Adler's ready to go. Do you mind taking her home?"

"Sure, be happy to." The deputy escorted the woman out to his car.

He turned back to Maggie, opened his mouth to question her further—and heard Belle crying.

A low groan slipped from her throat and before he could stop himself, he placed a hand on her shoulder. "I'll get her."

Grateful surprise lit her eyes, and she melted back onto the cushion.

Reese followed the wails down the hall to the nursery. It was tastefully decorated in pink-and-brown polka dots, and he couldn't help but smile.

The smile slipped when he saw the baby standing up, holding on to the railing, staring at him and blinking. A puzzled frown creased her forehead, and she looked as if she might start crying again. "Hey there, Belle. It's all right. It's just me."

His throat tightened as he recognized what he was doing. He was using the same voice he used to—

Oh, God, help me.

What had he been thinking? Volunteering to get the child from her crib. All he could see when he looked at her was his own baby daughter's lifeless face. The last baby he'd held, and she'd been gone. She'd never had a chance to pull in a breath this side of heaven. His hands shook, and he clenched them.

You can do this.

But he wasn't sure he could.

"Reese? Everything okay?" Maggie called from the other room.

He found his voice and some small measure of strength. "Yeah. Just fine."

When Belle's face scrunched up again as if she was getting ready to crank out a cry, he hurried across the room and lifted her from the crib. Her frown stayed as he held her at arm's length straight out in front of him.

And that's the way they walked down the hall into the den.

Belle's head swiveled and when she saw her mother sitting on the couch, her face brightened and she leaned toward her. Reese let her slide from his outstretched grasp into Maggie's embrace.

He backed up and perched on the edge of the recliner, his heart aching, memories fogging his thinking.

"Are you all right?" Maggie asked. She cocked her head, looking at him as though trying to figure out what was going on inside him.

She probably thought he was an idiot, based on how he carried Belle. He clamped down on his emotions and cleared his throat. "Yeah. Sure. I'm fine. I just…" He motioned toward a now-content Belle.

"Don't have much experience with babies?" she asked with a raised brow.

"Ah, no. I don't." Desperate for a change of subject, Reese touched the radio on his shoulder and got Eli. "Anything?"

"Nothing really. I'll be up there in a minute."

True to his word, Eli knocked about a minute later and let himself into the house. Wiping his shoes on the mat, he said, "I found some disturbed ground, but can't tell if it's recent or not."

"Like someone watching the house?" Reese asked.

A pause. "Yeah. Could be. But probably not. I don't think it was the robber."

Reese wasn't sure. "Maybe not. Maybe it was just a teenager or someone looking for an empty place to crash for the night. The more I think about it, the more I don't see how someone could have been waiting for her. How would they know who she was in the first place, much less where she lives?"

Maggie said, "So this was just a random thing? Someone tests the doorknob to see if I'm home and then runs off when I ask who's there?"

Eli sighed. "It could be some high school kids. We have our fair share of troublemakers. Nothing too serious, but..."

Maggie frowned and bounced Belle on her knee.

Reese said, "There hasn't been time for the guy who threatened you to find you. It was just a few hours ago."

"What if he followed us home?" she asked.

Eli and Reese exchanged a glance. "You mean these guys pretended to leave the bank and doubled back to watch the action?"

She shrugged. "Why not?"

Another exchanged glance with Eli and Reese rubbed his chin. "I can't say it's not possible. Highly unlikely, but not impossible." He paused. "Then again, you were really the one who made it possible for us to capture one of them."

She grimaced. "And he did threaten me—us."

Reese looked at Eli. "What do you think?"

Eli pursed his lips. "I think it's too soon to say, but I'd rather be safe than sorry." Reese nodded. Eli then said, "Why don't you keep an eye on things around here just until we know for sure."

"You mean while he's on duty, right?" Maggie asked. She swiveled her head back and forth between the two men. "I mean, I wouldn't expect him to volunteer his time or anything."

Surprisingly enough, the thought of volunteering to spend time with Maggie wasn't a hardship. If only looking at her with the baby didn't send shards of pain shooting through his heart.

"I don't mind. I live just across the lake. If you need me, just call." It was the least he could do, wasn't it? After all, she'd probably saved him from taking a bullet when she'd pulled the ropes and downed the bank robber who had his gun pointed at Reese.

He pulled out his cell phone. "What's your phone number?"

Maggie rattled it off. He punched it in his phone and soon heard hers ringing. He hung up and said, "Okay, now it's on your phone. Put it on speed dial and use it if you need it."

She bit her lip then said, "I don't want to put you out."

"You're not putting me out, I promise." But the faster he got away from here, the faster he could start figuring out how he was going to handle being around a baby on a regular basis. Because he already knew he wanted to get to know Maggie better.

Belle started squirming and Maggie stood with the infant on her hip. "Then if you don't mind, I'll take you up on the offer." She shot a look at the door. "Because whether you believe it or not, I have a feeling this is only the beginning."

Reese thought about what jailbird Pete had said and had a feeling she was absolutely right.

Chapter Three

Maggie's words echoed in her own ears long after the men left. She shivered, feeling scared and unsafe in the house for the first time since she'd moved in.

Knowing Reese was across the lake helped, but...

She fed Belle supper, played with her until her bedtime, then put her down.

In the quiet darkness, she now had time to think. To process everything that had happened over the course of the day.

As she thought, she checked the locks, tested the doors and peered through the blinds. She left every light outside burning.

Through a small copse of trees, she could see her nearest neighbor's den light burning. Mrs. Adler. Fondness filled her. The woman reminded her very much of her own grandmother, who'd passed away about five years ago. Maggie missed her. Almost as much as she missed her mother.

She'd never known her father.

A fact that weighed heavy on her heart.

While Maggie had had her grandfather the early years of

her life, she didn't want Belle growing up with the emptiness of not having a father figure in her life.

With that thought, she slid into the recliner, noticing the lingering scent of Reese's musky cologne. Drawing in a deep breath, Maggie felt a longing fill her.

And a loneliness.

She wanted someone in her life. Someone to share good times and bad. Someone to share Belle with.

But memories of her husband intruded, filling her with that familiar fear. What if she picked the wrong man again? What if there was something wrong with her judgment meter? She couldn't live through another abusive marriage. And she had more than herself to think of now. She wouldn't make decisions without first considering every consequence.

And why was she even thinking about this anyway?

Lord, we need to talk…

Her phone rang and she rose with a groan to answer it on the third ring. She frowned at the unfamiliar number displayed on her caller ID. "Hello?"

"Maggie, is that you?"

"Shannon?" Her sister-in-law. Her husband, Kent's, only sibling. "How are you? How did you get this number?"

"I'm fine and tracking you down wasn't easy, believe me. What are you doing? Hiding out?"

Guilt stabbed Maggie. She should at least have called Shannon and let her know that she and Belle were okay. "No, not hiding out, just living pretty simple. I'm sorry I haven't called."

"I'm sorry, too. How's my Belle?"

Maggie smiled. One thing for sure, Shannon doted on her niece. "She's fine. Sleeping right now, thank goodness."

"I want to see her. To see you."

Did Maggie want that? As much as Shannon loved Belle, she was also the sister of the man who'd liked to use Maggie as a punching bag. And Shannon had adored her brother, re-fusing to believe anything bad about him. "I…um…"

"Please, Maggie."

The quiet plea did her in. "Well, I suppose. When would you come?"

"I'm not sure. Let me…check on some things and I'll call you back."

"Okay."

Maggie said goodbye and hung up, her mind spinning, her heart pounding. Shannon had always intimidated Maggie. And Maggie wasn't even sure that she could explain why if some-one asked. The woman just seemed to have it all together. At least the world's view of "having it all together." A good job, a nice house and friends who held the same social status.

Social status that Maggie had never had, nor really wanted. And Maggie couldn't help the feeling that Shannon had looked down on her for being a stay-at-home mother.

Even though that's what Kent had insisted she do.

He hadn't wanted her to work, to have any way of being able to support herself. He'd wanted her totally dependent on him. And she'd bought into it for a while. He'd convinced her that he was all she needed. He would take care of her. Some-thing she'd missed since losing each and every family member. But once the abuse started, she knew she had to do something.

She'd had to sneak online classes to keep her teaching cer-tificate current. Though now, thanks to her grandfather, Mag-gie didn't have to work unless she wanted to.

Which she did. She loved her job.

Loved helping her students and earning a living that allowed her to provide for herself and Belle. The money her grandfa-ther had left her was there if she needed it. Otherwise, it would go to Belle. Satisfaction filled her. Maggie was so grateful she could leave that money to Belle, so the girl wouldn't have to scrape and scrounge and work three jobs while trying to go to school. And she'd never have to be dependent on a man to take care of her. Never.

A scratching at her window made her jerk.

Then a surge of anger flowed hot and heavy through her veins.

Enough was enough.

Reese tossed and turned. At 2:00 a.m., he felt frustrated and tired.

And worried.

Which was why he couldn't sleep.

After taking care of the situation at Maggie's, he'd gone back to Holly's café, ordered the daily special and taken it back to the jail for Pete.

The man looked surprised—and grateful.

Reese felt a twinge of sympathy for the fellow and had a feeling Eli often fed him his only hot meal of the day. He'd interrogated Pete while he wolfed the food down, but Pete had nothing else to add to his previous story.

So now, in the darkness, questions bombarded Reese. Questions about the bank robbery, the man Maggie had seen in her yard and questions about his attraction to a woman with a baby.

He'd promised himself he'd never put his heart on the line again. He'd had his shot at a family and happily-ever-after, and it had been snatched from him when his wife and child had died in childbirth.

So why couldn't he get the pretty mother out of his mind?

Tossing aside the covers, he padded to the window that overlooked the lake. Peering across, he could see Maggie's house lit up like a Christmas tree.

Realization hit him.

She was all alone and scared. The nights would be the worst. He knew this from experience. She would play the scene from the bank over and over in her mind, building it up, picturing what could have happened instead of what actually had happened. And she would work herself into a ball of nerves and fear. And with the threat the robber left ringing in the air, she would be jumping at every creak and moan of the house, wondering if the man was back to follow through on his promise.

Without a second's hesitation, he picked up his phone and dialed Maggie's number. She might be afraid of the phone ringing at this time of night, but his number and name were programmed in her phone. Once she saw it was him, she would be all right.

"Hello?" Her low, husky voice trembled over him.

"You can't sleep either?" he asked.

She gave a self-conscious little laugh. "I'm assuming you can see my well-lit house?"

"Reminds me of Christmas."

A sigh slipped through the line. "No, I fell asleep for a bit, but then started hearing things."

He frowned. "Hearing things? Like what?"

"Something scraping against my window." Another little laugh escaped her. One that didn't hold much humor. "I was angry enough to chew someone up and spit him out. I went flying out the door and no one was there."

"You did what?" He nearly had a coronary. "Maggie, may I just say that was incredibly stupid?"

"Oh, I know. What was even more stupid was the butcher knife in my hand. I used it cut the branch that was knocking against the window."

Some of his adrenaline slowed. But he still warned her, "Don't ever do anything like that again. Not after today."

She went silent.

He hurried to say, "Not that I have the right to tell you what to do, but—"

"No, you're right." This time her voice was soft. "I know you're right. It was stupid. I just let my fury get the better of me. It's just that the thought of being a victim again—" She stopped. "I won't do that again. I promise."

He felt slightly better. Then frowned as he realized what she'd said. Victim again? Unsettled, he started to ask her about it then stopped. She'd cut off her sentence. He took that to mean she wasn't ready to talk about it.

Instead, he said, "I tell you what. Since I'm going to be awake for the next few hours, I'll keep an eye on your place. You can rest easy."

For a moment she didn't respond. Then her voice, choked with tears or relief, he couldn't tell, reached his ear. "I really hate to say okay, but I...would truly appreciate it. That is, if you're sure you're not going to be sleeping anyway."

He let a sad smile curve his lips. "I'm not."

"Okay, then. I think I'll try to go to bed."

"Sweet dreams, Maggie."

She hung up, and he watched a few of her lights go off. The small manmade lake was probably only half a mile in diameter, but it would only take him about a minute to reach her house by motorcycle or car should he have to do so.

The dark night called to him. Slipping on his heavy coat and a pair of jeans and boots, he walked outside and down to the dock. Sitting there he wondered again at the strange things that had happened to Maggie that day.

And figured he might be losing a lot of sleep in the near future.

Reese walked into the sheriff's office a little later than usual Tuesday morning. He'd finally gone to sleep around 5:30 a.m.

when he'd noticed Maggie up and moving around, her shadow dancing across the window blinds. The bundle in her arms told him Belle was an early riser.

So here he was at nine o'clock instead of his usual eight o'clock. Fortunately, Eli didn't require his deputies to punch a clock. They all worked more than forty hours a week and if one of them needed a little flexibility, as long as someone was willing to stay a little longer on shift to cover, Eli was fine with that.

Reese decided he could learn to like that kind of schedule.

Eli looked up and turned from his computer at Reese's entrance. "You ready to question our prisoner?"

"He lawyer up?"

"Oh, yeah, first chance he got."

Reese shrugged. "Let's have at him then."

"After we take a crack at him, he'll move up to the larger prison in Bryson City where he'll wait to see the judge who'll set bail and all that."

"Where is he?"

"Talking to his lawyer in the holding cell." Eli stood and grabbed a ring of keys, which made Reese grin. In Washington, one simply pressed a button and the door opened. They still used keys here. Eli noticed the look. "We don't have a lot of crime here." He frowned. "Although, I have to say, it seems to be picking up lately." Then he shrugged. "But why spend the money to upgrade?" Eli passed him on the way to the back and said, "I'll get our prisoner and his lawyer and meet you in the interrogation room."

"Sure. Be there in a minute."

Reese noticed the brand-new laptop sitting on his desk and smiled. Now that was more like it.

He booted it up and pulled the sheet of paper from his

drawer that had his email address and other pertinent information he needed to do his job here in Rose Mountain.

Setting that aside to deal with later, he headed for the interrogation room.

A bald man in his late forties sat next to his client. Eli and the lawyer seemed to know each other and shook hands. Eli said, "This is Mr. Nathan Forsythe." Reese shook his hand then sat down and crossed his arms. The one thing he really hated about interrogations was giving up his weapon. He felt incomplete without the comforting weight of the gun under his left arm.

Once everyone was settled, the bank robber slouched in his chair, his hard eyes on the table in front of him.

Reese gave him a hard stare. "Hello, Charlie."

The man didn't even look up.

Eli said, "We ran your prints through AFIS. Welcome to Rose Mountain, Mr. John C. Berkley. Looks like you have a pretty nice rap sheet here."

Tension ran through Berkley as he finally lifted his gaze. He drilled Reese with a silent look filled with hate and a cold confidence that made Reese narrow his eyes.

Eli leaned forward. "Now, would you like to tell us who your partners are and where we can find them?"

Without expression, Berkley simply said, "No."

"Of course not." Eli nodded. "Well, then, I guess we'll send you on up to Bryson City. Oh, and I'm going to let it be known that you weren't just bank robbing, you were going after a baby."

That got Berkley's attention. His shoulders straightened and the surly attitude slid off his face. "Wait a minute, that's not true. You can't do that."

Eli shrugged and Reese admired the man's acting abilities. "I think it is true. What do you think, Reese?"

Reese rubbed his chin as though pondering Eli's question. "He told her to come with him. She had a baby she wasn't leaving behind. Yeah, at least attempted kidnapping." Reese kept his voice casual, as though he didn't have a care in the world. "Especially since we have someone who witnessed you saying something about 'The woman is mine.' Now, which woman were you talking about? There were only three in the bank."

Berkley's eyes narrowed. "I don't know what you're talking about."

"I don't believe you, but we can come back to that. I'm real interested in the fact that you didn't mind putting a child at risk and attempting to kidnap her mother. That might not go over so well in some prisons."

Berkley fidgeted, and Reese could tell he was working hard to keep himself under control.

Eli pressed the issue. "Lots of guys in prison, especially those with families of their own, don't take kindly to those who put children in danger—you know what I'm saying?"

A bead of sweat dripped from Berkley's forehead. He knew.

But he clamped his lips shut and looked at his lawyer, who said, "Don't say anything. I'll see what we can do with the judge." Forsythe nailed Eli and Reese with a glare. "That's pretty low, Eli."

"So is trying to rob my town's bank and kidnap a local resident." Eli stood and walked to the door.

Reese leaned forward toward Berkley, knuckles resting on the table. "And so is trying to shoot me. That tends to make me a little angry."

Barkley said nothing, just met Reese stare for stare. Then a slow smile slipped over the man's face, and he leaned back in his chair.

Reese stood, hoping his contempt for the man was obvious.

As he walked toward the door, Berkley gave a low chuckle. "You think you know everything don't you, Kirkpatrick?"

Reese paused, exchanged a glance with Eli and the silent lawyer. "What do you mean?"

"I don't mean anything." He looked at his lawyer. "Get me out of here."

Reese stepped in front of them. "*What* do you mean?"

For a moment the man simply stared at him, then sneered, "I *mean,* your little lady messed up when she decided to mess with our job. She'd better watch her back cuz this ain't over."

Chapter Four

Reese felt his blood boil as he watched Eli escort Berkley from the room. Was the man all talk? Or was there more to this than met the eye? Berkley's attitude suggested that he knew something they didn't, and it made Reese's palms itch. He wanted to watch the bank video, see if anything struck him.

Eli had said it was being sent over. So he'd wait for it.

He dialed Maggie's number and it went to voice mail. Then he dialed Mitchell's, the other deputy on duty.

"Mitchell here."

"This is Reese. What's your location?"

"I'm just on the edge of town, at the base of the mountain."

"Will you swing by Maggie Bennett's place?" He gave him the address. "Just check and make sure everything's all right?"

"Sure."

Reese's stomach rumbled, and he frowned. Although he felt better about sending Mitchell to check on Maggie, he couldn't help remembering Berkley's words. "It's not over yet." And why would one of the robbers talk about "the woman" being his *before* the robbery? Had Pete gotten his conversations mixed up? If not, which woman? One of the tellers?

Maggie?

But Maggie's trip to the bank had been spur of the moment. Hadn't it?

His stomach sent up hunger signals once again and Reese sighed. He'd grab a quick bite then get back to work. He'd left in a hurry this morning, which meant he hadn't taken the time to eat breakfast.

Reese headed for the door. "Hey, wait up." Eli came from the back. "Where you headed?"

"Thought I'd grab a biscuit at the diner. I missed breakfast."

"You mind if I come along? White's got the jail covered, and Alice is on the phones." Alice Colby, the department secretary, was a pleasant woman in her early fifties. She had salt-and-pepper-colored hair and blue eyes that sparkled all the time. Reese liked her. Jason White was the new hire who'd started the same day as Reese. Reese didn't like him as much as he liked Alice. But the deputy was competent, and Reese knew Eli was glad to have a full staff once again.

"Sure, come on," he said. "What's wrong? Holly didn't feed you this morning?"

Eli grinned. "Not this morning. Holly's not feeling all that great."

"Why does that put a smile on your face?"

"She'll feel better in a few weeks. After the first trimester."

"First tri— Oh." Holly was pregnant. A pang shot through him, and grief hit him in the gut. Covering the split-second reaction, Reese cleared his throat. "Ah, well, congratulations."

The smile slipped from Eli's face. "I'm sorry."

"For what?" Reese forced a lightness into his voice that he didn't feel.

"It still hits hard, doesn't it?"

Reese didn't bother to try to avoid the question. "Yeah. It does. Not as hard as it used to, so time's helping, but it still hurts." This time his smile was real. "But I'm happy for you and Holly. That's great. I hope it's a girl for her sake, though. Even things out with you males in the family."

Eli slapped him on the back and gave his shoulder a friendly squeeze. "Me, too. Come on, I'm starving. Let's eat while we have a chance."

On the way to the diner, Eli stopped residents of the town and introduced Reese to each one. Friendly faces welcomed him, and Reese felt a small sliver of peace slide into his heart.

Coming to Rose Mountain had been the best choice he'd made in a long time.

"By the way, don't forget about the church potluck dinner Wednesday night. When I was a bachelor, I looked forward to those things like a kid does Christmas. Best home cooking you'll find."

Reese nodded and smiled. "I heard the announcement in church last Sunday." One thing he'd done as soon as he'd moved to town was find a church. He'd settled into his house on Saturday a week ago and gotten up and gone to church with Eli and Holly and Cal and Abby the next morning.

He wondered if Maggie Bennett would be there.

When he walked into the diner, his eyes landed on the woman his thoughts couldn't seem to stay away from. Belle sat in her lap, picking Cheerios out of Maggie's hand and eating them one by one. Like a homing pigeon, he made his way to her, drawn by her deep brown eyes. He was vaguely aware of Eli following along behind. She smiled when she saw him. "Good morning, Reese."

"Morning. How'd you sleep last night?"

"Pretty well, thanks to you. Knowing you were watching was—well, it made a big difference. Thanks."

He returned her smile. "It was no problem."

Eli cleared his throat, and Maggie looked past him to greet the man. "Hi, Eli."

"Maggie. No classes this morning?"

"Not until 11:00 today. I started on paperwork about 6:00 this morning and decided I had definitely earned a break. So here we are."

Reese thought about that question he'd wanted to ask her. "Hey, do you go to the bank every Monday?"

She lifted a brow at him. "Yes. Usually. I get paid by electronic deposit on a weekly basis. I go to get my cash for the week and then go to the different places to pay my bills."

"You don't use checks? Pay online?"

She shook her head. "No. I do it this way on purpose. It gets me out of the house. I spend many hours online with my job." She shrugged. "I could do everything online, but I like getting out, visiting with people and…" She flushed. "I know it sounds silly. I just need that personal interaction."

"It doesn't sound silly," he reassured her. He understood what she was saying, and his mind was already clicking through what it meant.

Belle jabbered at Reese and held her arms out to him. He backpedaled, almost knocking Eli over. Maggie jerked and lifted a brow at him. Feeling like a fool, he stammered, "Um, well, I guess we'd better get a table. See you."

He turned and headed for the table in the far corner, feeling Maggie's puzzled gaze follow him until he was able to slide into the seat and out of her line of sight.

Eli seated himself on the opposite side and shook his head. "What in the world was that?"

A cold sweat broke across Reese's brow and he closed his eyes on a groan. "I don't know. I'm an idiot."

"Have you talked to anyone about this? Like a professional counselor?"

Eli's soft question sent darts through Reese's heart. "Yeah. I did."

"And?"

"It helped, but…"

"The grief is still there. And it will be for the rest of your life, I know, but…"

Guilt shook him. He opened his eyes and looked straight into Eli's compassionate gaze. "For Keira, the grief is less sharp. It's more of a sadness for what could have been, the loss of what we had. I miss her. A lot. And I'm sorry she died. I wish I could change that, but I can't." He sighed. "It's hard to admit it, but I'm ready to move on. To find someone to spend the rest of my life with. But…"

"But?"

"When it comes to babies, I just… It's hard. I don't know why it's so hard." Frustration at his inability to put his feelings into words washed over him. "It just is. And I need to find a way to move on, to accept the loss and deal with it, but…"

"You lost your wife and daughter, Reese. That's huge."

Reese swallowed against the lump in his throat. "I know." He stirred in his seat, restless with the direction of the conversation. Fortunately, the waitress arrived before he had to contribute further to it.

Then Eli changed the subject. "What was that about? Maggie and her trips to the bank?"

"She has a routine. A routine someone has figured out in her short time here in Rose Mountain."

Eli nodded, knowledge lighting his eyes. "And they hit the

bank at the time she was going to be there. Just as she was every Monday."

"Coincidence?"

"Maybe."

"But you don't think so?"

"I think time will tell. I also think we need to keep a really close eye on her."

Reese stared at the woman who'd already made such an impression on his heart. "I don't think I'm going to mind that." He also wouldn't mind finding out exactly why the pretty mother came to be in the wrong place at the wrong time.

In fact, finding that out might require spending a lot of time with her and getting to know her better.

He couldn't help the small smile that slipped across his lips.

Maggie pushed the sippy cup from Belle's grasping fingers, tired of the "throw it on the floor so Mommy can pick it up" game.

Belle protested with a loud squeal so Maggie stood, trying to juggle the baby, her purse and the diaper bag. Her wallet fell to the floor when it tipped out of her tilted purse.

With Belle on her hip, she squatted, attempting to keep her balance while she retrieved the wallet.

"Let me hold her a minute."

Maggie looked up to see Mrs. Adler standing behind her. Belle grinned when she saw her.

Grateful for the woman's intervention, Maggie handed Belle over. While Belle grabbed a handful of Mrs. Adler's graying shoulder-length hair and tried to get it in her mouth, Maggie picked up her wallet.

When she stood again, she nearly mashed her nose into the uniform-covered broad chest. "Oh!"

Reese's strong hands came up to grasp her upper arms,

and she shivered at the contact. He gave her a crooked smile that didn't match the look in his eyes. He handed her a dusty pacifier. "This fell out of your purse and bounced almost to my table. Would hate for you to need it and it not be there."

Maggie took it from him and stepped back to catch her breath. Being so close to him did crazy things to her pulse. She swallowed hard. "Thanks."

"No problem." He smiled at Mrs. Adler. "Good to see you, ma'am."

"And you, Deputy Kirkpatrick."

He smiled. "You can call me Reese."

Reese returned to his seat, and Maggie tucked the dirty pacifier in her purse to wash later. As Reese settled himself onto the plastic-covered seat, she saw Eli raise a brow at his new hire.

The flush on Reese's cheeks made her wonder if perhaps she triggered the same crazy feelings in him that he did in her.

While thankful for the return of the pacifier, she still frowned as she watched the two men engage in conversation. Because while Deputy Reese Kirkpatrick seemed to have a soft spot for her, she couldn't help but notice that when he offered her the pacifier and addressed Mrs. Adler, he never once looked at Belle.

In the small bedroom that served as her office, Maggie clicked out of her virtual classroom and took her headphones off. She was pleased with the five students who had shown up, and the class had gone well. In fact, all her classes this morning had had lively discussions and productive work. Satisfaction filled her.

Mrs. Adler entertained Belle in the den while Maggie worked. Now that Belle was getting older, Maggie needed someone to help out during her class times and for four hours a day, four days a week, Mrs. Adler was happy to do it. Not only that, the woman liked to cook. She seemed to feel as if it was her personal duty to keep Maggie in casseroles and pies. Maggie didn't argue with her.

She pictured the food-laden tables she knew would be spread out tomorrow night in the church gym and her stomach growled. The sandwich she'd downed in a hurry a couple of hours ago had worn off. She'd find a snack in a minute. Right now, she had something on her mind and needed to think a bit.

Maggie got up and walked toward the closet where she had a small portable file box. As she passed the window, movement caught her eye.

Stopping, she glanced out. The bedroom was in the back corner of the house. The view from the window was part lake to her right and part woods to her left. The sheer curtains allowed light to flood the room during the day. But now, Maggie wished she had something heavier and more concealing over the windows. She shivered and waited. Watching. Her mind flashed to the robber's threat that he would kill her.

Would he really? She remembered the look in his eye as he spewed the threat and decided, yes, he really would.

Fear trembled through her and she pulled in a deep breath. For the next few minutes, she simply stood and watched the area outside the window, then she moved to Belle's room and looked out. Again, she saw nothing that caused her concern. Before she left Belle's room, she checked the window latch. It was fastened securely.

Feeling a bit better, thinking it was just an animal or something that had captured her attention, she let herself relax slightly. Returning to her office, she went straight to the closet. The file box she wanted sat on the top shelf.

Maggie pulled it down and brought it to the desk.

Before she went any further, she couldn't resist one more glance out the window.

Nothing.

She turned back to the box, opened the latch and lifted the lid. Ever since the attempted bank robbery, she'd been troubled by the fact that she could have been killed. She wasn't ready to die, of course, but it wasn't so much the act of dying as it was dying and leaving Belle to face the world without her.

Maggie sorted through the files until she came to the one she wanted. The one marked WILL. When she'd lived with her husband, she'd learned fast to hide things she didn't want him to know about. He was suspicious and mean and went through her things often, accusing her of hiding money from him.

Guilt pulled at her. Well, he'd been right about that. She'd been hiding things from him. She'd been planning her escape from the man for several months because she knew if she didn't get away from him, she would eventually wind up dead. And now she had more than herself to think of. She had to take care of Belle.

Maggie pulled the one sheet of paper labeled LAST WILL AND TESTAMENT from the file, sat in the chair and simply looked at it. She really had to do something about guardianship for Belle in case something happened to her. The attempted bank robbery yesterday had hit home the fact that Maggie had no other living relatives. None.

Except for her deceased husband's sister, Shannon Bennett. And she wasn't even a blood relative. The woman was thirty-seven years old, had never married and seemed to prefer it that way. She was listed as the person who would get custody of Belle in the event of Maggie's death. And while Maggie knew without a doubt that Shannon was crazy about Belle, that she would take care of her, provide for her and love her, Maggie hesitated. She just wasn't sure she wanted to leave Belle with her. For a number of reasons.

The doorbell rang and she jumped.

Mrs. Adler called, "I'll get it."

Maggie relaxed and went back to trying to make a decision about what to do about Belle in the event of her death. Not something she planned on happening, but the bank robbery still had her shaken.

A high-pitched scream echoed through the house. Maggie jerked, bolted to her feet and raced down the short hall to find the woman standing in the doorway, hands clasped to her mouth.

"What is it?" Maggie's heart thudded as she stepped around Mrs. Adler and stared down at the dead squirrel on her porch. He lay on his back, feet in the air.

The words painted in red next to him read, "You're next."

Chapter Five

Maggie's shaky phone call still echoed in his mind as Reese stood on the porch looking down at the dead animal. The bright sun in the blue cloudless sky cast a cheery glow around him. A direct contrast to the chilling message next to the carcass.

Eli stepped forward and placed a hand on Mrs. Adler's shoulder. The woman still trembled as she twisted a tissue between her fingers. "Let me call Jim to come get you," Eli offered.

"No, I have my car. I'll be fine." She bit her lip. "I'd rather he not know about this. We're going to Asheville day after tomorrow for some heart tests. This wouldn't be good for him."

"I'm so sorry," Maggie whispered, her face pale and drawn.

Mrs. Adler reached over and took Maggie's hand in hers. "It's not your fault, honey. Someone is just getting his kicks in a twisted way." She fluttered her hand as though to say she was going to try to ignore it.

Reese wished he could.

But the would-be bank robber's threats still rang in his ears. He hadn't thought the two who'd escaped would have hung around the area. But maybe one had revenge on his mind. Maybe the person Maggie saw running from her home yesterday had indeed been the robber who'd threatened them. But why go after Maggie? Reese was the one who'd shot him.

Then again, if Maggie hadn't pulled the rope, everything would have ended differently. They would have gotten away with their money and Slim wouldn't have a bullet hole in him.

Eli looked up from the squirrel. "He was already dead. Been dead a couple of days, I'd say. Our joker probably came across him and decided it'd be a good way to scare Maggie."

She grunted. "It worked."

"Where's Belle?" Eli asked.

"In her playpen." Maggie glanced through the door and into the den. "She's content right now."

Eli looked at Mitchell, one of his deputies. "Anything on that red substance?"

"It's not blood." He held up the cotton swab he'd used to test the writing. "Maybe paint or some kind of marker."

"Let's get all this stuff bagged." He looked at Maggie. "We'll have to send it off to the lab in Asheville. It may take a while to hear back."

She nodded and ran a hand through her blond hair. She looked tired, the gray smudges under her eyes attesting to the fact that she hadn't gotten much sleep since the robbery. She asked, "What do I do now? If this person is determined to get to me, how do Belle and I—" she shot a glance at Mrs. Adler "—and everyone else in my life, stay safe?"

Reese's jaw firmed. "I live right across the lake, so I can help keep an eye on things." He looked at Eli. "Would it be possible to have deputies on duty drive by every couple of hours for the next few days?"

Eli blew out a sigh and was quiet while he thought about it. Then he said, "Fortunately, we're not short-staffed anymore. At least we won't be when Cal and Abby get back from Washington. They're due home any time now." Reese nodded. Cal McIvers was also a deputy on the small Rose Mountain police force. Abby, Cal's wife, was Reese's former sister-in-law. Their unconditional love and support had been instrumental in influencing his move to the mountain.

"That'll help."

Eli pulled out his notebook again and wrote as he spoke. "I'll set up a schedule for the drive-bys." He looked at Maggie. "And we can set up a check-in schedule for you."

"What's that?" she asked.

"You call either Reese or me throughout the day at designated times to let us know you're all right. It doesn't have to take long, just a simple, 'I'm fine.'"

Reese nodded. "She can call me." He looked into her eyes. "I'll be available, day or night. If you even feel uneasy, call."

He saw her throat work, the protest form on her lips. Before she could utter a word, he stated firmly, "It's not an imposition. Let me do this. If something happened to you—or Belle—I'd...probably blame myself for letting you talk me out of it. So let's just save me the guilt, okay?"

"Let him do it, honey," Mrs. Adler chimed in. "With the crazy stuff happening in this town lately, it wouldn't hurt." She shook her head. "First Eli has to take over for a crooked sheriff, then drugs being funneled through the elementary school then someone chasing down that sweet Abby McIvers and trying to kill her..." The woman trailed off, her muttered words making Reese wince.

He'd been part of Abby O'Sullivan McIvers's grief. His sister-in-law. He'd blamed her for his wife and daughter's deaths and she'd run from him. Straight to Rose Mountain, where she'd met and married Cal McIvers, one of Rose Mountain's deputies. Now she had a flourishing pediatric medical practice and the residents of Rose Mountain kept her busy enough that she'd started looking for a partner. Thankfully, Reese had been able to be friendly with her and Cal.

Maggie looked confused. "Dr. Abby?" So she hadn't heard the story of how he'd come to Rose Mountain.

He nodded. "Yes."

Before Mrs. Adler could add to her dialogue about all the bad things happening recently on the mountain, a cry sounded from inside the house.

Belle.

Maggie darted inside while Eli walked Mrs. Adler to her car. "Why don't you call it a day?"

"I believe I will." She climbed in and drove down the drive that would lead her to the two-lane mountain road.

Reese watched her go. The storm door squeaked open and Maggie stepped outside with Belle on her hip.

His heart flipped then settled.

Why was he reacting this way? He hadn't felt anything like attraction for a woman since Keira's death. And now this. He was developing feelings for the mother of a baby. He shook his head at himself and decided he'd better focus on her safety and not the fact that he wanted to push aside his insecurities and fears and lose himself in the possibility that God might have something planned for him and Maggie.

The thought was almost too much right now and something he would have to take the time to think about later.

Belle babbled, and Reese reached out to touch her cheek. When she grinned, he found himself smiling back. Then the sadness hit him once again. But the surprise in Maggie's gaze and the warmth that filled her eyes at his gesture helped ease the grief.

And he wasn't sure what to do about that, either.

"Reese?"

He spun to see Eli standing beside his cruiser. "Yeah?"

"I'm going to see how backed up the lab is." His gaze darted between Maggie and Reese. "Why don't you hang around here for a while and make sure everything's all right."

"Sure, I can do that." Reese felt the heat at the back of his neck and cleared his throat.

Maggie said, "Thanks, Eli."

"Anytime." Everyone cleared out and the sudden silence echoed around them.

Then Maggie nodded toward the door. "Come on in. I was just going to fix some lunch. You hungry?"

"I could eat."

She smiled. "Then let's see what we're having. I don't have another class for two hours. I can catch up on the paperwork tonight." She smirked. "Or at least attempt to. I honestly don't think I'll ever be caught up."

Thunder rumbled in the distance and he looked over his shoulder at the sky as he followed her inside. "It's going to rain tonight. You don't have to go anywhere tomorrow morning, do you?"

"No, why?"

"Because there'll be ice on the roads."

"Oh. No. I'll be right here teaching my classes. Mrs. Adler usually walks over, though. I'll give her a call and warn her not to come if it's icy. For her to fall is the last thing she and her husband need right now." She placed Belle in the high chair and gave her some Cheerios.

Reese stood awkwardly in the doorway. "What can I do to help?"

She studied him for a moment as though weighing whether or not she really wanted to help. "Do you like salad?"

"If it's got meat on it."

She laughed. "A chef salad it is, then."

He got the lettuce from the fridge and found ham, turkey and all the trimmings for an excellent salad. While Maggie sliced and buttered bread, Belle watched him with curious eyes.

And he found himself returning her stare, wondering what his little girl would have looked like if she'd lived. She would have been almost two years old by now. Biting his lip against the sharp slice of pain, he turned back to chopping the lettuce.

Maggie said, "It's weird having help in the kitchen, but you don't get in the way."

His pain faded and he grinned. "I love to work in the kitchen. Cooking, grilling..." He shrugged. "I like to eat good food and since I'm on my own, I'm responsible for it."

"Where'd you learn to cook?"

Maggie set the two large bowls of salad on the table while he grabbed the dressing and the jug of tea she'd pulled from the fridge. "Will you hand me those two jars of baby food by the microwave?"

He did and they settled down at the table with Maggie seated next to Belle so she could feed her daughter while she ate her own meal.

He blurted out, "I...grew up in foster homes."

She started and stared at him. "Oh. I didn't realize..."

He shrugged. "It's all right. In one of the homes, my foster mother was a gourmet chef." A smile curved his lips as he remembered. "She used to let me help her in the kitchen, and she taught me the ins and outs of cooking."

"How long were you there?"

His smile faded. "Long enough to get attached. Then my foster father died suddenly, and my foster mother sort of fell apart." He cleared his throat. "But it was a good place for about three years. I think I stayed there from the time I was fourteen until I turned seventeen. After that, the state sent me to live with a family who were nice enough, but it was clear that as soon as I was eighteen and finished with high school, I was on my own. After graduation, I joined the army. They paid for my college."

"How old are you?" she asked as she spooned another small glob of something green in Belle's waiting mouth.

He grimaced and answered, "Thirty-three."

Maggie caught his look and grinned. "I know it looks gross, but she likes it." After another spoonful and a bite of her salad, she asked, "And when you got out of the service, you decided to become a detective?"

He took a sip of tea and nodded. "Well, a cop first, then a detective."

"Why are you here in Rose Mountain, Reese? A big-city detective doesn't just one day decide to move to a small mountain town and become a deputy. It doesn't make sense."

He froze. But she deserved an answer. "I...was going through a tough time when Eli called and asked if I was interested in the job." Sympathy flashed in her pretty eyes, compelling him to tell her, "My wife and—" He let his gaze land on Belle and couldn't form the words. "My wife died about eighteen months ago."

She gasped. "Oh! I'm so sorry."

He blew out a breath. "After that, I sort of fell apart. I needed a change of pace. When Eli called, it was like a gift. I packed up and haven't looked back." At least not on purpose.

Belle thumped her cup on her tray and he flinched. The sippy cup spun on the edge then hit the floor. Belle let out a squeal. He bent to pick up the cup the same time Maggie did and they knocked heads.

Maggie yelped and jerked away from him.

Reese saw stars for a moment then turned his concern to her. "Hey, I'm sorry. Are you all right?"

Maggie held a hand to her head and he reached up to touch the small knot forming on her forehead. She opened her eyes and tears hovered on the edge. She blinked them back and gave a watery laugh. "Sorry, I don't know why I'm crying, but that stung a bit."

He winced. "I know. If I didn't want to permanently alter your perception of me as the tough cop, I'd shed a few tears myself."

That made her laugh and his heart twisted at the sound. He slid his hand from her small wound to cup her cheek. "You should do that more often."

Maggie's breath caught in her throat, and she stared up into his eyes that seemed so deep, if she wasn't careful, she'd find herself drowning in them. She swallowed hard. "What's that?"

"Laugh."

"Oh." She moved away from his touch and handed the cup back to the squirming, cranky Belle.

Who promptly tossed it across the kitchen.

Maggie pulled her child from the high chair and said, "It's nap time, I do believe."

"I guess I should leave." He looked at his watch.

Fear immediately settled around her like a wet blanket on a cold day. Unwanted and uncomfortable. She wanted to toss the fear aside, but wasn't sure how to go about doing that. She forced a smile. "Thanks for coming to the rescue."

Reese nodded and paced to the front door. "You know, why don't you put her down and I'll just hang around a few more minutes."

Relief slid over her, but she said, "Sometimes she's hard to get down. I might be a little while."

He pulled out his phone. "I can answer a few emails. It's no problem. I want to talk to you about some safety concerns."

So that's why he was offering to stay. Well, whatever the reason, she was glad. She hurried down the hall and into Belle's little room, which she'd decorated with such care. Kent, her husband, hadn't wanted Belle. And he sure hadn't wanted Maggie to spend time and money on decorating a nursery.

A shudder ripped through her as she remembered his violent anger when she'd told him she was pregnant.

Belle yawned and settled her head on Maggie's shoulder. That simple action by her sweet baby settled Maggie's nerves as she lowered herself into the rocker. Usually this was her favorite time of the day, rocking the child, but she now wanted Belle to hurry up and go to sleep. Her mind clicked as she wondered what Reese wanted to talk about. The fact that he'd been open with her and had discussed the loss of his wife was touching. Sympathy made her ache. They'd both lost a spouse.

Only Reese had loved his wife.

By the time Kent had died, the only things Maggie had felt for him were hate and fear.

And then she couldn't help wondering what it would be like to be loved by a man like Reese Kirkpatrick.

Chapter Six

Reese couldn't get Maggie off his mind. Not just because she was a lovely woman, but because she was a lovely woman who was in danger. The menacing message left on her porch drove that home to him, and he felt a responsibility to do something about it.

Reese pulled out the small notebook and pen that he carried everywhere. He started in the den and made notes about the location of the windows and the way the furniture was arranged. Then he moved on to the kitchen.

When he reached her office, he paused, wondering if he should ask permission to invade her space.

"Reese?"

At her quiet voice, he turned. The questioning look in her eyes had him flushing. "Hey." He held up his notebook. "I'm making some notes."

"On what?"

"On how to get you some security around here." He nodded to her office. "Do you mind if I take a look?"

"No, I don't mind. Go ahead."

"You need a security system." He looked at her. "I know they're kind of expensive, but I'll check with Eli and see if he knows someone who could give you a good deal along with excellent security."

Maggie gave a slow nod. "You're right. A security system would help me feel much safer."

"Also, you need motion sensors outside. I can put those up later tonight after I finish my shift." He could feel her eyes on him, watching him. He fidgeted, her fixed gaze making him a little uneasy. "What is it?"

"Why are you doing this? I don't think most deputies would take such an…interest in a victim."

But she wasn't just a victim to him. She was—well, he wasn't sure what she was to him yet, but it was more than a victim. "Because… I want to. Maybe it's because I was in the bank with you." Maybe it's because he was attracted to her and was trying to figure out his confusion about that fact. But one thing was certain. "None of this is your fault, and you shouldn't have to be afraid."

She bit her lip and looked at the floor. "If he really wants to get to me, he will."

Reese felt his jaw go tight. Reaching out, he lifted her chin to look into her eyes. "Don't think like that. We're going to do everything we can to keep you and Belle safe."

He wondered if his determination to succeed in that was a matter of leftover guilt that he hadn't been able to do anything for his wife or baby. His complete and total helplessness in the face of their deaths.

Probably.

But Maggie needed him, and he was going to be there for her.

Her eyes flickered and she swallowed hard as she gave a short nod. "Okay," she whispered.

"Okay." He walked past her into the master bedroom. His

first thought was: peace. The room was tasteful, warm and feminine. She'd done the room with colors that reminded him of peaches and cream, and he suddenly felt like a blundering intruder. He made his notes fast from the door. She said, "The window is stuck. I've tried to get it open, but short of using a crowbar, I think it's pretty secure."

He gestured to it. "May I?"

She frowned, but nodded. "Sure."

Reese walked over to the window and pushed the curtains aside. Two quick, sharp tugs and the window slid up.

Lightning flashed, the sound of rain pounding the earth filled his ears. Cold air rushed in, and he quickly shut the window. Over his shoulder, he said, "I think we'll add this window to the list."

She stared, the nonplussed expression on her face almost making him smile in spite of the reason for checking the window. "I guess I need to start working out," she said.

Before he could stop the words, he heard himself saying, "You're perfect just the way you are."

She flushed and cleared her throat as she walked toward him, then past him and into the hall. "You've been in Belle's room, so you know what it looks like."

"I think I've got everything I need." He paused. "I hate to ask this, but what kind of price range is doable for you?"

She tilted her head and shrugged. "It doesn't matter—" Maggie paused, then sighed. "Why don't you get me a couple of quotes, and I'll pick one."

Reese nodded. "I can do that." And then he'd make up the difference if he had to. She was going to have whatever security system it took to keep her safe. And give him a little peace of mind.

Later that afternoon, after Reese left with promises to check on her often and be back to install the motion sensors, Belle played in the playpen while Maggie tried to make a decision about her will. Flashes of the robbery danced across her mind, and she shuddered and tried to force the remembered terror away.

Maggie looked at the balance on the statement from her bank. She still couldn't believe her grandfather had left that much money for Belle.

All the time she'd been under Kent's thumb, been his prisoner in his beautiful house, she'd been so isolated, so afraid to make the wrong move, say the wrong thing or cook the wrong meal.

And getting a job wasn't even an option. A stockbroker, Kent had at first declared he didn't want his wife working because it would make him look unsuccessful, as if he couldn't take care of his own family. Later, Maggie realized it was just another way for him to control her. If he could have found a way to climb inside her mind and take over her thoughts, he would have.

But now she didn't have to worry about that.

There was something about making her own money to pay the bills, to take care of Belle and herself. She felt independent. Free in a way she hadn't been since childhood.

She put the bank statement into the file box and looked at the picture on her desk. Her grandfather and her mother stood arm in arm, smiling as if they didn't have a care in the world.

She missed them. Her grandfather had his faults, but he had loved Maggie.

She thought of the man who'd divorced her grandmother for another woman. "He's a hard, bitter man," her grandmother had told her. Her grandmother had gone to her grave praying for the man who'd hurt her so.

But Maggie had a different memory of her grandfather. She couldn't reconcile the man her grandmother described with the man she'd known the first eleven years of her life. The one who'd taken her for ice cream sundaes and walks in the park. The one who'd nursed her through the flu while her grandmother and mother had to work.

Maggie thought about all the people she knew—people she'd only met since coming to Rose Mountain. And made her decision.

Quickly, she pulled up the template on the computer and started working. Within minutes, she was finished, had the document printed and ready to mail to her lawyer, a nice man she'd met at church. He also represented Eli and Holly. Once done, she stared at the envelope and felt peace flood her. It was the right decision. She slid it under the heavy horse-head paperweight to the right of her computer and made a mental note to mail the envelope tomorrow when she didn't have to walk to the mailbox in the rain.

A knock on the door startled her. She hadn't heard a car drive up. Her eyes flashed to the knives on the kitchen counter, the heavy frying pan on the stove. Her fingers gripped the cordless phone, and she started to dial 911. Then realized if the person meant her harm, he probably wouldn't knock on the door.

Probably.

Although, he didn't seem to have a problem ringing the bell after leaving the dead squirrel and horrible message on the porch.

At the window, she glanced out and breathed a small sigh of relief when she saw Abby McIvers standing on her front porch. Then she frowned. What was she doing here?

Maggie opened the door. "Hello, Dr. McIvers."

The pretty woman smiled. "Please, call me Abby."

The rain slowed to a drizzle as Maggie motioned for her to come in. Abby stepped inside and shrugged out of her heavy winter raincoat. Maggie hung it on the hook beside the door and said, "Come into the den and sit down. What brings you by?" She glanced at the clock and figured she had about twenty minutes before Belle would demand her attention.

"I came to see a patient of mine who lives about three doors down from you. Susan Evans." Abby frowned as she sat on the sofa. "She's due any day now and is scared to death. I told her I'd come out and see her as often as I could." Abby's frown lifted into a smile. "I've heard a lot about you lately from Eli and Reese, and thought I'd come get to know you a bit better."

"A rainy day is always a perfect time for a visit," Maggie said. "Let me put on some coffee."

Abby followed her into the kitchen. "I noticed the police car outside. Cal told me what happened with the robber who escaped, so I'm glad they're keeping an eye on you. I'm sure the attempted bank robbery was incredibly scary."

"Very," Maggie agreed with a shudder.

"So I'll change the subject. How's Belle doing?"

"All recovered from her ear infection, thanks." Belle had suffered her fourth ear infection two weeks ago. Abby had been the physician who'd prescribed the antibiotics and numbing drops. "You saved my sanity. Belle finally fell asleep when we got home, and so did I. We both slept for eight hours straight." She measured the grounds and poured them into the filter.

Abby sat at the table. "I'm glad." A slight pause, then, "Reese thinks a lot of you."

Maggie looked at the woman out of the corner of her eye. "And you think a lot of Reese, don't you?"

A smile curved Abby's lips. "He's become one of Cal's best friends. He's my brother-in-law. Or former brother-in-law."

Maggie jerked. "That's something I didn't know."

"He was married to my sister, Keira."

"He told me she died." Maggie pulled two mugs from the cabinet. Then looked Abby in the eye. "I'm sorry."

Abby's smile turned sad. "I am, too." Then she sighed and her expression turned thoughtful. "It's been a year and a half, though, and I think he's ready to move on."

"Move on?"

The coffee finished brewing and Maggie rose to pour it into the waiting mugs. She handed one to Abby and motioned to the cream and sugar in the middle of the table.

While Abby spooned two heaping teaspoons of sugar, Maggie tried to figure out where the woman was going with this conversation.

Abby picked up where she left off. "Yes, move on. Find someone to spend the rest of his life with."

The speculative look in Abby's eyes caused Maggie to give a nervous laugh. "He and I just met, Abby. I think you might be rushing things a bit here."

"True, I probably am." She shrugged. "I just care about Reese and want to see him happy. And you're the first person he's—"

Maggie waited for Abby to finish. When she didn't, Maggie prompted, "He's what?"

Another shrug, another sip. "Expressed any interest in since my sister died." Her forehead creased. "At least as far as I know. He just moved here from Washington, D.C., about a week ago." She set her cup on the table. "But we've kept in touch on a regular basis and he's come to visit and stay with us a lot over the past year or so whenever he could get time off. Cal and I could tell he was looking for something different." She smiled. "Rose Mountain had gotten to him. He couldn't stay away. And now, according to Cal, Reese can't seem to stay away from you, either."

Maggie shifted, uncomfortable. "Reese is concerned that

I might be in danger—that's all it is. And I don't know that I'm ready for any kind of relationship with anyone anyway. I don't have a very good track record with men, and don't know that I trust my judgment anymore."

Sympathy flashed on Abby's face. "Sounds like you have a story to tell."

"Maybe one day." Spilling her guts to a stranger wasn't in her. But she already liked Abby and had a feeling they could become close friends.

Belle's cry came right on schedule. "Excuse me a minute."

"I need to get going anyway. Thanks for the coffee." Abby smiled as she rose and placed her half-finished cup in the sink. "Maybe we can do this again when I can stay longer? Or maybe you and Belle can come out for dinner one night?"

"I'd like that." And she would. She needed a friend here in Rose Mountain. It was time to start trusting people again.

Abby rested a hand on Maggie's upper arm and said, "I didn't mean to push and I'm not a nosy, interfering matchmaker." At Maggie's lifted brow, Abby laughed. "Okay, at least I'm not most of the time, and I promise I won't be from now on. I just wanted to…" She shrugged.

"Check me out?"

Abby laughed. "Okay, that'll do."

Belle hollered again and Abby gathered her coat. "I'll see you later." She let herself out and Maggie went to get Belle.

The baby grinned when she saw her mother, and Maggie felt love swell inside her just as it did every time Belle turned that smile on her.

"Come on, kiddo. Let's go play until supper time." She checked to make sure Abby had locked the door behind her, then, for the next hour, Maggie entertained her daughter.

But Maggie couldn't quite keep focused on the playtime as her mind kept going back to the attempted robbery, the ugly sneer in the robber's voice as he demanded that she and Belle go with him. The dead squirrel with the nerve-shattering message that she was next.

Fear rumbled through her, and she swallowed hard.

Glancing through the French doors, she watched the sun dip lower in the sky. Soon it would be hidden, darkness would take over, and she wondered if tonight would be the night that the robber would make good on his threat and be back to kill her and Belle.

"Hey, we got a hit on the vehicle used in the robbery."

Eli's voice came over the phone and Reese set the weight he'd been curling with his left arm on the floor.

"Who does it belong to?"

"A guy by the name of Glenn Compton."

Reese wiped the sweat from his brow and blew out a breath. "You track him down yet?"

"Not yet. I'm in contact with the Bryson City P.D. and the Asheville P.D. I've got a Be On the Lookout order out on him, so hopefully we'll hear something soon. I'll send his picture to your phone."

His phone beeped, and he pulled it from his ear to check it. A text from Maggie that read, I'm Fine.

He smiled and pressed the phone back against his ear. "Okay, Maggie just texted, checking in, and said she was fine. All is okay for now."

"Glad to hear it. Let's do our best to keep it that way."

"You know it. In fact, I'm going to go over and check on things in about an hour."

"Because you think you need to or because it's a good reason to see a pretty lady?"

Reese smiled at the smirk in his friend's voice. "I think we both know the answer to that one."

Eli turned serious again. "I think that's a good thing, Reese. Holly and I've liked Maggie from the moment we met her. She's a special lady."

"I agree."

Back to business, Eli said, "Cal will be back in the office tomorrow. We'll add him to the protection rotation. He'll want to help."

"Good." Satisfaction and relief surged through Reese. The more people Maggie had watching over her, the better off she would be. "Keep me posted, Eli."

"You know I will."

Reese hung up and within seconds his phone buzzed. Eli had sent him Compton's picture. Bushy brows, ruddy complexion and a hard blue-eyed stare. Reese made note of the features, tucked his phone back in his pocket and stared at the wall. He'd been doing a little research on the man they had in custody before deciding to get in his daily exercise routine. He usually did his best thinking while working out. This time was no different.

Two of John Berkley's known associates were missing. Compton and a man named Douglas Patterson. Reese had examined the picture of Patterson and couldn't tell for sure if it was Slim, the man he'd shot, or not.

"Could be, though," he muttered.

He'd gone on to read that the three of them had been busted for a robbery in a small town just outside of Asheville. But they'd gotten off on a technicality—and the unwillingness of the only witness to come forward and testify.

In fact, that witness was now missing and presumed dead.

Reese rubbed his chin. Interesting.

If they had intimidated that witness to the point of sending him running, Reese felt sure that was their plan now with

Maggie. Although, he frowned, he was also a witness and so far, everything had been directed at Maggie.

Was he next?

Or the tellers? No incidents with them had been reported, but that didn't mean something wasn't going to happen.

He made a mental note to ask Eli about keeping an eye on the tellers. He'd call and warn them to report anything suspicious. He'd also make an effort to stay extra alert.

The last thing he needed was to drop his guard and find himself with a bullet in his back.

Shaking off that thought, he glanced at his watch. Almost 5:30 p.m. He grabbed the bag that held Maggie's motion sensors and decided to make one more stop before heading her way.

Another knock on her front door didn't have the same effect on her heart rate as the earlier one. But she was still cautious as she placed Belle in her playpen and walked over to look out the window.

Reese was back. She couldn't help but think about Abby's comment that he was ready to move on.

But was Maggie? That was a question she didn't have an answer for right now. And didn't need to have one. She had time to get to know him and let him get to know her. And Belle.

She opened the door and he held up two bags from Holly Brody's Candy Caper shop and deli. "You were kind enough to feed me lunch, I thought I'd bring supper."

"Hmm...thank you. But...you really came to check on me, didn't you?" She smiled, not upset by that at all. She liked his company. She liked *him*. And she liked that he cared that she was safe. She felt as if she'd known him much longer than two days.

"Guilty as charged."

"Come on in."

He stepped inside and handed Maggie the bags of food and the motion sensors, then he shrugged out of his heavy coat, mimicking Abby's earlier actions. He hung the coat on the hook and moved into the kitchen while she placed the bags on the counter.

"I see you had company," he said. She lifted a brow at him and he grinned. "My awesome powers of observation. Two mugs in the sink."

Maggie smiled. "Abby came by."

He nodded. "She said she wanted to get to know you better. I'm glad she's making the effort to do so."

"It was nice having company. Gets kind of lonely around here with just Belle and me." She winced and prayed she didn't sound as desperate as she thought she did.

Reese gave a small, sad smile. "I know what you mean." Then shook off the melancholy her words seemed to bring on. Had she reminded him of his wife? Probably. "So let's eat. I'm starved."

"I'll get Belle."

Three hours later, Belle was asleep, and Reese was gone. Maggie smiled to herself as she thought about the evening. It had been nice. Pleasant.

Interesting.

She'd been able to forget everything that had happened over the past couple of days until Reese said, "I've got the alarm company scheduled to come first thing in the morning. I hope that's all right. He's a friend of Eli's and is fitting you into his busy day."

And she came back to earth with a thud. "It's fine."

Reality wasn't as pleasant as dinner with a handsome man, but she agreed that the alarm system was necessary. And she needed it fast.

Maggie glanced out the window to see the cruiser sitting in his usual spot. Who was it tonight? Mitchell or one of the other deputies? She couldn't tell because of the darkness and the tinted windows. But satisfaction and thankfulness filled her because she knew if anyone got close to the house, the lights would come on.

Eli had mentioned having a bit of turnover lately, but she couldn't remember the names he mentioned. Not that it really mattered. There was only one deputy she was interested in, and she wasn't likely to forget his name anytime soon.

As she prepared for bed, she checked her phone. One message. From her sister-in-law, Shannon. So the woman was serious about visiting. Maggie wondered how she'd found her, as she hadn't told Shannon or anyone else where she was headed. She'd even used some of the techniques her police officer friend had told her about to cover her tracks for a while. Even though Kent had been dead, Maggie supposed she'd still been scared enough to feel as if she needed to become invisible. Being anonymous had been important to her the last few months.

She'd needed time to heal, to figure out what she wanted out of life. To find out who she was underneath Kent's robot. She supposed when she'd applied for a credit card last month, it probably hadn't been too hard to track her down.

Making a mental note to call Shannon tomorrow, Maggie checked on Belle one more time before slipping between the covers. She sent one last text to Reese, letting him know she was safe and was going to bed.

Then she lay there, eyes closed, thinking. Her mind turned one way then twisted another. *Go to sleep.*

The order did no good. Her eyes popped open. She forced them shut. After two hours of this, Maggie was ready to give up, get up and do some work, when a sound from the hallway startled her into sitting straight up in the middle of the bed.

Heart thumping, she peered out of her open door. What had she heard? Not moving, she just listened. Heard the sound of her own breathing. Maggie swung her feet to the floor. The blanket slipped from her shoulders and she pushed it to the side. Rising from the bed, she padded on silent feet into the hall. Belle's door stood open the way Maggie left it every night. The nightlight glowed, casting shadows Maggie used to think were comforting. Now they taunted her, their eeriness causing the hair on the back of her neck to rise and goose bumps to pebble up and down her arms.

Shivering, she walked into the den and crossed to the front door.

She checked the knob.

Locked.

Her blood slowed its frantic race through her veins. Maybe she'd fallen asleep after all and had been dreaming.

She walked into the kitchen, her bare feet soundless on the cold hardwood floors. Taking a deep breath, she flipped on the light.

And let the breath out slowly. All looked like she'd left it before heading to her bedroom earlier. A quick glance at the clock on the microwave said it was a little after 1:00 a.m. She turned the light off and blinked until her eyes adjusted again. Turning, she stepped and nearly screamed. Something soft—and squishy—slid between her toes.

Only the thought of waking Belle kept the scream from erupting from her throat. Gasping, she slapped the light switch once again and looked down.

A dark brown substance stained the floor next to her foot. "What—?" she whispered. Her stomach turned and she grimaced.

Kneeling, she touched the brown goo, lifted her finger to her nose and sniffed.

Dirt.

Relief threaded through her. Not blood or anything else along those lines. Just dirt. She could handle dirt.

Then she stiffened. But how had it gotten here? Had Reese tracked it in? But no. It hadn't been there when she'd gone to bed.

Her gaze flew to the kitchen door that led out to the small porch that overlooked the backyard. Now she noticed the dark round spots on the dark floor. Small round wet drops and traces of mud led from the door.

Her heartbeats came faster. How? Who? She'd locked the door. Double-checked it even after Reese had given the knob a test from the outside.

She heard something coming from her office and froze, her breath hitching in her throat.

Was someone in her house?

Belle.

Maggie raced down the hallway and into the baby's room. The empty crib mocked her.

Chapter Seven

Reese rolled over and punched his pillow. He'd just checked with Jason White, the deputy assigned to guard Maggie's house tonight. Everything was fine. Quiet. She'd had her lights off now for a couple of hours.

It all sounded good. Maybe the robbers had decided to give it up. To stop hounding Maggie.

Right. He wished he believed that.

It would be nice, but he didn't live in a fantasy world. Reality was that Maggie was a target and until they caught everyone behind the attempted robbery, she would remain a target.

So the simple solution would be to find the other robbers. Hopefully, they'd hear something tomorrow. Reese glanced at the clock, sighed and rose. He walked to the window and pushed back the curtain just enough to look out across the lake. Maggie's place was lit up like a Christmas tree once again. He could make out the cruiser at the end of the gravel drive.

Reese couldn't say he was entirely comfortable with the placement of the cruiser. Where Jason sat, he could only see one side of the house. But when the man was making rounds, he walked the perimeter at least once an hour, staggering his timing so as not to have a pattern anyone could count on.

Reese rubbed his eyes and turned to head back to bed when a flash of red then blue flickering through the trees caught his attention.

"What's going on?" he whispered aloud. He waited, watching to see where the lights were headed.

Realized they were cruisers.

Cruisers heading toward Maggie's.

His gut clenched. Something had happened.

Bolting back to his room, he snagged his sweats and threw them on. Then he grabbed his gun and raced for his back door.

The sound of shattering glass brought him up short, and he turned to see a small round object on his bedroom floor. Reese's only thought was to make it out of the house before the bomb in his bedroom exploded.

Maggie felt her knees buckle. "Belle!"

Gathering her strength, she turned and raced to the front door and threw it open. The cruiser still sat at the end of her drive. "My baby's missing!"

At her frantic cry, Deputy Jason White opened the door and stepped out. The motion sensors blazed on. "What?"

Maggie felt tears slip down her cheeks. "Belle, she's not in her crib, she's...gone." The last word ripped from her throat and she thought she might throw up.

Before she could race back into the house, a loud crack ripped through the night air. Maggie spun around to see a bright flash light up the night sky. Across the lake.

Right where Reese's house was.

Reese's house?

She gaped then darted back into her house, desperate to

find Belle. *Please, let Reese be all right. And please, please let me find my baby.*

Sobs threatened to rip from her throat, but she couldn't afford the luxury of a good cry right now.

She went straight to the empty crib and gripped it with both hands as though touching it would allow her to touch Belle.

Deputy White stood behind her, speaking into his radio.

A high cry sounded. She froze as hope flooded her. "Belle?" she whispered as she ran toward the sound. The deputy again followed, his footsteps pounding right behind her.

Maggie rounded the corner of the door and raced into her office. She came to skidding halt on the hardwood floor. She blinked to make sure she wasn't seeing things. Belle stood in the playpen, holding on to the side, bottom lip quivering. Maggie rushed to her and snatched her against her. "Isabella, oh baby, you scared me to death."

"Is she all right?"

"Yes." Maggie inspected the little girl, running her hands over her head, her ears, her lips, her little fingers. "Yes, she's fine."

With the blinds drawn, flashing blue and red lights lit up the room as she carried Belle into the den. The deputy who'd been with her up to this point opened the door and let Eli Brody and Cal McIvers in.

"Maggie?" Eli asked. "What's going on?"

"What happened?" Reese demanded as he stepped inside behind Eli and Cal. "I heard the sirens then saw all the commotion over here and got here as fast as I could."

Maggie nearly lost it when she spotted Reese. "Your house?"

"Someone tossed an explosive in my bedroom as I was racing out. Fortunately, I got out before it went off." He glanced at Eli and Cal. "Fire trucks are on the way. We'll deal with that after we deal with this."

He'd left his own burning home to get to her, to make sure she was all right. The wild worry in his eyes conveyed a lot to her at that moment. She held herself together, clung to Belle and said, "Someone was in here. Someone moved Belle from her crib to the playpen in my office."

Eli and Cal exchanged a look. Deputy White nodded. Reese frowned. "Tell us what happened."

"I was trying to sleep," Maggie said, "and not being very successful at it when I heard a faint noise in the hall. I got up to check it and I came into the kitchen where I stepped in mud."

"Mud?" Cal lifted a brow.

"Yes. On the kitchen floor. Someone tracked it in." Reese went into the kitchen and the others followed. Maggie pointed to the floor. "See? It leads from this back door."

"Where does it go?" Eli asked.

Maggie shook her head. "I don't know. When Belle wasn't in her crib, I lost it."

"But she was in the playpen," Reese said. "Odd."

"Are you sure you didn't leave her in there and just thought you put her in the crib?" Deputy White asked.

Maggie stared at the deputy who'd been sitting in the cruiser outside her house while someone had been inside. "No, Deputy White. I didn't misplace my daughter. Someone moved her." The thought made her sick and she placed a kiss on top of the baby's head. Belle clapped her hands together and laughed, unaffected by the interruption of her sleep or the excitement going on around her.

Eli nodded then grimaced as he looked around. "Now that we've tracked all over it, let's make this an official crime scene. An attempted kidnapping. I'll get the kit. Maggie, I need you to take Belle back into the den and stay put while we see what we can do out here." He looked out the window toward Reese's home. "You'd better head back over there."

"I'll take care of that soon enough." He didn't look worried, but Maggie felt horrible that he was here with her when he was losing his home. His eyes softened as he looked at her, as though he knew what was going on inside her. "Go. It's all right. I didn't have anything too valuable anyway."

Maggie swallowed hard. She carried Belle into the den as ordered, but didn't sit. She hovered in the background to watch and listen. Because now she wasn't just scared...

...she was mad.

Reese slipped the mud from the kitchen floor into the evidence bag and ran his fingers across the top, sealing it. His thumping heartbeat had slowed considerably once he realized Maggie and Belle were safe, but his reaction to the flashing lights and sirens headed toward Maggie's house floored him.

He'd been terrified, more so than the moment he'd realized what was on the bedroom floor. His all-consuming fear of something happening to Maggie and Belle had nearly paralyzed him.

Reese looked at the deputy who'd been charged with keeping watch and wondered what the man had been doing while someone had been breaking into Maggie's house.

Anger rolled through him and he took a deep breath, pushing back the desire to lash out at the deputy and demand to know if he'd been sleeping on the job. Instead, he ran a hand through his hair and said, "Dust the doorknob for prints, would you?"

"Sure."

Reese followed the trail of dirt with his eyes then with his feet as it took him out of the kitchen, into the small foyer area and down the hall. A drop here, a drop there. The trail led straight into Belle's room. He was surprised Maggie hadn't stepped on either a water droplet or some of the mud before she'd found it in the kitchen.

Eli came up behind him. "Cal checked the door to the kitchen. No forced entry."

"Someone knows how to pick a lock?"

Eli shrugged. "Possibly. Or Maggie left it unlocked."

Reese was shaking his head before Eli finished the statement. "She's too careful about that. There's no way she left the door unlocked."

"The motion sensors didn't come on until Deputy White got out of his car," Maggie said.

"That means he didn't come through the front door. What about the door off the kitchen? That's where he gained access to the house."

Jason said, "I'll check."

Reese continued to follow the trail of mud, although it was faint now and he found fewer signs of the dirt as he went along to her office. But there beside the playpen was a trace of it. He could hear Belle starting to fuss and wanted to join her.

He looked inside the playpen and his eyes landed on a piece of paper. Snapping on the pair of gloves Eli handed him, he reached in and snagged the paper by the edge. He read aloud, "I could have taken her. Keep your mouth shut or you'll die like him."

He heard a quick, indrawn breath from behind him and turned to see Maggie standing in the hall, Belle on her hip. The baby rubbed her eyes and let out a wail. Maggie absently shushed her and asked, "What?"

Her pale face and trembling lips had him striding toward her. He handed the paper to Cal who bagged it. "Come back in here." Reese led her back into the den where she collapsed onto the couch.

Deputy White poked his head in the door. "The light over

the kitchen door is broken." He shook his head. "I never heard it. I was doing my perimeter check like I was supposed to, I promise." He frowned, his face pale. "I... I'm sorry."

Reese just shot him a dark look. He left the others to finish the evidence gathering and reached out to take a squirming, whining Belle. Shock crossed Maggie's face, but she let him take the baby. He settled her on his lap and she looked up at him with those big brown eyes, her fussiness forgotten for a moment.

He swallowed hard and focused on Maggie. "Whoever broke in had no intention of taking Belle. He wrote that note before he got inside."

Eli ran a hand down his face and agreed. "He came here first, left the note, then went straight to Reese's house. He didn't want to take a chance on the explosion waking you up before he got in here and left his little message."

Maggie swallowed hard. "So what does this mean?"

"He's afraid you'll testify."

"But he's not even in custody," she sputtered.

"But his partner is," Eli reminded her.

"But die like...who?" she asked.

Reese drew in a deep breath and looked in the direction of his home. "Me."

Maggie didn't sleep much that night after everyone left. Instead, she worried. She knew she shouldn't, but she did. Cal McIvers sat outside her home the rest of the night, and she worried about him being too tired to stay awake. She worried about Reese and his damaged house, and she worried about keeping Belle and herself safe.

She walked into her office and saw the envelope on her desk. The one she'd meant to mail, but had forgotten in the chaos of worrying about everything.

Maggie was tired of worrying.

"Be anxious for nothing," she whispered aloud. Then with more conviction. "Be anxious for nothing, but in everything by prayer and supplication, with thanksgiving, let your requests be made known to God and the peace of God, which surpasses all understanding, will guard your hearts and minds through Christ Jesus."

She needed that peace that surpasses all understanding. Peace. Something she'd been searching for all her life, it seemed. Something she found only when she prayed and focused on God.

Please give me that peace, God.

He could give it to her, she believed that. Just as she'd believed He'd somehow take care of her and Belle when she'd been at her lowest point.

And He had. In a way she never would have guessed.

He'd used her grandfather. The grandfather she hadn't seen or heard from in over fifteen years.

The one who'd left her this modest lake house and a good chunk of money to put in her checking account along with a sizable trust fund for Belle.

Surprisingly, the money hadn't brought her peace. Yes, it had been a huge relief, but the peace had come in knowing God cared about her. He'd provided.

The knock at her door jerked her from her thoughts— and prayers. Maggie looked over at Belle who was jabbering and playing with her pacifier. Soon the baby's happy chatter would escalate to demands to be fed. Maggie scooped her up and settled her on her hip. Belle laughed and Maggie couldn't help but smile. *Thank you for this child, God.*

She carried Belle to the front door and peeked out the window. The cruiser still sat at the end of her driveway. Reese's truck had pulled in next to hers, and now he was standing on her porch.

And she looked like a frump. Old sweats and her hair in a ponytail. She hadn't even brushed her teeth yet. She grabbed a peppermint from the candy dish on the mantel and popped it in her mouth. The sweet candy tingled on her tongue, and she took a deep breath.

Maggie opened the door and waited for her heart to do that swooping thing it did whenever Reese smiled at her. The way he was doing now. "How are you this morning?"

"Tired and grumpy and worried." She matched his smile, though. "But at least we're alive, Belle's safe and I still have a house. How's yours?"

He shrugged. "The insurance adjuster will be out sometime today. The crime scene unit that came from Asheville called me this morning. The tech said the bomb wasn't very well put together. Sloppy, homemade and possibly deadly, depending on my location and what debris hit me. If I'd been in the room when it went off, it most likely would have killed me or done some pretty bad bodily damage, but the destruction is mostly limited to the bedroom and part of the kitchen, so the house isn't a total loss."

Maggie shivered and moved so he could come in. Reese stepped inside, making the small foyer seem even smaller. "But it does tell us one thing."

"What's that?"

"Whoever is after you—and now me—is serious. He doesn't mind killing." He reached out and touched her cheek. "Which means you've got to be extra careful."

Maggie swallowed hard. Not just at his words, but at the trail of heat that followed his finger down her cheek. She wasn't sure what to think about her reaction to this man. "What about you?"

"I'll be careful, too."

Belle jabbered at him and after a moment of hesitation, he reached out and tapped her nose. "How are you this morning, Belle? Did you let your mama get some sleep after all the excitement?"

Belle ducked her head into Maggie's shoulder, and Maggie let happiness push aside the fear for a moment. Maybe he could learn to love Belle as well as…

She put a halt to those thoughts as she carried Belle into the kitchen. "She did. We both slept pretty well, considering everything that happened last night." She shook her head. "I moved her into my room, though. The terror I felt when I first saw she wasn't in her crib is still there."

"It may take a while for it to go away."

Maggie bent her head as Belle's bottle warmed on the stove. "I'll never forget that feeling," she whispered. "It's the same feeling I had once before, and I…" She trailed off and shuddered as she remembered the time she'd turned around in the grocery store for a bare minute. By the time she'd turned back, Belle and her stroller were gone. She'd found her the next aisle over, safe and sound with Shannon, her sister-in-law, hovering over her, but the feeling had been horrifying.

Another tremor rippled through her.

Reese's hands settled on her shoulder and she closed her eyes, relishing the comfort. Then Belle squirmed in her arms and reached for the bottle. Reese's hands fell away as Maggie juggled the baby and tested the milk on her wrist. She handed the bottle to Belle who promptly stuck it in her mouth.

"Let's go in the den so we can sit down."

He followed her and settled on the love seat while she took the recliner. Belle nestled in the crook of her arm, Maggie slowly rocked while the baby ate. He said, "Eli called me about an hour ago and said they got some footage off the bank's video cameras. It's not great, but he's hoping to get a response so he's circulating a picture of the robber I shot. His name may be Douglas Patterson, otherwise known as Slim. He's been known to hang out with Berkley and Compton. It looks kind of like him, but I couldn't say it's him for sure. Eli's also checked all the hospitals within a two-hour radius of us, but no one recognized Compton or the wounded man."

"He didn't get help, get his wound taken care of?"

"Probably not. The crime scene unit found the bullet in the wall by the door. It went straight through. I'm guessing Compton played doctor and patched him up."

Maggie shuddered.

Reese said, "We may even have a positive ID on the guy. Eli's checking it out."

"Who recognized him?"

"A gas station clerk in Asheville saw the newscast early this morning showing Compton's face and the picture from the bank camera. He called it in about three this morning."

Maggie felt a seed of hope sprout. "Maybe they'll catch them and this will all be over soon."

"I hope so." Reese was silent for a moment as he watched Belle eat. The creases in his forehead said he was thinking about something pretty deeply.

"What is it?" she asked.

"I was just wondering about you. We've spent quite a bit of time together, but I don't know a whole lot about you."

She lifted a brow at him. "I could say the same about you."

A flush appeared on his cheeks and she bit her lip on a smile. He nodded. "True enough."

Maggie studied him then said, "What do you want to know?"

"How did you come to live here? Where's your family?"

He swallowed. "And if you don't mind my asking—what happened to your marriage?"

Maggie blew out a sigh. "You don't pull any punches, do you?"

Reese winced. "Sorry if that's too direct. I just... I want to know you."

And she wanted to know him, too. "My family is all gone. First my mother, then my grandmother. I never knew my father—he left when I was two."

"I'm sorry."

She shrugged. "I never missed him. My grandfather was there for the first eleven years of my life. He was my father figure."

"And he died, too?"

"No, he disappeared."

Reese lifted a brow. "Where'd he go?"

"I didn't know it at the time, but he came here. He left my grandmother for another woman."

"Ouch. That had to be awful for you all."

She nodded and ran a hand down her thigh. "It was. My grandmother was very angry, even bitter for a while, but then as the years passed, she gave it to the Lord and let Him heal her. I've never forgotten that."

"What about Belle's father's family?"

Maggie snorted and pursed her lips. "Kent's parents didn't like me and didn't want anything to do with Belle. He married beneath him, you see." Reese grimaced. Then her face softened. "But his sister, Shannon, was pretty good to me. And Belle. Especially Belle. She loved and accepted her from the moment she was born." Shame filled her. "When I left, I never told Shannon where I was going. I was so filled with hurt, anger, uncertainty. I just wanted to leave it all behind and start over. Start fresh." She paused. "I probably should have told her what I was doing." Maggie sighed. "But I didn't. I didn't want to talk to anyone, to see anyone, to explain anything to anyone. I just wanted to be alone."

"Any brothers or sisters?"

"No. I was an only child of only children. As I said, my father left when I was two. My mom told me he'd been killed in car wreck when I was about six, I believe. My mother died of a rare heart disease just after my twenty-second birthday and my grandmother died in her sleep shortly before I met Kent four years ago."

"I'm so sorry."

So she'd been lonely and still reeling from all the tragedies in her life. Easy pickings for the wrong kind of guy.

Maggie pulled the empty bottle from Belle's hands and placed the baby on the floor. Maggie handed her a toy that made a quiet noise every time Belle shook it.

Then Maggie began to pace. Belle looked up and watched for a moment, then went back to the book she now had clasped in both hands. She shook it and laughed as she shoved a corner into her mouth.

Maggie said, "Long story short, I was an abused wife. By the time I woke up and realized what I was allowing Kent to do to me, I had no real friends left. I was spending most of my time alone in my house, becoming a shell of the person I used to be. When I found out I was pregnant with Belle, Kent reacted horribly. He ordered me to get an abortion. I refused. For the first time since I'd known him, I stood up to him." Just remembering that feeling brought a smile to her lips. "It felt good. He threatened to cause me to have a miscarriage. I went to Shannon, and she was outraged at her brother's behavior—and thrilled that she was going to be an aunt. She let me stay with her."

"So you left him."

"Briefly. Kent found me there and started hitting me. Shannon called the police and he left. I told Shannon I couldn't stay there any longer. She begged me not to leave, but I couldn't put her in danger. I had a friend who was a police officer. Practically the one friend I had left from the church I had attended before I married Kent. At her house I was able to finish the last two classes I needed for my degree to teach. And Kent knew better than to harass me while I was with Felicia." A frown puckered her brow. "At least I thought he did. But a few months later, Kent came knocking on my door, begging me to come back, wanting to prove he was a changed man. Shannon came with him and vouched for him." Tears flooded her eyes. "He promised he was once again the person I'd dated and fallen in love with. I wanted to believe him," she whispered.

"But he hadn't changed."

"No." She cleared her throat and frowned. "Well, yes, he seemed to. He never laid a hand on me the rest of my pregnancy and we got along pretty well. But two days after Belle was born, the abuse started again. I knew then I had to leave for good or I was dead. And I couldn't leave Belle with him."

Reese felt his gut clench. How he wished Kent Bennett wasn't dead so he could plant a fist in the man's face and give him a taste of his own medicine. Reese unclenched his fist and forced his fingers to relax.

"So…" she paced to the small table next to the fireplace and looked at the pictures she'd arranged in a nice display "… there you have it."

"But you left and ended up here."

She sighed and settled back into the recliner. Belle crawled over and pulled herself up on her mother's knee. Maggie stroked the baby's head as she talked. "When Kent started hitting me shortly after we were married, I knew I'd messed up and that at some point I might need a safe place to go. The only person I could think of as a possibility for refuge, someone Kent didn't know about and couldn't threaten, was my grandfather. But I had no idea if he still cared about me."

"So you found him."

She shrugged. "It wasn't that hard."

"You contacted him?"

"No, not at first," she whispered. "I couldn't work up the courage. I walked around the house with his number in my pocket for weeks." She gave a watery laugh and blinked back tears.

Reese swallowed hard. "You don't have to talk about it if you don't want to."

"No, it's okay. It's part of who I am. I've moved past it, but I can't deny it." She pulled in a deep breath. "So then I found myself pregnant, abused and basically lost. At some point, I knew I was going to die if I didn't get out. I called my grandfather. He was thrilled to hear from me. Apparently, he'd been forbidden to have any contact with me after my grandparents' divorce and he went along with it. His new wife didn't want him involved with anyone from his old life and he agreed. She died the year I married Kent."

"So he wanted to see you?"

She nodded. "But I couldn't let him come to my house. I put him off, not daring to introduce him to Kent. Kent didn't like people in his house unless he'd invited them." She paused. "And I didn't want Kent to know about Grandpa."

"You were already planning to get away from Kent and go to your grandfather."

Maggie gave a slow nod. "But I had to be careful. If I moved too fast or left a trail, I knew he'd find me and kill me."

Chapter Eight

And he would have, too. She had no doubts about that.

Her phone rang, distracting her from her thoughts. Reese motioned for her to answer it. She glanced at the caller ID.

"Hello, Mrs. Adler."

"Hello, dear, how are you? I heard you had some excitement out there last night."

"We're fine. Have you recovered from finding that nasty little gift on my porch? I guess some teenagers are the same all over and like to have fun at other people's expense." She gave a small laugh that fell flat. Primarily because she didn't believe her own words. Most of the teens she worked with were great kids and would never do something like leave a dead squirrel on someone's doorstep with a threat attached. But Maggie tried to make light of the incident, not wanting the woman to be worried or scared.

"I don't know who would do a thing like that, but you definitely need to be careful, dear."

"I know." She glanced at Reese. "Deputy Kirkpatrick is

working on helping me get a security system installed as soon as possible. In fact, the installers should be here soon."

A pause. "That's good." Another pause. "I, um… Well, the thing is, Maggie, ah…"

Suspicion hit Maggie. "Is there something you need to tell me?"

In a rush, the words came. "Oh, Maggie, Jim doesn't want me to come out to your house anymore because of everything that's happened. He's afraid I'll be involved and get hurt."

Maggie caught her breath. Then let it out slowly. "Oh."

"I'm so sorry. I tried to talk to him about it, but he was adamant and getting himself all worked up. I had to agree so he'd calm down. With his heart the way it is…"

"It's all right, Mrs. Adler. I really understand." Maggie didn't like it, but she did understand. "You have to take care of Mr. Adler."

"But what will you do with Belle while you're teaching?" she fretted.

"I… I'll figure something out. Your first priority is your husband. Once the police catch those bank robbers, all of this will stop and you can come back. I can make temporary arrangements for Belle."

"I'm just so sorry."

Maggie could tell the woman really was. Reassuring Mrs. Adler one more time that all would be okay, Maggie hung up, wondering what she was going to do about child care.

"You okay?"

Maggie picked Belle up and settled her into her lap. "Because of all that's happened, Mrs. Adler's not going to be able to take care of Belle while I teach anymore. I'm going to have to find someone else to watch her."

Reese frowned. "I'm sorry."

She gave a small shrug and frowned. "I'll figure something out."

"Are you still planning on going to the potluck dinner tonight?"

She bit her lip. "Should I?"

Reese didn't answer right away. Then he gave a slow nod. "I think it's all right. We'll be in public, and this guy's after you or me. No one else."

"But what if he does something that puts other people in danger?" She shook her head. "I don't think I should go."

Reese rubbed his chin and studied her. "No. You need to go. I want to watch the people there. I want to see how people interact with you."

She lifted a brow. "You mean use me as bait?"

"No, absolutely not. I just want to observe those you interact with. I'm not trying to catch anyone tonight." He paused. "And if I think there's even a hint of danger, I'll get you out of there faster than you can blink, all right?"

Maggie gave a slow nod. "All right."

The knock on her door pulled Reese to his feet. "Your alarm installers are here."

After the alarm system was installed, the afternoon passed in a blur of teaching and taking care of Belle. Finally, it was five o'clock and Reese would be there in fifteen minutes to take her and Belle to the potluck dinner. At the thought, her stomach rumbled in anticipation. But her nerves trembled.

Was she making a mistake? Should she stay home? But what was she going to do? Stay inside the rest of her life? Constantly worry that the bank robber would show up and make good on his threat?

Maybe.

Anger swelled inside her. Why did it seem as if the people

who tried to do the right thing always got knocked down while those who did everything they weren't supposed to do got off scot-free?

It wasn't fair.

Then again, nothing had been *fair* since she'd met and married Kent. And, truly, it wasn't about fairness. It was about living her life the way she'd determined to live it the day she'd decided to get away from the abuse.

She hadn't run from her marriage. In fact, she'd never planned to marry again as long as Kent was alive. But she wasn't going to be his punching bag, either.

Maggie lifted her chin as she thought about the dead squirrel and the nasty threat. Well, if she was *next* as the note said, she wasn't going down without a fight.

Maggie gathered Belle's bag of baby essentials and her purse and set them on the floor beside the door. Belle played in her playpen, happy to clean it out by throwing the toys on the floor. Then she'd yell and Maggie would fill it up again. Only to begin the game all over again.

But Maggie didn't mind. Belle was happy, and that was all that mattered.

When Reese's knock came, she was ready. She opened the door and swallowed hard. He had on jeans, a pullover sweater with his heavy coat thrown over it, but not zipped.

And he looked good.

Ignoring her heart's sudden increase in beats per minute, she smiled. "Right on time."

"I was ready to see you." His bluntness made her blink but his grin set her at ease.

"Well…thanks."

He laughed and bent to pick up her purse and baby bag. "I'll carry them to the truck while you get Belle."

She handed him the items. "I'll drive if you don't mind. I've already put the beans in the back of my truck. I don't want to have to transfer her car seat base to your truck and then back to mine. It's just easier to drive."

Reese nodded and walked to her truck. She unlocked it with the remote then went to get Belle.

The baby grinned up at her and Maggie felt love consume her. She picked up Belle and set her on her hip, saying a prayer of thanksgiving to God for blessing her with the child. Then she went to meet Reese.

In the car, she drove automatically while she noticed Reese watching the mirrors. "Are you sure this is a good idea?" she asked, her fingers tightening around the steering wheel as her stress level increased at the thought of being followed to the church.

He didn't take his eyes from the rearview mirror. "I think you'll be fine, Maggie. This guy has shown himself to be sneaky, preferring to leave things on your porch or try to get to you in the middle of the night. I really don't think we have anything to worry about at a church full of people." He reached over and covered her tense, cold fingers with his warm hand. "And don't forget, the entire Rose Mountain police force will be there. On duty and ready for trouble if it happens."

That did make her feel a bit better. "All right." She forced a smile. "Then let's go have a good time."

Reese wasn't quite as sure about the man who'd threatened Maggie as he'd led her to believe. Not that he doubted his reassurances, but he was making his judgments based on experience. Everything he'd told her was true. He just hoped this time didn't turn out to be the exception to the rule.

No, there was no hoping for that. He firmed his jaw. He'd make sure of that. He'd stick with Maggie and Belle like superglue to ensure they were safe and had a good time. In the meantime, he'd do his best to put her at ease. She needed to relax. But…he looked at her and said, "I meant what I said about believing you'll be safe, but…"

"But what?"

"But don't go anywhere alone. Even to the restroom, okay?"

Worry wrinkled her forehead once again and Reese grimaced. But as much as he wanted her to enjoy herself, she had to keep her guard up. Her lips flattened but she gave a short nod.

When Maggie pulled into the parking lot, Reese was surprised at the number of people there. "This must be a popular activity for the church."

Maggie nodded. "Holly said it's an annual tradition. The church supplies the turkey and everyone brings enough side dishes to serve a cruise ship."

Reese smiled at that picture. Maggie unbuckled her seat belt and climbed out to get Belle from the backseat. "But," she said, "the good thing about this is the church invites everyone in the community. They even have volunteers who deliver meals to people who can't get out to come eat. Which is why I brought that huge thing of green beans."

She set Belle's carrier on the ground beside her.

"Nice." He frowned. "I didn't realize that or I could have helped."

"I think you get a pass your first visit."

"This is your first dinner here and you didn't take a pass. You brought beans." She smiled at him and pulled the beans from the truck. His breath seemed to lodge somewhere between his chest and his throat as her eyes crinkled at the corners. She really was a beautiful woman. And a strong one, he thought, as, with beans in one hand, she lifted Belle's car carrier in the other. He quickly offered, "You want me to carry her?"

She lifted a brow at him. "Would you?"

"Sure."

"Then, thanks." She started toward the church and Reese glanced down at Belle, who looked like a miniature mummy wrapped in blankets. The small pink hat came down over her ears. Brown eyes studied him. He grasped the handle and lifted her. Carrying a baby in a carrier was different than carrying one in his arms. With his fingers wrapped around the handle, he didn't feel the sharp pang of grief and remembrance he did when he held a small body in his hands.

A small, fragile body, devoid of life—

He inhaled, his lungs protesting the sudden intake of frigid air. As he exhaled, he noticed Maggie almost to the door. She turned. "Are you all right?"

"Yeah." He forced a smile. "We're coming."

She waited until he caught up then held the door open. He let her pass in front of him and followed her inside.

Smells of home cooking tantalized him and his stomach rumbled. Home-cooked meals were few and far between unless he put forth the effort—which he rarely did. This was a real treat. He looked at the woman beside him and the baby carrier in his grip.

And swallowed hard at the picture the three of them made.

If the people in the small church didn't know the truth, they would probably think Reese, Maggie and Belle were a family.

The thought didn't bother him nearly as much as he thought it might. In fact, it just occurred to him that his first impulse had been to volunteer to carry Belle—not the beans.

He smiled and hope stirred. Maybe the big hole in his heart would one day heal after all.

★ ★ ★

Maggie set the green beans on the table with the other food. She unwound the scarf around her neck and shrugged out of her heavy coat. Pegs lined the wall near the door and she hung everything on one.

Reese stood beside her holding Belle, and she shivered at how they must look.

They could be a family.

Her stomach flipped at the idea and a small smile curved her lips. Then a niggling of doubt pressed in, causing her smile to droop. Memories of a bad first choice threatened to consume her. She refused to let it happen.

"Thanks for carrying her. She gets heavy."

"No problem." He set the carrier on the nearest table as people stopped by to speak to them. Holly and Eli were the first to greet them. Eli clapped Reese on the shoulder. "Glad you could make it."

Maggie released Belle from her safety restraints and smiled as Mrs. Adler started toward her, arms open, delight—and determination—in her eyes. "Jim may not want me to come over and watch her at your house anymore, but I can enjoy her here at the church all I want. I'll take her while you eat if you like. I'm not the least bit hungry right now."

"Nibbled a little too much when you were helping put the stuff out?" Maggie teased.

Mrs. Adler grinned. "You know it."

"Then, sure, I'd love for you to entertain Belle for a while. Thanks." Maggie watched the sweet woman take Belle over to another woman with a baby about the same age as Belle. She couldn't begrudge Mrs. Adler time with Belle just because her husband was worried about her being at the house where all the strange things were happening.

She knew Mrs. Adler loved Belle as if she were one of her own grandchildren.

Grief pierced her with a sudden jab. It should have been her mother, Belle's natural grandmother, coddling and kissing her.

Reese's hand on her arm pulled her from her sad thoughts. "Are you all right? Something wrong?"

Maggie shook her head. "No. It's nothing. Nothing I can do anything about." She pulled in a deep breath and smiled at Holly. A pale and wan-looking Holly. "How are you feeling?"

"Sick." The woman grimaced then grinned as her eyes trailed after the teen who had volunteered to entertain her almost three-year-old son, Daniel.

Maggie felt her heart lighten. "I remember the feeling well."

"But I'm glad to be here where I can let someone else chase that rascal for a bit."

A pretty blond woman walked up and gave Holly a hug. She looked at Maggie and offered a friendly smile. "I'm Paige Seabrook."

"Dylan's wife. I've heard about you. Nice to finally meet you," Maggie said.

"I hear you're having some trouble since the bank robbery," Paige said, then grunted as a toddler hurled himself at her legs. She bent down and picked him up as a boy about ten years old came rushing up.

"I was chasing him. He's fast!"

Paige grinned. "Maggie, these are my two boys, Will and David."

Will held out a hand and Maggie shook it. He smiled. "Nice to meet you." Then he was gone, chasing after a buddy who'd tagged him, leaving David for Paige to wrestle with as he wanted to go with Will.

Paige shook her head, motioned to Dylan to watch the boy as she set him on his feet and watched him go. Dylan started off after him. "They grow so fast." Then her expression turned serious as she returned to the conversation they'd been having before the interruption. "Have you had any more incidents since yesterday?"

Maggie frowned. "No. I was worried about coming here, afraid my presence might put everyone in danger, but Reese said we'd be safer here than at home." She sighed and shook her head. "I really hate that they went after Reese, too."

Holly nodded. "Eli told me about the bomb in Reese's house." She gave a shudder. "How awful."

"I know. Now he's living out of his boathouse and checking up on me every hour or so." Maggie's gaze homed in on Reese and her heart flipped that crazy little cartwheel it liked to do whenever she looked at the man. He still stood with Eli and Dylan. Cal had joined them. "Where's Abby?"

Holly kept one eye on the teen carrying her son, Daniel, around. "She had a delivery at the hospital in Bryson City." Holly turned back to Maggie. "Eli's briefed me each night about the latest happenings, then given me descriptions of who to watch for and orders to keep my doors locked, don't answer the door if I don't know who's there, and so on." She said it with amusement, but the concern in her eyes was real.

Maggie shivered and looked around, wondering if her attacker had followed her to the potluck dinner. She bit her lip, praying she hadn't led trouble to the doorstep of these innocent people.

"Looks like Pastor Collins is getting ready to say the blessing," Holly murmured. As if on cue, the crowd quieted and Pastor Collins blessed the meal.

When he was done, everyone made a beeline for the food-laden tables. Maggie hung back, eyeing the crowd, wondering if the man who'd been terrorizing her was here.

Was he watching?

Waiting for a chance to strike?

Fear tightened her gut and her breath wanted to short out.

"You ready to get a plate?"

Reese's quiet voice settled her nerves immediately. She nodded, eyes on Belle's happy face. "That sounds good."

He led her to the line and she savored his presence beside her.

She just couldn't help feeling that someone was watching. And waiting.

Waiting for a chance to make his move.

"I'm going to get a high chair," Holly said from behind her. "Do you need one for Belle?"

"Yes, that would be great." She frowned. "I guess I could feed her in her carrier, but she likes a high chair better."

"I'll get them for you," Reese offered. "Where are they?"

"In the—"

"Sorry to interrupt. I need to speak to Reese for a minute. We may have a lead on the bank robbery." Eli motioned Reese to the side. Reese smiled an apology and followed Eli to a far corner where Cal waited, phone pressed to his ear.

Holly shrugged. "I can get them."

"I'll come with you," Maggie insisted. "You can't carry two high chairs at the same time."

"True. They're down the hall in the closet next to the bathrooms."

Maggie followed Holly from the fellowship hall into the corridor. As the door shut behind them, the loudness of so many people in one room was muted to a low buzz. Maggie laughed. "My ears are ringing."

Holly grinned then grimaced as she placed a hand over her stomach.

Concerned, Maggie touched the woman's shoulder. "Are you all right?"

"Just really queasy. I've eaten my weight in crackers and it helps, but…" She pulled in a deep breath and swallowed hard. "I'll be all right. Let's get those high chairs." She started down the dark hall. "There's a light switch around here somewhere. Try your side, I'll try this one."

Maggie felt along the wall and a few seconds later, her fingers found the switch. "Here it is."

She flipped it and light flooded them.

"That's better. It's spooky in here without any light." Holly gave a small laugh, but Maggie had to shake off an uncomfortable sudden fear of being separated from the rest of the group.

But she was with Holly. They'd be fine.

Her footsteps echoed as she followed Holly past the restrooms on the right then around the corner to a room labeled Kitchen Storage. "Here we are," Holly said as she pulled the key from the band around her wrist. She inserted it into the lock and opened the door. Reaching in, she flipped the light on.

Then turned with wide eyes and a distinctly green cast to her pretty face. "I'll be in the bathroom for a few minutes." She bolted back down the hall to the restroom, leaving Maggie standing in the storage room.

"Poor thing," Maggie whispered aloud. She'd been a little nauseous with Belle, but hadn't had Holly's problem. She looked around and spied a row of high chairs. They didn't look very heavy and she thought she might be able to carry both at the same time if she balanced them right.

Maybe.

When the hallway behind her went dark, Maggie froze.

Chapter Nine

"Holly?" Maybe she'd come back and hit the light switch by mistake. "Holly? Are you there?"

Silence.

Okay, it wasn't Holly. She would have answered. Maggie's stomach twisted. What should she do? Venture into the dark hall and look for the light switch? Or stay here and wait for Holly to come back from the restroom?

Then she remembered Reese's instructions. Don't go anywhere alone. Stay with someone, even when you go to the restroom.

Trembling started from deep within. Had he followed her here? To the church?

A resounding yes echoed inside her. It was him. The light going off wasn't an accident. And he could probably see her standing in the doorway of the lighted storage closet.

She slapped the switch and plunged them into darkness.

A light footfall fell to her right. From the direction of the restroom.

She moved further inside the small room.

But what about Holly? What if she came out of the restroom and the man attacked her?

Maggie stepped back out into the hall. The hair on the back of her neck stood at full attention. Should she scream and bring everyone running?

Would anyone even hear her through the thick doors that separated the roar of the crowd from this hall?

No, no one would hear, except maybe Holly.

She knew it.

He knew it.

Maggie moved on silent feet down the hall, all sense tuned to the area around her. She prayed to feel any air shift, a hint of cologne or body odor, anything that would tell her he was near.

On trembling legs, she continued her slow tread to the restroom where Holly was. Her fingers trailed the wall even as her mind pictured the door. The first one she came to would be the bathroom.

Fingertips hit the doorjamb just as the bathroom door flew open.

Holly let out a surprised squeal as Maggie pushed her inside, slammed the door shut and locked it.

A heavy fist crashed against the thin wood and Maggie stared at a still-shocked Holly, knowing they didn't stand a chance if the attacker outside decided to kick it in.

"Hey," Reese asked Eli. "Where did Maggie and Holly go?"

Eli looked around and shifted Daniel from his shoulders to the floor. "I don't know. I've been so busy keeping up with this guy I didn't notice that she was missing." He gave a rueful smile then a sympathetic grimace. "She's probably in the bathroom being sick again."

Reese winced at the thought. "But where's Maggie?"

"Oh, she went to get a high chair for Belle. I think Holly went with her," Paige said. "When they came back, I was going to get one for David." She let her eyes scan the crowd. "But they're not back yet." A frown pulled her lips down. "And they should be. The closet is just outside in the hall."

Reese and Eli exchanged a glance. A bad feeling swept through Reese before he could stop it. He headed for the big double doors without another word. Eli was on his heels. He told himself he was just being paranoid, but that didn't stop his blood pressure from skyrocketing and his worry meter from jumping into high.

Pushing through the doors, he stepped into darkness. "Maggie?"

Running footsteps sounded. "Eli, where's the light?"

"Right here."

The hallway lit up. Empty.

Where were they?

A door slammed from the hall that branched to the right. Eli took off in that direction. "I'll check that out. You find Maggie and Holly!"

Reese placed a hand on his weapon and scanned the hallway once again. His eyes landed on the bathroom door just as his cell phone started ringing.

Maggie's tone.

He grabbed his phone from the clip on his belt. "Maggie, are you all right?"

"Someone's in the hallway. Holly and I are in the bathroom." Her terror-filled voice came through the line, singeing his brain and firing his fury at the person doing this to her.

"I'm right outside the door." No sooner had the words left his lips than the door flew open and Maggie's scared face stared up at him. Holly's wide eyes and pale cheeks sent his tension level soaring. "Go back into the crowd and stay there. Tell Cal what's going on and to listen to his radio. I'm going to go after Eli and see if I can help him find whoever was in the hall." Reese spoke into his radio. "I've got Maggie and Holly. They're fine. You catch the guy?"

"Not yet," Eli's disgusted response came back. "I'm at the back of the church. Check the front."

Reese's left hand curled into a fist and he had to make an effort to relax it as he watched as Holly and Maggie safely made it back through the double doors.

Then he spun on his heel and made his way to the side door that led outside. Darkness covered him. Silence made his ears ring.

He stood for a moment to let his eyes adjust. Then he opened them to scan the area. Nothing but the church parking lot. But lots of cars to hide behind.

Reese made his way down the steps, around the side of the building, his gun ready, senses alert. Eli's voice came over the earpiece he'd tucked into his left ear in order to keep the radio quiet. "Hey, any luck?"

"Nothing," he said, keeping his voice low. At the front of the church, he probed each and every shadow, the bushes, the cars on the curb. "He's gone."

"Or hiding, watching us chase our tails," Eli grunted.

"Yeah, I'm feeling a bit exposed. Let's get back inside and check on Maggie and Holly." Eli pulled his cell phone from his pocket. "Jason's on duty, but I noticed he's not here tonight. He said he was going to stop by and grab some food." Eli shook his head. "Guess he changed his mind. I'll get him over here to do a sweep with the big light."

Reese nodded. "I'll meet you back inside." He itched to make sure Maggie was all right. Within seconds, he was in the social hall and standing at the edge of the crowd, searching for her blond head.

Finally, he spotted her at a table in the back, Belle in her lap, spooning food into the little one's mouth. He made his way to her and noticed that Holly had Daniel seated on some hymnals. Holly shrugged as she noticed the direction of his glance. "I wasn't going back to get a high chair."

"Me, either." Maggie shuddered, her eyes troubled.

Reese didn't have any problem figuring out what it was that bothered her. "It's not your fault, Maggie."

"If I hadn't come, then none of this would have happened." She kept her voice low, but he caught the slight tremble that shook her words.

Reese rested a hand on her shoulder and squatted in front of her and Belle. He looked into her eyes and said, "You have every right to be here. Letting him scare you into taking precautions is smart. We did that tonight and you're fine. Letting him ruin your life is not going to happen. Not as long as I'm around. Got it?"

He saw her swallow then give a slow nod. "I agree, but I can't put other people in danger anymore, either. If something had happened to Holly tonight..." She bit her lip. "I can't do that anymore."

Reese glanced around, then sighed. "You may be right. He's escalating, becoming more bold. Trying to get to you in the middle of a crowd like this..." He shook his head. "I didn't think... I'm sorry. I really thought it would be fine for you to come. I'll stay right by your side for as long as you want to stay, then I'll take you home and make sure you're safely inside."

"Then what?"

"Then we keep our eyes open, watch our backs and catch him the minute he lifts his head."

★ ★ ★

For the next week, Maggie's nerves stayed wound up tight. At night, her adrenaline surged at the slightest sound. During the day, she kept the doors locked, the alarm on and only took Belle outside if the deputy on duty was by her side.

A lot of times that deputy was Reese.

In fact, it was more times than not, she'd noticed. As the days passed and she spent more and more hours in his presence, getting to know him and finding out the little things that made him tick, Maggie realized she could fall hard for this man.

If it wasn't for his reluctance to be around Belle. True, he'd held the baby the night someone had broken in, but she didn't think he'd really wanted to.

And that hurt.

Maggie sighed and logged off the computer. For the past few days, she'd juggled her classes and Belle, while trying to find child care. Fiona, Cal's sister, had volunteered to watch Belle today at their ranch while Maggie worked. It was Cal's day off, and he was there to keep an eye on everyone, including his nephew, one-year-old James. Abby was working late and Joseph, Fiona's husband, was on a horse-buying trip. Brother and sister would hold down the fort and take care of the two children.

Now that her classes were done for the day, the house echoed its silence. She missed Belle and her baby chatter, but Maggie had to admit that she was looking forward to enjoying the time to herself for the next two hours.

The phone rang and she jumped. Placing a hand over her racing heart, she wondered if she'd ever be able to fully relax again.

"Hello?"

"I hear you have some free time."

She smiled at Reese's statement. "How'd you hear that?"

"Cal told me. He offered extended babysitting services if you were to accept my invitation."

"Invitation?" The blood started to hum in her veins.

"I wondered if you might like to have dinner with me."

A date? Maggie felt her stomach start to twist itself in knots. *No* hovered on the tip of her tongue.

But she wanted to go.

The week had been slow and had seemed to drag on forever as she'd waited for something else to happen. Something bad. Nothing had happened and she still couldn't let go of the tension.

"Maggie?"

She'd been silent too long. "That sounds lovely, Reese. I'd love to, thanks."

A relieved sigh filtered through the line. "You had me worried there for a minute. How about five o'clock? We'll drive in to Bryson City."

"I'll be ready."

Maggie hung up and just sat there for a moment. It was a little past three o'clock. She had two hours. She wondered if it would be enough time to figure out what she was going to wear.

An hour and a half later, she was ready. Maybe.

Nervousness twisted inside her.

The knock on the door startled her. A quick glance at the clock said four-thirty. Was Reese early?

Hurrying to the door, she peered out the window.

And nearly fell over in shock.

Maggie twisted the knob and threw the door open. "Shannon?"

The pretty brunette smiled. "Hello, Maggie." The woman

looked Maggie up and down and then nodded. "You're look-ing good. Widowhood seems to agree with you."

Maggie threw her guard up. "At least it doesn't leave bruises," she snapped.

"Very true. My brother was a rat. You're well rid of the man. Now may I come in before the officer in your driveway decides to arrest me?"

Maggie stepped back and got a good whiff of Shannon's strong perfume as the woman whipped past her and into the den. Her jeans hugged her perfect figure, the aqua-blue blouse brought out the color of her eyes, and her makeup had been applied with an expert hand.

Shannon looked amazing. As always.

Maggie said, "I've had some…trouble. The officer is there to make sure a certain bank robber doesn't follow through on his threat."

"Bank robber?"

"It's a long story. I didn't know you'd be coming so soon. I thought you'd call or let me know when to expect you."

"I know. I'm sorry. I just managed to get away faster than I thought. I didn't want to waste any more time than necessary in getting here." She plopped on the couch. "Now, where's my Isabella? I can't wait to see her." The excitement in Shan-non's eyes melted Maggie's ire with her high-handed ways and airs of superiority.

"She's not here."

Disappointment fell all over the woman. "Oh, well that's just not what I wanted to hear. Where is she?"

"With some friends. I have a…" What did she have? Did she dare call it a *date*? "I'm having dinner with a friend. He should be here soon."

"Dinner with a friend? A male friend?" Shannon let out a small laugh. "My dear, that's called a date."

Maggie resisted the urge to roll her eyes. But she couldn't help the small smile. "Maybe that's what you call it, but I'm simply calling it dinner. If it becomes more than two friends getting together for a meal…well, we'll just see how it all plays out before we put a label on it, okay?"

"Sure, whatever you say."

"Now, where are you staying?"

With a manicured fingernail, Shannon picked at nonexistent lint on her jeans. "I've got reservations at that quaint little B and B on Main Street, but I'm not sure how long I'll stay there. It's ridiculously expensive for a rinky-dink town like this."

Maggie's brow rose. Shannon worried about money? That was a new one. "Rose Mountain is a wonderful town, Shannon. If you'll give it a chance, I think you'll come to love it."

Shannon pursed her lips. "Hmm. Maybe." She sighed. "I suppose I don't have a choice. I sold my house."

Maggie gaped. "You what? Why would you do that?"

A delicate shrug lifted the woman's shoulder. "I was tired of it. I wanted to do something new."

"But what about your job?"

"I quit. It was boring."

Concerned, Maggie simply stared at Shannon. Would the woman never grow up? Granted, she didn't have to work, but from what Maggie remembered, she'd seemed to enjoy it. And this was the woman she was going to leave Belle with if something happened to her? She sighed. No, she needed to figure that out soon. Shannon's impromptu visit just reinforced that decision.

The doorbell chimed and Maggie rose. "That's probably Reese." She walked to the door and peeked out. In spite of herself, her heart picked up its pace and her palms went slick. Pulling in a steadying breath, she twisted the knob. "Hi."

He grinned down at her. "Hey, there. You look gorgeous."

"So do you." The words slipped out before she could stop them and she felt a flush creep up the back of her neck. His grin widened and his eyes held a decidedly pleased look.

Maggie cleared her throat and stepped back, motioning him in. "There's someone here I want you to meet." Curiosity had him lifting a brow and stepping inside. "I wondered who the car outside belonged to."

She led him into the den and said, "Reese Kirkpatrick, meet my former sister-in-law, Shannon Bennett."

The two shook hands. Maggie thought Shannon allowed her grip to linger a bit longer than necessary and was surprised by the little dart of jealousy she felt. Shannon was a beautiful woman. Would Reese...

He turned to Maggie and she could see conflict on his face. Before he had a chance to say anything, Maggie said, "Shannon, you're welcome to stay here if you like."

"Oh, no. I'll just get checked in to my room at the B and B and see you later." She frowned and bit her lip, looking uncertain. A very un-Shannon-like look. "Will you call me tomorrow?"

"Sure. I have your number from when you called me last week."

"Okay, thanks. Y'all have fun." And then she was gone, leaving Maggie blinking at her sudden perfume-laden departure.

"Wow," Reese said.

"Exactly."

"I don't think Rose Mountain is prepared for her."

"I don't think it's possible to prepare for Shannon. I think all you can do is hang on and hope you don't get tossed off the life raft when the waves start crashing in."

Reese laughed, but Maggie wasn't so sure she meant her

statement to be funny. She had enough chaos in her life right now. Adding Shannon into the mix was enough to twist her stomach in knots and set her nerves on edge.

Maggie hung up the phone after checking on Belle, and Reese wondered if she would stay deep in thought the whole night or just during the ride to Bryson City. "Anything you want to talk about?"

Maggie started. "Oh, sorry. Just thinking."

"About?"

She let out a sigh. "Everything." Then seemed to shake it off. "But tonight's supposed to be fun. I don't want to talk about worries and troubles. Belle is in good hands, and I'm going to dinner for the first time since she's been born without her on my hip. It feels good." She smiled at him and his heart lightened. He really liked this woman.

A lot.

But he wanted to tell her about his baby girl and how she'd died. He needed to explain why he was so uncomfortable around Belle. Although, he had to admit, he was getting better the more he was around her.

But Maggie said she didn't want to talk about worries and troubles. He reached over to grasp her hand. "Okay, I have one thing we need to talk about and then we can put all serious stuff aside and just focus on enjoying ourselves. You want to talk about it now or at the end of the da—er, dinner?"

She turned slightly in her seat to face him and squeezed his hand. "We can talk about anything you want."

"Okay." He pulled in a deep breath and prayed he could get the words out without tearing up. Clearing his throat, he said, "You know my wife died about eighteen months ago."

"Yes."

"Well, what I didn't tell you was that she died in childbirth."

A gasp whispered from her lips and her hand tightened even more around his. "Oh, Reese, I'm so sorry."

"She had an aneurysm. The baby, a little girl we'd named Emma, died, too." He cleared his throat again, hoping to dislodge the knot that always formed there when he talked or thought about his baby.

When Maggie didn't say anything, he looked over at her to see tears standing in her eyes. He quickly looked back at the road. Taking the longer route on the back roads to Bryson City had seemed like a good idea at the time. He'd gotten off I-74 and turned onto the Blue Ridge Parkway. His purpose had been to keep her in the car with him as long as possible in order to give him plenty of time to get the words out. Now they were out and he wished he'd taken the shorter route. At least in the restaurant, there wouldn't be the silence surrounding him.

He finally heard Maggie draw in a deep breath. "Well, that explains a lot."

"Like what?"

"Like why you're so reluctant to hold Belle and be around her."

"Oh. You noticed that, huh?"

She flashed him a watery smile. "It's kind of hard not to."

"I'm sorry, Maggie. Belle is a beautiful child. It's just hard sometimes because when I'm around babies, the memories seem to crash in with more force. The memories, the emotions, the…loss, it just all seems magnified."

"I'm sure."

He drove in silence for the next few miles then asked, "Have I ruined our evening by telling you this?"

For a moment, she didn't answer, then she gave his hand another squeeze and said, "No way. We both need this. I'm glad you told me." More silence, then, "So how's living in the boathouse working for you?"

He gave a surprised laugh at the change of subject. "It's fine for the next couple of weeks until my house is put back together."

Reese caught sight of headlights coming up fast behind him. Keeping his eye on the rearview mirror, he sped up. The person following him jammed the gas, and before Reese could do the same. The impact slammed him forward against the seat belt.

Chapter Ten

Maggie screamed as the seat belt cut into her right shoulder and jerked her back against the seat. Reese's truck swerved to the right then back into the lane as he fought for control. "Get your phone and call Eli!"

Maggie bent and grabbed her purse from the floor, slipped her fingers into the side pocket and pulled out her phone. She didn't know if she'd be able to hear over the pounding of her heart and the squealing tires.

"Here he comes again," Reese warned, his voice tight, knuckles white on the wheel.

Maggie felt her muscles brace for the next impact and sent up a desperate prayer. Metal crunched metal as she kept a tight grip on the phone. She slammed forward then back, her elbow hitting the door. Pain raced up her arm and she ignored it as Reese jerked the car to the left, pressed the gas pedal and zoomed forward.

Her fingers found the touch pad of the phone and it lit up. "What's Eli's number?" she gasped.

He told her and she punched it in then held the phone to her ear. "No, call 911. Eli's too far away."

She hung up and hit the three digits that would bring help. She hoped. Her heart beat fast, adrenaline made her fingers tremble.

The car swerved left, then right. She didn't even want to know where they were on the mountain. She was almost glad for the dark. At least she couldn't see how far she had to fall if the car shot through the guardrail.

The phone rang. Then cut off. "No cell signal, Reese."

"That's why he waited until this moment to attack. I'm an idiot. I should have stuck with the highway."

A car whizzed by on the left and Reese muttered, "We've got to stop this guy or someone's going to get killed."

Trembling, she tried the phone again. "911. What's your emergency?"

"Someone's trying to run us off the road. We're on the Blue Ridge Parkway about..."

"A mile from Highway 19!" Reese hollered.

He swerved around the next bend then jerked the wheel to the left to hit the next curve. The car behind them closed the distance and Reese slammed on the brakes as he rounded the curve on two wheels. Maggie squelched a scream and simply held on as she prayed.

Sparks flew from the car behind them as it ran along the guardrail. It fell back a few feet and Reese raced to make the turn onto the highway.

"Look!" She gestured to the blue lights heading their way.

"Thank God."

Reese approached the intersection of Highway 19 and slowed. Maggie kept an eye on the car behind them. It raced up and Reese jerked to the left at the last minute into the on-coming-traffic lane.

Their attacker roared past and squealed around the corner onto Highway 19, barely missing an oncoming car. Horns blared and the Bryson City police cruiser took up the chase.

Reese braked to a stop on the side of the road. Maggie leaned her head against the window and closed her eyes, offering a hearty thank-you prayer that they were still alive.

"That was scary." Reese's rumble filled the car.

"I can't believe you didn't go over the side."

"I was number one in my class when it came to defensive driving."

"That's good. You did good."

The inane conversation helped to calm her. Reese finally opened the door and flashed his badge at the approaching officers. Maggie climbed out the passenger side and almost hit the ground as her knees buckled. She sank back into the seat to marshal her strength and wait for the shaking to stop.

When she finally gathered herself together enough to get out of the car, she shivered. Pulling the edges of her coat more tightly around her, she watched Reese talk with the officers. As she approached them, his eye caught hers. Frustration glinted in them. Her heart dropped. "He got away?"

"Yeah. He lost them on a curve."

Maggie didn't have enough energy to be upset. She felt drained, wiped out, empty. An effect of the ebbing of the adrenaline rush, she felt sure.

Reese caught her fingers in his. "Come on. Let's let them worry about this guy for a while. Eli's going to fax over another copy of the bank robber's picture. They'll be watching for him. As for us, we have a dinner to eat."

She stared up at him. "You still want to go?"

"Absolutely." The firm set of his jaw said he wasn't going to let the harrowing mountain ride ruin the evening. Some of her energy began to seep back in.

★ ★ ★

Reese hung up the phone, pulled into the restaurant parking lot and cut the engine. He'd called Eli to fill him in about the accident. Once Eli was satisfied no one was hurt, he'd given Reese an update on the robbery investigation. Reese planned to give Maggie the details, but first asked, "You okay?"

Maggie drew in a deep breath. "I think so. You?"

He nodded. "Come on. Let's get a table and I'll tell you what Eli said."

They headed toward the entrance and Maggie breathed in the night air. "It'll be Thanksgiving soon," she said.

"I know. Next week."

They stepped inside and Reese gave his name to the hostess, who led them to a table for two at the back of the restaurant. Maggie smiled and he thought he caught sight of a small dimple in her right cheek. "This is nice," she said as she took in the log cabin atmosphere.

"They have amazing steaks. Eli brought me out here about a year ago. I'd just recovered from a gunshot wound and—"

"You were shot?" Shock rippled across her face.

"Yeah. It's a long story, but my sister-in-law, Abby, was in trouble, and I was trying to warn her. By the time I got out here, trouble had already found her and he shot me for good measure."

"Oh, my goodness."

"I know. So anyway, after I recovered, before I went back to Washington, Eli brought me here. Told me I needed to slow down and move to a small town."

Maggie lifted a brow as the waitress filled their water glasses. After several minutes studying their menus, Maggie asked, "What did you say to that?"

"I laughed at him."

"And yet here you are."

Reese gave a rueful chuckle as he remembered that day. "I think Eli and God had a conversation that I wasn't privy to at the time."

Maggie was quiet for a moment as she studied the table. Then looked up at him. "How do you feel about God after everything you've been through?"

Reese was glad for the brief interruption as the waitress took their order. After she left, he said, "At first I was really angry with God. Blamed Him, blamed Abby, blamed everyone I thought had a part in Keira and Emma's deaths." He sighed. "I was so sure I had a right to seek revenge, but through that whole process of blaming Abby I found I didn't like myself very much. Anger was eating me up inside. Fortunately, I recognized what it was doing to me and was able to find forgiveness and peace."

She looked shocked at his confession. "That doesn't sound like you."

"It wasn't me." He frowned and sighed. "It's difficult to explain, but in my quest for answers, God showed me that wasn't what He had planned for me. He showed me that I was designed for more than that. That I had a purpose, a reason for being here. And one of those reasons was to help save Abby. Once I was able to focus on that, my heart changed."

He saw her swallow hard and wondered if he should have bared so much of his soul. Would it send her running? He tensed as he gave her time to process everything. Then she gave him a gentle smile, the empathy and concern shining in her eyes making him relax. She said, "That's quite a testimony."

"It's just what happened." He took a sip of water. "I'd rather hear about you. Will you tell me what happened with you and your husband?"

She studied him for a moment and he wondered if she'd

let him change the subject. Then she shrugged. "At first, I was just dumbfounded that he'd turned out to be an abuser. I couldn't believe he'd managed to hide that part of himself the entire time we dated and were engaged. That I hadn't seen something to set off warning bells in my head. But there was nothing. Even now, looking back at that time, I can't think of anything he might done that I should have noticed as...off." She twisted her fingers and placed her elbows on the table. Settling her chin in her palms, she sighed. "Of course, I realized at some point that he was pushing the relationship along at a pretty fast clip, but..." She shook her head, the confusion on her face snagging his heart and giving it a twist. "But I have to say, I just went along with him. I couldn't believe someone like Kent was interested in me. And—" she swallowed hard "—I was lonely. I let him sweep me off my feet." She gave a grimace.

"So how do you feel about finding someone else? Trusting again?" He tensed, waiting for her answer.

A flush crept into her cheeks. "I think the right man could convince me to try again." Then the flush faded and she said, "I made a really bad choice the first time. I won't do that again." She stared into his eyes. "The right man would have to be patient, take things slow and prove himself." A shrug lifted her shoulders. "I hate that I feel that way, but I guess I just don't know that I trust myself. My judgment. If I could be so wrong before, where do I find the discernment to know that I won't make the same kind of mistake again?"

Reese gave a slow nod. "I guess I can understand why you would feel that way."

"You can?" She seemed surprised.

"Sure. People do it all the time. Not just in relationships like a marriage, but any kind of situation where you're required to make a judgment call or a decision. When you make the wrong one, it's hard to trust that you'll make the right one next time you're faced with the same choice. And now it's not just you who'll be affected by your decision. You have Belle to think of, too."

Maggie dropped her eyes to the plate that the waitress set in front of her, and he could almost see her mind spinning.

For the next several minutes after Reese said the blessing, they ate in comfortable silence.

Then Maggie said, "You haven't filled me in on what Eli had to say about the robbery."

Reese nodded. "They caught the owner of the getaway vehicle."

"Really? Did he tell them the name of the man you shot?"

"Not yet. They caught him in Asheville, but they're bringing him to Bryson City and we're going to play him and Berkley off against each other."

"What do you mean?"

Reese smiled at her as anticipation threaded through him. "Just a little cop game that usually nets some pretty good results. We let them 'accidentally' see each other in the station and then let them know that each of them is being questioned individually. At some point, we usually have enough info on one that we can 'let it slip' to the other that his partner is squealing on him and if he wants to make a deal, now's the time to spill it."

She smiled at him, the admiration in her gaze making him feel ten feet tall. She nodded. "Clever."

"One of the oldest tricks in the book, but it still works when it's done right."

She frowned and Reese could see her mind working. "But that means that it wasn't him who tried to run us off the parkway."

"No, I'm guessing it was his buddy—the one I shot."

"Wounded, but not hurt badly enough to need time to recover."

Reese lifted a brow. "Exactly."

"So he's alone and out for revenge—or he simply wants to shut us up so we don't testify when his partners go to trial."

"Right."

He glanced out the window behind Maggie—a window he made sure was far enough to her left that no one outside could see her sitting at the table—and saw the Rose Mountain cruiser sitting in the parking lot. Probably Mitchell or the new guy, Jason. He smiled. Eli was making sure he had backup should anything else happen on the way home.

His smile slipped into a frown. Maybe this had been a bad idea. From a safety standpoint. Then he looked at the woman across from him, her soft blond hair falling over her shoulders, her delicate lashes fanning her cheeks, and he couldn't regret the time alone with her.

When they'd finished their dinner, Reese felt that he had a better grasp of Maggie and what made her tick. He didn't think he had the whole picture, but at least he had one that wasn't so blurry.

She wanted to trust him, trust her judgment that he was a good guy, but she was still unsure, still hesitant to take that leap of faith yet. And he didn't blame her. He would have his work cut out for him to prove he wasn't like her dead husband. And while he was proving that, he had to find a way to make sure he kept her safe.

He drew in a deep breath. "What do you think about moving to a safe house until we catch this guy?"

Chapter Eleven

Maggie stepped into her house and shut the door behind her. Full of emotions and feelings from the date—and it *had* been a date—she'd decided against inviting Reese inside. Especially after that question he'd dropped on her at supper. A safe house?

She didn't think so. At least not yet.

He seemed to understand what was going on inside her and hadn't pushed. Instead, he'd made sure there was no awkward moment on the front porch. He'd simply hugged her and said, "I enjoyed the time with you. Sleep well." He'd gestured to the cruiser now in his spot at the end of her driveway. "You've got a good watchdog, rest easy."

She'd nodded and smiled and wondered how she would sleep tonight. Without Belle in the house. Fiona had called to say Belle had fallen asleep, and she was welcome to leave her there for the night. She'd also offered, "You can come here for the night, if you want."

Maggie thought about it. "No, someone's after me, Fiona. I

wouldn't feel right about staying with you. I might just bring a truck full of trouble to your door if I do that."

Fiona had simply laughed. "Wouldn't be the first time." Then she'd sobered. "I understand. Belle will be safe here, I promise."

Cal would drop her off on his way in to work in the morning. Maggie had mixed feelings about leaving her daughter there, but, truthfully, she wondered if Belle wasn't safer on Fiona's ranch than in the little house with Maggie.

The question tore at her. And if she hadn't been so conflicted, she would have gone right over to the ranch and picked Belle up. But she wanted her baby to be safe. And the fact was, she might be safer away from her mother.

Maggie sank onto the couch, pushed that depressing thought away and let her mind drift to Reese. The man intrigued her, drew her...and scared her. Not in a physical way, as Kent had, but on a deeper, emotional level. He could be dangerous to her heart.

The phone rang.

Maggie snatched it from the end table. "Hello?"

"I'm not going away."

At first, she didn't understand the whispery voice. "What?"

"I'll be back. No one can protect you from me."

Maggie's thumb pressed the button to hang up the phone. She pressed it twice for good measure. Trembling, her heart thudding from the sudden adrenaline rush, she checked the caller ID.

Private call.

She stood on shaky legs and walked to the window to look out. The cruiser still sat there at the end of her driveway.

Walking into the kitchen, she checked the door, then each room of the house, one by one. All were fine. The bathrooms were empty. No one was hiding in her house. The phone call had her spooked. Her heart still raced and her palms were slick with sweat.

She dialed Reese's number with one hand and peered out at the cruiser once again. She didn't want to go outside and expose herself, even if the cop car was just a few steps from her door.

"Hello?"

"Reese, I just got a phone call that worries me."

His tone sharpened. "What did he say?"

"'I'll be back. No one can protect you from me.'" Just saying the words made the trembling start anew.

A harsh mutter came through the line. Then he said, "I see why you're scared. All right, I'm going to get Eli to see if he can trace the number that called you. Is Jason still outside?"

"Yes."

"I'm going to give him a heads-up and tell him to come inside with you. Then I'm going to talk to Eli. I'll get back to you."

"Okay." She hated the fear that came through that one small word.

"Hey." His voice softened. "You're going to be okay."

Tears threatened. "I know. Thanks, Reese."

"I enjoyed tonight, Maggie."

That made her smile. "I did, too."

He hung up, and she slowly placed the phone on the counter. Deputy White knocked on the door within a minute. She let him in and he scoured the house again. She wasn't surprised that he insisted on searching and came up empty, too. She supposed searching her house by herself had been rather stupid. What if there *had* been someone inside?

Her phone rang again.

She jumped and this time checked the caller ID. Relief swept through her when she saw Shannon's number. "Hello?"

"Oh, Maggie, I'm so glad I got you. My reservation at the B and B fell through. I need a place to stay. Could I use your spare room?"

Maggie hesitated. She wouldn't mind having Shannon there, but... "Shannon, someone seems to be trying to hurt me. A bank robber has threatened me. I don't know that you'll be safe here."

A pause. "Well, there's safety in numbers, right? Plus you have a cop sitting outside your house. I'm not worried about it."

Maggie fidgeted, wondering if she dared allow Shannon to stay. If something happened to the woman while she was here... "I don't know..."

"Please? I don't have anywhere else to go tonight. Tell the nice deputy that I'm coming so he won't shoot me, okay?"

Maggie sighed. With Shannon, it was always easier to give in than to argue. "Okay, fine. I'll see you soon."

Shannon's knock on the door came thirty minutes later. Maggie answered it and stared at her sister-in-law in surprise. The woman looked a bit more worn than she had before Maggie left with Reese for supper. "Are you okay?"

"Oh, yeah, just very tired and a little frustrated." Shannon rolled her suitcase inside and waved a hand. "When I got to the B and B, they had apparently lost my reservation. Or given it to someone else—or something. Thanksgiving is just a week away and they're filled to capacity."

She placed her hands on her hips and rolled her eyes. "It was too late to find another place to stay."

"So you called me." Maggie smiled, her nerves easing at the woman's presence. Maybe this would be a good idea after all.

"Yes."

"Well, you'll have to take my bedroom. Belle's room is next door and then my office is across the hall."

"Oh, no," Shannon groaned. "I'm putting you out, aren't I?" She grabbed her suitcase handle and the small toiletries bag she'd set on the floor.

As she did, the toiletries bag hit the floor with a thump and the small clasp fell open. Makeup, toothpaste and a small aspirin bottle rolled out. With a grunt, Shannon bent to pick them up. "I'll just drive into that little town that's not too far from here and—"

"Don't be silly," Maggie said as she grabbed the aspirin and handed it Shannon. The woman tucked everything back in the bag and fastened the clasp. Maggie pursed her lips and motioned toward her room. "Go on, I'll be fine. I have a very comfortable daybed in my office." She shrugged. "I spend more time in there than my bedroom anyway."

Shannon continued to look torn and Maggie asked, "You really want to drive to the next town?"

Her sister-in-law shuddered. "No." She pulled the suitcase closer. "Okay, if you're sure."

"I'm sure."

"I'm going job hunting tomorrow. As soon as I get a job, I'll be out of your hair, I promise."

Maggie pointed to her room. "Go."

Shannon didn't hesitate a moment longer. She rolled her suitcase into Maggie's room then darted into the nursery. Maggie followed, curious.

Then watched with amusement as Shannon peered into the crib. Maggie didn't want to laugh at Shannon's disappointment, she knew the woman loved Belle and had missed her over the last few months they'd been gone, but her disgusted expression was quite funny. "She's at a friend's house for the night," Maggie explained.

"Bummer." Shannon pouted. "I wanted to see her."

"I know you did. You can see her tomorrow. My friend

Cal's dropping her off first thing on his way in to work." An idea occurred to Maggie. "Speaking of seeing Belle. How would you like to watch her for me while I'm teaching to-morrow?"

Delight lit up Shannon's face. "Are you kidding? I'd love to. We'll stay right here and play, but we won't get in your way."

Relief filled Maggie. "Wonderful." Then she frowned. "But what about your job hunt?"

"Are you crazy? Hunt for a job or take care of my niece?" She lifted a brow. "Hon, that's a no-brainer."

On impulse, Maggie hugged the woman. "I'm glad you're here, Shannon, I've missed you."

"Me, too, Maggie. Very glad I'm here." She frowned. "Al-though, I should be completely furious with you for running off without a word."

"I left a note."

"It's not the same thing. I looked for you for a month. I thought about hiring a private detective, but decided to wait and see if you called."

Maggie sighed. "I know. And I'm sorry, but I did what I had to do at the time." She forced a smile. "Forgive me?"

"Maybe." Shannon's lower lip jutted.

Maggie's smile this time was real. "Good night, Shannon."

"Night." Shannon disappeared into Maggie's bedroom. Maggie had spent the thirty minutes between Shannon's call and subsequent arrival changing the sheets and cleaning the bathroom. Shannon should be fine for the night.

Maggie walked into her office, now her bedroom, and shut the door. Shannon didn't seem bothered by the police officer sitting outside Maggie's house or the fact that Maggie had a need for him. And Maggie had to admit that having another adult in the house eased her fears tremendously.

Walking over to her desk, she picked up the envelope she'd

meant to mail today and sighed. She'd get it in the mail to-morrow first thing.

Placing the envelope right where she would see it, she laid down on the daybed and closed her eyes.

Worry took over, making them shoot wide open. Would having another woman in the house deter the man who seemed determined to terrorize her into silence? Or would he just go through Shannon to get to Maggie, if that's what it took?

Maggie forced her eyes closed and prayed for safety.

Reese walked into the office the next morning and sat at his desk while he smothered a yawn.

"You know you can come stay with us, don't you?" Cal asked from the doorway.

Reese snapped his jaw shut and sniffed. "I smell coffee. Good coffee. And I know I can. I appreciate the offer, but I want to stay close to Maggie."

The white foam cup appeared in front of him. He snatched it and took a careful swig. "Ahhh. Thanks. My coffeemaker didn't survive the blast." He shook his head. "The bomb goes off in my bedroom, and the coffeemaker takes a hit in the kitchen." He rolled his eyes. "Nothing else in the kitchen. Just the coffeemaker."

"No explaining how or why blasts destroy the things they destroy and leave the things they leave."

"Yeah."

"How's Maggie?"

Reese frowned. "She was all right. I'm getting ready to take my turn watching her house."

"I've got the shift after you."

Reese nodded. "I'm wondering if we should consider moving her to a safer place."

Cal perched himself on the edge of Reese's desk and took a sip of his coffee. "Might not be a bad idea. Got kind of quiet there for a while then the attempt to run you off the road and a threatening call all in one night." He shook his head. "Not good."

"I know." He smiled. "But on the bright side, Maggie's not alone right now. She has a visitor."

"Who?"

"Her former sister-in-law, Shannon Bennett."

"That's good to know. She the one driving that white Mercedes around town?"

"Yep."

"Nice." He paused and his expression turned thoughtful. "She was in the diner last night and caused quite a stir in some of the regulars. Several men were tripping over themselves trying to buy her a drink or her supper."

"It's a small town, where the men outnumber the women by five to one. She's bound to stir things up as long as she's here."

"Better keep our eyes open."

"And our backs to the wall," Reese grunted.

Maggie turned off her computer and stretched. Wednesday was her busiest day with four classes practically back to back, time for a quick lunch then two more classes. Her stomach rumbled, and she glanced at the clock. Time to think about dinner.

She could hear Shannon singing a silly song about horses and cowgirls to Belle. The two had hit it right off the minute Cal had dropped Belle at the house this morning. Maggie had watched them for a little while and then gone to work with a smile.

She'd joined them for lunch, then heard Shannon in Belle's room rocking the baby to sleep. All in all, Maggie felt good about the situation. Good enough to wonder if Shannon might consider doing this for a while.

At least until she found another job.

If she intended to find one. She still couldn't believe Shannon had quit her job back in Spartanburg. She thought she'd planned to just take a leave of absence or some vacation time.

Belle was still sleeping, and Maggie found Shannon in the den reading a novel. "Would you like to stay for Thanksgiving?" she found herself asking.

Shannon looked up, surprise on her face. Then pleasure. "I'd love it."

Maggie felt warmth start to thaw the area around her heart. Shannon really did seem different than when she'd last been around her. Softer, more content. Happy.

"Great." Then she frowned. "What about your parents? Won't they expect you to be with them?"

A grimace crossed Shannon's face. "My parents. I suppose we need to talk about them."

Maggie lifted a brow. "What do you mean?"

"I told them I was going to be moving to Rose Mountain to be closer to you and Belle, and they flipped."

"Flipped?"

"They weren't happy with me."

"Well—" Maggie gave a soft sigh "—they've never liked me and never wanted anything to do with Belle, so that's not surprising, is it?"

This time it was Shannon's turn to look surprised. "What do you mean? Of course they wanted something to do with Belle. But you're right, they didn't approve of you." She shrugged. "No offense, it's just a fact."

Maggie was beyond taking offense at something she'd known and accepted for years. But to hear they wanted to be part of Belle's life?

"But Kent said—"

Shannon waved off her protest with a sharp jab of her hand. An angry glint sparked in the woman's eyes. "Every word out of my brother's mouth was a lie. Haven't you figured that out yet?"

Maggie sank onto the couch. Yes, she'd figured it out before the first year of her marriage had passed. But his parents... "Then why didn't they ever let me know that they wanted to see her?"

"Because Kent wouldn't let them."

Maggie's jaw dropped. "Wouldn't let them?" She knew she sounded like a parrot, repeating Shannon's words, but shock had frozen her brain.

Shannon shook her head and narrowed her eyes. "Kent needed money. He asked them to give it to him. They wouldn't."

More shock settled over her. She wilted into the pillow behind her. "Money? But we weren't hurting for money. You saw the house we lived in, the car Kent drove." He hadn't allowed her to drive, but spared no expense when it came to his own automobile. Fortunately, they lived within walking distance of a small grocery store. When he left for work, she often went walking, sometimes to the grocery store, sometimes to the small church on the outskirts of the neighborhood.

Shannon gave a small, uncharacteristic snort. "It was all image with him. And, yeah, he made good money as a stockbroker, but he also liked to gamble, and that wasn't a good thing for his bank account."

"Gamble?" Maggie felt the blood drain from her face. "I never really knew him at all, did I?"

"No, unfortunately, you didn't."

Belle's "I'm awake" cry sounded and Shannon jumped to

her feet, the book tumbling onto the floor. "I'll get her," she said as she raced toward the nursery.

In spite of the things she'd just learned about her former in-laws and the disturbing news about Kent, Maggie smiled and shook her head as she picked up the book. It might be nice having Shannon around.

She thought about the envelope still sitting on her desk to be mailed and looked down the hall where Shannon had disappeared into Belle's room.

Maybe she'd wait another couple of days before mailing it after all.

Reese knocked on Deputy White's cruiser window. The glass lowered and Reese caught the man on the tail end of a yawn. "Sorry," White said. "It's just boring as all get out watching this place."

"Wasn't boring a few nights ago."

"Yeah. I know." He said it as if he wished something would happen.

"Reese?"

He turned to see Maggie standing in the doorway. Her flushed cheeks and the white substance on her nose and cheeks said she'd been busy in the kitchen. He tapped the door and said to Jason, "You can take off. I've got the evening covered."

"You don't have to say it twice." Deputy White started the car and left, a spray of gravel spitting up behind him as he turned out of the driveway.

Reese gave the area around him a good look as he walked toward Maggie. He admired her beauty, and wondered what she saw in him. Then decided he didn't care as long as she liked what she saw.

The look in her eyes said she did.

A strange, peaceful feeling flowed through him, taking him by surprise. And making him smile.

"Would you like to join us for dinner?" she asked.

"Shannon's still here?"

"She is."

He swiped a finger down her nose. "What did that belong to?"

Maggie giggled. And his heart did strange things. Things it hadn't done in a very long time. She backed up and motioned him inside, saying, "I made cookies for dessert. I haven't baked in a while and decided we needed some sweets."

"I'm always up for cookies." He followed her into the small foyer and saw Shannon holding Belle. She smiled and he nodded. "I'm glad you're here to keep Maggie company."

"Me, too."

Reese felt the hair on the back of his neck rise. Uneasiness flowed through him and he shivered at the sudden unexpected feeling.

The foyer window shattered inward and Reese felt a sting under his right eye even as he dove for Maggie, heard Shannon scream, and two more bullets pound the wooden door.

Chapter Twelve

Maggie whirled, her first thought to grab Belle and cover her. A hard arm around her waist stopped her midflight and took her to the floor. She cried out. "Belle!"

"Stay here," Reese demanded. Maggie flipped around to see him pull Shannon and Belle to the floor behind the recliner in the den.

He was already reaching for his phone when the glass on the other side of the door mimicked the first one, shattering all over the foyer floor and spraying into the den.

Reese barked, "Shooter at Maggie Bennett's house with a good view of her front door."

Trembling, breaths coming in pants and tears blurring her eyes, she crawled toward Belle and Shannon, her only thought to get to her baby and cover her, protect her.

"Maggie! Stop! Stay still!"

She froze.

And realized she was crawling over the glass on the floor.

And her arms were bleeding. "Belle," she cried as she frantically searched for Shannon and the baby.

"She's fine, Maggie. I have her. She's fine," Shannon reassured her. Maggie wasn't reassured. She wanted to see her baby for herself, hold her in her arms and keep her safe.

A bullet hit just above her head. She ducked with a scream.

Glass crunched under Reese's feet as he moved toward her. What was he doing? He'd be exposed. She felt him gently grasp her upper arm and pull her up and way from the line of fire. "Down the hall, into the bedroom and under the bed."

She jerked from his grasp. "Not without my baby."

"I'll get Belle and bring her to you, but go."

Three more shots beat a staccato beat against her door, and one whizzed by Reese, who flinched and pulled her down once more. "Go!"

She went. Crying and begging God to spare the life of her child.

And everyone in her house.

Anger, hot and furious flowed through her, drying her tears, fueling her determination, even as she heard footsteps behind her. She turned to see Shannon leading the way, followed by Reese who had Belle tucked up against his chest, shoulders hunched over her.

Maggie slipped into the bedroom and sank to the floor next to the bed, making sure she was out of sight of the window on the opposite wall.

Shannon burst through the door and dropped beside her. Maggie held her arms out for Belle and flinched when Reese hesitated, then handed the crying baby to Shannon. He stumbled back so fast he nearly tripped and fell. Her stomach dipped as she realized how hard it was for him to hold Belle even in this crazy situation. But to give the baby to Shannon, that hurt. Then she saw her outstretched arms and knew why he'd hesitated.

Blood covered her arms from elbow to wrist where she'd tried to crawl army-style across the glass in her foyer.

"We'll get you some medical help soon," he promised.

"I'm fine. I'll be fine." But the trembling wouldn't stop, and the terrible nerve-shattering fear just kept building. Shannon looked pale, but surprisingly calm as she huddled over a now-screaming Belle. Maggie's heart wrenched at her daughter's angry and scared cries, but with her arms the mess they were, Maggie couldn't do anything but whisper comforting words in her ear.

"I'm going after him," Reese said. "Stay put and stay away from the windows."

"Reese, no! You can't! Not without your backup." She blinked. "Where is your backup? Why are they taking so long to get here?"

"It's not taking them that long," he grunted as he pushed the tall dresser in front of the window. "It just seems like it is when you've got bullets whizzing all around you."

And then he was gone, locking the bedroom door behind him.

The sudden silence made Reese's ears ring. No more bullets came his way, but that didn't mean the shooter was gone. In the foyer, he waited by the door, his gun ready. Where was Jason? When no more shots sounded, he headed for the kitchen door and threw it open, staying off to the side, well clear of the opening.

More silence.

Reese waited then said into his phone, "How far away are you?"

"You should hear us coming in about a minute."

"I'm going after him, Eli."

"Reese…" The warning in Eli's voice didn't deter him.

"He's already stopped shooting. If I wait any longer, he's going to be long gone."

"Where's Jason?"

"Good question." Reese looked out the window and saw the deputy behind his car, weapon drawn. "I see him. The two of us will get started looking for him."

"Where's he shooting from?"

He looked across the lake. "My house." Reese stiffened as he saw a lone figure racing along the edge of his property, a rifle clutched in his right hand. Reese shoved his Bluetooth piece into his ear and kept his phone on so Eli could hear what was going on. "I see him. He's at the edge of the lake. I'm using the trees for cover."

Over the radio, Reese said, "Jason, watch the house."

"Copy that." Jason's voice sounded a bit wobbly. Could be he'd gotten a little more excitement than he'd wanted. *Lord, don't let him get shot.*

Slipping the phone into his pocket, he kept his eyes on the figure who still moved along the edge of the lake.

He was heading this way, toward Maggie's house, not away from it. Coming to check and make sure his bullets hit home?

Reese frowned at the man's uneven gait. He kept weaving, unsteady, losing his footing every now and then.

Now at the top of the semicircle the cove made, the shooter kept up his awkward pace and came toward Maggie's house at a good clip, then stumbled and went down on one knee. He got up and continued on the same path. Coming straight toward Reese, who stayed hidden in the edge of the trees.

Then the silence was broken by the sound of sirens in the distance. Eli was on his way. Jason had the house covered. Maggie, Belle and Shannon were safe as long as Reese had eyes on the shooter. The man stopped, and Reese finally got a good look at him. The one named Slim. His indecision was plain to see from where Reese stood.

Keeping to the trees at the top of the property, Reese started making his way toward the shooter. Soon he would be in the exposed grassy area that led toward the muddy area of the lake.

Then Slim was moving again, having come to an apparent decision on what he planned to do.

And that was to run.

Reese quit trying to be quiet and took off after the now-fleeing shooter, leaving the cover of the trees and praying Slim didn't turn and start taking shots at him. Slim probably had a car waiting near Reese's house and wanted to get back to it now that he could hear that help was on the way. Reese felt sure that the man hadn't planned on leaving anyone alive to call the cops. Fortunately, Slim didn't seem to be such a great shot.

Heart thumping, Reese heard his feet pounding over the hard ground. He broke through the dense tree line, playing tag with the trees scattered along the edge of the crescent-shaped shoreline, using them for cover as he kept pursuing the fleeing figure. Slim glanced back over his shoulder, and Reese was close enough to see determination stamped on the man's features.

Then he stumbled and went down. Propped himself up and tried to keep going. Fell again, then turned the gun on Reese who came within thirty yards. Reese darted behind the nearest tree as he lifted his weapon and yelled, "Freeze! Drop your gun!"

Slim slung the rifle around and pulled the trigger. Bark flew from the tree, and Reese flinched as he felt his cheek sting. As the man took a few precious seconds to aim for a better shot, Reese squeezed the trigger. Slim screamed and went down, his rifle landing beside him as he clutched his leg.

Reese looked over his shoulder to see Eli and backup racing toward him. Keeping his weapon trained on the man now writhing on the ground, he strode to him and kicked the rifle out of reach.

As Slim cried out his agony, Reese stated, "You're under arrest. You have the right to remain silent." As Reese quoted him the Miranda rights, another siren bit through the winter air. An ambulance, guided by Eli on the phone, headed their way. Fortunately, the injured party was the one on the ground and not any of his intended victims.

As Eli reached his side, Reese holstered his weapon. Eli patted the suspect down and came up with nothing but a piece of paper with a phone number on it in the man's left front pocket.

Reese pulled his cell phone out and called the number.

"Anything?" Eli asked.

"Straight to voice mail. Phone's turned off and the voice mail is an automated one."

EMTs approached on Eli's signal and went straight to the moaning man. Cal stood next to him to make sure he didn't try anything, but Reese didn't think he had the ability to do much. The bright flush on the shooter's cheeks and the harsh panting breaths didn't fit with the short sprint along the edge of the lake.

"Reese, are you okay?"

He turned to see Maggie jogging toward him, concern and fear on her face.

The blood on her arms was still there. He said, "I'm fine, but let's get you looked at." Reese gestured toward one of the EMTs, who came over. "Can you take a look at her arms?"

She flushed. "They look worse than they are, I think. They just sting really bad." She frowned. "You're bleeding."

He lifted a hand to his cheek. "It's nothing. We need to get your arms taken care of."

A protest still on her lips and concern in her eyes, she walked with the paramedic toward the truck, Reese close on her heels. When they passed the man who'd tried to kill her, she came to a stop and looked down at him. The shooter met her gaze and smirked through his pain. Maggie's expression didn't change. She simply stared at him.

It seemed to unnerve him. "What?" Slim gritted out.

"Was it worth it?"

Confusion flickered in his bloodshot eyes. "What are you talking about?"

"The bank robbery. Trying to kill us? Possibly killing a baby. Everything. Was it worth it?"

He grunted then glared. "If you hadn't interfered, everything would have gone as planned. And yeah, it would have been worth it."

Maggie didn't flinch, didn't blink, didn't move. She simply stared as she processed the man's words. Reese frowned, wondering what was going through her head. Then she said, "But you got away. You could have kept going and never looked back. You could have hit another bank and probably gotten away with the money. Why keep coming after us? Why take a chance on getting caught when you knew I had deputies watching my every move?"

He shut his mouth and looked away.

"What's your name?"

"None of your business."

Maggie didn't budge, just kept her gaze on the man.

Again, her unwavering stare seemed to make him uncomfortable and he sighed, then coughed, a harsh hacking cough. A groan escaped him and he said, "I'm in the system. All you gotta do is run my prints."

"So what's your name?" she pressed.

"Doug Patterson. Can I have some water?"

Reese wrapped his hand around Maggie's upper arm and gently pulled her toward the waiting paramedic. This time, Maggie didn't protest, but the frown between her brows remained.

"We got him. It's over."

A laugh sounded from behind him. He turned to see the EMT working on Patterson, but the man's hard eyes said he had something else to say. Reese lifted a brow in his direction.

"Over?" Patterson gave a humorless snort then licked his dry chapped lips. "You think this is over? You ruined the chance of a lifetime for me," he snarled. "It's far from over. A lot of money was lost on this job." Fury turned his blue eyes to chips of ice. "And my boss isn't going to let it just be over. So you'd better watch your back and sleep with one eye open."

"Shut up!" Shannon yelled as she stomped toward them, Belle in her arms. "Just shut up! How can you do this to people? To a baby? You could have killed her!"

Reese stepped in between Shannon and the man now glaring at her. She looked mad enough to do him bodily damage. Belle sucked on her pacifier and seemed content until she spotted Maggie with the EMT. Belle let out a cry and held her arms out toward Maggie.

Reese reluctantly took the baby from a glowering Shannon and walked over to Maggie. Another officer led a still-furious and vocal Shannon away.

Belle squirmed in Reese's arms, wanting her mother. Maggie looked at Belle and crooned, "Just a minute, baby."

Her wounds didn't look as bad as he'd feared when he first saw all the blood. Now that they were almost cleaned up, he could see that the cuts weren't too deep. As the EMT began to bandage the worst ones, he concentrated on soothing Belle, knowing his attempts were awkward and unwanted.

Screeching, Belle strained against him and lunged for Maggie. Reese prayed the paramedic would hurry up.

Maggie finally pushed the helping hands away with an apology and reached for Belle.

Reese let her go, the heat from her small body nearly singeing his palms. The baby quieted the moment her mother's arms closed around her. Maggie placed a kiss on her daughter's forehead and whispered soothing words in her tiny ear. Reese's heart jerked in his chest, and he swallowed hard. What would it be like to be on the receiving end of Maggie's love?

The thought nearly overwhelmed him and he turned away to concentrate on what he needed to do to get information out of the now-subdued Patterson.

Subdued due to pain medication. Reese wanted to jerk the IV out of the man's arm.

The EMT working on him looked at Reese. "This guy has a bad infection in his left shoulder. Looks like it's from a previous gunshot wound. He's got a fever and is one sick dude."

"Yeah, well, today's not the first time I've shot him."

The EMT lifted a brow. "Ooo-kay."

Reese didn't bother to explain as they loaded Patterson into the back of the ambulance. Cal holstered his weapon and said, "I'll go with him."

"I'm going to get Maggie and Shannon settled back inside the house." He looked at Eli. "Then we've got to talk."

Eli nodded. "Yeah, because while we've caught all the robbers, this is obviously not over."

"Exactly."

Maggie paced the floor of her kitchen, her sneakers making a squeaking noise on the linoleum with each step. It wasn't over. Why not?

Reese said to give him a few minutes to finish things up and he'd be in. He'd also called someone to come over to patch up the window that had been shattered by the bullets. Maggie had gotten Belle to sleep with very little trouble, but she was afraid the hammering and banging would soon wake her. She'd practically had to pry the baby out of Shannon's arms to put her to sleep. "But I haven't seen her in six months," she'd whined. "I'm playing catch-up for all the time I lost with her and she's had a rough night. Let me put her down."

"No." Maggie had needed to hold Belle, needed her reassuring weight in her arms, her soft baby breath blowing on her neck. "She needs her mother tonight."

So Shannon had agreed with a grimace then glanced at her watch and gave a low shriek. "I've got to go."

"What? Where?" Maggie frowned. How could the woman think about going somewhere after all that had happened?

But Shannon was already in her bedroom.

Maggie shook her head and walked into the kitchen. She peered into the refrigerator and wondered what she would fix for dinner. But she didn't want any food right now. What she wanted was a nap.

Shannon entered the kitchen, hair swept up into a professional bun. She wore a knee-length skirt and a white blouse and brown blazer. Matching brown pumps completed her outfit. Maggie stared. "What are you all dressed up for?"

"I have a meeting in Bryson City. I'm thinking of getting a job nearby so I'm heading over there to talk to the CEO of an advertising firm there. Guess it's time to see if I can put my degree to work again." She shrugged. "I don't have to work, of course, but what will I do all day without a job?" She held up a hand as though to forestall any protestations. "Don't worry, I'll help you out with Belle until then, but I need to find a job or I'll be bored silly."

"Oh." Maggie blinked. "All right. Do you want to eat first? I was just thinking about fixing something."

"No, thanks. It's a dinner interview. I may be late."

With a wave and a smile, she turned on her heel and went out the door.

Relieved to have some time for herself to just think, Maggie's brain tumbled like crazy as she'd rocked Belle to sleep.

Once Belle was down, Maggie grabbed a quick shower. Coming out of the bathroom, weariness tugged at her. Her bed tempted her. She sighed and rubbed her eyes. She'd like nothing more than to curl up on her own bed, pull the covers over her head and hide from the world.

But she couldn't. Because something kept niggling at her. She pulled her still-damp hair up in a ponytail and walked into her office. She spent the next forty-five minutes working on school paperwork to prepare for the three meetings she had next week.

Maggie shivered. The hole in her window had been covered with plastic, but it was still cold in the house. She hoped the window was fixed fast.

A knock on her door pulled her from the computer and into the foyer. She opened the door to find Reese standing there looking battle-worn and tired. "Hi."

"Hi." He held up several bags of food.

She inhaled and her stomach rumbled. "I smell something good."

"I didn't figure you felt much like putting together anything, so I had one of Holly's helpers bring this out."

Touched by his thoughtful gesture, she opened the door wider. "You seem to like bringing food to my house."

He lifted a brow and smiled. "Gives me an excuse to see you."

Maggie felt the flush rise on her cheeks. "You don't need an excuse. And don't worry, I'm not complaining. I appreciate it. Come on in." She took the bags into the kitchen, set them on the counter and said, "Come with me."

At his questioning look, she pointed to his cheek. "You never had anyone clean that up, did you?"

He raised his hand and touched the wound, surprise in his eyes. "No, I guess not. I forgot about it."

"I have a first aid kit in my bathroom. Let's wash that before it gets infected."

"I can take care of it later."

She paused and looked into his eyes. "Reese, I can't stop bank robbers and I can't chase down men with guns, and I can't even do much to protect myself against someone who wants to hurt me and Belle." She bit her lip. "But this is one thing I can do for you. Will you let me?"

At her gentle question, his expression turned tender. He gave a slow nod. "Sure."

He followed her into the master bedroom and on into the bathroom where he seated himself on the edge of the tub. "It's cold in here. Are you sure Belle's warm enough?"

Maggie smiled. "I put the little portable heater in her room. She's fine."

Maggie opened the small linen closet, pulled out the hard plastic box that held all her first aid items and placed it next to the sink. She held a washcloth under the warm water and felt Reese's eyes following her every movement.

It made her extremely self-conscious, and her fingers trembled as she held the washcloth to the wound, soaking away the dried blood. His hand came up to cover hers and he said, "Thank you."

Her smile felt shaky, but she forced it wider. "Sure." She pulled the washcloth away and tossed it into the dirty clothes basket. After applying some antibiotic cream, she opened a small bandage and placed it over the cut. His hands came up to rest on her shoulders, his face inches from hers.

All of a sudden the bathroom felt too small, his size dwarf-

ing her, his presence surrounding her. His right hand slid from
her shoulder to cup her chin. Then he leaned down and placed
his lips over hers. A gentle caress filled with gratitude, comfort...and a restrained passion.

She went still, savoring his nearness, the security he represented, relishing everything about him. When he lifted his
head, she simply stared up at him. He gave a small sigh. "I've
been wanting to do that for a while now, but was afraid if I
did you'd smack me."

Maggie couldn't help the smile that slid across her tingling
lips. "I'm not going to complain."

Full-fledged laughter rumbled from his chest and he pulled
her close for a hug. She rested her head against him. "Thank
you for all you're doing, Reese. If it wasn't for you, I don't know
what—"

His finger over her lips cut her off. "I wouldn't want to be
anywhere else."

Maggie nodded. Another rumble sounded and she giggled.
"Are you hungry?"

"Starved," he admitted with a self-conscious quirk to his lips.

She closed the first aid kit and opened the linen closet once
again. She moved aside a few towels and placed the box on
the shelf.

Then Reese looked up, studying her. "You okay?"

"I will be." Maybe. When time passed and this was all behind her. Assuming she was still alive at that point. Together,
they walked into the kitchen.

"I need to ask you a few questions," he said.

She frowned. "Okay."

"I've been thinking about something for about the past
thirty minutes."

"What's that?"

"Your husband's murder."

Chapter Thirteen

He saw her flinch and regretted the lack of finesse in his delivery. Reese rushed to apologize. "I'm sorry. Let me back up a bit."

She waved his apology away as she set the food on the table. Maggie waited while Reese said grace then asked, "It's all right. What do you want to know?"

"I've been going over and over this bank robbery in my mind. Plus I've watched the security videos. I've played it scene by scene. The robbery, your response. My response. And something keeps nagging at me."

"What?"

"That's the problem. I don't know. I always say the best way to solve a case is good investigative work and listening when your gut sends you warning signals. My gut is sending signals and is telling me to find out more information about your husband and the possible suspects involved. Will you tell me what happened? Everything you remember about the night he died? Who the police questioned—everything."

Maggie wiped nonexistent crumbs from the table and sighed. "You could look it up. It's all in the police report."

"I want to hear it from you. You'll give me stuff I can't get from the file."

Maggie glanced down the hall toward the nursery and he figured she was calculating how much time she had before the baby woke. "Fine." She paused to take a bite of her sandwich.

While she nibbled at her food, Reese devoured his. He couldn't remember if he'd had lunch or not.

He ate the last fry on his plate and studied her. She appeared fragile on the outside, but he'd witnessed her inner strength more than once. He realized that he admired her.

Once they were finished, she placed the dishes in the dishwasher while he tossed the empty food bags. She turned to say something.

And Belle hollered for attention.

Maggie snapped her mouth shut and started for the hall. Reese snagged her arm and took a deep breath as he felt the words hover on the tip of his tongue. He finally spit them out. "Let me."

Before she had a chance to ask all the questions brewing in her eyes, he was down the hall and in the nursery.

Belle wasn't unhappy. She was just awake and ready to get out of the crib. And Reese figured she probably needed a diaper change. When he'd found out Keira was pregnant, he'd read everything he could get his hands on about pregnancy and the first year with a baby. If he remembered correctly, the books said to change the baby upon waking.

"Hey, there, Belle, did you have a good nap?"

Her brown eyes went wide, then she smiled at him and his heart stuttered a beat.

Reese took a deep breath then slipped his hands under the

small arms and picked her up. Then grimaced. Yep, the books were right on. A change would be the first order of business.

He laid her on the changing table and got to work while he talked to her. "Wish I could take a nap. You have it easy, kid. Hope you appreciate all your mom does for you."

She waved a tiny fist at him and he caught it, staring at the perfect miniature. Small, perfect fingers and a beautifully shaped hand. Delicate. Fragile. Breakable.

And yet strong. Just like her mother.

Belle tried to roll off the table and Reese held her, keeping her in place. Keeping her safe. "Can't do that darling," he said. "You'd land on the floor and that would hurt."

He shuddered at the thought of her being hurt. By accident or by someone who didn't believe life was a precious gift and was willing to snatch it away. He fastened the first tab on the diaper, pulled her other leg down and managed to close the diaper and fasten the second tab. "Practicing on dolls doesn't compare to the actual experience. Dolls don't wriggle. You were a tough customer, sweetheart."

He leaned over the baby and stared her in the eye, face to face, nose to nose. Belle went still as a rock, looking at him as if she wondered if he'd done everything right and if she dared move. He gave a low laugh, his heart light for the first time since he'd seen Maggie and Belle in the bank. "You're awfully cute."

As though she understood, Belle grinned, her brown eyes sparkling. Reese decided at that moment he'd never get his heart back.

Tears flooded Maggie's eyes. Without a moment's hesitation, she snatched the camera she'd left on Belle's small table by the door and snapped a picture.

Still resting on his forearms, Reese looked over his shoulder and smiled. "What? You checking up on me? You think I need some help corralling a mere fifteen pounds of baby?"

His teasing words chased the tears away, and she shrugged, "Maybe." Reese straightened and pulled Belle into his arms. To Maggie's surprise, the baby seemed happy to be there. And Reese seemed fine having her there. "She's nine months old today."

He lifted a brow. "I'm guessing time goes fast."

Maggie nodded. "Very."

Belle kicked her legs and caught Reese in the stomach. He grunted. "I think she's going to be a soccer player."

"You would have been a great dad," Maggie whispered the words.

Reese stilled. Then a huge sigh filtered from him and he dropped his head. Maggie wished she could snatch the words back. Then he lifted his head, a sad smile on his face. "I sure would have done my best."

Relieved that her words hadn't plunged him into the depths of sadness, Maggie nodded toward the den. "While Shannon is gone, you want to have that conversation?"

"Sure." He handed Belle to her and she started down the hall to the den.

Reese rubbed his head and said. "Hey, do you mind if I help myself to a couple of those aspirin I saw in your medicine cabinet?"

She turned back to face him. Concern immediately clouded her eyes. "Of course I don't mind. I'll get them for you."

"I can get them." He smiled and headed to her bedroom. Once inside her bathroom, he opened the medicine cabinet and saw the bottle of aspirin sitting on the shelf to the side. He helped himself to two, almost took them, then stopped. They didn't look right. Small round yellow tablets. He frowned and put the bottle back. Carrying the pills, he walked into the kitchen to find Maggie preparing a bottle for Belle. "Hey, these were in your aspirin bottle, but I don't think they're aspirin."

Her brows pulled together in a frown as she studied the little yellow pills. "I've never seen those before. They must belong to Shannon."

Still frowning, he said, "I'll put them back. Just be careful when you go to get some aspirin."

"Okay."

Reese put the bottle back where he found it and returned to the kitchen to find Maggie standing there with a glass of tea and two little white pills. "I had these in my purse. I know for a fact that these are aspirin."

He smiled his thanks and downed the two pills.

The door opened and shut and Reese saw Shannon stomp into the foyer. She paused when she saw him, turned on her heel and started down the hall.

Maggie lifted a brow in his direction and went after her sister-in-law. Keeping her voice low so she wouldn't wake up Belle, he heard her ask, "Shannon? What's wrong?"

"Nothing. Just…nothing."

"Something is," he heard Maggie insist.

"My plans…changed." A thud sounded and he imagined her tossing a shoe. "I sat there and waited and waited and he stood me up. Not even a stinking phone call." He heard the woman blow out a disgusted sigh followed by another thud. "I'm just upset that I can't do anything about it. Don't worry about it, I'll get over it."

"I'm sorry. There's some food in the fridge. There was plenty, and we couldn't eat it all."

"Thanks. I'm going to go change first."

Maggie returned to the den where Reese now sat on the

couch. She took the bottle of juice she'd carried with her from the kitchen and set it on the end table, then perched on the edge of the recliner, her eyes serious, face thoughtful as she tapped one foot against the floor. Belle sat in the exersaucer, bouncing and slapping at the various toys attached to the device.

Reese watched Maggie's restlessness with compassion. He hated making her relive what he could tell were some pretty awful days. He seated himself on the couch. "Tell me about Kent's job, his habits, who he hung around with."

"Why?"

"Because someone's after you. It may be related to the bank robbery—or it may be something else."

She lifted a brow. "You think whoever killed him would wait six months to come after me? What would be the purpose of that?"

"I don't know." He stood and walked over to place his hands on her shoulders. "I'm just saying we need to consider everything. I don't want to be blindsided, surprised because I ignored my gut. Sometimes what seems obvious…"

"…isn't?"

"Yes. Exactly."

Maggie bit her lip. "His and Shannon's parents didn't like me. They made no effort to be even halfway civil to me. They had in mind the girl they wanted him to marry. But for some reason, he wasn't interested." She snorted. "Well, I know now why he wasn't interested. He knew he couldn't browbeat her—" She chopped her sentence off and looked away.

Reese felt his gut clench and hastened to reassure her. "You were vulnerable, Maggie. Kent saw that and used it to his advantage. It's not your fault."

She blinked away the tears and nodded. "I know that now." A sniff and a sigh and she had herself back under control. "So anyway, he was home a lot at first after we were married, but then I guess I started to bore him and he...um, found other ways to alleviate the boredom."

"He had a girlfriend?"

"Girlfriends," she whispered.

Reese clenched a fist and wished he could plant it in the dead man's face. "How did he die?"

"A hit-and-run car accident."

"Only it wasn't an accident."

She blinked. "No. There was a witness, a homeless man who said he saw a man arguing with someone. He said the person Kent was arguing with stayed inside the car, so he couldn't see the person. But then Kent slammed a fist on the hood of the car. He shouted something like 'That's final. That's the way it's going to be, get over it.' And then started to walk away. The car with the other person accelerated and slammed into him. Kent died instantly. The car never stopped after it hit him."

Reese rubbed his eyes. "I'm sorry, Maggie."

"I don't know who could have done that. One of the women he strung along. An irate husband or boyfriend. Someone he punched out in a bar." She shrugged and shook her head. "It could have been any of a hundred people, Reese. There's just no way to tell."

"I don't suppose your homeless guy got a license plate?"

She gave a humorless laugh. "No. He just said it was a green car."

Reese frowned. "Sounds like a crime of passion, of opportunity."

"What do you mean?"

"I mean, it doesn't sound planned, premeditated. Like Kent was supposed to meet with the person in the other car, they had an argument and the person didn't like what he had to say and acted in a fit of anger or rage."

"Maybe."

"Or not." He shrugged. "It's all speculation, but I'm really wondering if all this doesn't have something to do with his murder."

"Why are you going through all this? Why don't you just let Kent rest in peace?" Shannon spoke from the door, her tone low, voice tight.

Maggie jerked her gaze to her sister-in-law. "Because if Reese is right, connecting Kent to the events going on around me will help us figure out exactly why someone is out to get me."

Shannon sniffed then reached up to rub her eyes. "Are you listening to yourselves? How in the world could Kent's death be linked to what's going on with you?"

Maggie shook her head and looked at Reese. "I don't know. Her question is a good one. How could Kent's death six months ago have anything to do with a bank robbery gone wrong?"

He stood. "I have no idea, but I'm going to find out."

The next morning, Reese sat at his desk working on the paperwork that comes with a shooting. It was being investigated even as he typed.

Eli opened the glass door and a gust of cold air blew in with him. "Hey, guys, let's have a little powwow in the conference room."

Reese lifted a brow at Cal and his friend shrugged. They followed Eli, with Jason bringing up the rear. Mitchell was the deputy assigned to Maggie's house this morning. He'd just called to say Maggie's broken window was fixed and all was well.

Once inside the conference room, Eli shut the door. "Have

a seat." He slapped a file folder on the table in front of him. "Well, we've got them all."

Reese felt satisfaction run through him for a brief moment, but that satisfaction quickly turned to concern. Yes, they'd captured all three robbers. But they didn't have the boss. "When do we get to question Patterson?"

"He's at the hospital now. I tried talking to him last night, but he was drugged up and out of it. He's got a nasty infection from your first gunshot wound. Asheville P.D. has a guard on his door. We'll be making a little visit to the hospital shortly."

Reese stood. "I'm going to call Maggie." He stepped outside the conference room and dialed her number.

She answered on the third ring. "Hello?"

"Good morning, pretty lady."

A low laugh reached him. "You sound awfully cheerful this morning."

"Maybe that's because we're getting ready to go over to the hospital to question Patterson."

For a moment, silence filled the line. Then she said, "What about the boss he mentioned? Have you found out anything about him?"

"Not yet, but I've got some ideas I plan to work with as soon I get back to the office. Eli's still going to keep someone on your house. Right now it's White. He was real apologetic for taking this assignment lightly."

"He was?"

"Yeah. He caught me this morning. He apologized several times and promised he'd be vigilant in watching out for you. I believe him."

"Okay, thanks…" She seemed at a loss for words.

"But don't drop your guard yet, Maggie. I don't think Patterson was all hot air when he was saying it's not all over yet."

"I won't." She paused. "Thank you," she whispered. "Thanks for everything."

His throat tightened and he cleared it. "You're welcome." He hung up and pressed the phone into his forehead while he replayed Patterson's parting comments.

He had a lot of thinking to do.

But first, he wanted to get over to the hospital and talk to the man he'd shot. Because while it was good news that all three robbers were now in custody, Reese couldn't shake the feeling that he was missing something important. Something he needed to put together before someone else got hurt. Or killed.

Chapter Fourteen

Maggie looked up to see Reese and Eli walking toward the nurses' station. When Reese's eyes landed on her, he couldn't hide his surprise. She shrugged at the unasked question on his face. "I wanted to be here. I want to hear what he has to say."

He looked over her shoulder.

"Jason brought me, but don't be mad at him. I told him I was coming with or without him."

"Maggie—"

"Reese, don't try to talk me out of it. If you'll leave the door open a crack, I can just listen in." She swallowed hard. "That bullet in the bank came real close to my head. The bullets he fired tore up my house and could have killed my daughter. Or you. Or Shannon. He bombed your house partly because of me. I think I have a right to hear him talk."

The men exchanged a look and Reese said, "It's fine with me. If I were in her shoes, I'd be doing the same thing."

Reese blew out a sigh and said to her, "All right. By the door. But you don't say a word, okay?"

She nodded. "Thank you." Maggie followed the men to the prisoner's room. Reese reached up to squeeze her arm and then the two officers entered the room, leaving the door slightly ajar so she could listen in.

"How you feeling, Patterson?"

The man uttered a crude phrase, and Maggie flinched. He was never going to talk. Despair hit her. She wanted to be safe. She wanted to be free to take Belle for a walk down the street without wondering if someone would try to kill her. She wanted—

Reese was speaking again. "You know this would all go easier for you if you'd just tell us the story. Who's the boss you were talking about?"

Maggie inched her head to the right so she could see into the room. She could make out Patterson's feet at the foot of the bed. She could see Reese clearly as he faced the door. Eli had his back to her, but she could see his head and the right part of his body. And if she looked a little to the left, she could see the whole room in the mirror on the far wall. Doug Patterson looked rough. His cheeks were still flushed and he looked like a very sick man.

"No boss. It must have been the fever talking. I don't have a boss." He leaned his head back against the bed and closed his eyes. His throat worked.

Silence as she saw Reese lift his eyes to Eli. There must have been some kind of silent cop communication because Reese dropped his head and nodded. "Right. No boss."

"So…" Eli took a deep breath "…guess we'll just send you up to Marion Correctional Institute."

"Whatever."

"And let it be known that the three of you were trying to kill a baby," Reese stated, his voice low. Lethal.

"What?" Doug's eyes popped open and he stared at the men

at the foot of his bed. "No way. Wasn't trying to kill a baby. Are you crazy?" The man protested long and loud. Reese simply stood there. Then shrugged.

"So you say. I don't know that. Do you know that for sure, Eli?"

Eli shook his head. "Nope. Those bullets came awfully close to that baby."

Maggie heard Eli's phone ring over Patterson's protests. Eli pulled it out of his pocket with his right hand and spoke into his phone. "Brody here." He listened as Reese and the prisoner fell quiet. Then Eli let out a short laugh. "Really? They did? Sang like canaries, huh? Thanks for the update."

He hung up and looked at Reese. "We don't need this guy. Station says the two down there are seeing which one can talk the fastest."

"Right," Patterson sneered. "Like I'm going to fall for that."

Eli simply lifted a brow. "So the three of you never met at your father's ranch to work out the deal?"

Uncertainty flared. "No."

"Right. And Compton also said you're the ringleader who was going to deposit ten grand in his account so he could party it up in Mexico."

Full-blown panic crossed his face. "How do you know all that?"

Eli snickered. "Looks like you're going to come up with the short end of the draw." He motioned to Reese. "Let's go."

The men started toward the door and Maggie pulled back.

"No!" Patterson hollered. "Wait! I want a deal. I... I'm not taking the fall for this!"

A slow smile crossed Reese's lips. And he and Eli exchanged smug grins before they wiped them off and turned back to the man in the bed.

Reese shook his head. "I don't know. What do you think you can offer that these guys can't?"

"I was the main contact. I was contacted first and never said anything to those guys about the fact that the robbery was a cover-up."

Maggie saw Reese go still. "A cover-up for what?"

The right foot under the sheet shifted, a restless move that said the prisoner didn't want to say another word. "What kind of deal are you offering?"

Eli shrugged. "I don't know yet. Depends on who offers us the best information."

The man groaned. Then finally said, "We were supposed to grab the woman with the baby."

Maggie's lungs deflated. The hallway darkened for a brief moment before she inhaled enough air to keep herself conscious.

She forced herself not to run screaming down the hall and kept her eyes trained on Reese, whose relaxed posture had disappeared. Tension radiated from him as his hands curled into fists at his side. "Why?"

The low word sent shivers down her spine. She could see the steel in his eyes from where she stood.

"I don't know why. We were just told to watch her then grab her and the kid. While we were watching, we noticed she went to the bank once a week. So we came up with the plan. The money from the bank was a bonus. But we had to make it look like a hostage situation."

"Then what?"

"Then we were to take her to an address."

"Where?" Eli demanded.

"An abandoned warehouse on the edge of town." He gave them the address. Maggie heard him say, "Now, you're going to give me a deal right? What kind of deal? I told you everything I know."

"You still haven't given us a name," Reese said. "Who's your boss?"

"I don't know, I never got a name. Just a contact number with a note in my mailbox saying if I wanted to make a lot of money to call it."

Eli snorted. "And of course you couldn't turn that down, could you?"

Silence echoed through the room for a moment and Maggie began to shake. She couldn't comprehend what she was hearing. Someone had paid to have her and Belle kidnapped. Under the guise of a fake bank robbery?

And if it hadn't been for Reese being in the right place at the right time, that someone would have succeeded.

She shook off the thought as one question took up residence at the forefront of her mind.

Who?

Chapter Fifteen

Reese paced the office and jammed his hands into his coat pockets. The police station heater was broken, and it was cold. He blew out, watching his breath form small clouds in front of his face. He shook his head and shivered.

Sitting at his desk netted him nothing and he thought about heading over to Maggie's and giving Cal a break. At least Maggie's house would be warm. Or maybe he'd go sit in his cruiser.

But he was waiting for a phone call.

He stood and walked into Eli's office. The man had a wool scarf wrapped around his neck, and he had his warm Sherpa coat buttoned up. A small space heater at his feet ran full blast. Eli looked up and Reese asked, "How'd you know about Patterson's dad's ranch?"

"His father finally called me back and said he hadn't seen his son since the night he and his buddies were over there. I took a shot in the dark."

"Good shot. Same with the money in the bank?"

Eli held up a report. "I got this from Spartanburg P.D. Alice scanned and emailed it to my phone right before we got to the hospital. They found an account number in Compton's apartment along with a brochure about Mexico. Another shot."

Reese smiled. "You're pretty good at that."

Eli shrugged. "It worked. Sometimes it does, sometimes it doesn't."

Reese changed the subject. "What do you know about Maggie's husband?"

Eli's eyes clouded as he leaned back in his chair to give Reese his full attention. "He wasn't a very nice man, and he was killed about seven months ago. Hit and run." The flat response said he knew more than he was letting on.

"I'm not asking you to betray a confidence. In fact, Maggie's told me most of it, I think. And I've been thinking about what she's told me."

"Tell me what you're thinking."

"All right." He hunched his shoulders and leaned forward. "Her husband was killed. The killer was never caught. We know that the bank robbery was a cover as an attempt to kidnap her and Belle. What if we need to do a little more digging into her husband's death?"

Eli was silent for a few moments and Reese held his tongue as he let the man think. Finally, his boss said, "You think it's all connected?"

"I don't know." Reese grimaced. "Might be a long shot."

"But it might not be a bad idea. I can't think of anything else that would have someone after her. What was he involved in? Did she tell you that?"

"No. I did a background check on him and it's pretty spotless. A couple of parking tickets, but nothing major. I don't know. I mean, it's just a thought. Probably a crazy one, but one I don't want to overlook and regret later."

Eli gave a slow nod. "Why don't you take that and run with it?"

Reese offered a small smile. "I'm waiting for a phone call now."

No sooner had the words left his lips than the phone on his desk rang. He bolted from Eli's office and snatched it to his ear. "Kirkpatrick here."

"Hey, Reese. I think I've got what you're looking for." Colt Harris, a friend of his from Maggie's hometown of Spartanburg, South Carolina.

"What did you find out?"

"A lot. How much time do you have?"

Reese shivered and said, "Call me back on my cell." He rattled off the number, hung up and hollered to Eli. "I'm going to find someplace warm."

Eli's laugh drifted to him. "Don't blame you a bit."

As Reese exited the police station, his cell phone rang. He answered, "Go ahead. Fill me in."

"All right, first of all, it looks like your lady's in-laws have filed a custody suit."

Reese stopped dead in his tracks, ignoring the swirling white snow that had started to come down. "What? You're kidding!" Just what Maggie needed.

"Yep. While I was checking out your guy, Kent Bennett, I came across his folks and decided to see what they had to say about his death."

"And?"

"At first, I thought they were a cold couple. Showed no real emotion when I started questioning them. Then I mentioned Maggie and the baby and the woman starts weeping, saying she can't believe their son is gone and they're going to do everything they can to get their granddaughter."

Reese closed his eyes then clicked the remote to unlock

his truck. He climbed in and slammed the door. Jamming the key into the ignition, he shivered. The engine caught and he reached over to turn the heat on full blast. As the cold air turned warm, he concentrated on the information Colt was sharing.

"It's been seven months. When did they start the process on all of this?"

"A couple of months ago, but no one seemed to be able to track Maggie down. She didn't have a credit card in her name until about a month ago. She uses cash for everything and she put all the utilities in her maiden name."

"She was hiding?" He hadn't gotten that impression.

"Looks like it."

"I'll ask her about that. What else?"

"Still working on the hit-and-run with Bennett."

"I told you about the witness that heard him arguing with someone that night. Did you track the witness down to question him again?"

"I did. Found him in the soup kitchen." Reese heard a page flip in Colt's notebook. "He described Bennett as angry, stomping up and down and flapping his hands like a 'chicken gone crazy' while the other person sat in the car and listened, then started screaming back at him."

"What about who Bennett was arguing with? Did you get a description?"

"Not a good one. I looked for any cameras that might have gotten everything on tape, but there weren't any on that block. But our witness says the person was smaller than Bennett, that he was wearing all black with a heavy overcoat and a black hat. The witness never got a look at the guy's face."

"Huh, of course. It's couldn't be that easy," Reese grunted. "I wonder whose idea it was to meet there then. Isolated, off the main road…could be more than a crime of opportunity. Maybe it was planned?"

"I know, I thought about that. But we won't know that answer until we catch this person Bennett met with. So anyway, the parents hired a P.I. to find Maggie and when she got her cell phone last month and that credit card, he found her. She should be getting a letter about the custody thing sometime this week."

"He was watching her credit."

"Yep."

"Why wait this long to contact her?" Reese rubbed a hand down the side of his cheek and turned the heater down a notch.

"They've been trying to build a case against her, I think. From what I can tell, they're saying she's an unfit mother."

Reese sat up in the seat. "On what grounds?"

"Based on an incident that happened in a store about two weeks after Belle was born."

"What happened?"

"Maggie apparently went shopping and left her baby unattended in an aisle. The sister-in-law happened to be in the store and watched the baby until Maggie came back to get her."

"I don't believe it," he stated flatly.

"Ask her about it. See what she says. I mean these people seemed nice enough once they warmed up to me and I think they really do want the baby. If the mother's not fit, I think they'd give Belle a good home."

Reese didn't speak for a moment as his mind raced with all the new information. "Well, she's fit. More than fit. I'm not really worried that they would win. But I hate for Maggie to have to go through the whole drama of them suing for custody." He paused and tapped the steering wheel. "Okay, keep me updated. See what you can find out about that green car. And check out where his family was the night he was killed."

"Will do."

Reese frowned as he hung up. He had to warn Maggie that her in-laws had filed for custody before she got the lawyer's letter.

Maggie walked into the den and dropped the mail onto the coffee table. Cal had played delivery man for her so she didn't have to walk to the mailbox. Frankly, she could use a little fresh air, but it wasn't worth risking if someone was still after her. And Reese seemed to think someone was.

Shannon had taken Belle grocery shopping for their Thanksgiving dinner. Shannon said Maggie needed some time for herself and besides, Maggie really should stay put and not put anyone in danger by leaving the house and having someone try to kill her again.

"Thanks bunches, Shannon," Maggie muttered as she paced from one end of the den to the other. But she couldn't deny the truth in the woman's words, so she'd relented.

As a result, Maggie had finished her classes, had one Individualized Education Plan meeting on a student and written another IEP for the meeting that would be held first thing Monday morning. Working with special education high school students was a challenge that fulfilled her in a way she'd never dreamed possible.

But it involved a lot of paperwork. While she'd worked on that, she'd managed to push thoughts of being a target out of her mind.

Now, as she paced, she thought. Was Reese right? Did Kent's death have something to do with everything that was happening now? The bank robbery was a setup. She and Belle were supposed to be kidnapped.

And then what?

Why?

They were supposed to deliver them to an address. What had Reese found out about that location? Who could be behind such a horrible thing?

She let out a groan, dropped to her knees and let her chin fall to her chest. "Father, I don't know what to do now. I pray You're working behind the scenes here because I'm lost and floundering and I'm so tired. Please help us."

A tear slid down her cheek, but her heart felt lighter. As if some of the burden had been lifted from her shoulders.

The presence of God. Her troubles and worries weren't magically gone, but she had help. She didn't have to do this alone. Maggie drew in a deep breath. "Thank You," she whispered.

God never promised that life would be easy for those who chose to trust Him, but He did promise to walk through the hard times with them.

And she was certainly going through a hard time.

The doorbell rang and she rose to walk into the foyer. Peeking through the window, she smiled.

Another thing she had to give God the credit for.

He'd sent Reese into her life just when she needed him.

She opened the door with a smile. "Hi."

"Hi."

The serious look on his face sent her smile into a nosedive. "What is it?" Snow drifted down in a gentle veil of white outside as he stepped inside and shrugged out his coat. "Oh, goodness, I didn't realize it was snowing so much. I'm going to call Shannon and ask her to get on back here before the roads get bad."

He nodded. "Good idea. Then we need to talk."

"All right."

She led him into the den then picked up the phone to dial Shannon. Reese settled himself on the couch while Maggie listened to the phone ring. When it went to voice mail, she frowned, but said, "Shannon, it's snowing pretty hard out there. Why don't you go ahead and bring Belle on home. I'm a little worried about your getting stuck on the road. Call me as soon as you get this." She hung up and looked at Reese. "Hopefully, she'll call me back soon. Or see the snow and realize she needs to get home." Maggie took a deep breath to settle her nerves. Belle and Shannon would be fine. But she sent up a silent prayer for their safety. "Okay, so what has you looking like you have bad news?"

"I had a conversation with a buddy of mine who lives in Spartanburg."

"Okay."

"After all the crazy stuff going on around here, I asked him to look into a few things."

"Kent's hit-and-run?"

"Right."

Maggie rubbed her suddenly sweaty palms on her jean-clad thighs. "And?"

He blew out a breath. "There's no easy way to say this."

"You're scaring me, Reese."

"Your in-laws plan to sue you for custody of Belle by proving that you're an unfit mother. The letter's on the way—if you haven't already gotten it."

The bottom dropped out of her stomach. Stunned, she simply looked at him. Then she shot to her feet and grabbed the mail from the coffee table. One by one, she went through the envelopes, tossing them aside. Until she came across one that said Billings and Jordan, Attorneys at Law.

Maggie ripped the envelope open, read through the information that Reese had just delivered. She tossed the paper onto the table and shook her head. "How can they do this?" She paced to the mantel then back. "They can't take her away from me. I won't let them."

Reese stood and placed his hands on her shoulders. "Calm down a second. I said they were suing. I didn't say they'd win."

She paused and looked up at him. Tears hovered on the edges of her lashes, but she refused to let them fall. "I'll fight them," she whispered. "Every step of the way, no matter what I have to do or how much it costs. I have money, Reese, a lot of money that my grandfather left me. They will *not* have her."

He blinked at her statement about the money, but addressed her last comment. "I don't think they have any grounds. They'd have to prove that you're an unfit mother. An investigation would be carried out and once they realized there's no evidence, they wouldn't have a case."

At his reassuring and confident words, Maggie felt herself start to relax a fraction. "But they could still cause us a lot of grief."

"Unfortunately, yes. They could."

"They've never seen her, Reese. Not even once. They didn't come to the hospital, they never called, they don't know who she is or—"

He placed a finger over her lips. "I know. I really don't think you have anything to worry about." He gave a tug on her shoulders and she slipped into his arms to rest her head on his chest. She felt him place a kiss on the top of her head. Maggie closed her eyes and allowed peace to wash over her for just a moment. So this was what it felt like to be loved, to be cared for by a man who didn't feel the need to control and hurt.

But she'd thought Kent was this way in the beginning, too. She tensed and moved away. Reese let her go without protest, but the question in his eyes hurt.

He cleared his throat. "I'm fall—" He stopped and shoved his hands in his pockets. "I care about you a lot, Maggie. More than a lot. I want us to see if we have a chance at a relationship. I want to see if we maybe have a future together."

The words hit her like a punch to the gut. "Oh, Reese."

"You don't have to say anything right now. Just think about it."

She wanted to yell, "I have thought about it." But didn't. Because she still had doubts about her ability to make a sound judgment when it came to men.

Kent would have demanded an immediate answer. And if it wasn't the one he liked, he would have pouted and sulked or simply beat her until she gave in. No, Reese wasn't anything like Kent. Even by comparing them, she was insulting Reese. And in that instant, she knew Reese would never raise a hand to her. They might fight and argue, even raise their voices to one another. But he'd never hit her—or hurt her on purpose.

Maggie stepped forward and wrapped her arms around his neck and brought his lips to hers. After a long, sweet moment, his surprise melted into a tender response. When they parted, she smiled at him. "I care about you, too, Reese."

He gave a relieved laugh. "Good."

She glanced at the clock then at the phone. Her smile flipped into a frown. "I'm worried."

He walked to the window and looked out. "It looks like the snow is slowing down, but the temperature's hovering around freezing. Shannon probably should be on her way back."

Maggie dialed Shannon's number again. When Shannon still didn't pick up, Maggie swallowed hard. "I don't like this."

"Wait a minute." He cocked his head to the right. "Call it again."

She frowned, but pressed the redial button. And then she heard what he did. She walked down the hall, the faint sound growing louder with each step. By the time they reached Maggie's bedroom, the ringing continued then stopped.

Maggie walked into her room and saw Shannon's overnight bag beside the bed, packed in a haphazard fashion. Shannon's cell phone lay on the end table. But it wasn't the phone that captured her attention, it was the large manilla envelope sticking out of Shannon's bag.

Her grandfather's name was on the return address portion. And she had seen this envelope before. She reached out with only a twinge of guilt about invading her sister-in-law's privacy, pulled the envelope from the bag.

"What is it?" Reese asked.

A bad feeling churned in her gut. "It's the information my grandfather sent me," she whispered. "After we got in touch and I said I wanted to visit, he sent me all this information on Rose Mountain, this house, everything about his will and what to do when he died. Everything." She swallowed hard. "He said he sent it, but I never received the first package. So he sent a second one. We just assumed the first one got lost in the mail. Unless—" She rose and hurried past Reese and into her office. She dropped the package she'd found in Shannon's bag onto the floor and fell to her knees. She opened the small file cabinet beside her desk. Maggie reached in and pulled out a matching manilla envelope. She looked up at Reese. "He sent the first package about three months before I was due with Belle. When it didn't come, he sent another one." She bit her lip, worry and that bad feeling in her stomach gnawing away at her. "Why would Shannon have this first package?"

A frown drew his brows together over his nose. "I don't know. Maybe she found it in Kent's things and decided to give it to you. Because it's highly likely that your husband got to the mail first and took it."

"I thought about that," she said, "but when he didn't confront me with it, I figured it had gotten lost after all." She paused. "And if Shannon found it, why hasn't she given it to me yet?"

"Good question." He shrugged. "Maybe she forgot."

"Maybe." She glanced at the clock again and a pang of fear shot through her. "Reese, I'm getting scared that Shannon and Belle aren't back yet."

He nodded. "Let me put a BOLO out on her car and see if I get some answers." He walked to the window and looked out. "At least it's not snowing anymore."

"But the roads are wet, and it's a little below freezing. That's not good."

His phone rang and he snatched it, listened for a moment then paled. "I've got to go. There's been an accident just outside of town. I'm a first responder. They may need my skills before an ambulance can get out there."

Her knees went week. "It's not Shannon's car is it?"

"No, a black Ford Taurus. Jason's going to be here and will keep a watch on you. I'll be looking for Shannon on my way out to the accident. If I see her, or if I get a report of anyone else seeing her, I'll call or text you."

Maggie nodded. "All right. They're probably fine. Maybe she got to talking to someone in the grocery store."

"Maybe."

Maggie walked with him to the front door and saw him jog to the cruiser still sitting in the driveway. He spoke to Jason who nodded then, with a wave in her direction, Reese climbed into his own cruiser and left.

She ached at his absence. Having him around made her feel safe. Confident that things would work out. When he left, he took that feeling with him.

"Which is why I don't need to rely on my feelings, right, God? That's why I need to trust in You. In Your constant and abiding promise to be with me no matter what. Lord, please watch over Belle and Shannon. Bring them safely home," she whispered. Saying the words helped, even though the worry lingered.

For the next thirty minutes, she paced the floor. No word from Shannon, nothing from Reese.

The phone rang and Maggie jerked. She didn't recognize the number, but snatched her handset from the coffee table. "Hello?"

"Oh, Maggie, I'm so glad I got you."

"Shannon! Where are you? Is Belle all right?"

"Yes, we're fine."

Maggie's pulse slowed. She walked to the window to look out, half expecting to see Shannon driving up the drive. "Where have you been? I expected you an hour and a half ago." She sighed. "And now it's snowing again."

"I know. But don't worry, we're fine. We're just stuck."

"Stuck? Stuck where?"

"Near a little country store. I left my cell phone at the house so I had to walk a little ways to find this pay phone."

"Is Belle warm enough?"

"Of course she is," Shannon snapped. "I know how to take care of her."

Maggie blinked at the woman's sharp tone. Then Shannon said, "Sorry, sorry. I didn't mean to be crabby. It's been a rough couple of hours with the snow, the cold and the car that quit on me."

"Of course," Maggie soothed. "Don't worry. I'll come get you. Give me directions."

Maggie listened as Shannon described how to find her. For someone who didn't know the town very well, Shannon gave her pretty good directions. Maggie had never been where Shannon directed her, but thought she could find it easily enough.

"I'll be there as fast as I can."

Before she left, she sent a text to Reese to let him know Shannon and Belle had been found and were safe. She waved to Jason. "I need to go somewhere. You want to follow me or drive?"

His eyes went wide. "Hop in."

Chapter Sixteen

Reese placed a call to his buddy in Spartanburg and got him working on a hunch. The faster he got some answers to the questions running through his head, the better off they'd all be.

He arrived at the scene of the accident and winced when he saw the family of four sitting off to the side of the road. Mom, Dad and two kids. A boy about six and a little girl who looked to be around nine. They looked cold and miserable, but otherwise not seriously injured.

EMTs hadn't arrived yet. Eli had a first aid kit out and was patching up a nasty-looking cut over the little girl's eye. Reese grabbed a handful of blankets he always kept in the truck for emergencies.

Cal drove up and Dr. Dylan Seabrook got out of the cruiser.

"Paul, Stacy, are you guys all right? What happened?" Dylan hurried toward the shaken family.

Cal looked at Eli. "I figured it wouldn't hurt to pick him up on my way out here."

Eli nodded. "Good idea."

Reese helped Dylan wrap the blankets around the shivering family and escort them to sit in the warm cruiser. Then he looked at the black Ford Taurus kissing the large oak tree on the side of the road. He leaned into the cruiser and looked at the man Dylan had called Paul. "What happened?"

A shock of red hair fell over the man's forehead. His blue eyes narrowed, his brow furrowed as he spoke. "I was just telling Eli that this car came out of nowhere and ran us off the road."

Reese pulled his green notebook from his front pocket, ignoring the blast of wind trying to sneak down the back of his heavy coat. "Someone in a hurry?"

"Must have been."

"No," his wife said from the backseat. "It was deliberate. Someone ran us off the road on purpose."

Reese lifted a brow. A three-way stop lay just ahead in the direction the family had been traveling. Another side road connected to the main road about fifty yards from the intersection. "Looks like the car that hit you was coming out of that side road, you rounded the corner and got slammed."

"That's exactly what happened," Paul said. "But I don't think it was deliberate."

Stacy's expression said she disagreed.

Reese noticed that Cal had the little boy in his arms, wrapped in a blanket and was walking him over to join his parents and sister in the car. The child appeared unhurt, just scared. But he seemed willing to be entertained by Cal's badge.

Reese walked to the damaged Taurus. The front hood had crumpled up and now rested against the spiderwebbed windshield.

He checked the side that had been hit. Ran his fingers along the dented metal. He returned to the cruiser. Paul held his son in his lap now. One of the father's arms dangled, useless, to rest on the seat. Pain drew the man's brows down and a muscle ticked in his jaw. His good hand held his son against his chest. Reese asked, "Do you know what kind of car hit you?"

Paul shook his head. "No, sorry. I just had a flash of something coming toward me, then we hit the tree."

The little girl looked at him, opened her mouth to say something then closed it. Reese moved to her side of the car to look past Stacy and focus his attention on the child. "What's your name, sweetheart?" Her blue eyes looked extra large under the white bandage now covering the gash in her forehead. She moved closer to her mother, but didn't take her gaze from him. Reese tried again. "Can you tell me what you saw?"

Stacy wrapped an arm around her daughter's shoulder. "Lisa, if you saw the car, will you tell the deputy what it looked like?"

"It was white," she said then pulled the blanket up over her lips and nose. Her eyes stayed on him.

Reese smiled at the girl. "Thanks, Lisa, that helps. Was it a truck like mine or a car like yours?"

"It was just a car."

"It was a Mercedes," the little boy stated.

Reese lifted a brow. "It was?" He looked at the boy's father. "Would he know that?"

Paul nodded. "Yeah. He knows all the car symbols. I travel a lot and we make a game out of it when he comes with me. The person who spots the most Beemers wins a milk shake. Then we do Toyotas or Mercedes or Fords. Then we both get milk shakes." He shrugged, winced and went pale.

Dylan, who had walked up to peer into the cruiser, grunted. "Keep that shoulder still, Paul. I'm pretty sure it's dislocated." He looked at the shaken family. "Good thing you all had your seat belts on."

Sirens sounded to his left and Reese looked up to see two ambulances barreling toward them. They'd come from Bryson City.

Then his mind went back to what Paul's son said. Cold dread settled in his gut. Shannon drove a white Mercedes. Of course there was more than one white Mercedes in the state, but...

"Eli, how many people around here drive that kind of car?"

Eli met his gaze. "I can only think of one."

Reese blew out a breath and nodded. "I was afraid of that." He rubbed his gloved hand against his thigh. "I already have an unofficial BOLO out on her because she's got Belle, and Maggie was getting worried." Small towns did that kind of thing. Just one more thing Reese liked about Rose Mountain.

"Yeah, I heard that," Eli said. He pulled out his radio. "Well, now it's official. If it wasn't her, at least we can rule her out."

Reese's phone buzzed.

His buddy from Spartanburg. "Trevor, what do you have?"

"Nothing yet on that pill you sent, but it's coming."

"Then what?"

"You know how you're always saying go with your gut?"

"Yeah."

"I did and it paid off."

Excitement began to hum in Reese's veins. "Tell me."

"Everything you've told me about what's going on with your lady friend had me suspicious. Especially after you sent that pill in the aspirin bottle and Maggie said it must belong to her sister-in-law."

Reese frowned. "All right. And?"

"And so I started looking into the night Maggie's husband was killed. You may already know some of this, but here's what I got. First of all, the witness wasn't reliable. A homeless guy who saw two people arguing. After checking out Kent Bennett's background, it came to light that he was deeply in debt."

"To whom?"

"To some pretty nasty characters."

"Right. So it's safe to assume that he was probably killed by one of them?"

"That would be the first assumption. I decided to keep looking. And when I got to his family, things turned real interesting."

"How?" He wished the man would just hurry up and spit it out.

"Turns out the nasty characters didn't do the killing." Reese didn't even want to know how Trevor could be certain of that. He knew his buddy had contacts better left under their rocks. Reese had been in that territory a few times in his career and he never cared to go back. Trevor said, "They were furious the man was dead."

"Because they'd never get their money, right?"

"Right."

"So if they didn't kill him, who did?"

"Someone driving a green car. The paint chips the ME found embedded in Mr. Bennett's clothing told us that much."

"But you have something up your sleeve. What is it you're not telling me?"

"Because of my highly suspicious nature, I decided to check into whether anyone in the family had a green car. No one did."

"What about—"

"A rental. Yeah, I thought about that. And I hit pay dirt."

"Who?"

"A woman by the name of Shannon Bennett rented a green BMW from the airport the night her brother was killed."

Chills that had nothing to do with the cold weather raced up his spine. "Anything else?"

"Nope. I'll let you know when the report comes back on the pill."

"Thanks."

No sooner had he hung up than the phone buzzed again. A text from Maggie.

SHANNON CALLED. HER CAR BROKE DOWN. ON THE WAY TO MEET HER AT SIMON'S STOP AND GO. JASON IS WITH ME.

He looked up. "Hey, Eli. Just got a text from Maggie. She said she was on the way to meet Shannon. Her car broke down."

"Where?"

"Simon's Stop and Go."

Reese frowned. Why did that sound familiar.

Eli's head snapped up and Reese saw a flash of worry darken his eyes. "What is it?"

Reese said, "That's the place where Maggie and Belle were supposed to be delivered after the bank robbery."

Maggie squinted through the still-falling snow. At least it wasn't too heavy. Hopefully, she would have Belle and Shannon back home safe and sound before too long, and then it could snow all it wanted.

Jason slowed the cruiser, his head nodding to the right. "Should be right around here. I come out this way every once in a while, but not often."

"There aren't any lights on. Is it closed?"

"Probably. Around here businesses close up if it's snowing and dropping to the freezing mark. No one wants to try to get home on icy roads."

"Right."

She bit her lip and glanced up at the sun. In an hour it would be gone. And the temperatures would drop fast. But she was here now and in an hour would be home.

Nothing to worry about.

Except the place looked deserted. "Where are they?" Maggie wondered as she climbed from the vehicle.

Jason got out and glanced around the area. "Kind of creepy, isn't it?"

Maggie shot him a perturbed look. "Well, I didn't think so until you pointed it out." He gave her a sheepish smile and hitched his pants up as he walked toward the front door. Maggie followed him, uneasiness making her skin ripple. "Shannon? We're here." Where was she? Why hadn't she met them at the door? Had someone else come along and rescued her and Belle?

Confusion and a renewed anxiety to see Belle overshadowed her skittish nerves and Maggie rushed through the door after Deputy White.

She could see him standing in the middle of the store looking around. "Ms. Bennett?"

A loud pop sounded.

Maggie flinched and spun toward the sound. A second passed before she realized Jason had been shot. Surprise settled on his face and he lifted a hand to cover the rapidly spreading red stain on his chest.

Chapter Seventeen

The minute Eli finished his statement, Reese was headed for his cruiser. Eli was right behind him in his own car. Over the radio, Eli told him, "I'm getting Cal and Mitchell for backup. I don't like this any more than you do."

Reese cranked the car and let Eli pull out first. Eli knew the fastest route to the place. With one hand on the wheel, he dialed Maggie's number. A number he'd programmed into his phone. Speed dial number one.

He held the phone to his ear and listened to it ring. "Come on, Maggie, pick up."

Her phone went to voice mail.

Reese hung up, and his worry meter shot off the chart. She'd just texted him thirty minutes ago. Why wasn't she answering?

Eli made a left, then a right, then they were on the main road going toward the edge of town. Reese wanted to floor it, but there were too many side roads, the sun was sinking behind the mountain to his right and he didn't want to take

a chance on hitting someone who may decide not to come to
a complete stop at the numerous stop signs lining the road.

So he gritted his teeth and kept it ten miles over the speed
limit.

"Jason!" Maggie screamed as she raced to the fallen deputy's
side. She dropped to her knees beside the man and felt for a
pulse. She looked up and saw Shannon standing in the doorway that looked like it might lead back into a pantry. "Get
down!" Maggie yelled. "Someone's shooting!" Then Maggie noticed the gun in the woman's hand and froze. "You?"
she whispered.

"Me." She lifted the weapon and Maggie screamed and
ducked, rolling toward the counter, searching for any kind
of cover she could find. The bullet shattered the glass display
behind her.

"Stop! What are you doing? Why?" Maggie felt the terror
choke her, closing her throat, numbing her reflexes, freezing
her brain. "Shannon, stop! Talk to me!"

"He promised me the baby." The flat monotone spiked
Maggie's fear. Horror flooded her as she tried to piece together what Shannon was saying.

"What baby? Who promised you a baby?"

"Kent. He promised to give me the baby when she was
born."

Realization dawned. "What? Give you my baby? Are you
crazy?"

"Actually, yes. At least that's what the doctors tell me."
Shannon moved and Maggie could see her in the round mirror above the door. Shannon held the weapon like she knew
how to use it. But then she'd already taken Jason down with
no trouble. The deputy lay still, pale as death. Maggie wanted

to go to him. Help him, but knew if she moved Shannon would shoot her.

She licked her lips. "Where's Belle?"

"Belle's fine. Don't worry about Belle. Belle's mine now. I'm going to take care of her like I should have all along."

"Why did he promise you Belle, Shannon? You should know I'd never give up my baby."

"You were negligent! I proved that in the store."

Maggie knew immediately what the woman referred to. She'd been desperate to get out of the house. So, when Belle was about three weeks old, Maggie had strolled her up to the shopping center. In one of the stores, Maggie had turned to look at something and when she turned back, Belle was gone. "You took her."

"I wanted to teach you a lesson. Show you that you couldn't take care of her."

"You scared me to death."

"We were one aisle over. You should have realized that you were in no shape to take care of her."

"She's mine!"

"No, she's mine." It wasn't the words that sent sheer fear shuddering through her, it was the without-a-doubt certainty with which Shannon said the words that scared her senseless.

"Why did he promise to give her to you? Why?" Shannon knew her husband hadn't wanted the baby, but to think he'd schemed to get rid of her...

"I can't have children, and I can't adopt. Belle was my one hope to be a mother." Shannon's voice cracked, then steadied. "And I *will* be her mother. He was going to give her to me. Then he took her away." She paused. "He took her away!"

Maggie flinched. "So you killed him." Somehow she knew it. She didn't know why, she just knew it was true.

A perfectly arched brow lifted over one cold eye. "I did.

He found the envelope your grandfather sent you. He came home early that day and found it in the mailbox. When he looked inside, he knew your baby was going to rescue him from the gambling debts he'd managed to rack up. If you were dead, the money would go to whoever got custody of Belle."

Maggie's breaths came in pants. She had to get out of here. Had to do something to save herself. Save Belle. But Belle wasn't here.

She froze as something warm touched the back of her neck. Shannon's voice hissed in her ear. "Now it'll be my money. And Belle will be mine, too."

"Not without my signature," Maggie blurted out.

The woman behind her froze. "What do you mean?"

"I changed the will. I changed everything. Unless you have my signature on a new will, my death means nothing."

"You're lying." But Maggie could hear a faint thread of worry in her voice.

"Then kill me and find out," Maggie bluffed, keeping her words low and steady.

A slight pause. "Go."

"What?"

"In the car. Go."

Maggie stood on trembling legs, using the counter to pull herself up. The gun jabbed her lower back and she stumbled out from behind the counter. Her gaze fell to Jason, bleeding on the floor. Maggie moved toward him. "Let me help him."

"No." Shannon shoved her once again and Maggie tripped over Jason, landing with a thud half on top of him, half on the floor. His weapon still in his holster, her fingers closed over the butt.

"Get up!" Shannon screamed. "I'm sure you told someone you were coming here! Now move! Into the police car."

Maggie pulled on the gun. But it wouldn't move, still

strapped into the holster. And she didn't have time to figure out how to release it. "I'm sorry, Jason," she whispered. But she'd had no idea that Shannon was so unstable.

"Let's go now!"

Maggie thought fast. "I need the keys. They're in his pocket."

"Then hurry up and get them!" Shannon screamed at her. Maggie dug into the pocket with her right hand, hoping Shannon wasn't paying attention to her left.

Maggie got the keys, stood, stumbled and got her balance. She shoved her hands into her pockets and made her way to the door. "Take me to Belle, Shannon."

"Not a chance. Into the driver's seat."

Maggie stepped out into the cold, the wind biting at her bare face. She made her way through the swirling snow, got to the car, opened the door and slid behind the wheel.

She pulled the keys from her right pocket and jammed them into the ignition. "Where am I going?"

"To get the paper you need to sign so that I get Belle and all the money."

Maggie swallowed hard. "It's at my house."

Shannon simply glared at her, the gun never wavering. "Then go home."

Reese pulled into the parking lot of Simon's Stop and Go and stared at the dark building. His heart sank. He didn't have to examine the structure to know they weren't there.

Eli sidled up beside him. Cal and Mitchell turned in, too. Reese opened the door and raced toward the store, leaving the car running, the car door open.

He pushed the unlocked door open and stepped inside. His eyes landed on Jason. "Oh, no."

Reese launched himself to the deputy's side and felt for a pulse. Faint and weak, but there.

As he was reaching for his radio to call for help, Eli and the other officer came through the door. When Eli saw Jason on the floor, he gave a harsh exclamation and dropped to the floor opposite Reese. "Is he alive?"

"Barely." Speaking into the radio, he gave their location. "Officer down, send a helicopter." He looked at Eli. "It can land in the parking lot."

"Absolutely."

He spotted something on the floor near the counter and got to his feet. He reached down and picked up a scarf. "It's Maggie's. She was here."

Eli still had his finger on Jason's pulse. He looked up and nodded. "I'll get Mitchell to stay with Jason. The rest of us need to figure out where Maggie and Shannon went. His keys are missing and his cruiser's gone."

Reese nodded. "They're in his car. You got a GPS tracker on that thing?"

"Yeah." While Eli called that in, Reese gave the store another once-over, but didn't see anything else that might give him a clue as to where Maggie might be going.

"His radio's gone."

"What?"

Eli looked up. "Jason's radio. It's missing."

Reese frowned and wondered what that meant.

He turned his up and listened.

Nothing but police chatter about the nightmare he was living. "I'll keep listening. Someone took that radio for a purpose. If he—or she—wants to get in touch with one of us, we need to be paying attention."

"Good idea. I'm just going to—"

Reese cut him off with a wave as he lifted the radio to his

hear. Maggie was saying, "...knows I'm with you, Shannon, he'll know you're involved in this."

"You're lying. Now shut up and drive."

Reese looked at Eli. "Maggie has it."

With her left hand in her pocket, holding down the button to transmit, she drove with her right hand. She'd managed to turn the volume all the way down on the radio so Shannon wouldn't be able to hear any transmissions coming through, but if there was someone listening, they'd hear her and Shannon talking.

Please God, let there be someone listening.

"Tell me why you killed Kent. He was your brother."

"He was a liar," Shannon snarled, spittle flying from her tense lips.

"But to kill him..." Maggie bit her lip. "Did you plan it all along?"

"No, of course not. It was something we planned together. I wanted a baby. He didn't want 'the brat.'" Maggie glanced out the corner of her eye and saw Shannon frown in disgust. "To call that beautiful baby a brat was awful. *Kent* was awful. I begged him to let me have her, and he agreed."

"But why? There had to be something in it for him."

"He got to keep you," she said with a shrug.

Maggie flinched. She never would have survived living with Kent if he'd given Belle away. And she never would have seen her baby again if Shannon had had her way.

And now she was in the same situation. Unless she got Shannon to give up, she'd never hold Belle again. The thought was enough to freeze her muscles. Maggie swallowed hard and focused on driving.

"He found that letter from your grandfather. He was planning to kill you—did you know that?" Shannon said it conversationally, as though her words didn't hold the power of a boxer's punch.

"What?" Maggie gaped long enough to run off the road onto the edge. Tires crunched and the wheel jerked from her grasp.

Shannon screamed and waved her weapon. "Pay attention!"

Maggie got control of the car. "How do you know that? I thought you just said he planned to give you Belle and keep me. Why would he want to kill me?"

"For the money. That's why he had to die."

"Money?" Maggie blinked. "I'm confused."

Shannon gave a long-suffering sigh. "You haven't put it together yet? He found the envelope in the mail after he promised me Belle."

The envelope. Realization dawned. "And once he saw that Belle came with the money only upon my death, he knew he had to keep her and get rid of me," Maggie whispered.

"Exactly."

"So he backed out of your agreement."

"And I threatened to tell you." Shannon shook her head. "Two weeks before I killed him, he tried to kill me, can you believe it? He grabbed me around the throat and…" She gulped and shuddered. "I got away from him, but knew it wouldn't be the last time he tried. I knew I had to get rid of him."

"So you hit him with a car?"

"I did." A hard, determined expression crossed Shannon's face. A look so scary that Maggie winced. "The opportunity just was suddenly there and without even really thinking, I just…did it. I pressed the gas pedal and…" A slight smile curved her lips. "I did it and it was so easy." The smile disappeared and she gave Maggie a bitter look. "I knew I was in your will to be guardian of Belle if something happened to you and Kent. Well, something happened to Kent. Now it's your turn."

The woman was sick, mentally ill. Maggie whispered, "You really think you'll get away with killing me, too?"

"After you sign that paper, I will."

"They're going to Maggie's house," Reese said over the radio to Eli. "Shannon killed her brother and it looks like she plans to kill Maggie." He shuddered at the information he'd just overheard.

His phone buzzed, and he glanced at it. A text message from Trevor, his buddy in Spartanburg.

Eli took the next turn. "Is Belle with them?"

"No. Doesn't sound like it. Keep listening."

As they drove, Reese prayed. He snatched his phone and read the text.

And felt dread center itself in his gut. With a whispered prayer, he tossed the phone onto the passenger seat and grabbed his radio once again.

He knew Eli had called for backup from Bryson City, even Asheville, but that didn't mean they'd get there in time. "Eli, I don't know how volatile Shannon is. I found an aspirin bottle in Maggie's cabinet, only it wasn't aspirin in the bottle. I sent a pill to Asheville to be tested and it's medication used for people with schizophrenia."

A low whistle came through the radio as Eli processed what that might mean.

"But there are other reasons someone takes that kind of drug. Schizophrenia's just one of them." Reese said the words, but his gut didn't believe Shannon was taking the medication for anything else. If Shannon was truly mentally ill, Maggie had a whole different set of problems on her hands. And even if Shannon wasn't having a schizophrenic episode, she still had a gun and planned to get rid of Maggie. The only plus would be Shannon might be in a frame of mind to be reasoned with.

Maybe. Hopefully. His heart shuddered at the thought of Maggie being in a hostage situation. A SWAT team from Asheville was already en route.

Then again, if he and Eli got to Maggie's house in time, they could just stop Shannon in her tracks and be done with it. He liked that plan.

Chapter Eighteen

Maggie pulled into her driveway and shut off the car, wishing she had a switch for the terror racing through her.

Shannon nudged her with the gun. "Now get out. And remember, I've got Belle."

"I don't need a reminder." Maggie released the radio in her left hand and opened the car door. Her mind spun as she tried to figure out what she was going to do. How she was going to get away and alert Reese. She prayed he was listening in and was on his way to her house, but she couldn't count on that.

What was she going to do? What about the will? A cold shudder ripped through her. She'd never mailed the envelope. The envelope containing the new will. If Maggie died now and Shannon got away with it, she would get custody of Belle.

"Inside." Shannon gave her a shove toward the door. Maggie walked, but her mind spun.

"This was all supposed to be taken care of before now," Shannon said. "I wasn't even supposed to be here. You were never supposed to see me." The pout in her voice scared Maggie. The woman sounded put out that she was being so inconvenienced. Maggie opened the door and stepped inside. She disabled the alarm and sent prayers heavenward. Shannon still muttered, waving the gun. Maggie slipped her hand in her pocket and pressed the button while Shannon continued her rant. "Those idiots I hired couldn't even follow a simple plan. Rob the bank, grab you and Belle and get out."

"And then what, Shannon? Kill me?"

"Yes. Exactly."

The flat statement in the annoyed tone made Maggie gulp. How could the woman talk about killing her as though she were just squashing a bug in her house?

Fear made her nauseous.

She had to hold it together. Think. Think. Where could Belle be? The only thing that kept Maggie from screaming the house down was the fact that she felt certain Shannon wouldn't hurt Belle.

"Where is it?"

The barrel of the gun kissed her lower back.

Her knees threatened to buckle.

She locked them and forced herself to walk toward her office.

Reese got on the radio to Eli. "Don't pull in the driveway. Stop before you get to her house. I want to case the place and see if I can possibly go in unarmed, pretend like I don't know anything is wrong."

The radio crackled then Eli asked, "You think that's a good idea? From what you've said, that woman is unstable."

"Right now, it's the best thing to do."

He rolled his car to a stop where the gravel began its crawl to Maggie's house. Eli pulled up behind him. He looked at Eli. "Keep your radio on."

"I'm right behind you."

Reese took off his heavy coat, but left his gloves on for now. He needed to be able to move easily, unencumbered by the heavy material of the Sherpa coat. But he needed his hand warm in case he had to use his weapon. Cold fingers were slow fingers. Once he got a look at the house, he'd decide whether or not to pull his glove off his right hand.

The gravel crunched under his feet. His eyes scanned the driveway, the house, the woods beyond. He could hear the water lapping against the dock in a silent soothing rhythm.

Jason's cruiser sat in the driveway. They were here. His heart thumped in a mix of anticipation of getting Maggie away from the woman and terror that he wouldn't be able to do so.

Eli's footfalls echoed behind him. Reese called Maggie's cell phone once again. And again, it went to voice mail.

He looked at Eli. "What's Shannon's number?"

Eli shook his head. "I have no idea, I'll get Alice to get it ASAP." He pressed the earpiece further into his ear and Reese knew he was listening to the sounds coming from Jason's radio. "Sounds like they're at the back of the house. Maybe in her office?"

Reese crept to the front of the house, then rounded the corner to the office window. She had the curtains pulled but if he peered in at the corner... There.

He had a perfect glimpse of the gun in Shannon's left hand.

Maggie's hands shook as she pretended to go through the files. "I had it in here."

"Why did you change it?"

Maggie paused and looked up, past the barrel of the gun into Shannon's mad, snapping eyes. "Because I just wasn't sure about you. And then you were here, living in my house, taking care of Belle and I thought..."

"What?" The gun lowered a fraction.

"I thought that you really loved Belle. That maybe I was wrong to change the will."

Confusion flickered through the madness. "Of course I love Belle. She's my only chance... Mom said that..."

"Your chance at what, Shannon?"

"Motherhood." Her jaw tightened and the confusion fled. So did the madness. Sanity now stared at Maggie as Shannon went on. "I had an abortion when I was twenty-four. A back-alley type thing that led to a hysterectomy when I didn't stop bleeding. I've been diagnosed with a mental illness, too, so adoption is out of the question." She snorted. "It's so unfair. As long as I take my medication, I'm fine."

Medication. The strange pills in the aspirin bottle that Reese had almost taken?

"So you decided to make Belle yours."

"From the minute I found out you were pregnant." She waved the gun. "Now get the paper."

But Maggie didn't move. "That's why you were so nice to me," she whispered. "You wanted my trust. You wanted me to think you were on my side and that you would help me..."

"And it was working just fine until Kent showed up and scared you off."

"I thought he would hurt you if I stayed." She remembered how Shannon had begged her not to leave, said she wasn't scared of Kent and didn't care what he thought about Maggie staying there. But Maggie had cared. Maggie had wanted to protect the woman from the violence that followed Kent wherever he went. Especially if he was displeased with someone. And he'd been very displeased with Maggie.

Shannon's grip tightened on the weapon. "I know. I was furious with him. All he had to do was stay away and..." She broke off and screamed, "Now get the paper! I don't have time for this. They're probably looking for you right now."

Maggie could only pray that was so. She'd had to release the radio button to search the file box. It would have been too obvious if she'd left her hand in her pocket. However, she managed to snag the envelope addressed to the lawyer with the new will in it. With subtle ease, she maneuvered it into her pocket with the radio. "Tell me where Belle is, Shannon. I need to know where my baby is."

"She's safe. And she'll be with us. That's all you need to know."

"Us?" Before Shannon could answer, Maggie bent back over the file drawer and in one smooth move, snagged the horse-head paperweight in her right hand and brought it around to catch Shannon in left shoulder.

The woman screamed and dropped the gun. Maggie kicked it under the bed and bolted for the door.

Reese watched Shannon fall back against the wall as he threw himself through the window. Glass shattered around him, his back stung and his neck felt like someone had drawn a razor blade across it, but none of that mattered as Shannon's back disappeared through the doorway. "Now!" he yelled into the microphone.

The crash of the front door greeted his order.

"Shannon! It's the police! Drop your weapon!" He hollered the words, but didn't hold out hope they'd have any effect on the woman.

Scrambling to his feet, he bolted from the room.

He raced into the den and came up short. Shannon had managed to snag Maggie's blond ponytail and now had her at gunpoint in front of the fireplace.

Eli and Cal stood, weapons drawn.

A standoff.

Heart in his throat, Reese watched Shannon's eyes, looking for sanity. His stomach dropped as he saw the trapped look of a wild animal. A desperation that made her incredibly dangerous.

"Let Maggie go, Shannon."

Her eyes cut from the officers in the doorway to Reese. She drew herself up and yanked on Maggie's hair. Maggie winced and met his gaze. Terror mingled with fury.

"Tell them to get out!" Shannon screeched at him. "Out! Out! Or you'll never find Belle!"

Reese jerked his chin at Eli. The man shook his head. "Go," Reese said. "Shannon doesn't want to hurt anyone, do you? She just wants to be with Belle."

Shannon drew in a deep breath and some of the wildness left her eyes. "That's right. My Belle. Mine."

"Kent was going to take her away from you, wasn't he?"

Her lips tightened and she jerked a quick nod. Sorrow replaced the madness in her eyes. "He said I could have her. Then he said I couldn't." Confusion, then anger flashed. "But I got her anyway."

"You planned to kill him, didn't you? The night you hit him with the rental?"

"No." Shannon shook her head, the frown deepening the lines in her forehead. "No, I didn't plan it. It just…happened."

"Tell me how it happened," Reese coaxed, drawing on his negotiation skills. Skills he hadn't had to use in a long time. *Please, God, give me the words.* "Tell me."

She nodded to Eli and Cal who'd backed up, but hadn't left or lowered their weapons. "Tell them to leave."

Reese shot a glance at Eli then the window behind Shannon. Maggie's dark eyes stayed on him and he tried to convey his determination to make sure she got out of this alive.

Because Shannon had killed once. He had no doubts she would kill again.

Chapter Nineteen

Maggie did her best not to struggle. Staying still was almost impossible with her head cocked at such a strange angle and her neck muscles protesting. But Shannon was talking to Reese. She was listening. And Maggie thought Shannon had lowered the gun a fraction. Shannon's grip on her hair wasn't quite so tight.

Eli and the others backed up. Eli met Reese's eyes briefly for a moment of silent communication that Maggie wished she understood. Then they were gone, leaving her alone with Reese and Shannon.

Shannon relaxed a bit, enabling Maggie to move her head slightly and ease her screaming neck muscles. Then Reese coaxed, "Tell me how it happened."

"My car was in the shop. I... I got a rental car that day and was going to a party that night." As she talked, she tensed again and Maggie winced as pain shot through her skull. Reese's eyes narrowed, but he didn't take them from Shannon.

"A party? Right, I saw that in the police report. You had

an alibi for that night. They questioned you and the people at the party. You left the same time everyone else did."

From the corner of her eye, Maggie could see a sly grin cross the woman's lips. "I didn't plan it that way, it just…" Shannon shrugged. "It just worked out perfectly. Like God was telling me I was right and everything was going to be all right."

God? Maggie wanted to scream at the woman. *God doesn't condone murder.* She bit her lip and swallowed the words. So far Shannon hadn't killed her and Maggie didn't want to do anything to provoke her.

Reese said, "The police questioned you. Everyone said you were at the party all night and that you left when everyone else did."

"Of course. I felt ill and went to lie down. The hostess escorted me to a room on the second floor and told me to take as much time as I needed." Tension shook her. "The longer I lay there, the madder I got. I couldn't stand it. I called Kent and told him to meet me." Her words took on a singsong tone as she said, "He said he couldn't, he was busy. I knew what he was doing. He was gambling. Gambling away more money." A tremor shuddered through her. "He'd called earlier that day and told me I couldn't have the baby. I was shocked. I didn't understand. But I'm not stupid. I'm not stupid!"

"No one thinks you're stupid, Shannon." Reese's voice soothed, his body language conveyed confidence and an easygoing manner. But Maggie could see the coiled tension just below the surface. She didn't think Shannon would notice.

"Better not think I'm stupid. I'm not."

"You slipped out of the house, took the car and met him. And no one saw you leave?"

"No, apparently not. I didn't sneak out, but I didn't tell anyone I was leaving either. No one saw me slip out the back door, I guess."

"Or sneak back in," Reese said softly. "What happened? You met Kent…"

"And he told me that I couldn't have the baby. Just…flat out said I couldn't have her. He'd decided to keep her."

"Because of the money."

A growl erupted from Shannon's throat. "Yes, he'd found the envelope from Maggie's grandfather. And he said he had to keep Belle and kill Maggie and all his problems would be taken care of."

Maggie wanted to vomit. That someone could think so little of her life. Someone who'd professed to love her at one point. A wave of dizziness swept over her, and her neck cramped. And yet Shannon seemed to have forgotten about her. The woman was lost in her story, her memories, her hurt.

Maggie brought her hands to her chest and clasped them as though to pray. Reese's gaze flicked to her, then back to Shannon.

Shannon shifted, growing agitated. "But what about me? What about the fact that he'd promised me Belle? What about me! He didn't care about me! He laughed at me." Her voice dropped, chilling, the fury radiating as she remembered. "He laughed. Said I wasn't fit to be a mother anyway. And I just… lost it. I got in my car and while he was standing in the road laughing, I ran over him." She gave an eerie chuckle. "He stopped laughing."

The gun dipped and Maggie acted. She slammed her elbow back into Shannon's midsection.

Air whooshed from her lungs. The gun dropped to the floor and Maggie was finally free from the iron grip on her hair. She sank to the floor next to the gun and grabbed for it.

"No!" Shannon's screech cut off as Reese tackled her. Shannon's foot caught Maggie's hand and the gun skittered away from her.

Right next to Shannon's hand.

Shannon snagged it.

Reese's hand clamped down on her wrist, but still Shannon wasn't ready to give up. "Let me go! You can't do this to me! She's mine!"

Maggie's fist shot out, and she clipped the woman on the chin, stunning her. Shannon's eyes shot wide, and she went still as Reese stared at Maggie in shock—and pride.

Knuckles throbbing, Maggie silently thanked her police officer friend from church for her lessons in self-defense as she stared down at the woman who had caused her so much grief. "Belle and I were supposed to be kidnapped that day at the bank," she said, her voice low, terror for her own safety fading. "And then they were supposed to kill me, right?"

Shannon nodded, her eyes narrowing. "And then Belle would be found by the police and she would be given to me."

"Because my will stated that you would get Belle and the money that came with her. When that failed, you simply wanted that man, Douglas Patterson, to kill me. He shot at my house, Shannon. He could have killed all of us, including Belle!"

Shannon snorted. "That never should have happened. He was incompetent and stupid." Her eyes changed, glazed over as she said, "But it doesn't matter now. I have Belle. I'll always have Belle. She's mine." Then Shannon laughed. And laughed.

Maggie wanted to slug her again. "Where's my baby!"

But Shannon was beyond talking as Reese called for Eli to come in and take her away. The words *Psych ward* reached her ears as a violent tremor shuddered through her. Where was Belle?

Maggie felt as if she was going to fall apart. Reese rushed to her and wrapped his arms around her. "We're going to find her."

"She's okay. She's not hurt. Shannon may be mentally ill, but she wouldn't hurt Belle."

Eli stepped back inside. "Cal's here. He got Jason to the hospital and he's in surgery. Looks like he's going to make it. He's going with Shannon to the hospital to see if he can get any more information about Belle from her." He looked at Maggie. "We'll find her."

"Please," she whispered. The thought of never seeing her child again was more than she could bear. Tears flowed down her cheeks, and she allowed herself to lean against Reese, allowed him to comfort her for a brief moment.

Then she sniffed, stiffened and pulled away from him. "What can I do?"

"What?"

"I need to be doing something to find her. What can I do?"

He stared down at her and for a moment she thought he would tell her to let them handle it. But she couldn't. She needed to do something.

Eli said, "You can think. Think back on every conversation you had with Shannon. Did she ever tell you anything, say anything that would indicate that she was planning something? Where she could leave Belle while she dealt with you?"

Eli's phone rang and he answered it while Maggie forced her brain to cooperate. "I don't…" She shook her head. "I don't know. She talked a lot about missing Belle. She quit her job…"

"She was fired. We already looked into that."

"Oh."

Eli looked up from his phone. "And she bought four one-way tickets to Paris."

Maggie flinched. "Four?"

Simultaneously, Maggie and Reese said, "Her parents."

Eli hung up, dialed and barked orders. He looked at Maggie and Reese. "Let's head for the airport. Their flight leaves in forty-five minutes. Shannon may have told them to go on if she didn't make it."

"It's at least and hour and fifteen minutes to the airport. Can you stop the plane?" Maggie asked as she rushed out the door toward the police car.

"I'm working on it," Eli grunted as he slipped into the backseat. "Drive, Reese, while I try to stop that plane and give descriptions to security."

Reese drove. Maggie prayed and Eli consulted with airport security. She watched the clock. For the next forty-five minutes, she prayed and listened.

Eli finally said, "They're holding the plane."

"Have they found Belle?"

"Asheville P.D. is there looking for her. I had them pull up driver's license photos so they know what the Bennetts look like."

"It's not a very big airport. Why haven't they found them yet?" She bit her lip and closed her eyes on the panic threatening to swamp her.

"They could be in disguise."

"No, no, no. Please, God," she whispered. Reese reached over and grasped her hand with his. She drew comfort from his warmth, but felt his tension. She shuddered. "What if they see people looking for them? What if they get suspicious? What if—"

His hand tightened. "No what-if's. We're going to get her back."

Maggie clamped down on the fear and her panicky words. "Right. Of course we are. We have to."

Within minutes, Reese pulled up to the curb, lights flashing on top of the car. He held up his badge to security and the man waved them on.

Eli was back on the phone. "Where? Got it." He looked at Maggie and Reese. "This way."

They hurried through the crowd. Thanksgiving was in two days, she realized. People packed the airport. Rushing to the gate, they were met by TSA security officials who cleared them within minutes then escorted them to the gate. Airport security had been briefed and was anxious to help.

Maggie drew up short.

Sitting twenty yards away were Mr. and Mrs. Bennett. In Mrs. Bennett's lap was Belle. Security sat on either side of them.

Maggie rushed forward and dropped to her knees in front of her daughter. Belle squealed when she saw her and launched herself at her mother. Maggie caught her and rocked backward landing on her rear end, but holding Belle as close as she could without squeezing too hard. She breathed in her little girl scent, set her on the floor in front of her and ran her hands over every inch of her child.

She looked up at her former in-laws. "Why?"

"We didn't realize we were kidnapping her," Mr. Bennett said. "Security found us and told us what was going on. Shannon called and said she might not make the plane and for us to just go ahead and she'd catch up later. She said she had custody, that you signed her over. She showed us the will and spun a story that—" He broke off and a lone tear slid down his cheek. "We're sorry. I think we knew something was wrong, that there was no way you'd just sign her over, but we hoped… we wanted to believe so much…we're sorry."

She could see their grief, their pain. It all looked real, as if they truly had no idea what Shannon was doing. Maggie drew in a deep breath and felt some of her anger and bitterness toward this couple start to fall away. She stood and picked up Belle. To Reese, she said, "Will you check out their story? Make sure it's true?"

She nodded and looked at the grief-stricken husband and wife. "If what you say proves to be true, then I won't keep Belle from you. You can see her whenever you want."

Twin expressions of shock greeted her announcement. Mrs. Bennett blinked. "What?"

"Shannon was a con artist—and mentally ill. I can see how she could play on your grief for Kent and your desire to see Belle. I can't hold that against you." She paused and studied them. "If what you say is true."

"It's true," Mr. Bennett whispered. "I promise, it's true."

Mrs. Bennett gave a small cry and leaped to her feet. Throwing her arms around Maggie's neck, she whispered, "Thank you."

Maggie felt hope sweep through her. And relief. It was over. Her eyes met Reese's and the tender expression there made her gulp.

Chapter Twenty

Maggie stood beside Belle's crib and simply watched the baby sleep. It had been three months since Shannon had tried to kill her and kidnap Belle, and Maggie still didn't like to take her eyes off her daughter.

But the fear and anxiety were fading. Reese had been a big part of helping her accept that the danger was over and she and Belle were safe.

All three bank robbers were serving time. Shannon was in a hospital for the criminally mentally ill and getting help. Maggie hadn't been able to bring herself to go see the woman yet, but she hoped one day she could do it. Reese assured her he thought she could.

Reese.

Love filled her heart.

"Hey." Warm hands settled on her shoulders and she turned to see the man she'd been thinking about.

"Hey."

"I got your groceries put away. I'm going in to work in about an hour. Are we still on for dinner?"

Maggie wrapped her arms around his waist. "I love you, Reese."

He froze, then a small sigh slipped from his lips. "I've been wanting to hear those words for a while now."

She looked up into his eyes. "I've been wanting to say them for a while now."

"So why now?"

She smiled. "Because it was time."

He looked at the sleeping baby then pulled her into the den. The fire crackled in the fireplace and through the window she could see a light layer of snow covering the ground.

Excitement flooded her. She'd finally said the words and now that she had, she was surprised at how easy it had been. And how much she wanted to say them again.

"I love you, too, Maggie."

The air in the room suddenly seemed too thin. "You don't have to say it just because—"

His finger covered her lips, cutting her off. "I've been wanting to say it since we found Belle at the airport." He reached into his pocket and pulled out a small box.

Maggie drew in a much-needed breath. She whispered, "Reese?"

"You and Belle have wriggled your way into my heart and…" He shrugged. "I have something I've been wanting to ask you, but didn't want to rush you."

Her stomach flipped. "What's that?"

He dropped to one knee. "Well, I was going to be a little more creative about this, but since you've provided the opening, I'm going to go ahead and step through."

"Reese?" She couldn't seem to say anything else. She felt

shaky and light-headed and oh so happy. But first... "You're really okay with Belle, aren't you?"

He gave a sad smile. "I'll always miss Emma, but Belle is a beautiful little girl with her own personality, who makes me smile and has captured my heart. She's a part of you. How could I not love her?"

Maggie already knew that. She'd watched the two of them bond like superglue over the past three months. They'd celebrate Belle's first birthday tomorrow and Reese had been like a kid in a candy store picking out the perfect present for her. "I know. I have no more doubts that you'll love her like your own." Eyes swimming with tears, she cupped his cheek. "You're already a father to her."

Reese's green eyes widened and he opened the box to pull out a beautiful diamond ring. "Will you marry me, Maggie?"

Her throat closed and all she could do was nod. "I would be honored."

He slid the ring on her finger and stood.

Belle's cry sounded and he placed a gentle kiss on her lips. "Hold on a minute, I'm not done."

Maggie sank onto the couch and studied the ring on her finger. Joy surged through her and she sent up a silent thank-you to God, who'd allowed Reese to come into her and Belle's life.

Reese walked back into the den with Belle on his hip. Belle lay her head on his shoulder and smiled at Maggie. Then Maggie noticed something on her daughter's tiny finger. A small silver ring.

She glanced at Reese. "One for her, too? How sweet."

He took it from her hand and said, "We'll keep it somewhere safe for when she's older. Right now, she'll just want to eat it." Maggie gave a watery laugh. He pulled her up from her seat on the couch and wrapped an arm around her shoulders. "This is my promise to be the kind of dad she needs. I promise to love her and teach her and train her in the ways God says fathers are to love, teach and train their children."

Her heart shook with emotion as he lifted her hand and kissed the ring he'd just placed there only moments before. "And I promise to be the kind of husband I'm supposed to be. I don't promise to be perfect, but I promise you'll never have reason to fear me."

She felt a tear slip down her cheek. "I can't believe I'm crying this much." He smiled and she said, "I love you."

"And I love you." He leaned over and placed another tender kiss on her willing lips.

Belle giggled and clapped and Maggie grinned through her tears. "Welcome home, Reese."

"Welcome home, Maggie." And she thought she heard him whisper, "Thank You, God, for my family." He planted a kiss on her forehead. "What's the first thing you want to do now that you don't have to worry about someone trying to kill you?"

Maggie thought about it then grinned. "Kiss you."

"I like that plan."

His head lowered but before his lips touched hers, she muttered, "Then put you in my will."

His laughter was music to her ears.

* * * * *

STRANGER IN THE SHADOWS

Shirlee McCoy

To Brenda Minton, who makes me laugh when I want to cry. Thanks for the brainstorming sessions and the pep talks, but mostly thanks for being you.

And to Bob and Jan Porter and Dick and Carolyn Livesey, who are true encouragers. Thanks for always cheering me on!

Send forth your light and your truth, let them guide me;
let them bring me to your holy mountain, to the place where you dwell.
—*Psalms* 43:3

Chapter One

It came in the night, whispering into her dreams. Silent stars, hazy moonlight, a winding road. Sudden, blinding light.

Impact.

Rolling, tumbling, terror. And then silence.

Smoke danced at the edges of memory as flames writhed serpentlike through cracked glass and crumbled metal, hissing and whirling in the timeless dance of death.

Adam! She reached for his hand, wanting to pull him from the car and from the dream—whole and alive. Safe. But her questing hand met empty space and hot flame, her body flinching with the pain and the horror of it.

Sirens blared in the distance, their throbbing pulse a heartbeat ebbing and flowing with the growing flames. She turned toward the door, trying to push aside hot, bent metal, and saw a shadow beyond the shattered glass; a dark figure leaning toward the window, staring in. Dark eyes that seemed to glow in the growing flames.

Help me! She tried to scream the words, but they caught in

her throat. And the shadow remained still and silent, watching as the car burned and she burned with it.

The shrill ring of an alarm clock sounded over the roar of flames, spearing into Chloe Davidson's consciousness and pulling her from the nightmare. For a moment there was nothing but the dream. No past. No present. No truth except hot flames and searing pain. But the flames weren't real, the pain a fading memory. Reality was...what?

Chloe scrambled to anchor herself in the present before she fell back into the foggy world of unknowns she'd lived in during the weeks following the accident.

"Saturday. Lakeview, Virginia. The Morran wedding. Flowers. Decorations." She listed each item as it came to mind, grabbing towels from the tiny closet beside the bathroom door, pulling clothes from her dresser. Black pants. Pink shirt. Blooming Baskets' uniform. Her new job. Her new life. A normality she still didn't quite believe in.

The phone rang before she could get in the shower, the muted sound drawing her from the well-lit bedroom and into the dark living room beyond.

"Hello?" She pressed the receiver to her ear as she flicked on lamps and the overhead light, her heart still racing, her throbbing leg an insistent reminder of the nightmare she'd survived.

"Chloe. Opal, here."

At the sound of her friend and boss's voice, Chloe relaxed, leaning her hip against the sofa and forcing the dream and the memories to the back of her mind. "You've only been gone a day and you're already checking in?"

"Checking in? I wasn't planning to do that until tonight. This is business. We've got a problem. Jenna's gone into labor."

Opal's only other full-time employee, Jenna Monroe, was eight months pregnant and glowing with it. At least she had been when Chloe had seen her the previous day. "She's not due for another four weeks."

"Maybe not, but the baby has decided to make an appearance. You're going to have to handle the setup for the Morran wedding on your own until I can get there."

"I'll call Mary Alice—"

"Mary Alice is going to have to stay at the store. We can't afford to close for the day and between the two of you, she's the better floral designer."

"It doesn't take much to be better than me." Chloe's dry comment fell on deaf ears, Opal's voice continuing on, giving directions and listing jobs that needed to be done before the wedding guests arrived at the church.

"So, that's it. Any questions?"

"No. But you do realize I've only been working at Blooming Baskets for five days, right?"

"Are you saying you can't do this?"

"I'm saying I'll try, but I can't guarantee the results."

"No need to guarantee anything. I've already left Baltimore. I'll be in Lakeview at least an hour before the wedding. We'll finish the job together."

"If I haven't ruined everything by then."

"What's to ruin? We're talking flowers, ribbons and bows." Opal paused, and Chloe could imagine her raking a hand through salt and pepper curls, her strong face set in an impatient frown. "Look, I have faith in your ability to handle this. Why don't you try to have some, too?"

The phone clicked as Opal disconnected, and Chloe set the receiver down.

Faith? Maybe she'd had it once—in herself and her abilities, in those she cared about. But that was before the accident, before Adam's death. Before his betrayal. Before everything had changed.

Now she wasn't even sure she knew what the word meant.

It didn't take long to shower and change, to grab her keys and make her way out of her one-bedroom apartment and into the dark hallway of the aging Victorian she lived in.

Outside it was still dark, brisk fall air dancing through the grass and rustling the dying leaves of the bushes that flanked the front porch. Chloe scanned the shadowy yard, the trees that stretched spindly arms toward the heavens, the inky water of Smith Mountain Lake. There seemed a breathless quality to the morning, a watchful waiting that crawled along Chloe's nerves and made the hair on the back of her neck stand on end. A million eyes could be watching from the woods beside the house, a hundred men could be sliding silently toward the car and she'd never know it, never see it until it was too late.

Cold sweat broke out on her brow, her hand shaking as she got in the car and shoved the keys into the ignition.

"You are not going to have a panic attack about this." She hissed the words as she drove up the long driveway and turned onto the road, refusing to think about what she was doing, refusing to dwell on the darkness that pressed against the car windows. Soon dawn would come, burning away the night and her memories. For now, she'd just have to deal with both.

Forty minutes later, Chloe arrived at Grace Christian Church, the pink Blooming Baskets van she'd picked up at the shop loaded with decorations and floral arrangements. It was just before seven. The wedding was scheduled for noon. Guests would arrive a little before then. That meant she had four hours to get ready for what Opal and Jenna had called the biggest event to take place in Lakeview in a decade. And Chloe was the one setting up for it.

She would have laughed if she weren't so sure she was about to fail. Miserably.

Cold crisp air stung her cheeks as she stepped to the back

of the van and pulled open the double doors. The sickeningly sweet funeral-parlor stench nearly made her gag as she dragged the first box out.

"Need a hand?"

The voice was deep, masculine and so unexpected Chloe jumped, the box of wrought iron candelabras dropping from her hands. She whirled toward the sound, but could see nothing but the deep gray shadows of trees and foliage. "Thank you, but I'm fine."

"You sure? Looks like you've got a full van there." A figure emerged from the trees, a deeper shadow among many others, but moving closer.

"I can manage." As she spoke, she dug in her jacket pocket, her fist closing around the small canister of pepper spray she carried. She didn't know who this guy was, but if he got much closer he was going to get a face full of pain.

"I'm sure you can, but Opal won't be happy if I let you. She just ordered me out of bed and over here to help. So here I am. Ready to lend a hand. Or two." His voice was amiable, his stride unhurried. Chloe released her hold on the spray.

"Opal shouldn't have bothered you, Mr...?"

"Ben Avery. And it wasn't a bother."

She knew the name, had heard plenty about the handsome widower who pastored Grace Christian Church. Opal's description of the man's single-and-available status had led Chloe to believe he was Opal's contemporary. Late fifties or early sixties.

In the dim morning light, he looked closer to thirty and not like any pastor Chloe had ever seen, his hair just a little too long, his leather jacket more biker than preacher.

"Bother or not, I'm sure you have other things to do with your time, Pastor Avery."

"I can't think of any offhand. And call me Ben. Everyone

else does." He smiled, his eyes crinkling at the corners, the scent of pine needles and soap drifting on the air as he leaned forward and grabbed the box she'd dropped.

Chloe thought about arguing, but insisting she do the job herself would only waste time she didn't have. She shrugged. "Then I guess I'll accept your help and say thanks."

"You might want to hold off on the thanks until we see how many flower arrangements I manage to massacre."

"You're not the only one who may massacre a few. I know as much about flowers as the average person knows about nuclear physics."

He laughed, the sound shivering along Chloe's nerves and bringing her senses to life. "Opal did mention that you're a new hire."

"Should I ask what else she mentioned?"

"You can, but that was about all she said. That and, 'It'll be on your head, Ben Avery, if Chloe decides to quit because of the pressure she's under today.'"

"That sounds just like her. The rat."

"She is, but she's a well-meaning rat."

"Very true." Chloe pulled out another box. "And I really could use the help. This is a big job."

"Then I guess we'd better get moving. Between the two of us we should be able to get most of the setup done before Opal arrives." Ben pushed open the church door, waiting as Chloe moved more slowly across the parking lot.

"Ladies first." He gestured for her to step inside, but Chloe hesitated.

She hated the dark. Hated the thought of what might be lurking in it. The inside of the church was definitely dark, the inky blackness lit by one tiny pinpoint of light flashing from the ceiling. She knew it must be a smoke detector, but her mind spiraled into the darkness, carried her back to the accident, to the shadowy figure standing outside the window of the car, to the eyes that had seemed to glow red, searing into her soul and promising a slow, torturous death.

She swayed, her heart racing so fast she was sure she was going to pass out.

"Hey, are you okay?" Ben wrapped a hand around her arm, anchoring her in place, his warmth chasing away some of the fear that shivered through her.

"I'm fine." Of course she wasn't fine. Not by a long shot. But her terror was only a feeling, the danger imagined.

She took a deep breath, stepped into the room, the darkness enveloping her as the door clicked shut. Chloe forced herself to concentrate on the moment, on the soft pad of Ben's shoes as he moved across the floor, the scent of pine needles and soap that drifted on the air around him.

Finally, overhead lights flicked on, illuminating a wide hallway. Hardwood floors, creamy walls, bulletin boards filled with announcements and pictures. The homey warmth of it drew her in and welcomed her.

Chloe turned, facing Ben, seeing him clearly for the first time, her heart leaping as she looked into the most vividly blue eyes she'd ever seen. Deep sapphire, they burned into hers, glowing with life, with energy, with an interest that made Chloe step back, the box clutched close, a flimsy barrier between herself and the man who'd done what no other had in the past year—made her want to keep looking, made her want to know more, made her wish she were the woman she'd been before Adam's death.

His gaze touched her face, the scar on her neck, the mottled flesh of her hand, but he didn't comment or ask the questions so many people felt they had the right to. "The sanctuary is through here. Let's bring these in. Then I'll make some coffee before we get the rest from the van."

Chloe followed silently, surprised by her response to Ben and not happy about it. She'd made too many mistakes with Adam, had too many regrets. There wasn't room for anything else. Or anyone.

"Where do you want these?" Ben's question pulled her from her thoughts and she glanced around the large room. Rows of pews, their dark wood gleaming in the overhead light, flanked a middle aisle. A few stairs led to a pulpit and a choir loft, a small door to one side of them closed tight.

"On the first pew will be fine. I'll start there and work my way back." She avoided looking in Ben's direction as she spoke, preferring to tell herself she'd imagined the bright blue of his eyes, the warm interest there. He was a pastor, after all, and she was a woman who had no interest in men.

"Am I making you nervous?"

Startled, Chloe glanced up, found herself pulled into his gaze again.

"No." At least not much. "Why do you ask?"

"Sometimes my job makes people uncomfortable." He smiled, his sandy hair and strong, handsome face giving him a boy-next-door appearance that seemed at odds with the intensity in his eyes.

"Not me." Though Ben seemed to be having that effect on her.

"Good to know." He smiled again, but his gaze speared into hers and she wondered what he was seeing as he looked so deeply into her eyes. "And just so we're clear. Florists don't make me uncomfortable."

Despite herself, Chloe smiled. "Then I guess that means we'll both be nice and relaxed while we work."

"Not until we have some coffee. I don't know about you, but I'm not much good for anything until I've had a cup."

His words were the perfect excuse to end the conversation

and move away from Ben, and Chloe started back toward the sanctuary door, anxious to refocus her thinking, recenter her thoughts. "I'll keep unloading while you make some."

Ben put a hand on her shoulder, stopping her before she could exit the room. "If the rest of the boxes are as heavy as the last one, maybe you should make the coffee and I should unload."

"I'll be fine."

"You will be, but I won't if Opal finds out I let you carry in a bunch of heavy boxes while I made coffee."

"Who's going to tell her?"

"I'd feel obligated to. After all, she's bound to ask how things went and I'm bound to tell the truth."

For the second time since she'd met Ben, Chloe found herself smiling at his words. Not good. Not good at all. Men were bad news. At least all the men in Chloe's life had been. The sooner she put distance between herself and Ben, the better she'd feel. "Since you put it that way, I guess I can't argue."

"Glad to hear it, because arguing isn't getting me any closer to having that cup of coffee. Come on, I'll show you to the kitchen." He strode out of the sanctuary, moving with long, purposeful strides.

Chloe followed more slowly, not sure what it was about Ben that had sparked her interest and made her want to look closer. He was a man, just like any other man she'd ever known, but there was something in his eyes—secrets, depths—that begged exploration.

Fortunately, she'd learned her lesson about men the hard way and she had no intention of learning any more. She'd just get through the wedding preparations, get through the day, then go back to her apartment and forget Ben Avery and his compelling gaze.

Chapter Two

The industrial-size kitchen had a modern feel with a touch of old-time charm, the stainless steel counters and appliances balanced by mellow gold paint, white cabinets and hardwood floor. Chloe hovered in the doorway, wary, unsure of herself in a way she hadn't been a year ago, watching as Ben plugged in a coffeemaker and pulled a can of coffee from a cupboard. He gestured her over and Chloe stepped into the room ignoring the erratic beat of her heart. "This is a nice space."

"Yeah, it is, but I can't take credit. We remodeled a couple of years ago. The church ladies decided on the setup and color scheme. Opal pretty much spearheaded the project."

"That doesn't surprise me. She's a take-charge kind of person. It's one of the things I admire about her."

"Have you known her long?" He leaned a hip against the counter, relaxed and at ease. Apparently not at all disturbed by the fact that he'd been called out of bed before dawn on a cool November day to help a woman he didn't know set up flowers for a wedding he was probably officiating.

Strange.

Interesting.

Intriguing.

Enough!

Chloe rubbed the scarred flesh on her wrist, forcing her thoughts back to the conversation. "Since I was a kid."

"You grew up in Lakeview?" His gaze was disconcerting, and Chloe resisted the urge to look away.

"No, I visited in the summer." She didn't add more. The past was something she didn't share. Especially not with strangers.

Ben seemed to take the hint, turning away and pulling sugar packets from a cupboard. "It's a good place to spend the summer. And the fall, winter and spring." He smiled. "There's cream in the fridge if you take it. I'd better get moving on those boxes."

With that he strode from the room, his movements lithe and silent, almost catlike in their grace. He might be a pastor now, but Chloe had a feeling he'd been something else before he'd felt a call to ministry. Military. Police. Firefighter. Something that required control, discipline and strength.

Not that it mattered or was any of her business.

Chloe shook her head, reaching for a coffee filter and doing her best to concentrate on the task at hand. Obviously, the nightmare had thrown her off, destroying her focus and hard-won control. She needed to get both back and she needed to do it now. Opal was counting on her. There was no way she planned to disappoint the one person in her life who had never disappointed her.

She paced across the room, staring out the window above the sink, anxiety a cold, hard knot in her chest. New beginnings. That's what she hoped for. Prayed for. But maybe she was too entrenched in the past to ever escape it. Maybe coming to Lakeview was nothing more than putting off the inevitable.

Outside, dawn bathed the churchyard in purple light and deep shadows, the effect sinister. Ominous. A thick stand of trees stood at the far end of the property, tall pines and heavy-branched oaks reaching toward the ever-brightening sky. As the coffee brewed, the rich, full scent of it filled the kitchen, bringing memories of hot summer days, lacy curtains, open windows, soft voices. Safety.

But safety and security never lasted. All Chloe could hope for was a measure of peace.

She started to turn away from the window, but something moved near the edge of the yard, a slight shifting in the darkness that caught her attention. Was that a person standing in the shadows of the trees? It was too far to see the details, the light too dim. But Chloe was sure there was a person there. Tall. Thin. Looking her way.

She took a step back, her pulse racing, her skin clammy and cold. This was the nightmare again. The stranger watching, waiting on the other side of the glass. Only this time Chloe wasn't trapped in a car and surrounded by flames. This time she was able to run. And that's just what she did, turning away from the window, rushing from the kitchen and slamming into a hard chest.

She flew back, her bad leg buckling, her hands searching for purchase. Her fingers sank into cool leather as strong arms wrapped around her waist and pulled her upright.

"Careful. We've got a lot to do. It's probably best if we don't kill each other before we finish." Ben's words tickled against her hair, his palms warm against her ribs. He felt solid and safe and much too comfortable.

Chloe stepped back, forcing herself to release her white-knuckled grip on his jacket. "Sorry. I didn't mean to run you down."

"You didn't even come close." His gaze swept over her, moving from her face, to her hands and back again. "Is everything okay? You look pale."

"I…" But what was she going to say? That she'd seen someone standing outside the church? That she thought it might be the same person who'd stood outside her burning car, watching while the flames grew? The same person who'd been in jail for eleven months? "Everything is fine. I'm just anxious to get started in the sanctuary."

He stared hard, as if he could see beyond her answer to the truth that she was trying to hide, the paranoia and fear that had dogged her for months. Finally, he nodded. "How about we grab the coffee and get started?"

Go back into the kitchen? Back near the window that looked out onto the yard? Maybe catch another glimpse of whoever was standing near the trees. No thanks. "You go ahead. I'll start unpacking boxes."

She hurried back toward the sanctuary, feeling the weight of Ben's gaze as she stepped through the double wide doors. She didn't look back, not wanting him to see the anxiety and frustration in her face.

She'd been so sure that moving away from D.C., leaving behind her apartment, her job, starting a new life, would free her from the anxiety that had become way too much a part of who she was. Seven days into her "new" life and she'd already sunk back into old patterns and thought processes.

Her hands trembled as she pulled chocolate-colored ribbon from a box and began decorating the first pew. Long-stemmed roses—deep red, creamy white, rusty orange—needed to be attached. She pulled a bouquet from a bucket Ben had brought in and wrestled it into place, a few petals falling near her feet as she tied a lopsided bow around the stems.

"Better be careful. Opal won't like it if the roses are bald when she gets here." Ben moved toward her, a coffee cup in each hand, sandy hair falling over his forehead.

"Hopefully, she won't notice a few missing petals."

"A few? No. A handful? Maybe." He set both cups on a pew and scooped up several silky petals. "I brought you coffee. Black. You didn't look like the sugar and cream type."

He was right, and Chloe wasn't sure she was happy about it. "What gave it away?"

"Your eyes." He didn't elaborate and Chloe didn't ask, just lifted the closest cup, inhaling the rich, sharp scent of the coffee and doing her best to avoid Ben's steady gaze.

Which annoyed her. She'd never been one to avoid trouble. Never been one to back away from a challenge. Never been. But the accident had changed her.

She took a sip of the coffee, pulled more ribbon from the box, forcing lightness to her movements and to her voice. "They say the eyes are the window to the soul. If you're seeing black coffee in mine, I'm in big trouble."

"I'm seeing a lot more than black coffee in there." He grabbed a bouquet of roses, holding it while Chloe hooked it in place and tied a ribbon around the stems, feeling the heat of Ben's body as he leaned in close to help, wondering what it was he thought he saw in her eyes.

Or maybe not wondering. Maybe she knew. Darkness. Sorrow. Guilt. Emotions she'd tried to outrun, but that refused to be left behind.

She grabbed another ribbon, another bouquet, trying to lose herself in the rhythm of the job.

"The flowers look good. Are they Opal's design, or Jenna's?" The switch in subjects was a welcome distraction, and Chloe answered quickly.

"I'm not sure. They were designed months before I started working at Blooming Baskets."

"Do you like it there?"

"Yes." She just wasn't sure how good she was at it. Digging into the bowels of a computer hard drive to find hidden files was one thing. Unraveling yards of tulle and ribbon and handling delicate flowers was another. "But it's a lot different than what I used to do."

"What was that?"

"Computers." She kept the answer short. Giving a name to her job as a computer forensic specialist usually meant answering a million questions about her chosen career.

Former career.

"Sounds interesting."

"It was." It had also been dangerous. Much more dangerous than she ever could have imagined before Adam's death. But that was something she didn't need to be thinking about when she had a few dozen pews and an entire reception hall left to decorate.

Chloe pulled out more ribbon, started on the next pew and wondered how long it was going to take to complete the decorations on the rest. Too long. Unless she started working a lot faster.

She moved forward, more ribbon in her hand. Ben moved with her, his sandy head bent close to hers as he helped hold the next bunch of roses in place, his presence much more of a distraction than it should have been. "Maybe we should split up. You take the pews on the other side of the aisle. I'll finish the ones over here."

"Trying to get rid of me?"

Absolutely. "I just think we'll get the job done more quickly that way."

"Maybe, but we seem to be making pretty good headway together. Two sets of hands are definitely helpful in this kind of work."

He had a point. A good one. If she had to hold the flowers and tie the ribbons it would probably take double the time. And time was not something she had enough of. "You're probably right. Let's keep going the way we are."

"Silently?"

Chloe glanced up into Ben's eyes, saw amusement there. "I don't mind talking while we work."

"As long as it's not about the past?"

"Something like that."

"I bet that limits conversation."

Chloe shrugged, tying the next bow, grabbing more ribbon. "There are plenty of other things to talk about."

"Like?"

"Like what Opal's going to say if she gets here and we're not done."

The deep rumble of Ben's laughter filled the air. "Point taken. I'll lay off the questions and move a little faster."

Four hours later, Chloe placed the last centerpiece on the last table in the reception hall; the low bowl with floating yellow, cream and burnt umber roses picked up the color in the standing floral arrangements that dotted the edges of the room. Roses. Lilies. A half a dozen other flowers whose names she didn't know.

"You did it! And it looks almost presentable." Opal Winchester's voice broke the silence and Chloe turned to face the woman who'd been surrogate mother to her during long-ago summers, watching as she moved across the room, her salt and pepper curls bouncing around a broad face, her sturdy figure encased in a dark suit and pink shirt.

"I didn't do it alone."

"I know. Where is that good-looking young pastor?"

"Home getting ready for the wedding. Which he's officiating after spending almost four hours helping with the floral decorations."

"Did he complain?"

"No."

"Then I don't expect you to, either." Opal slid an arm around Chloe's waist and surveyed the room. "It's beautiful, isn't it?"

"It is. You and Jenna did a great job."

"So did you and Ben." Opal cast a sly look in Chloe's direction, her dark eyes sparkling. "So, what did you think of him?"

"Who?"

"Ben Avery. As if you didn't know."

"He's helpful."

"And?"

"And he's helpful." Chloe brushed thick bangs out of her eyes and limped a few steps away from Opal, smoothing a wrinkle out of a tablecloth, determined not to give her friend any hint of how Ben had effected her. "How was your drive?"

"You're changing the subject, but I'll allow it seeing as how I'm so proud of what you've accomplished this morning. The drive was slow. I thought I'd never get here." Opal adjusted a centerpiece, straightened a bow on one of the chairs. "But I'm here and happy to announce that Jenna had a bouncing baby boy fifteen minutes ago."

"That's wonderful!"

"Isn't it? A wedding and a birth on the same day. You can't ask for much better than that. I'm going to stop by the hospital after the reception is over. Maybe slip Jenna a piece of wedding cake if Miranda and Hawke don't mind me bringing her some. Speaking of which," She paused, spearing Chloe with a look that warned of trouble. "You're going to have to attend."

"Attend?"

"The wedding."

"No way." She had no intention of staying to witness the marriage of two people she didn't know, two people who, according to both Jenna and Opal, were meant to be together.

Meant to be.

As if such a thing were possible. As if meant to be didn't always turn into goodbye.

"I understand your reluctance, Chloe, but it's expected."

"You know I never do what's expected."

"I know you never did what was expected. You're starting fresh here and in a small town like Lakeview, doing what's expected is important."

"Opal—"

"Don't make me use my mother voice." She glowered, straightening to her full five-foot-three height.

"I'm not ready for a big social event."

"Well, then you'd better get ready. The entire church was invited to the ceremony and the reception. It's a community event."

"I don't attend this church."

"But Jenna does. You'll be taking her place, offering support to the couple and representing Blooming Baskets."

"I'm sure—"

"I won't listen to any more excuses. I don't like them." The words were harsh, but Opal's expression softened, her dark eyes filled with sympathy. "It's been a year, Chloe. It's time to move on. That's why you're here. That's what you want. And it's what I want for you. So, ready or not, you're attending the wedding."

Much as Chloe wanted to argue, she couldn't deny the truth of Opal's words. She did want to leave the past behind, to focus on the present and the future. To create the kind of life she'd once thought boring and mundane but now longed for. "Okay. I'll stay. For a while."

"Good. Now, I'm going to make sure everything is perfect in the sanctuary. You grab yourself a cup of coffee and put your leg up for a while."

"I'll come with you."

"You'll do exactly what I told you to do." Opal bustled away, leaving Chloe both amused and frustrated. Opal was a force to be reckoned with. In her absence, the room felt empty, the hollow aloneness of the moment a hard knot in Chloe's chest, the beauty of the flowers, the tables, the bows and ribbons reminding her of the wedding she'd almost had.

Almost.

All her plans, all her dreams had died well before the accident. Now her dreams were much simpler and much less romantic. She wanted to forget, wanted to move on, wanted to rebuild her life. Maybe with God's help she could do that, though even here in His house, she felt He was too far away to see her troubles, too far away to care.

And that, more than the flowers and decorations and memories, made her feel truly alone.

Chapter Three

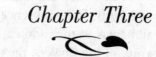

Ben Avery's attention should have been on the bride and groom, the wedding party, the guests who joked and laughed, ate and talked as the reception wound its way through hour three with no sign of slowing. Instead, his gaze was drawn again and again to Chloe Davidson. Straight black hair gleaming in the overhead light, slim figure encased in a fitted black pantsuit, she smiled and chatted as she moved through the throng, her limp barely noticeable. On the surface, she seemed at ease and relaxed, but there was a tension to her, a humming energy that hadn't ebbed since he'd first seen her unloading the van.

He watched as she approached Opal Winchester, said a few words, then started toward the door that led outside. Maybe she needed some air, a few minutes away from the crowd, some time to herself. And maybe he should leave her to it. But he'd seen sadness in her eyes and sensed a loneliness that he knew only too well.

And he was curious.

He admitted it to himself as he smiled and waved his way across the reception hall and out the door. Already the day was waning, the sky graying as the sun began its slow descent. The air felt crisp and clean, the quiet sounds of rural life a music that Ben never tired of hearing.

He glanced around the parking lot, saw Chloe leaning against Blooming Baskets' pink van and strode toward her. "It looks like the flowers were a big success."

"Opal is pleased, anyway." Her eyes were emerald-green and striking against the kind of flawless skin that could have graced magazine covers. Only a deep scar on the side of her neck marred its perfection.

"She should be. You worked hard." He leaned a shoulder against the van, studying Chloe's face, wondering at the tension in her. Opal had told him almost nothing about the woman she'd hired a week ago. Only that Chloe was recovering from surgery and working at Blooming Baskets. There was more to the story, of course. A lot more. But Ben doubted he'd get answers from either woman.

"So did you. Thanks again for all your help." She smiled, but the sadness in her eyes remained.

"It was no problem. People in my congregation call me all the time for help." Though he had to admit he'd been surprised by Opal's early morning summons. Flowers? Definitely not his thing.

"That may be true, but being woken up before dawn and asked to do a job you're not getting paid for goes way beyond the call of duty."

"But not beyond the call of friendship."

"If that's the case, Opal is lucky to have a friend like you."

"In my experience, luck doesn't have a whole lot to do with how things work out."

"You're right about that." She straightened, brushing thick

black bangs from her eyes. "Opal came into my life just when I most needed someone. I've always thought that was a God thing. Not a luck thing."

"But?"

She raised an eyebrow at his question, but answered it. "Lately it's been hard to see much of God in the things that have happened in my life."

"You've had a hard time." The scars on her neck and hand were testimony to that, the pain in her eyes echoing the physical evidence left by whatever had happened.

Chloe's gaze was focused on some distant point. Maybe the trees. Maybe the last rays of the dying sun. Maybe some dream or hope that had been lost. "Yes, but things are better now."

He was sure he heard a hint of doubt in her voice, but she didn't give him a chance to comment, just shrugged too-thin shoulders. "I'd better get back inside before Opal sends out a posse."

The words and her posture told Ben the conversation was closed. He didn't push to open it again. Much as he might be curious about Chloe, he had no right to press for answers. "I'm surprised she hasn't already. There must be at least five unmarried men she hasn't introduced you to yet."

"Is that what was going on? I was wondering why almost every person she introduced me to was male." She laughed, light and easy, her body losing some of its tension, her lips curving into a full-out grin that lit her face, glowed in her eyes.

"You should do that more often."

The laughter faded, but the smile remained. "Do what?"

"Smile."

"I've been smiling all day."

"Your lips might have been, but your heart wasn't in it."

She blinked, started to respond, but the door to the reception hall flew open, spilling light and sound out into the deepening twilight.

"There you are!" Opal's voice carried over the rumble of wedding excitement as she hurried toward them. "Things are winding down. It won't be long before Hawke and Miranda leave."

"Are you hinting that we should get back inside?"

"You know me better than that, Ben. I never hint."

It was true. In the years Ben had been pastoring Grace Christian Church, Opal had never hesitated to give her opinion or state her mind. A widow who'd lost her husband the same year Ben lost his wife, she was the one woman Ben knew who'd never tried to set him up with a friend, relative or acquaintance.

She had, however, told him over and over again that a good pastor needed a good wife. Maybe she was right, but Ben wasn't looking for one. "So, you're telling us we should get back inside?"

"Exactly." She smiled. "So, let's go."

There was no sense arguing. Ben didn't want to anyway. He'd come outside to make sure Chloe was okay and to satisfy his curiosity. He'd accomplished the first. The second would take a little more time. Maybe a lot more time.

That was something Ben didn't have.

Much as he loved his job, being a pastor was more than a full-time commitment. Opal's opinion about a pastor needing a wife aside, Ben had no room for anything more in his life. That was why he planned to put Chloe Davidson and her sad-eyed smile out of his mind.

Planned to.

But he knew enough about life, enough about God, to know that his plans might not be the best ones. That sometimes things he thought were too much effort, too much time, too much commitment, were exactly what God wanted. Only time would tell if Chloe was one of those things.

He pushed open the reception hall door, allowing Chloe and Opal to step in ahead of him. Light, music, laughter and chatter washed over him, the happy excitement of those in attendance wrapping around his heart and pulling him in.

"Ben!" Hawke Morran stepped toward him, dark hair pulled back from his face, his scar a pale line against tan skin.

Ben grabbed his hand and shook it. "Things went well."

"Of course they did. I was marrying Miranda. Thank you for doing the ceremony. And for everything else. Without your help we might not be here at all." The cadence to his words, the accent that tinged them, was a reminder of where he'd grown up, of the life he'd lived before he'd come to the States to work for the DEA, before he'd been set up and almost killed. Ben had met him while he was on the run, offered the help Hawke needed, and forged a friendship with him.

"There's no need to thank me. I was glad to help."

"And I'm glad to have made a friend during a very dark time." He smiled, his pale gaze focused on his wife.

"Are you returning to Thailand for your honeymoon?"

"We are. I want Miranda to experience it when she's not running for her life."

"Try to stay out of trouble this time."

"I think my days of finding trouble are over." He paused, glanced at the hoard of women who had converged on his bride. "Miranda is finally going to toss the flowers. Come on, let's get closer. My wife doesn't know it, yet, but as soon as she finishes, she's going to be kidnapped."

That sounded too good to miss and Ben followed along as Hawke moved toward the group. Miranda smiled at the women crowded in front of her, turned and tossed the bouquet. Squeals of excitement followed as the ladies jostled for position, the flowers flying over grasping hands and leaping bridesmaids before slapping into the chest of the only silent, motionless woman there.

Chloe.

Her hands grasped the flowers, pulled them in. Then, as if she realized what she was doing and didn't like it, she frowned, tossing the bouquet back into the fray. More squeals followed, more grasping and clawing for possession. Chloe remained apart from it all, watching, but not really seeming to see. Ben took a step toward her, hesitated, told himself he should let her be, then ignored his own advice and crossed the space between them.

Chapter Four

"I think that's the first time I've ever seen a woman catch the bouquet and throw it back." Ben Avery's laughter rumbled close to Chloe's ear, pulling her from thoughts she was better off not dwelling on. Hopes, dreams, promises. All shattered and broken.

She turned to face him, glad for the distraction, though she wasn't sure she should be. "I didn't throw it. I tossed it."

"Like it was a poisonous snake." The laughter was still in his voice and, despite the warning that shouted through her mind every time she was with Ben, Chloe smiled.

"More like it was a bouquet I had no use for." She glanced away from his steady gaze, watching as a little flower girl emerged triumphant from the crowd of wannabe brides, the bouquet clutched in her fist. "Besides, it seems to have gone to the right person."

Ben followed the direction of her gaze and nodded. "You may be right about that, but tell me, since when do flowers have to be useful? Aren't they simply meant to be enjoyed?"

"I suppose. But I'm not into frivolous things." Or things that reminded her of what she'd almost had. That was more to the point, but she wasn't going to say as much to Ben.

"Interesting."

"What?"

"You're not into frivolous things but you work in a flower shop." His gaze was back on Chloe, his eyes seeming to see much more than she wanted.

To Chloe's relief, a high-pitched shriek and excited laughter interrupted the conversation.

"Look," Ben cupped her shoulder, urging her to turn. "Hawke told me he was going to kidnap his bride. I wasn't sure he'd go through with it."

But he had, the broad-shouldered, hard-faced groom, striding toward the exit with his bride in his arms, the love between the two palpable. Chloe's chest tightened, her eyes burning. At least these two had found what they were seeking. At least one couple would have their happy ending.

For tonight anyway.

The cynical thought weaseled its way into Chloe's mind, chasing away the softer emotions she'd been feeling. She brushed back bangs that needed a trim and stepped away from Ben, ready to make her escape. "I'm going to start cleaning things up in the sanctuary."

"You most certainly are not." Opal appeared at her side, a scowl pulling at the corners of her mouth. "You're going home. I'll take care of things here."

"I'm not going to leave you to do all this alone."

"Who said I'd be alone?" As she spoke a white-haired gentleman stepped up beside Opal, his hand resting on her lower back. Opal glanced back and met his eyes, then turned to Chloe. "This is Sam. He and I go back a few years."

"A few decades, but she won't admit it." The older man

smiled, his face creased into lines that reflected a happy, well-lived life. "Sam Riley. And you're, Chloe. I've heard a good bit about you."

"Hopefully only good things." Sam Riley? It was a name she hadn't heard before. That, more than anything, made her wonder just what kind of relationship he had with Opal.

"Mostly good things." He winked, his tan, lined face filled with humor. "But I promise not to share any of the not-so-good things I heard if you'll convince Opal to go for a walk with me after this shindig."

"Sam Riley! That's blackmail." Opal's voice mixed with Ben's laughter, her scowl matched by his smile.

"Whatever works, doll."

"How many times do I have to tell you not to call me that?" But it was obvious she didn't really mind; obvious there was something between the two. A past. Maybe even a future.

And no one deserved that more than Opal. "If you agree to go for a walk with Sam, I'll agree to go home without an argument."

Opal speared her with a look that would have wilted her when she was a scared ten-year-old spending the night with her grandmother's neighbor. "And that's blackmail, too. I thought I'd taught you'd better than that, young lady."

"You tried."

Opal looked like she was going to argue more, then her gaze shifted from Chloe to Ben and back again. She smiled, a speculative look in her dark eyes. "Of course, I'll need the van and you'll need a ride back to the shop. Ben, you don't mind giving Chloe a ride to Blooming Baskets, do you?"

"Of course not."

"I appreciate that, Ben, but we've put you out enough." It was a desperate bid to gain control of the situation. One Chloe knew was destined to fail.

"You're not putting me out at all."

"Good." Opal smiled triumphantly. "It's all settled. We'd better get started, Sam. It's getting colder every minute and I don't plan on freezing just so you and I can go for a walk." She grabbed Sam's arm and pulled him away.

"I guess we've got our orders." Ben's hands were shoved into the pockets of his dark slacks, his profile all clean lines and chiseled angles. He would have fit just fine on the cover of GQ, his sandy hair rumpled, his strong features and easy smile enough to make any woman's heart jump.

Any woman except for Chloe.

Her heart-jumping, pulse-pounding days of infatuation were over. Adam's betrayal had ensured that. Still, if she'd had her camera in hand, she might have been tempted to shoot a picture, capture Ben's rugged good looks on film.

"Trying to think of a way out of this?" Ben's words drew her from her thoughts. She shook her head, her cheeks heating.

"Just wishing Opal hadn't asked you to give me a ride. Like I said, you've already done enough."

"Why don't you let me be the judge of that?" His hand closed around her elbow, the warmth of his palm sinking through the heavy fabric of her jacket as he smiled down into her eyes.

And her traitorous, hadn't-learned-its-lesson heart skipped a beat.

She wanted to pull away, but knew that would only call attention to her discomfort, so she allowed herself to be led out into the cool fall night and across the parking lot toward the trees that edged the property. Evergreens, oaks and shadows shifted and changed as Chloe and Ben moved closer. Was there someone watching? Maybe the same someone she'd seen that morning.

Chloe tensed, the blackness of the evening pressing in around her and stealing her breath. "Where's your car?"

"It's at my place. Just through these trees."

Just through the trees.

As if walking through the woods at night was nothing. As if there weren't a million hiding places in the dense foliage, a hundred dangers that could be concealed there. Chloe tried to pick up the pace, but her throbbing leg protested, her feet tangling in thick undergrowth. She tripped, stumbling forward.

Ben tightened his hold on her elbow, pulling her back and holding her steady as she regained her balance, his warmth, his strength seeping into her and easing the terror that clawed at her throat. "Careful. There are a lot of roots and tree stumps through here."

"It's hard to be careful when I can't see a thing."

"Don't worry. I can see well enough for both of us." His voice was confident, his hand firm on her arm as he strode through the darkness, and for a moment Chloe allowed herself to believe she was safe, that the nightmare she'd lived was really over.

Seconds later, they were out of the woods, crossing a wide yard and heading toward a small ranch-style house. "Here we are. Home sweet home."

"It's cute."

"That's what people keep telling me."

"You don't think so?"

"Cute isn't my forte, but my wife, Theresa, probably would have enjoyed hearing the word over and over again. Unfortunately, she passed away a year before I finished seminary and never got a chance to see the place."

"I'm sorry."

"Me, too."

"You must miss her."

"I do. She had cystic fibrosis and was really sick at the end. I knew I had to let her go, but it was still the hardest thing I've ever done."

Chloe understood that. Despite anger and bitterness over Adam's unfaithfulness, she still mourned his loss, and desperately wished she could have saved him. She imagined that years from now she'd feel the same, grieving his death and all that might have been. "I understand."

"You've lost someone close to you?" He pulled the car door open, and gestured for her to get in, his gaze probing hers.

"My fiancé." Ex-fiancé, but Chloe didn't say as much. "He died eleven months ago."

"Then I guess you do know." He waited until she slid into the car, then shut the door and walked around to the driver's side. "Had you known each other long?"

"Three years. We were supposed to be married this past June." But things had gone horribly wrong even before the accident and they'd cancelled the wedding a month before Adam's death.

"Then today's wedding must have been tough."

Chloe shrugged, not wanting to acknowledge even to herself just how tough it had been. Dreams. Hopes. Promises. The day had been built on the fairy tale of happily-ever-after and watching it unfold had made Chloe long for what she knew was only an illusion. "Not as hard as it would have been a few months ago."

"That's the thing about time. It doesn't heal the wounds, but it does make them easier to bear." He smiled into her eyes before he started the car's engine, the curve of his lips, the electricity in his gaze, doing exactly what Chloe didn't want it to—making her heart jump and her pulse leap, whispering that if she wasn't careful she'd end up being hurt again.

Chapter Five

It was close to seven when Chloe pulled her Mustang up to the Victorian that housed her apartment. Built on a hill, it offered a view of water and mountains, sky and grassland, the wide front porch and tall, gabled windows perfect for taking in the scenery. When Opal had brought her to look at the place the previous week, Chloe had been intrigued by the exterior. Walking through the cheery one-bedroom apartment Opal's friend had been renting out, seeing its hardwood floors and Victorian trim, modern kitchen and old-fashioned claw-foot tub, had sealed the deal. She knew she wanted to live there.

Unlike so many other places she'd lived in, this one felt like home.

Tonight though, it looked sinister. The windows dark, the lonely glow of the porch light doing nothing to chase away the blackness. Her car was the only one in the long driveway and Chloe's gaze traveled the length of the house, the edges of the yard, the stands of trees and clumps of bushes, searching for signs of danger. There were none, but that didn't make her feel better. She knew just how quickly quiet could turn to chaos, safety to danger.

She also knew she couldn't stay in the car waiting for one of the other tenants to return home or for daylight to come.

She stepped out of the car, jogging toward the house, her pulse racing as something slithered in the darkness to her right. A squirrel searching for fall harvest? A deer hoping for still-green foliage?

Or something worse?

Her heart slammed against her ribs as she took the porch steps two at a time. The front door was unlocked, left that way by one of the other tenants, and Chloe shoved it open, stumbling across the threshold and into the foyer, the hair on the back of her neck standing on end, her nerves screaming a warning.

Shut the door. Turn the lock. Get in the apartment.

The lock turned under her trembling fingers, her bad leg nearly buckling as she ran up the stairs to her apartment. She shoved the key into the lock, swung the door open. Slammed it shut again.

Safe.

Her heart slowed. Her gasping terror-filled breaths eased. Everything was fine. There was nothing outside that she needed to fear. Even if there was, she was locked in the house, locked in her apartment.

A loud bang sounded from somewhere below, and Chloe jumped, her fear back and clawing up her throat.

The back door.

The realization hit as the step at the bottom of the stairs creaked, the telltale sound sending Chloe across the room. She grabbed the phone, dialed 911, her heart racing so fast it felt as though it would burst from her chest.

Blackness threatened, panic stealing her breath and her oxygen, but Chloe refused to let it have her, forcing herself to breath deeply. To take action.

She grabbed a butcher knife from the kitchen, her gaze on the door, her eyes widening with horror as the old-fashioned glass knob began to turn.

Chloe clutched the phone in one hand and the knife in the other, praying the lock would hold and wondering if passing out might be better than facing whatever was on the other side of the door.

Ben Avery bounced a redheaded toddler on his knee, and smiled at his friend, Sheriff Jake Reed, who was cradling a dark-haired infant. "I'm thinking we may be able to go fishing again in twenty-one years."

"You're going next weekend." Tiffany Reed strode into the room, her red hair falling around her shoulders in wild waves. Three weeks after having her second child, she looked as vivacious and lovely as ever. "Jake needs a break."

"From what?" Jake stood, laid the baby in a bassinet and wrapped his arms around his wife. "This is where I want to be."

"I know that, but Ben's made two week's worth of meals for us. It's time for you to take him out to thank him."

Ben stood, the little girl in his arms giggling as he tickled her belly. "I made the meals because I wanted to. I don't need any thanks."

"Of course you don't, but you and Jake are still going fishing next weekend. Right, honey?"

Jake met Ben's eyes, shrugged and smiled. "I guess we are. What time?"

Before Ben could reply, Jake's cell phone rang. He glanced at the number. "Work. I'd better take it."

Tiffany pulled her daughter from Ben's arms, shushing the still-giggling child and carrying her from the room.

Ben made himself comfortable, settling back onto the sofa and waiting while Jake answered the phone. Whatever was happening couldn't be good if Jake was being called in.

"Reed here. Right. Give me the address." He jotted something down on a piece of paper. "Davidson?"

At the name, Ben straightened, an image of straight black hair and emerald eyes flashing through his mind.

"Okay. Keep her on the phone. I'll be there in ten." Jake hung up, grabbed a jacket from the closet.

"You said Davidson?"

"Yeah. Lady living out on the lake in the Richard's place is reporting an intruder in the house. My men are tied up at an accident outside of town, so I'm going to take the call."

"Did you get a first name?"

"Chloe."

"I'm coming with you."

Jake raised an eyebrow. "Sorry, that's not the way it works."

"It is this time. I'll stay in the squad car until you clear things, but I'm coming."

"Since I don't have time to argue or ask questions, we'll do it your way."

It took only seconds for Jake to say goodbye to his family, but those seconds seemed like a lifetime to Ben, every one of them another opportunity for whoever was in the house with Chloe to harm her. As they climbed into the cruiser and sped toward the lake, Ben could only pray that she'd be safe until he and Jake arrived.

Sirens sounded in the distance and Chloe backed toward the window that overlooked the front door, her gaze still fixed on the glass knob. It hadn't turned again, but she was expecting it to and wondering what she'd do if or when the door crashed open.

"Chloe? Are you still there?" The woman on the other end of the line sounded as scared as Chloe felt.

"Yes." She glanced out the window, saw a police cruiser pull up to the house, lights flashing, sirens blaring. "The police are here. I'm going to hang up."

"Don't—"

But Chloe was already disconnecting, tossing the phone and knife onto the couch and hurrying toward the door. The stairs creaked, footsteps pounded on wooden steps and a fist slammed against the door. "Ms. Davidson? Sheriff Jake Reed. Are you okay?"

"Fine." She pulled the door open, stepping back as a tall, hard-faced man strode in, a gun in his hand.

"Good. I'm going to escort you to my car. I want you to stay there until I'm finished in here."

"Finished?"

"Making sure whoever was here isn't still hanging around."

Still hanging around?

Chloe didn't like the sound of that and hurried down the stairs and outside, the crisp fall air making her shiver. Or maybe it was fear that had her shaking.

"I won't be long. Stay in the car until I come back out. I don't want to mistake you for the intruder."

"And I don't want to be out here alone." She might not like the idea of someone being in the house, but she liked the idea of staying outside by herself even less.

"Then it's good you don't have to be." As he spoke a figure stepped out of the cruiser. Tall, broad-shouldered and moving with lithe and silent grace.

Chloe knew who it was immediately, her visceral response

announcing his name, her betraying heart leaping in acknowl-
edgement. "Ben, what are you doing here?"

"How about we discuss it in the cruiser?" He wrapped an
arm around her waist and hurried her down the steps. Strong,
solid, dependable in a way Adam had never been. The comparison didn't sit well with Chloe. Noticing how different
Ben was from the man she'd once loved was something she
shouldn't be doing.

"Climb in." He held the cruiser door open for her, then slid
in himself, his knee nudging her leg, his arm brushing hers.

She scooted back against the door, doing her best to ignore
the scent of pine needles and soap that drifted on the air, but
he leaned in close, his jaw tight, his face much harder than it
had seemed earlier. "Are you okay?"

"Just scared."

"Jake said someone was inside the house with you. Did he
make it into your apartment?"

"No, but it looked like he was trying to get in." She shuddered, watching as the lights in the attic area of the Victorian
flicked on.

"Did you see the person?"

"I saw something before I went in the house, but if it was a
person, I couldn't tell. There was no way I was going to open
the apartment door to take a look."

"I'm glad you didn't. That would have been a bad idea." The
porch light flicked off, then on again, and Ben pushed open
the car door. "That's Jake's all clear. Ready to go back inside?"

"Of course." But she wasn't really. Sitting in the car with
Ben seemed a lot safer than stepping back into the darkness.

He rounded the car, pulled open her door and offered a
hand. "It'll be okay, Chloe. Whoever it was is long gone."

Chloe nodded, not trusting herself to speak, afraid anything she said would be filled with the panic and paranoia that

had chased her from D.C. Nightmares. Terror. The feeling of being watched, of being stalked. She'd been plagued with all of them since being released from the hospital nine months ago. Post-traumatic stress. That's what the doctors said. That's what the police said. Given enough time, Ben and Jake would probably say the same.

She braced herself as she stepped back into the house, sure that Jake would tell her he'd found nothing, that her mind had been playing tricks on her, that nothing had happened. She was only partially right.

Jake seemed convinced that something had happened, but his list of evidence was slim—an unlocked back door, a smudge of dirt on the back deck that might have been a footprint, fingerprints that might have belonged to the intruder, but more likely belonged to someone who lived in the house.

"We'll get prints of the other tenants. See if I've picked up anything that doesn't belong to one of you. Can you come to the station Monday?"

"I've got to work, but I'm sure Opal will give me the time off."

"Good. In the meantime, keep the doors locked and don't take unnecessary risks. I'm thinking this is probably a kid playing a prank or hoping to find some quick cash, but you never know."

"No, you don't." Chloe shifted her weight, trying to ease the ache in her leg, trying to convince herself that the sheriff was right and that what had just happened had nothing to do with her former life.

Tried, but wasn't successful.

He must have sensed her misgivings. His gaze sharpened, going from warm blue to ice. "Is there something you're not telling me? If so it's best to get it out in the open now."

"I'm just not sure what happened tonight was random."

There. It was out. For better or worse. If it made her look crazy, so be it.

"And you have a reason for thinking that?" His tone was calm, but there was an edge to his words, a hardness to his face that hadn't been there before.

"This isn't the first time I've been followed into a building. It's not the first time I've felt like I was in danger."

"It sounds like there's a lot more to the story than what happened tonight. Maybe we should finish this discussion in your apartment." He started up the stairs, giving Chloe no choice but to follow.

Which was fine.

It was better to get everything out on the table now rather than later. And Chloe was pretty sure there would be a later. As much as she'd hoped things would be different here, she hadn't been convinced she could leave all her troubles behind. Apparently, she'd been right.

"Do you want me to wait outside?" Ben spoke quietly as he followed her up the stairs and Chloe knew what her answer should be. Yes, wait outside. Yes, keep your distance.

Unfortunately, knowing what she should say didn't make her say it. "No. You're fine. I'm going to get some coffee started. Then we'll talk."

She stepped into the living room, limped to the kitchen, and pulled coffee and a package of cookies from the cupboard. If she had to talk about the past, she might as well have sugar in her while she did it.

"Cookie, anyone?"

The sheriff shook his head, a hint of impatience in his eyes. "You were going to tell me why you don't think tonight was a prank."

Chloe nodded, forcing her muscles to relax and her tone to remain calm. Sounding hysterical was a surefire way to make herself seem unbalanced. "Eleven months ago someone tried to kill me. He failed."

The words had an immediate effect. Both men straightened, leaned toward her. Intent. Focused. Concerned.

Now if they'd just stay that way through the entire story, Chloe might believe that things really were going to be different.

"Who?" Jake pulled a small notebook from his pocket, started scribbling notes in it.

"A man named Matthew Jackson."

"Do you know where he is now?"

"Federal prison serving a life sentence for murder."

"Murder?" Ben reached over and took the cookies from her hand, pulled two out of the package and handed her one.

"My fiancé was killed in the accident Jackson caused."

Jake glanced up from the notepad. "And you think that has something to do with what happened tonight?"

"I don't know. I just know that ever since the accident, things have been happening."

"Things?"

Was there a tinge of doubt in Jake's voice, a look of disbelief on his face? Or was Chloe just imagining what she'd seen so many times on the faces of so many other police officers. "Like I said, I've had the feeling that I was being followed. A couple of times I was sure someone had been in my apartment."

There was something else, too. Something that she didn't dare bring up.

"You contacted the police?"

"Yes. They investigated."

"And?"

"At first they thought I was being stalked by some of Jackson's friends. He was part of a cult that I'd helped close down a few months earlier."

"The Strangers?" Ben took another cookie from the pack.

Surprised, Chloe met his gaze, saw the interest and concern there. "Yes."

"I remember hearing about it in the news. A computer forensics specialist was investigating a cult member's death and found evidence that implicated the leader. He went to jail for money laundering, but they couldn't prove that he'd killed his follower."

"The deceased's name was Ana Benedict. She started working as an accountant for the cult's leader and was dead a few months later. Her death was ruled a suicide, but her parents didn't believe it."

"You seem to know an awful lot about it." Jake was still writing, a frown creasing his forehead.

"I worked freelance for the private investigator Ana's parents hired. They had her laptop, but there wasn't much on it. I was hired to search for deleted files and I found plenty. Ana had documented everything. The Strangers were involved in the drug trade and were laundering money through their organization. I brought the information to the FBI."

"And Jackson blamed you when the cult dispersed."

"Yes."

"You said that after the attempt on your life, you felt like you were being followed and that someone had been in your apartment. The police suspected other cult members?"

"For a while."

"And then?"

Chloe grabbed mugs and poured coffee into them. Anything to keep from facing the two men who were watching her so intently. "They decided it was all in my head."

"I see." Jake spoke quietly, but Chloe knew he didn't see at all.

She turned back around, handing a cup to each man. "Look, Sheriff Reed—"

"Call me Jake."

"Jake, there may not be evidence proving I'm being stalked, but that doesn't mean it's not happening."

"I don't think I said it wasn't." He sipped his coffee, exchanging a glance with Ben, one that excluded Chloe and conveyed a message she couldn't even begin to figure out.

"No, you didn't, but I've been told it enough times to imagine that's what you're thinking."

"What I'm thinking is that I don't know what happened in D.C. Whatever it was, it's not going to happen here." He placed his coffee cup on the counter. "I'd better head out. If you think of anything else that might be helpful, give me a call."

"I will." Chloe followed him to the door, holding it open as he stepped out and started down the stairs.

Ben held back, the concern in his eyes obvious. "Will you be okay here alone?"

"I've been living alone since I was eighteen."

"That doesn't mean you'll be okay."

"Of course I'll be okay. What other choice do I have?" She tried to smile, but knew she failed miserably.

"You could stay with Opal."

And bring whatever danger was following her into her friend's life? Chloe didn't think so. "No, I really will be fine."

Ben watched her for a moment, his gaze so intense Chloe fidgeted. Then he nodded. "All right. Keep the doors locked and be safe."

He stepped out into the hall and pulled the door shut behind him, leaving Chloe in the silent apartment.

Be safe?

She didn't even know what the word meant anymore. She

sighed, grabbed a cookie from the package and collapsed onto the easy chair. Maybe she'd figure it out again. Maybe. Somehow she doubted that would be the case.

Chapter Six

"Sounds like your friend has a big problem." Jake's comment echoed what Ben had been thinking since he'd walked out of Chloe's apartment.

"Really big."

"Unless the police in D.C. are right and the stalker is all in her head."

"She seems pretty sure about what's been going on."

"Being sure of something only means we've convinced ourselves that it's true. I don't put much stock in it." Despite the gruff words, Jake sounded pensive and Ben knew he was leaning toward Chloe's version of things.

"You seemed to believe someone was at her apartment."

"I do. I'm just not convinced it has anything to do with what happened in D.C. It could just as easily have been a kid, or someone out to steal a few bucks."

"It could have been."

"But you don't think so?"

"I think there's more to the story than Chloe is telling. I

think that until we have all the information, it'll be hard to know exactly what's going on."

"Agreed. I'm going call some friends that are still on the D.C. police force and see what they have to say." He paused as he pulled into the driveway of his house. "Regardless of what they say, I'm treating this like any other investigation until I can prove it's not one."

"I didn't expect anything less."

"And I didn't expect to be as curious about you and Chloe as I am." Jake grinned, pushed open his door. "So, are you going to tell me what's going on between you two, or am I going to have to speculate?"

"I met her at the wedding today."

"And?"

"And I would have introduced the two of you if you'd been there."

"I'm almost sorry I missed it."

"Almost?"

"Tiffany isn't ready to take the baby out or leave him with a sitter yet. I'm not ready to spend my Saturday away from her."

"Who'd have thought marriage would make you into such a romantic?" Ben grinned and got out of the car. "I'd better head home. I've got to work tomorrow."

"Good avoidance technique, but I still want to know about you and Chloe."

"You've been living small-town life for too long. You're getting nosy."

"Only when it comes to my friends."

"Sorry to disappoint, but you know as much about Chloe as I do."

"I'm not interested in what you know about her. I'm wondering what you think of her."

"Right now? I think she's a nice lady who's been hurt a lot."

"Look, Ben, if you were anyone else, I'd keep my nose out of it, but you're not, so I'm going to say what's on my mind."

"Go ahead."

"Chloe does seem like a nice lady, but I know trouble when I see it. I see it when I look at her."

"And?"

"And be careful. I don't want that trouble coming after you."

"Thanks for the worry, but I'm pretty good at taking care of myself. I'll be fine."

Jake nodded, but his jaw was tight, his expression grim. "I've got a bad feeling about this. Really bad. Watch your back."

With that he walked away, stepping into his well-lit house, into the warmth of family and home, and leaving Ben to himself and his thoughts.

Thoughts that were similar to Jake's.

Trouble did seem to be closing in on Chloe. If Ben were smart, he'd keep his distance from it and from her. Unfortunately, he didn't think that was going to be possible. Something told him that Chloe was about to become a big part of his life. He might not want the complication, might not like it, but that seemed to be where God was leading him. If that were the case, Ben would just have to hold on tight and pray the ride wasn't nearly as bumpy as he thought it was going to be.

Apparently, Chloe's intruder was big news in Lakeview, and at least half a dozen customers converged on the flower shop minutes after it opened Monday morning. Opal seemed happy about all the business, but by noon Chloe was tired of the sometimes blatant, sometimes subtle questions. How many times and how many ways could a person say "I don't know" before she went absolutely insane?

Not many more than Chloe had already said.

She pulled a dozen red carnations from the refrigerated display case, grabbed some filler and headed back to the shop's front counter, doing her best to tamp down irritation as she listened to two elderly women discuss the "incident" in loud whispers.

"Here they are, Opal." She spoke a little more forcefully than necessary, hoping to interrupt the women's conversation.

It only seemed to make them think she wanted to be part of it.

The taller of the two smiled at Chloe. "Those are absolutely lovely, dear. I'm impressed that you could focus on picking the perfect flowers after such a harrowing experience."

"Thank you." What else could she say? "I try to keep my mind on the job."

"But aren't you terrified?" The shorter, more rotund woman shuddered, her owl-eyed gaze filled with both fear and anticipation, as if she were hoping for a juicy tidbit of information to pass along.

"Not really." At least no more than she'd been before she'd come to Lakeview. "The sheriff assured me he'd do everything he could to find the person responsible."

Though Chloe wondered if he'd be saying the same after he talked to the police in D.C. She wasn't looking forward to the conversation they were going to have when he found out about her recent hospitalization and its supposed cause.

She refused to worry about it and tried to focus on her job instead, shoving the carnations into a vase and scowling when two stems broke.

"Keep it up and I'll be out of business in no time." Opal took the flowers and vase from her hands, smiling at the women who were watching wide-eyed and interested. "I'll finish this up. Aren't you supposed to go to the police station today?"

"Yes, but it can wait."

"You know how I feel about procrastination. It only makes more work for everyone. Go punch out and head over there. Since we don't know how long it's going to take, I think you should just take the rest of the day off."

"We've had a lot of business so far, Opal. Are you sure you want to handle the rest of the afternoon alone?"

"I handled it alone for two years before I hired help. Besides, I've hired a kid from church to come in after school until Jenna gets back. Laura's her name. She's a senior trying to save money for college. It should work out well for all of us. Now, go ahead and do what needs doing. Then go have some fun."

"Fun?" Fun was puppies and kittens, laughter and friendship. Relaxation. Fun was something Chloe wasn't even sure she knew how to do anymore.

"Yes, fun. Go shopping. Get your nails done. Better yet, go to Becky's Diner and have a slice of warm apple pie with a scoop of ice cream on it. That's fun."

"It does sound good." But being at home sounded better. Safe behind closed doors and locked in tight.

"But you won't do it."

"I might."

"Hmph. We'll see, I guess. Now, get out of here. I've got work to do and you're distracting me."

"Destroying flowers and distracting you. I don't know why you keep me on."

"Because you bring in so much business. Now, shoo."

Chloe laughed as she stepped through the doorway that led to the back of the shop.

It didn't take long to punch out and gather her jacket and purse. Outside, the day was misty and cold, the thick clouds and steely sky ominous. Several cars were parked in the employee parking lot behind the building, but Chloe was the only person there. In the watery afternoon light, the stillness seemed unnatural, the quiet, sinister, and she was sure she felt the weight of someone's stare as she hurried toward her car.

She shivered, fumbling for her keys, the feeling that she was being watched so real, so powerful, that she was sure she'd be attacked at any moment. Finally, the key slid into the lock, the door opened and she scrambled in, slamming the door shut, locking it.

Against nothing. The parking lot was still empty of life. The day still and silent.

"You're being silly and paranoid." She muttered the words as she put the car into gear. "Being afraid because an intruder is in the house is one thing. Being afraid to cross a parking lot in the middle of the day is ridiculous."

But she was afraid.

No amount of self-talk, no amount of rationalization could change that.

She sighed, steering her vintage Mustang toward the parking lot exit. Opal was right. She needed to do something fun, something to get her mind off the tension and anxiety she'd been feeling since Saturday night, but she hadn't had time to make friends since she'd come to Lakeview and she had no intention of going anywhere or doing anything by herself. The fact was, despite what the D.C. police had told her, despite what her friends, doctors and psychologist had said, she couldn't shake the feeling that danger was following her. That the accident hadn't been the end of the violence against her. That eventually the past would catch up to her. And when it did, she just might not survive.

No, she definitely didn't want to go anywhere by herself, but she didn't want to go with someone, either. Look what had happened to Adam because he was with her when a murderer struck.

Hot tears stung her eyes, but she forced them away. Tears wouldn't help. Only answers could do that and Chloe didn't have any. She'd been living her life, doing what she thought was right, trying her best to be the person God wanted her to be. Then the rug had been pulled out from under her, the stability she'd worked so hard for destroyed. All her childhood fears had come to pass—death, heartache, pain, faceless monsters stalking her through the darkness. Now, it seemed that God was far away, that her life had taken a taken a path that He wasn't on and that no matter how hard she tried to get back on course, she couldn't. As much as she wanted to believe differently, as much as she knew that God would never abandon His children, abandoned was exactly how she felt.

Abandoned and alone, her mind filled with nightmare images and dark shadows that reflected the hollow ache of her soul.

Chapter Seven

By the time she finished at the police station and returned home, it had started to rain. First a quick patter of drops, then a torrential downpour that pinged against the house's tin roof and seemed to echo Chloe's mood. Outside, the clouds had turned charcoal, bubbling up from the horizon with barely contained violence.

Chloe put her mail on the kitchen table, grabbed a glass of water and opened sliding glass doors that led to the balcony off her living room. From there she could see the stark beauty of the lake as it reflected gray clouds and bare trees. Winter would arrive soon, bringing with it colder air and a starker landscape. It would be good to capture those changes on film, to hang a few new photos on the wall. The thought brightened her mood.

It had been a long time since she'd photographed anything. In the aftermath of the accident, she hadn't had the time or the inclination. Now, with surgeries and physical therapy behind her, she did. She just hadn't had any desire to.

276 Stranger in the Shadows

Except once.

An image flashed through her mind—sandy hair, vivid blue eyes, a half smile designed to melt hearts.

"Enough!" She grabbed her digital camera from the top drawer of her dresser, refusing to think about Ben and determined to do what she should have months ago—regain her life. Get back into her routines. Enjoy the hobbies she'd found so much pleasure in before the accident. Maybe she couldn't go rock climbing anymore, but she could shoot pictures. And she would.

A soft tap sounded at the front door and Chloe jumped, her heart racing. She wasn't expecting company. Anyone could be out there, waiting to finish what was started almost a year ago.

She sidled along the wall, imagining bullets piercing the door and knowing just how ridiculous she was being. "Who's there?"

"Ben Avery."

"Ben?" Surprised, relieved, Chloe pulled open the door and stepped aside so he could walk in. "What are you doing here?"

"Carrying out my orders." He smiled, rain glistening in his sandy hair and beaded on his leather jacket, the scent of fall drifting into the room with him. Fall and something else. Something masculine and strong.

Chloe took a step back. "Orders?"

"Opal and I ran into each other at the diner. She asked me to bring you this." He held out a brown paper bag, and Chloe took it, catching a whiff of apples and cinnamon.

"Apple pie?"

"And ice cream. She had Doris put that in a separate container."

"Fun in a bag?"

"I guess you could call it that."

"Those are Opal's words. Not mine. She said I should have

a little fun today. I guess she wanted to make sure I did." Chloe smiled, touched by her friend's thoughtfulness, though she wasn't sure she was happy with her methods. "Thanks for bringing this over. I'm sure you had better things to do with your time."

"It seems like we had this conversation before. And I'm going to tell you the same thing now that I did then—I can't think of any." He leaned his shoulder against the wall, his vivid blue gaze steady. "Of course, bringing it here was only part of my job."

"What was the other part?"

"I'm supposed to make sure you eat it."

"Tell me you're kidding."

"I'm afraid not. She said that if you faded away to nothing she wouldn't have any reliable help at the shop."

"She's conveniently forgetting Mary Alice and the new girl she hired."

"Laura. She mentioned that she'd left her to watch the store for a few minutes and had to hurry back."

"You and Opal must have had a long conversation."

"Not too long." He didn't seem inclined to say more, and Chloe decided not to press for details. Knowing Opal, she'd said more than she should have. Eventually, she and Chloe would have to talk about that. For now, the pie smelled too good to ignore.

"Since you've been ordered to make sure I eat this, maybe we can share." She moved into the small kitchen and set her camera down, grabbing two plates from the cupboard.

"I was hoping you'd say that. I brought enough for both of us." Ben moved toward her, an easy grin curving his lips and deepening the lines near his eyes. Was he thirty? Thirty-five? Older?

She shouldn't be wondering, but was.

And that didn't make her happy.

"You knew I was going to invite you?"

"No, but I was hoping." He pulled a large plastic container from the bag, opened it up to reveal two slices of apple pie. "It's my day off. Apple pie, ice cream and interesting company seemed like a good way to spend part of it."

"What if I hadn't asked you to stay?"

"Then I would have gone home and had a couple of oatmeal cookies in front of the TV."

"No way."

"No way what?" He served the pie, scooped ice cream onto both slices.

"No way would you be sitting home in front of the television eating oatmeal cookies."

"You're right. I would have gone back to the diner and bought more pie. It's much too good to pass up. Then I would have gone home and watched TV." He smiled and Chloe's pulse had the nerve to leap.

"Funny, I picture you as more the outdoor type. Hiking. Camping. Boating."

"Good call, but today is too rainy for outdoor activities."

"Then I guess I'm glad I could provide you with something to do. I'm going to have to have a talk with Opal, though. She can't keep asking you to come to my rescue."

"Who says I'm rescuing you? Maybe you're rescuing me."

"From an afternoon of boredom?"

"Exactly." He smiled again and dug into the pie, his hair falling over his forehead, his broad hands making the fork look small.

Chloe resisted the urge to pick up her camera and shoot a picture, choosing instead to fork up a mouthful of pie, the flaky crust and tart apples nearly melting in her mouth.

"You're right. This is too good to pass up. I guess I'll have to thank Opal instead of lecturing her."

"She cares a lot about you."

"And I care a lot about her."

"You said you spent summers on the lake. Is that how you two met?"

"My grandmother rented a cottage next to Opal's property."

"Your grandmother, not your mother?"

Chloe hesitated, then shrugged. "My mother preferred to leave my upbringing to other people."

"And your grandmother filled in?"

"Not really." She scooped up another bite of pie, not willing to say any more about her childhood. "How about you? Was your family the Father Knows Best type?"

"It was as far from that as you can get. Absent father. Drug-addicted mother. My sister and I were in foster care by the time I was thirteen."

"I'm sorry."

"Don't be. It was the best thing that ever happened to me. My mother may not have cared much about me, but God did, and He used her neglect to get me to people who did care."

"You must have been a great kid."

He paused, his fork halfway to his mouth, his eyes so blue they seemed lit from within. "I was a little hoodlum. By the time my parents stepped in I'd been in ten foster homes, a group facility, and was about to be thrown into a juvenile de-tention center."

"Are you kidding?"

"Not even close to kidding. My foster parents got my case file from a social worker they knew. A few days later they came to visit me and told me I had a choice—come stay with them and straighten up my life or stay on the path I'd chosen and end up in jail or worse."

"So you decided to straighten up."

"I wish I'd made it that easy on them. The fact is, I thought Mike and Andrea were softhearted enough to be taken advantage of. I agreed to go home with them, but had no intention at all of changing my life. Fortunately, they stuck with me." He stood and put his empty plate in the sink. "I'd better get out of here. You've probably got things you need to do."

Agree. Send him on his way. Forget the story he just told and the new light it cast him in.

But Chloe had never been great at listening to advice. Even her own.

Especially not her own.

"Nothing pressing. I was just going to take some photographs."

"A florist, a computer expert and a photographer? What other surprises are you hiding?" Ben settled back down into his chair and Chloe could almost imagine him as a kid, sitting in one kitchen after another, searching for someone to believe in him. To love him.

"No surprises. What you see is what you get."

"Somehow I doubt that." He steepled his fingers and stared at her across the table, his gaze somber and much too knowing.

But Chloe didn't plan on sharing more about her life, her hobbies, her past or the shadows that lived in her soul. "Doubt it all you want, but it's the truth. How about you? What surprises are you hiding?"

"The fact that I cook surprises people, but it's not something I hide."

"I wouldn't have thought a widowed pastor in a small town like this would ever have to cook. Aren't the church ladies knocking on your door begging to cook you a meal?"

"They were. That's why I had to learn to cook. By the time I'd been in town a month, I had so many casseroles in my refrigerator there wasn't room for anything else. No milk. No eggs. No vegetables or fruit. Learning to cook was a matter of self-preservation."

Chloe laughed, relaxing into the moment and the conversation. Enjoying the company. The man.

"You're laughing, but it was a serious issue." His eyes gleamed with humor as he lifted Chloe's camera. "Now it's your turn."

"My turn?"

"To tell why you got into photography."

"I moved around a lot when I was a kid. Taking pictures helped me remember where I'd been." So she would know where she didn't want to go, the kind of life she didn't want to have.

"So you do landscape photography."

"And architectural. The pictures on the wall are mine." She gestured to a black-and-white photo of the White House and a colored photo of Arlington National Cemetery.

"They're good. Mind if I take a look at the ones on your camera?

"Only if I get a chance to sample your cooking." The words were out before she could stop them and Chloe regretted them immediately. "What I mean is—"

"That you'd like to have dinner with me?" His eyes dared her to accept the offer.

"I don't think that would be a good idea."

"Really? Two friends sharing a meal sounds like a great idea to me."

She should refuse. Friendship with Ben wasn't a good idea. Friendship with anyone wasn't a good idea. "I don't want to drag you into my troubles, Ben."

"I'm not the type of person who gets dragged anywhere I

don't want to go." He leaned across the table, and squeezed her hand. "So, how about that dinner?"

Say no.

But once again Chloe ignored her own advice. "All right. A meal with a friend."

There was no harm in that.

She hoped.

Ben smiled and released her hand, turning his attention to the camera. As she watched, his smile faded, a frown creasing his brow.

"Interesting choice of subject matter." His voice was tight, his frown deepening.

"What?" She leaned toward him, curious to see what he was looking at. It had been months since she'd used the camera. There might be photographs of Adam, of the house they'd planned to buy. Of the church where they were going to be married.

But the photo wasn't of any of those things.

Bright flowers. Dark wood. Adam lying in white silk, his face almost unrecognizable.

Ben scrolled back and the same picture appeared again. And again.

Chloe gagged, shoving away from the table and stumbling backward, her mind rebelling at what she'd seen, her body trembling with it. Panic throbbed deep in the pit of her stomach, stealing her breath until she was gasping, struggling for air.

"Hey. It's okay." Ben's voice was soothing, his hands firm on her shoulder. "Chloe, you're fine. Take a deep breath."

"I can't." Blackness edged her vision, the shadowy nightmare coming closer with every shallow breath.

"Sure you can." His hands smoothed up her neck, cupped her cheeks, forcing her to look up and into eyes so blue, so clear, she thought she could lose herself in them. "You're a survivor. A couple photos can't take that away from you."

His words were warm, but she sensed the hard determination beneath them. He had no intention of letting the nightmare take her, and that, more than anything, eased the vise around Chloe's lungs.

"Right. You're right. I'm sorry."

"Don't apologize." His words were gruff, his hands still warm against her cheeks. "Tell me what's wrong."

"I didn't take those pictures."

He stared into her eyes for another minute, then nodded. "I'd better call Jake."

His hands dropped away and he strode to the phone, leaving her in the kitchen with the camera and the horrifying images.

Chapter Eight

"When was the last time you used the camera?" The question was the same one Jake Reed had asked fifteen times in the past ten minutes. If he were hoping for a different answer than the one she'd already given, he was going be disappointed.

Chloe's fist tightened around the coffee mug she held, but she kept her frustration in check. "I don't know. A few months before the accident."

Jake lifted the camera in gloved hands, staring at the image. "And you didn't take these photos?"

"No!" Her tone was sharper than she'd meant and she reigned in her emotions. "They're sickening."

"Sickening, but fake."

"Fake?"

"Take another look. The guy in the casket is in a different position in each photo. The 'casket' is too wide. Looks like a twin bed with pillows and white silk on top of it."

"I'll take your word for it."

"You thought it was your fiancé?"

"Yes."

"It's not. The date on the photos is September of this year. Months after your ex-fiancé's funeral. And he was your ex-fiancé, right?"

Apparently, he'd been talking to people in D.C. What else had they told him? Chloe's hands were clammy, but she looked him straight in the eye as she answered. "Yes, but I don't think that's relevant."

"What you think is relevant doesn't matter, Chloe. What matters is finding out what's going on. The only way to do that is to get all the information available. You didn't provide me with that Saturday night."

"I provided you with what I thought was important. My relationship with Adam was complicated. We were friends before we started dating and were trying to maintain that after we broke up." He'd wanted more than that, but Chloe hadn't been able to forgive.

"You broke up because he'd been seeing another woman."

Chloe's cheeks heated, but she nodded, refusing the urge to glance at Ben. "Adam was a nice guy. He collected friends like other people collect knickknacks. A lot of those friends were women. One became a little more than just a friend."

"You're leaving out a lot of details." Jake leaned back in the kitchen chair and tapped gloved fingers against the table. "Like the fact that you did freelance work for Adam's P.I. company. That the two of you had testified at a criminal trial the day he was killed."

"I'm sure the D.C. police were glad to fill you in."

"I would have been happier if you'd been the one to do it."

"Jake, you're not dealing with a suspect here." There was a subtle warning in Ben's voice.

"And I don't want to be dealing with a body, either. Chloe

needs to be open and honest. Hiding information is never a good idea."

"I wasn't hiding information. It's just hard to talk about Adam." Chloe stood and grabbed a bottle of aspirin, her hand shaking as she tried to pry open the lid.

"Here. Let me." Ben leaned in, his shoulder brushing hers, his hands gentle as he took the bottle and popped the lid. He placed two in her hand, closed her fingers over them, his palm pressing against her knuckles, the warmth of it chasing away the chill that seemed to live in her soul. "It's going to be okay."

She wasn't so sure he was right. "Maybe."

"Things will be okay once we find out who's after you." Jake's voice was hard, his face grim. "Can you tell me who had access to your camera."

"Anyone who visited my apartment. I usually kept it out near my workstation."

"Can you give me a list of those people?"

"Probably, but the past few months are blurry. I had surgery on my leg a month ago and the recovery was brutal. There were people in and out all the time trying to help out."

"Do the best you can. I'll also want a list of anyone who had a key to your place in D.C."

"That's a shorter list. Jordyn Winslow. James Callahan. They both worked with Adam. Morgan Gordon had the apartment next to mine. They took turns taking care of things while I was in the hospital during the months after the accident."

"Good. We'll start there." Jake pulled a pen and small notebook from his pocket, jotted the names down. "Do you know the name of the woman Adam was involved with?"

"No. He wouldn't tell me and I didn't press for the information. Maybe I really didn't want to know."

"You didn't leave a forwarding address with the police in D.C."

"There didn't seem to be any reason."

"But you did leave it with friends?"

"I left it with some of my former employers. Com-panies that owed me money. No one else knows where I am. I was hoping that would keep me safe. I guess I was wrong."

"Let's not jump to conclusions yet. It's possible that who-ever took the photos doesn't know where you are."

"I don't believe that. I don't think you do, either."

"There's only one thing I believe. Matthew Jackson has nothing to do with what's been happening to you. The rest I plan to find out." He closed his notebook and stood. "Do you have any other cameras?"

"A Nikon."

"Is there undeveloped film in it?"

"Yes."

"Do you mind if I take that one, too?"

"Not at all." As a matter of fact, she'd rather have it out of the house than spend the next few days wondering what might be on the undeveloped film.

She limped to her room, pulled the camera from a storage box in her closet and brought it out to Jake. "Here you go. I think I used it the week before Adam and I broke up. We'd gone on a picnic to Great Falls. The day was perfect. We…" Her voice trailed off and she shook her head. "Those should be the last pictures on the roll."

"I'll develop the film, see if there's anything there that shouldn't be. In the meantime, try not to worry too much." He smiled and she was surprised by the warmth and genuine concern in his eyes.

"I appreciate it, Jake. Thanks."

"Hold off on the thanks until I figure out what's going on."

He strode to the front door and pulled it open. "I'll see you this weekend, Ben."

"Saturday, 6 a.m. Unless that's too early."

"The baby has us up at five every day. Six won't be a problem."

Jake stepped out into the hall, hovering near the top of the steps as Ben turned to Chloe.

"I've got to head out, too, but before I leave, tell me something?"

"What?"

"Do you like fish?"

"Fish?" She'd expected a question about Adam, about their relationship. His death. She hadn't expected to be asked about fish.

"Yeah, fish. Trout. Catfish."

"Sure."

"Good. That's what I'll make, then."

"Make?"

"For dinner. We had a deal. I still need to fulfill my end of the bargain."

"That's not necessary, Ben." All thoughts of a quiet dinner spent with a friend were gone, replaced by cold dread. Something terrible had followed her from D.C. Something that was determined to destroy her and anyone who got near her.

"Isn't it?" He smiled, brushing her bangs out of her eyes and tucking long strands behind her ear.

Her stomach knotted and she stepped away. Surprised. Uncomfortable.

Afraid.

For herself. For Ben.

"No. It really isn't."

"You're chickening out."

"I'm not. I'm just..." Terrified that something terrible was going to happen. Scared that she'd be hurt. That Ben would be hurt.

"Just going to have dinner with a new friend. Is that so bad?"

"I don't want to get hurt again, Ben. And I don't want you to be hurt."

"How can having dinner hurt either of us? How does Saturday night around six sound?"

He was purposely ignoring the point and Chloe frowned. "You'll be fishing with Jake that day."

"Right. Fresh fish for dinner. What could be better?" He smiled, his eyes flashing with humor and inviting her to join in.

And despite herself, despite the warnings she knew she should heed, she relaxed. "You have a lot of faith in your ability to catch fish."

"No. I've got a lot of faith in my ability to track down a meal. If I don't find it in the lake, I'll get it from the grocery store."

"Won't that be cheating?"

"Only if I try to pass it off as my own." He grinned. "Your place or mine?"

"Mine." She answered without thought, and knew she wouldn't take the word back.

"Great. See you then." He stepped out into the hall, joining Jake there.

The other man nodded at Chloe, but she couldn't miss the concern in his eyes. Obviously, he was as worried about Ben's safety as she was. "I'll be in touch, Chloe. In the meantime, don't hesitate to call if something comes up."

"I won't."

Jake hesitated, rubbing a hand against the back of his neck. "Listen, my wife is part of a quilting circle that meets at Grace

Christian on Wednesday nights. Seven o'clock. They make blankets for NICU babies and little bears for kids who have to stay at Lakeview General. They'd love to have another set of hands."

"I've never quilted before." But she couldn't deny the small part of her that longed for something new, something more than flowers and bows and evenings spent alone.

"They'll teach you everything you need to know."

"I don't usually go out at night."

"Understandable, but you'll be with a large group of people. That might be better than being here alone. Think about it. Here's my home phone number. Call my wife if you've got any questions." He scribbled the number on the back page of his notebook and tore it out.

"I will, thanks."

"No problem. Now, I really do need to get out of here. You coming? Or are you planning to spend another half hour saying goodbye?" He glanced at Ben and the amusement in his eyes was unmistakable.

"Knock it off." Ben growled the words, but smiled at Chloe, waving as he and Jake started down the stairs.

Chloe closed the door on their retreating figures, shutting out the sounds of their lighthearted banter and pacing across the living room.

She'd thought the room cozy before. In the wake of Ben and Jake's departure, it seemed empty and hollow, a sad reflection of her life.

She grimaced, moving into her bedroom, flicking on the light and turning on the CD player she kept near her bed. An upbeat modern tune filled the room, the thrumming, strumming tempo of it doing nothing to lift Chloe's mood.

"Get over yourself, Chloe. Things could be worse."

She flopped onto the bed, knowing she should get up and

do something. Television. A good book. Anything that would take her mind off the loneliness that she was suddenly feeling.

Her gaze caught on the Bible lying abandoned on the bedside table. Opal had given it to her when she was twelve and she'd had it ever since. Lately, though, she hadn't spent much time reading it. She picked it up, thumbing through it, skimming some of the passages Opal had highlighted in yellow. Little by little, she was drawn into what she was reading, her loneliness slowly fading away. She might feel as if God had abandoned her, but the truth was much different. Despite the trials and troubles she'd faced, she had to hold on to that certainty, had to believe that He was there, working His perfect will for her life. Had to trust that in the end everything would turn out okay.

But would it?

As much as she wanted to believe, to trust, Chloe couldn't imagine things getting better. She could only imagine them getting much, much worse.

She shook her head, closing the Bible, setting it back on the table and praying that she was wrong. That somehow everything would be okay. That what she imagined wasn't what would be and that eventually the nightmare would be over and she'd be able to rebuild her life.

Chapter Nine

Maybe quilting wasn't such a good idea after all.

Chloe stood in the doorway of the reception hall and eyed the people gathered there. Old and young, tall and short, thin and stout, they were a swarm of bees, humming with energy as they performed a dance that had meaning only to them.

She took a step back, pretty sure she'd made a poor decision when she'd left Blooming Baskets and headed toward Grace Christian. She'd come on a lark, another night alone at the apartment appealing to her about as much as a root canal. Now she was thinking a root canal might not be so bad.

"You must be Chloe." A tall redhead stepped from the throng, a broad smile creasing her face.

"That's right."

"I'm Tiffany Reed. My husband told me he'd invited you. I wanted to call and tell you a little more about what we're doing here, but Jake refused to give me your number. He said you might not be ready to face the Lakeview Quilters."

"He might have been right."

Tiffany laughed, the sound full and unapologetic. "We're not as scary as we look. Come on. I'll introduce you to a few of the ladies. Then you can get started."

"I've never quilted before in my life. I barely know how to sew."

"Not a problem. We've got people doing everything from cutting squares to stuffing bears."

"I might be able to handle that."

"Of course you can. Jake tells me you're a computer forensics specialist." She started toward the group and Chloe followed, moving fast to keep up.

"I was one. Now I'm a florist." Though if she smashed one more of Opal's intricate bows, she might not be that for long.

"You and I have a lot in common, then. I was a computer tech before I opened my quilt shop. I'd love to hear more about your old job. Why don't you come over after work one day? We can have a cup of coffee and chat. Of course, you'd be exposed to my noisy munchkins, so…" She blushed. "Sorry, I'm speed-talking again. I've got a two-year-old and a newborn at home. When I talk to adults, I'm so excited to actually have people that understand me, I feel like I've got to get it all out at once."

"Talking fast is better than talking to yourself. Which is what I've been doing lately."

Tiffany laughed again, looping an arm through Chloe's. "You know. I think you and I are going to get along fine. Now, let's get to work before Irma Jefferson sees us chatting and cracks the whip."

"She's the group leader?"

"No, she just thinks she is."

Chloe laughed and allowed herself to be tugged deeper into the buzz of activity.

★ ★ ★

Ben typed a sentence. Deleted it. Typed another one. Deleted it.

Disgusted with his lack of focus, he stood and walked to the small window that looked out over the churchyard. Fall had ripped the leaves from the tall oak that stood in the center of the lawn. Its broad branches were clearly visible in the moonlight. Beyond that, the parking lot was still half full. Wednesday night's prayer meeting was over, but there were plenty of other activities. Choir. Youth Bible study. The quilting circle.

The quilting circle where Chloe might be.

He'd thought about calling her several times during the past few days, but had decided against it. They'd have dinner Saturday night and catch up then. Anything else seemed like...

Exactly what it was. Interest.

Ben ran a hand over his hair, rubbed the tension at the back of his neck. There were fifteen single women at Grace Christian Church. All of them were nice, sweet and as uncomplicated as women could be. Which was much more complicated than Ben wanted to deal with. Friends and acquaintances had set him up with dozens of their female relatives during the past six years—daughters, nieces, cousins, aunts. Mothers. None of them had caught and held his attention the way Chloe seemed to be doing.

He wasn't quite sure how he felt about that and was even less sure that how he felt mattered. Chloe seemed to be the direction his life was heading. Whether or not that was a good thing remained to be seen.

"Busy?" Jake's deep voice pulled Ben from his thoughts and he turned to face his friend who stood in the doorway of the office.

"No. Come on in." He waited while Jake stepped across the threshold and closed the door. "I'm surprised to see you here. I thought you'd be on child-care duty."

"I got called into work. Tiffany's mom is babysitting the kids."

"Anything serious going on?"

"Kyle Davis is feuding with his neighbor again, insisting Jesse Rivers is stealing mail from his box."

"That does sound serious." Ben grinned, gestured to the chair across the desk. "Want to have a seat?"

"I've only got a minute. I just wanted to check in on Tiffany, make sure she's not overdoing it."

"Is it possible to overdo it while quilting?" Ben tried not to smile but failed. The gruff, hardened police officer who'd come to Lakeview five years before had definitely been softened by love.

Jake scowled. "Go ahead and laugh, my friend, but from my vantage point, it seems your time has come."

"Does it?" Ben lifted a pen from the desk, tapped it against his palm.

"You brought Chloe pie."

"Opal insisted."

"I've seen you refuse other insistent matchmakers."

True, and Ben didn't deny it. "Chloe's had a tough time."

"And is still having one." There was tightness to Jake's voice that Ben didn't like.

"You've got more information?"

"I spoke to someone else on the D.C. police force. He was willing to tell me a little more than just what's in the records."

"Like what?"

"Chloe was diagnosed with post-traumatic stress disorder a couple of months after the accident."

"And?"

"The complaints she filed were vague—things being moved around in her apartment, someone following her. She reported her laptop stolen. Then found it in the trunk of her car."

"So, they assumed she was making it up?"

"No. Both men I spoke to have worked with Chloe in the past. Her skills in computer forensics have helped close some difficult cases. Both said she was professional, intelligent, easy to work with. Neither thinks she was making things up."

"Then what do they think?"

"That losing her fiancé in an accident that was meant to take her life left her... unbalanced."

"She doesn't seem unbalanced to me. Just scared."

"I told the guy I was talking to today the same thing. He disagrees. The brake line on Chloe's car had been cut. She was driving. After the accident she told several people that she wished she'd died instead of Adam." Jake raked a hand through his hair, ran it down over his jaw. "Look, I don't know if this is something I should be sharing, but I can trust you to keep it quiet and you might have better luck getting more information about it from Chloe than I will."

"What?"

"Chloe attempted suicide two weeks before she left D.C."

Ben stilled at the words, his fist tightening around the pen he held. "No way."

"She refused to admit it, but paramedics found an empty bottle of antidepressants in her trash can. The prescription was filled less than a week before."

"Chloe called for help?"

"No. A friend called to see how Chloe was feeling and thought she sounded odd. She called an ambulance. That saved Chloe's life."

"Was the friend Opal?"

"I didn't ask, but it's possible. Chloe left D.C. less than two weeks later. Didn't bother leaving a forwarding address or telling the police that she was going. According to the guy I talked to today, Chloe insisted someone had tried to murder her. Investigation revealed nothing. No sign of forced entry into the apartment. No fingerprints but Chloe's."

"And your thoughts on this?"

"The same as they were before—I think there are missing pieces to the puzzle. I think something is going on that we don't understand. I also think I could be wrong, that maybe I'm misreading Chloe and she really does have some deep-seated problems."

Ben nodded. "I can see that."

"But you don't agree?"

"No. I don't. Chloe doesn't seem depressed enough to try and end her life."

"Maybe she isn't anymore."

"That kind of depression doesn't just go away, Jake." He dropped the pen back onto the table, rolled his shoulders trying to ease the tension in his neck. "What's the next step?"

"One of us needs to ask Chloe what happened that night."

"You're the police officer."

"I can't see upsetting the woman and that's probably what my blunt questions would do."

"You're not that bad.

"Sure I am. Even my wife says so. Speaking of which," He smiled, frustration and worry draining from his face. "I've got a redhead to track down before I go home."

"I'll walk with you, see if Chloe showed up at the quilting circle."

"Call me once you two talk."

Once they talked? Ben doubted there'd be much talking going on once he asked Chloe if she'd attempted suicide. No matter how he tried to couch the question, he was pretty sure it wouldn't be taken well.

They stepped into the reception hall, the buzz of activity and enthusiasm washing over Ben. He loved watching the women and men as they worked, the busy, almost frantic pace they set like an intricately choreographed dance to the music of chattering voices and laughter.

"There's my wife." Jake's soft smile and quick, eager steps as he moved toward Tiffany brought back memories of Ben's own happiness with Theresa, his own eagerness to be with her.

Now, he had no one to rush to. No one waiting for his return home. No one to ask about his day. He'd had seven years to get used to that, but sometimes it still bothered him. Sometimes he still felt the aching pain of loss and loneliness.

He shook aside the thoughts, not willing to dwell on what he didn't have. The key to happiness and contentment, he'd found, was in dwelling on what he did have. A home. Friends. A job he loved.

He scanned the room, searching for Chloe's coal-black hair and slim figure, not sure he'd be able to spot her in the crowd if she were there. A few men were interspersed among the women, mostly widowers, though some were young teenagers or college students. One or two die-hard bachelors were in the mix as well, looking for someone new to set their sights on. Ben searched their faces, wondering if Brian McMath were there. If he was, he'd probably hightail it to the only single woman in attendance who didn't know his reputation.

It took only a few seconds to spot the doctor, his buttoned-up white dress shirt and dark tie setting him apart from the rest of the crowd. Standing at the stuffing table, shoving filler into a quilted bear, Brian looked like a fish out of water. The woman beside him looked more comfortable, her faded jeans and dark sweater more in keeping with what the rest of the group was wearing.

Chloe.

Both surprised and pleased to see her there, Ben strode toward the two. "Hi Brian. Chloe. Mind if I join you?"

"Actually, we were discussing some medical issues that Chloe would probably prefer to keep private." McMath's dismissal was curt.

Ben ignored it.

"Sounds fascinating." He smiled at Chloe and she returned the gesture, her lips curving, her eyes begging for intervention.

"Not even close. Here," She handed him a flat bear patchworked in various yellow prints. "You can stuff Cheers. He's starting to feel left out."

"Cheers?"

"He's bright enough to cheer anyone up."

"Did you name yours, too?" He gestured toward the purple-toned bear she held.

"Of course. This one is Hugs."

"Because he'd make any kid want to hug him?"

"You catch on quick, Ben." This time her smile was real.

"I hate to break the news to you two, but they're stuffed bears. They don't require names."

Chloe met Ben's eyes and her smile widened. "Of course they do. That's the whole point of having a stuffed animal. You give it a name. Pretend it's your friend."

"Must be a girl thing." Brian grumbled and grabbed another handful of filler.

"I don't know about that. I can remember having a stuffed bear when I was maybe five. I called him Brown Bear." He'd given it to his sister when she was a toddler and she'd recently passed it to her one-year-old.

"Brown Bear. Very creative, Ben. My toys were more educational. Puzzles. Word games. Those kinds of things. How about you, Chloe? I'm sure a computer forensic expert…"

"I'm a florist, Brian."

"But you were an expert in computer forensics. I'm sure

the kind of intelligence it takes to do that sort of work starts in early childhood."

"Actually, I didn't have many toys when I was a kid. Just a stuffed turtle that Opal gave me. A floppy green and brown one that was perfect for cuddling."

"And you named him, of course." Ben shoved a handful of stuffing into the yellow bear, wondering if the bright, relaxed woman next to him was really the tragically broken woman the D.C. police had painted her to be.

"Of course. I called him Speedy."

"That's a strange name for a turtle." Brian frowned, tossed the green bear he was stuffing onto the table where another group was stitching closed openings. "But let's talk about something that is more grown-up. Like those scars. There are ways to correct some of the damage, Chloe."

"I'm sure there are, but I'm not interested." Chloe finished stuffing the bear she was working on and grabbed the last one off the table, slashes of color staining her cheeks.

"Surely a woman as beautiful as you—"

"Knows her own mind." Ben spoke firmly, hoping to put an end to Brian's pushiness.

"Like I said when you joined us, the conversation is confidential. Something between patient and doctor."

"You're right, Brian. I think that's exactly what I'll do. Discuss things with my doctor." Chloe finished filling the last bear and set it on the to-be-stitched table, her smile sweet as pecan pie, but not quite hiding the bite to her words.

"I'm sure you haven't had time to find one yet."

"My surgeon recommended someone. I've got an appointment for next week."

"I see. Who with?"

"I think that's probably confidential, Brian." Ben smiled at the doctor, then gestured to the empty table. "It looks like we've finished the last bear. How about joining me for a cup of coffee, Chloe?"

Chloe's brow creased, a frown pulling at the edges of her mouth. Ben thought she'd refuse. Then she glanced at Brian and nodded. "Sure. It was nice talking to you, Brian."

"Maybe we'll see each other next week."

"Maybe."

"I'll see you Sunday, Brian."

The doctor's nod was curt, his shoulders stiff as he moved away.

"I guess we should go get that coffee." Chloe sounded tired, the dark shadows under her eyes speaking of too many sleepless nights.

"You don't seem too enthusiastic."

"It's been a long day."

"Opal's working you too hard?"

"You know that isn't even close to the truth."

"I do." He led her into the office, gestured for her to have a seat. "So maybe she's not working you hard enough."

"Boredom can make the day long, but I wasn't bored today. We're almost too busy this week what with half of Lakeview coming in to hear about what happened Saturday night."

"So if it's not boredom maybe there were too many thorns on the roses. Too many petals in your hair."

She smiled, shook her head. "Too many nightmares last night."

"I'd like to say that was going to be my next guess, but it wasn't." He poured coffee from the carafe on the coffeemaker and handed her a cup. "Want to tell me about them?"

"Not really." She smiled again, lowering her gaze and tracing a circle on the desk with her finger. "You and Jake walked into the reception hall together."

"He stopped by to see his wife."

"He had news, though. About me, right?"

"He did say he'd spoken to D.C. police again."

"And?" She met his gaze, her eyes shadowed, whatever she was thinking well-hidden.

He could beat around the bush or he could lay it all out on the table. The latter was more his style and Ben couldn't think of a good reason to change it now. Much as he might want to avoid the issue, he wasn't going to hide the truth. "The guy he spoke to today said you tried to commit suicide."

"I knew that would come up eventually."

"Yet you didn't mention it to Jake."

"And give him reason to doubt me? I lived with that for almost eleven months. I didn't want to live it here, too." She brushed her bangs off her forehead, her eyes flashing emerald green fire.

"Like Jake told you before, he can't help you if he doesn't have all the necessary information."

"He knows everything I do."

"Everything except whether or not you actually were attempting suicide."

"If I'd been trying to kill myself, I wouldn't have picked up the phone and had a conversation with Opal." Her words were blunt, her gaze direct, but there was a forced quality to both, as if she were trying to convince herself of the very things she wanted him to believe.

"I believe you."

"Do you? Because lately I'm not even sure I believe myself." She stood abruptly. "I've really got to go. Like I said, it's been a long day."

Ben stood, too, putting a hand on Chloe's arm and holding her in place when she would have walked out the door. Her skin was pale, her mouth drawn in a tight line, the moisture in her eyes tempting Ben to wrap her in a hug that he knew she wouldn't appreciate. "Whatever is going on, Chloe, you don't have to face it alone."

"I appreciate the thought, but all the platitudes in the world can't change the fact that I am facing it alone."

"I don't believe in placating people. I believe in telling the truth."

"What truth? That you and Jake are going to help me? That God is looking out for me? I've trusted the police before. I've trusted God. But it hasn't done me any good. The nightmare is still chasing me. Eventually, it's going to catch up." There was no anger in her voice, just a weariness that Ben knew all too well. "I really do need to go."

He nodded, reluctantly letting his hand slide from her arm. "Your apartment is only five minutes from here. If anything happens and you need help fast, give me a call." He grabbed a sheet of paper from his desk and scribbled his home and cell phone number on it.

"Thanks."

"I'll be praying for you, Chloe."

"Thanks for that, too. I guess I'll see you Saturday?"

"I wouldn't miss it."

She nodded and stepped out of the office.

Ben pulled the door closed, wishing he could do more than offer words and friendship, wishing she would accept more. But he couldn't, she wouldn't, and he knew the best thing he could do for both of them was pray.

Lord, I don't know why my life has intersected with Chloe's. I don't know what Your purpose is for us, but I know there is one. I pray that Your will be done in both our lives and that in Your infinite mercy You will give Chloe the faith she needs to overcome whatever obstacles and challenges she faces.

The prayer was simple, the peace that washed over Ben a

familiar friend. He took a seat behind his desk, tapping a pen against his palm, the glimmer of an idea forming. He smiled, grabbed the phone and dialed.

Chapter Ten

Chloe paced the length of her living room for the fifth time, the walls pressing in on her, the darkness beyond the window preventing her from doing what she wanted to do—leave.

Exhaustion dragged her down, but the bone-deep ache in her thigh wouldn't allow her to sink into sleep. The skin on her neck felt tight, the bands of scars uncomfortably stiff. She wanted to blame both on her work at Blooming Baskets, but being on her feet for a few hours a day wasn't the cause. Neither was bending over flower arrangements. Anxiety. Tension. Fear. They haunted her days and filled her nights with dreams that stayed in her mind long after she woke.

She moved toward the computer that sat on the desk against one wall of the living room. Maybe she should e-mail a few friends, catch up with them. Make a few phone calls. See how everyone was, but that would mean explaining all that had happened in the past month. Explaining that she'd left town because she hadn't attempted suicide. Explaining that someone wanted her dead.

The story sounded far-fetched even to her.

She grimaced, stalked into her bedroom and picked up her Bible before returning to the living room and pushing open the balcony door. The full moon cast bluish light across the yard and reflected off the lake, painting the world in shades of gray. If she'd had her camera, she would have taken a picture, but she didn't and instead she tried to soak it all in, memorize it, pack it away in her mind so that she could take it with her if she was forced to run again.

The phone rang, the sound drifting out onto the balcony and offering a welcome distraction.

She hurried to pick it up. "Hello?"

"Chloe? It's Ben." The warmth of his voice washed over her, and she sank down into the recliner, relaxing for the first time in what seemed like hours.

"Hi. What's up?"

"I was just out for a ride and thought I'd give you a call."

"Opal must have put you up to it."

"No, but she did give me your number."

"I bet you didn't have to twist her arm for it."

"Not even a little."

Chloe smiled, enjoying the conversation more than she knew was good for her. "So, if Opal didn't put you up to calling me, who did?"

"Me. I had a thought after you left the church the other night and I wanted to share it with you."

"I'm all ears."

"It'll be hard to explain over the phone. What would you say to going for a ride with me?"

"Now?"

"You're not busy. I'm not busy. What better time than now?"

Chloe glanced toward the still-open balcony door and the

darkness beyond. "I don't usually go out at night. The darkness hides too much."

She spoke without thinking, her cheeks heating as she realized what she'd said. "What I meant was—"

"No need to explain. Let's do it another time."

"You haven't even said what it is."

"And ruin the surprise?"

"I'm not much for surprises." Most of the ones she'd had weren't good.

He chuckled, the warmth of it seeping through the phone line and tugging at Chloe's heart. "I had a feeling you were going to tell me you didn't like surprises. So, here's the thing, I have a friend who's a veterinarian. She's got a litter of puppies she needs to find homes for."

"Puppies?"

"Puppies. As in little yapping bundles of fur."

"Should I ask what this has to do with me?"

"I thought you might like some company at night. A puppy seemed perfect."

"I've never had a dog. I wouldn't know the first thing about taking care of one." Though she had to admit, the idea held a certain appeal. The past few nights had been long, filled with odd noises and sinister shadows, nightmares and memories. A distraction might be just what she needed.

"There's a first time for everything, Chloe." There was a smile in Ben's voice and Chloe's lips curved in response.

"My landlady might not allow pets."

"The Andersons across the hall from you have one. They've brought it to a couple of church picnics."

"The little mop they dress in a sweater doesn't qualify as a pet."

His laughter rumbled out again. "Tell you what, why don't

you think about it? You can give me a call, or we can talk about it when we get together for dinner."

She should definitely think about it. Rushing into something like a puppy could only lead to trouble and regret, and she had enough of both of those to last a lifetime.

She didn't want to think about it, though, because saying no would mean spending another night alone in the apartment. Another night jumping at every sound, wondering about every shadow. "Is the offer still open for tonight?"

"Sure."

"Then I think I'll take you up on it."

"Great. I'll be there in five."

Five minutes was just enough time for Chloe to check her copy of the rental agreement she'd signed, pull on shoes, pop two aspirin and waffle back and forth on the puppy idea a dozen times.

By the time Ben knocked, she'd driven herself crazy with indecision. Over a dog. But she couldn't deny the excitement she felt. The sense of fun and adventure that had been missing from her life for far too long and now welled up inside as she pulled the door open. "Five minutes on the dot."

"I'm a stickler for being on time. Ready?" His easy smile was as familiar as an old friend's and just as welcome.

"Indecisive." She limped over and grabbed her purse off the couch, pulled on a jacket.

"Then it's good you don't have to decide anything tonight." Despite his smile, Ben seemed more subdued than usual, his normally abundant charm overshadowed by something dark and sad.

"Is everything okay?"

"Yes." But it wasn't. Fatigue had darkened his eyes from sapphire to navy. Tension bracketed his mouth. "We'd better get going. Tori said she'd be at the clinic until eight-thirty. I don't want to keep her longer than that."

Chloe nodded, stepping out into the hallway and moving down the steps toward the front door, knowing she shouldn't ask the questions that were clamoring through her mind, but unable to stop herself. "Were you working today?"

"Friday's the day I do visitations. We've got several house-bound members of the congregation and a few in the hospital." He paused, ran a hand over his hair. "I also conducted a funeral for a two-year-old boy."

"Just a baby. That's terrible."

He nodded, his jaw tight. "It's hard enough to say goodbye to someone who has lived a long, full life. Saying goodbye to a child who has barely begun to live is devastating."

"I can't even imagine what that must be like for the parents."

"Me, neither." He pushed open the front door, his movements stiff. "Talking to people who are so devastated, so desperate to know why the tragedy happened, how God could have allowed it, is tough, because there are no answers. We live in a fallen sinful world. Tragedy is part of that. We know that God loves us, that He wants what's best for us. That makes accepting things like a child's death even more difficult."

He ran a hand over his face, then stepped out onto the porch. "Maybe tonight isn't such a good night for this, after all. I came to cheer you up, not drag you down into the pit with me."

Chloe hesitated, then put her hand on his arm, feeling the rigid tension of the muscles beneath his sleeve. "I was already in the pit before you arrived. Since we're both in it together, we may as well hang out. Who knows? Maybe we'll manage to hoist each other out."

Ben stared down at her, his eyes dark, the angles of his

face harsher in the porch light. He looked harder, tougher, much more like the teen he'd said he'd been than the man he'd become.

Finally, he shrugged. "Then let's go look at puppies."

He started down the porch steps and Chloe followed, the coolness of the evening seeping through the long-sleeved blouse and lightweight jacket she wore. She shivered, stumbling down the first step, her bad leg buckling.

Ben grabbed her arm before she could fall the rest of the way. "Whoa! Careful. If you fall and break your leg, Opal will have my hide."

"And my surgeon will have mine." She limped down the last two steps, pausing at the bottom to let the aching pain in her thigh ease. "She spent a lot of hours putting it back together. She won't be happy if I undo all that work."

"Then we definitely need to make sure it doesn't get broken again."

"I don't think we have to worry about it too much. I've got enough rods and screws in it to set off a metal detector."

"Sounds pretty indestructible, but let's not take any chances." He put a hand under her elbow and led her to his sedan, his slow pace matching her limping stride.

Even with Ben beside her, Chloe felt fear creeping close, breathing a dire warning in her ear. Something was out here with them. Something dark and evil. Something ready to strike. Ready to kill.

She glanced around the yard, searching for signs of danger. There was nothing there. At least nothing she could see.

As if he sensed it, too, Ben stilled, his body tense. "Something seems off."

"Off?"

"Yeah. Off. And it's crawling up my spine and shouting a warning in my ear." He glanced around the yard, the hardness Chloe had seen while he stood on the porch even more pronounced.

"Come on." He hurried her toward the car, pulled open the door. "Get in."

Chloe did as he asked, sliding into the sedan and expecting him to do the same.

"Lock the door. I want to take a look around." He pushed the door closed, but Chloe caught it before it could snap shut, pushing it open once again.

"Look around? For what?"

"For whatever it is that's out here with us."

"Ben, I don't think that's a good idea. Let's go inside and call the police."

"Use my cell phone to call. It's in the glove compartment. I've got Jake's number on speed dial. Lock the door and stay in the car until I get back."

"Let's call him together. You can't go running after whoever is out there by yourself."

"Why not? It won't be the first time I've gone running after something lurking in the darkness."

"I didn't realize that was part of a pastor's job description." Chloe wanted to grab Ben's hand and keep him from leaving.

"It isn't. Good thing I haven't always been a pastor." He brushed the bangs from her eyes and smiled, his teeth flashing white in the darkness. "Now, stop worrying and stay put."

With that he shut the door and started across the yard toward the lake.

Chloe watched him go, sure that at any moment someone would swoop down on him. Instead, he seemed to disappear, blending into the shadows and fading into the night. Chloe found the cell phone, scrolling through the contact numbers until she found Jake's.

He picked up quickly, his gruff voice filling her with relief. "Reed here."

"It's Chloe. Davidson."

"Calling from Ben's cell phone. Is he okay?"

"I don't know," she explained quickly, her words rushing
out so that she wasn't sure Jake would be able to make any
sense of them.

"You're at your place?"

"Yes."

"Stay where you are. I'll be there in ten."

Ten minutes. Six hundred seconds. Plenty of time for a shot
to be fired, a knife to be buried deep in a chest. A man to die.

Images filled Chloe's head. Black night. Fire. A shadowy
figure. Danger. Pain.

Fear.

She wanted to sink down in the seat, hide her head until
help arrived. Wanted to embrace the weak-willed, wimpy
woman she'd become and let Ben and Jake handle the problem.

Wanted to, but couldn't.

Adam had died because of her investigation into the death
of Ana Benedict, had died because of what that investigation
had uncovered about The Strangers. She had no intention of
letting the same thing happen to Ben. Fear or no fear, she was
getting out of the car and she was going to face whatever was
hiding in the darkness.

Hands shaking, she shoved open the car door and took a
gulping breath of cool air. The yard was silent and still, waiting for whatever would come. Chloe waited, too, breathless
and watching, hoping to see Ben return before she actually
had to go after him. Finally, she couldn't put it off any longer
and she stepped away from the car, leaves and grass crunching
under her feet, releasing the heavy scent of earth and decay.

Up ahead, the dark water of the lake washed over rocks

and wood, lapping against the shore in rhythmic waves that should have been soothing but weren't.

I could really use some help right about now, Lord.

The prayer chanted through her mind as she skirted a thick grove of trees and approached the lake. The shoreline was empty, tall reeds and thick grasses heavy and overgrown, tangled in bunches near the water's edge. A boat bobbed on the surface of the lake, the rickety dock it was tied to barely keeping it from floating away.

"Ben?" She whispered his name as she moved toward the dock, peering into the shadows afraid of what she might find there.

"I thought you were staying in the car."

He spoke from behind her, his voice so unexpected, Chloe bit back a scream, whirling to face him, her heart in her throat. "I didn't want you to be out here by yourself."

"So you decided to come out by yourself?" The moon was behind him, casting shadows across his face, making his expression impossible to read.

"It seemed like a good idea at the time."

"It wasn't." He cupped her elbow, tugging her back toward the house.

"Did you see someone?"

"No, but that doesn't mean someone wasn't here."

"What do we do now?"

"We go back to the car and you get in it and lock the door. I walk around the house and see if there's any evidence that someone has been hanging around. Maybe talk to the downstairs tenant, see if he's heard anything. Once Jake gets here and checks things out, we'll head over the veterinary clinic."

"It's getting a little late for that."

"It's not late at all." His hand rested on her back, the warmth of it seeping through her jacket and warming her chilled skin.

"I hear sirens. Jake is on the way. Stay in the car this time, okay?"

"Okay."

The door shut again and this time Chloe stayed where she was, watching Ben move around the perimeter of the house as the sound of sirens drifted into the car and her rapidly beating heart subsided.

Chapter Eleven

By the time Jake and Ben finished searching the property, Chloe had come up with several excuses to return to her apartment and lock herself in for the night. Her head ached. Her leg throbbed. She really didn't think a puppy was a good idea.

All of them fled her mind as Ben pulled open the car door and slid in, a woodsy, masculine scent floating into the car with him. "We're all set."

"Did you find anything?"

"Nothing but a few smudged footprints near the window under your apartment. They could be from anyone and could have been there for a few days." He started the engine. "Someone was out there tonight, though. I'm sure of it."

"You saw someone?"

"Felt someone. Whether or not that someone has anything to do with what's been happening to you, I can't say."

"How could it not? It's exactly what's been happening to me for months."

"It started after the accident?"

Had it? It seemed that what had happened after the accident was crystal clear, the threat she felt like a waking nightmare she couldn't escape from. What had come before was less clear and Chloe couldn't say for sure that she hadn't felt the same way. She couldn't say she had, either. "I don't know."

"The man who was convicted of murder—"

"Matthew Jackson." His pale face and coal-black eyes were tattooed into her memory, his skeletal frame standing outside the burning car, something she would never forget.

"According to the news reports I heard, Jackson never admitted to sabotaging your car. It's possible he didn't."

"He was there, Ben. Standing outside the car while it burned around us. He had a gun." The police speculated that he'd been planning to kill Chloe if she got out of the car. The fire that had scarred her, had saved her life. The bent metal that had held her inside the burning wreck had kept her from certain death.

The thought made her shudder and she wrapped her arms around her waist. "Jackson wanted me dead. He was at the scene of the accident. It seems pretty obvious he had something to do with it."

"Maybe he did, but maybe the accident has nothing to do with what's happening now." Ben turned into the parking lot of a well-lit building and turned to face her. "What if the D.C. police were heading in the wrong direction? What if they couldn't find evidence that you were being stalked because they were looking for a connection to Jackson and couldn't find it?"

She rubbed the ache in her thigh, wincing a little as bunched muscles contracted even more. "They looked in every direction. My old caseload, my personal relationships. They investigated thoroughly but couldn't find anyone else who had a grudge against me."

"Did you?"

"Did I what?"

"Investigate." His eyes were liquid fire in the dim light, his face carved from stone, but his hand was gentle as it wrapped around hers, his fingers skimming across her palm and settling there. "It's what you do. It would seem natural for you to check things out yourself."

"I was too sick at first. By the time I was healthy enough to think about investigating, Jackson was in jail and it seemed the police had covered all the bases."

"If it were my life on the line, I don't think I'd rely solely on the police to investigate." His hand dropped away from hers and he opened his door. "This is it. Tori's clinic. Let's head in and see what those puppies are like."

Chloe grabbed his arm before he could get out, scowling as he turned to face her. "You're good, Ben Avery. Really good. But I know exactly what you're up to and…" She planned on saying it wasn't going to work, that she had no intention of digging into her old caseloads, no intention of searching for someone who might want her dead. But he'd planted a seed and it was already growing in the fallow soil of her heart.

"And what?" His gaze touched her hair, her cheeks, her lips, lingering there for a second before he met her eyes.

Her skin heated, but she ignored it and the wild beating of her heart. "And it's working. But I use computer forensics to investigate crime. If someone is really coming after me, that won't be hidden in a computer file or found in a deleted e-mail."

"But his reason might be."

He had a good point and Chloe mulled it over as she got out of the car. "I'll have to look through my open cases. Maybe I'll find something there."

"If you do, go to Jake with it. Don't try to confront the person yourself."

"I'm not that crazy. One near-death experience in a lifetime is more than enough."

He chuckled and pressed a hand to Chloe's lower spine. "Come on. Tori is probably pacing the floor wondering what's taking so long."

"Maybe she's left." Which might be a good thing.

"Maybe, but it's doubtful. She's got to find homes for these puppies before her grandfather finds another litter."

"Her grandfather brought her the puppies?"

"Yeah. That was this week. Last week, he found an abandoned potbellied pig. The week before he found a goat."

"What's he do? Ride around looking for strays?"

"When he's not riding around looking for Opal."

"Opal?"

"Yeah. Sam's got a thing for her. You probably remember meeting him the night of the wedding. Tall, gray hair, smitten look on his face."

"I remember. I tried to find out what's going on with them, but Opal is keeping mum."

"That's probably for the best."

"Why's that?"

"It'll give you an excuse to keep mum about what's going on with us." He shouldered open the clinic door, gesturing for Chloe to precede him into the brightly lit reception area.

"Nothing is going on with us."

"I'm not so sure you're right about that, Chloe." He smiled, the gentle curve of his lips spearing into Chloe's heart.

She blinked, took a step back, denying what she was feeling. Refusing it. She didn't need to add a man to her already complicated life. She wouldn't add a man to it. "Ben—"

"You're finally here. I was beginning to wonder if you were

coming at all." A woman strode toward them, her movements brisk despite what looked like an advanced pregnancy. Tall and striking with bright red hair and green eyes, she exuded confidence and warmth as she offered a hand to Chloe. "You must be Chloe. I'm Tori Stone. You met my grandfather the other night."

"I remember."

"Yeah, well, Sam is hard to forget. The puppies are this way. I've only got two left. This litter has been pretty easy to place. The last one..." She paused, shuddered. "Not so much."

"Was something wrong with them?"

"Wrong? No. They were just homely. Poor little guys. Eventually we found some people who were willing to overlook that." She smiled, led them to a closed door. "Here we are. I've got a few patients to check on. I'll let you two take a look. Then come back in a few minutes to see what you think."

She pushed open the door and motioned for Chloe to go in. "Feel free to take them out of the crate, but close the door if you do or they'll be down the hall and into trouble before you know it. See you in a few."

Chloe stepped into the room. It housed an exam table, cabinets, a counter. The crate sat on the floor near the far wall, the wiggling, squirming balls of fur inside it looking more like overgrown dust bunnies than dogs.

"Those are puppies? They look more like miniature mops or giant dust bunnies to me." Ben's comment neatly mimicked what Chloe was thinking, and she smiled.

"Except for the tails."

"There is that." Ben knelt down. "Which do you want to see? The fuzzy one or the fuzzier one."

"Either."

Ben reached in and pulled out a handful of wiggling cream-colored puppy. "Try this one."

She lifted it to her chest, stroking silky fur and feeling the vibrating excitement of the puppy surge through her. It strained against her hold, licking her hands and neck and rolling sideways for a belly rub. "It's awfully cute."

"So's this one." Ben lifted out the second pup and set it on the floor. Its paws were black, its torso dark brown, its tail wagging so fast, Chloe thought it might knock itself over.

"If I were to decide to bring one home I wouldn't know which to choose." Chloe set the one she was holding down, and watched as it scampered across the floor, rushing from wall to wall, skidding on the tile floor and slamming into the door.

Chloe laughed, kneeling down, her bad leg protesting the move. She ignored it, picking up the brown puppy and holding it up so she could look in its eyes. "This one is quieter."

"Definitely."

She put it back down, smiling as it climbed up her legs and settled down for a nap. "I don't know, Ben. They're both adorable, but I'm not sure I'm ready for a pet."

"Ever have one before?"

"Not even a fish. The closest I came to it was Speedy."

"The stuffed turtle."

"Exactly."

Ben lifted the cream-colored puppy and rubbed it under its chin as he settled down beside Chloe. "Like I said before, there's a first time for everything."

"I'm just not sure now is the right time for this particular first."

"It's your decision to make." He placed the puppy down on the floor, watching as it raced away. "But it might be fun to have a quirky little guy like that racing around the apartment."

A soft knock sounded on the door and Tori strode in. "I see you've met Cain and Abel."

She knelt down next to Chloe, smoothing the fur on the dark puppy's back. "They're brothers, but the similarity ends there. Cain is full of energy and life. Lovable but constantly in trouble."

"Then this one must be Abel." Chloe stroked the puppy's head.

"Yes. Sweet as pie. Cute as a button. Smart as a whip." She grinned. "But lazy."

"They're both sweet as pie."

"You're right about that, Chloe, but their personalities are very different. If you decide you want to take one, you need to think about which will fit better with your lifestyle."

Chloe nodded, watching Cain as he chased his tail. His energy level high, his exuberance appealing. A year or two ago, he would have been her choice. Now, though, she wasn't sure she could keep up with the wiggling ball of energy. The quieter puppy, on the other hand, was more her speed, his slow movements as he finally roused himself to join his brother's play made her smile.

"You don't have to make up your mind tonight, of course. I can hold them both for a few days while you decide." Tori started to rise and Ben hurried to offer a hand up. "Thanks, Ben. Why don't I give you a couple more minutes with the puppies? Then we'll call it a night."

The door closed behind Tori's retreating figure.

"What do you think?" Ben lifted Cain and rubbed his belly.

"I think you should take that one home with you."

"We didn't come here to pick a puppy for me. We came for you. You need some company, remember?"

"And you don't?"

"My life is busy. I don't have time for a puppy."

"Mine is, too, and neither do I."

"So, I guess we leave them here."

"I guess we do." She lifted the brown puppy who'd come to sit in her lap again, surprised by the disappointment she felt. "Sorry, guy."

"Of course, there's another option." Ben knelt down in front of Chloe, lifting Abel from her arms and setting him on the floor.

"What's that?"

"We could make time for them." He grabbed Chloe's hand and tugged her to her feet, his hands wrapping around her waist to hold her steady.

"Come on, Chloe. You know you want to." His grin was just the right side of wicked, his eyes flashing with amusement and a challenge Chloe knew she should ignore, but couldn't.

"So you're saying if I take Abel, you'll take Cain?"

"I'm saying if you take one I'll take the other. Which one of us gets the hyperactive guy is up for debate."

"Debate? I think it's pretty obvious that the more active puppy should go to the more able-bodied person. My bum leg won't let me chase after anything much faster than Abel."

"You may have a point. One way or another, we'll have to work out visitation. A couple of walks a week. Maybe a playdate or two." He leaned a shoulder against the wall. "Just because you and I aren't together, doesn't mean the boys shouldn't be able to spend time with each other."

He looked serious, his face set in somber lines, sandy hair falling over his forehead, but laughter danced in his eyes.

Chloe's own laughter bubbled out, spilling into the room, the feeling of it new and fresh. Life, hope, joy. So many things she'd thought she'd never have again, but that suddenly seemed possible. Here, in the brightly lit room, two puppies scampering near her feet, Ben's amused eyes staring into hers, she could almost forget the darkness that waited outside, the shadows that seemed determined to follow her wherever she went.

Almost.

"Don't stop." He brushed strands of hair from Chloe's cheeks, his fingers lingering for a moment before dropping away.

"Stop what?"

"Laughing. It's good for the soul."

"I guess I need to find more things to laugh about, then."

"You will. Sorrow fades in time."

"Sorrow I can handle. It's the guilt that's eating me alive."

"You've got nothing to feel guilty about."

"Don't I?" She leaned down and scooped Abel into her arms, the fuzzy warmth of the puppy comforting. "My investigation caused Adam's death."

"The person who sabotaged your car caused his death."

"No matter which way you try to paint the picture, it'll always be the same. I found information that I passed on to the FBI. Because of that The Strangers dismantled. Because of that, Matthew Jackson tried to kill me and killed Adam instead."

"It seems to me you're taking a lot of responsibility for something you couldn't know would happen."

"I'm not taking responsibility. I'm just…"

"What?"

"Wishing I'd made different choices. Wishing that Adam hadn't died in my place."

Ben's hands framed her face, the rough calluses on his palms rasping against her skin. "He didn't die in your place, Chloe. He was killed in a tragic accident that had nothing to do with you and everything to do with someone else's sin."

"The words sound good, Ben, but they don't feel like the truth."

"Then it's good that how we feel doesn't actually determine the facts." His hands slid to her neck, his thumbs brushing against the tender flesh under her jaw and spreading warmth in their wake.

Chloe's heart jumped, and she stepped back, refusing to put a name to what she'd promised herself she'd never feel again. "We should find Tori and tell her we've decided to take the puppies."

For a moment, she didn't think Ben was going to acknowledge her comment. His vivid eyes stared into hers, secrets and shadows hidden in their depth.

Finally, he nodded. "Let me corral Cain first."

Chloe waited at the door, Abel sleeping in her arms, his fuzzy head pressed into the crook of her elbow, her heartbeat slowing, the places where Ben's hands had rested cooling. She shouldn't be letting him affect her so much, shouldn't be having this kind of reaction to him.

Shouldn't be, but it didn't seem she had much of a choice. No matter how much she might want to tell herself differently, Ben was becoming a fixture in her life. She wasn't sure she liked it and was even less sure she could change it. All she could do was pray that Ben wouldn't eventually suffer for being her friend and that she wouldn't eventually be left heartbroken again.

Chapter Twelve

Having a puppy in the apartment proved to be as much of a distraction as Ben had said it would be. The cozy rooms Chloe loved so much were even more inviting with a ball of fur keeping her company in them.

And company was definitely something she needed at three in the morning when nightmares woke her and fear kept her from returning to sleep.

She shifted in the easy chair, hoping a change in position would alleviate the ache in her leg. Abel whined, moving into a more comfortable spot, his body heat seeping through the flannel pajamas Chloe wore and easing the knotted muscles of her thigh.

"You're a living heating pad, puppy." His tail thumped, his eyes opened briefly before he went back to sleep again.

Chloe wished she could do the same, but the dream she'd woken from refused to release its hold and her heart hammered in response, the quick, sickening thud enough to convince her she was having a heart attack. She wasn't. Despite the pressure in her chest, the too-rapid throb of her pulse and the cold sweat that beaded her brow, she knew she was suffering from nothing more than panic.

She wanted to get up and move, pace the floor, run a mile, talk to someone. She lifted the phone, realized what she was doing and set it down again. She couldn't call Opal at this time of the morning. Not when Opal was already so worried about Chloe's mental health. She wouldn't call Ben. All she could do was sit and wait while seconds became minutes and minutes hours.

Or she could use the time to do what Ben had suggested. She could pull her laptop from the closet where she'd shoved it when she'd moved in and revisit the cases she'd been working on around the time of the accident. As much as she wanted to believe that Matthew Jackson had been convicted of a crime he had committed, Ben had planted a seed of doubt and Chloe couldn't ignore it no matter how much she wanted to.

And the fact was, she really didn't want to.

It was a surprising change to the head-in-the-sand attitude she'd taken for so long; Chloe's mood lifted as a small spark of the person she'd once been took hold, urging her to face the situation, sort out the facts and find out for herself what was what, who was who and just how she could keep herself alive.

Maybe coming to Lakeview had given her back some of her old confidence and enthusiasm. Maybe talking to Ben had. Or maybe as her physical health and strength returned, her will to survive was kicking in stronger than ever. Whatever the case, Chloe was an investigator. She'd spent almost a decade of her life seeking evidence and answers. She'd found them for the FBI, for private investigators, for the police. Now she was going to find them for herself.

"Sorry, pup, you're going to have to move." She stood, setting Abel down on the ground and moving to her bedroom. The puppy scampered after her, waddling into the closet when she opened the door, pawing at the box she pulled out.

"This is mine, Abel. Tomorrow we'll get you some fun toys to play with."

Abel tilted his head to one side as if he were actually listening, Chloe smiled. "It's good to know I won't be talking to myself anymore. Come on. We've got work to do."

She grabbed her laptop from the box and carried it to the kitchen. Her hands were shaking as she set it up on the tiny table there. It wasn't fear that made them tremble. Excitement, anticipation, the drive to succeed—all the things that had made her good at computer forensics—those were what had her hands shaking and her heart racing.

Her elbow hit the Bible she'd set on the edge of the table and she shoved it away, then paused, pulling it back toward her, the yearning she'd felt since she'd come to Lakeview as real and as tangible as anything she might find stored on the computer.

After Adam's betrayal, she'd prayed for understanding, prayed that she could accept what had happened and move on. In those dark moments, she'd felt sure that God was listening, that He understood and cried with her. Then Adam had been killed and that certainty had been ripped away, a gaping hole all that remained of her fragile faith.

But maybe faith couldn't disappear or fade away. Maybe it couldn't be ripped from a life. Maybe, like the information she pulled from computer systems, it was only hidden from sight, waiting for a little effort, a little attention, to bring it back into view again.

She pushed the laptop toward the center of the table, opened her Bible to the first chapter of John and started reading.

"You've caught the biggest fish again, friend." Ben eyed Jake's cooler full of fish and his own empty one.

"Again? If I remember correctly, you've brought in the biggest catch three times running."

"You may be right, but that doesn't make my loss this time any less painful." He stepped out onto the dock, tied the boat. "I guess I'll be heading to the grocery store before I cook dinner for Chloe. Preparing store-bought fish after a fishing trip isn't a very manly thing to do, but I'll swallow my pride and do it."

"Your pitiful act is falling on deaf ears."

"Anyone ever tell you you're coldhearted?"

"Not coldhearted. Practical. The way I see it, if you want a couple of my fish, you'll have to trade for them."

"A trade or a trip to the grocery store? I don't even need time to think about it. What do you want?"

"A babysitter. Tiffany's birthday is next week and I want to take her out. Unfortunately, her parents are going out of town and she doesn't trust just anyone to watch the kids."

"And you think she'll let me do it?"

"I know she will. I asked."

"You've got to be pretty desperate to be asking me, Jake. You do know I haven't changed a diaper in years? I'll probably end up putting it on backward or upside down."

"Desperation has nothing to do with it. You're the closest thing to a brother I've ever had. I trust you. Besides, Isaac is four weeks old. He won't care what way his diaper goes on."

"Since you put it that way, I guess I'll do it. No fish necessary."

"Thanks." Jake slapped him on the back and handed over the cooler filled with fish. "And just so we're clear, I would have given you these anyway."

"You say that after I've already committed to hours of diaper duty and baby-doll play." Which he had to admit he'd probably enjoy. If Isaac and his sister, Honor, didn't spend the entire time crying for their parents.

"Amazing how that worked out, isn't it?" Jake grinned and started toward his car. "Is six-thirty Friday okay with you?"

"I'll be there."

"Great. And now we'd both better get moving. I don't want to miss Honor's bath and I'm sure you don't want to be late for your date."

"Whoa! Hold up there. I'm cooking dinner for Chloe. That's not the same as a date."

"Then what is it the same as?"

"Cooking dinner for you and Tiffany or for my sister and Shane."

"Really? Because the way I see it, when you cook dinner for me and Tiffany or Raven and Shane, you're cooking for family. Chloe isn't family. So you cooking dinner for her doesn't seem like the same thing at all."

"She needs a friend. I'm being one."

"You just keep telling yourself that." Jake grinned and got into his car, his face sobering as he ran hand over his hair. "I hate to even ask, but did you ask Chloe about the suicide attempt?"

"She denied it."

"Do you believe her?"

"Yeah, I do."

"Then so do I. Which means we're dealing with a second murder attempt. We just have to find a way to prove it."

"Did the police in D.C. collect evidence?"

"It seemed like a cut-and-dry suicide attempt. They weren't looking for evidence of murder. When they went back in afterward, the place had been cleaned by some friends who were getting it ready for her return from the hospital."

"Convenient for the murderer. Do we know who those friends were?"

"You'll have to ask Chloe when you're there tonight. Or I'll give her a ring tomorrow."

"I'll ask."

"And I'll keep searching for answers. If Chloe's in danger, I plan to figure out where it's coming from.

"That makes two of us."

"You just be careful, friend. I'm a cop. You're not."

"I can handle myself." He might have left the military years ago, but he hadn't forgotten what he learned there.

Jake nodded, but the concern in his eyes didn't fade. "There's something going on here I don't like. Chloe's brought trouble into town. Big trouble. The fact that you're involved with her—"

"I'm not involved with anyone."

"You're cooking her dinner. You went and picked out puppies with her. You're involved, Ben, and that makes things all the more complicated." He scowled. "Like I said, be careful."

The car door shut before Ben could respond. That was probably for the best. There wasn't much left to say. Denying that he was involved with Chloe wouldn't convince Jake. The truth was, Ben wasn't all that convinced, either. Much as he might tell himself he wasn't interested in Chloe beyond wanting to help her adjust to her life in Lakeview, the truth seemed much more complex. He was intrigued, compelled, drawn into the sadness he saw in her eyes, the laughter that must have come much more frequently before the tragedy.

Despite what she'd been through, she was strong, determined and dedicated to creating a better life for herself. Ben understood that. He'd lived it. Even her struggles with faith and trust were familiar to him. He understood Chloe and that wasn't something he could say about many of the women he'd met.

Whether or not that meant anything, whether or not he wanted it to mean anything remained to be seen. For right now, he'd enjoy spending a few hours with an interesting woman and not worry about what would come next. God had everything under control.

Ben just wasn't sure he did.

He sighed, hefted the cooler containing the fish and strode toward his car. Like Jake, he had a bad feeling about Chloe's situation. Her story was like a puzzle with missing pieces. Until the last one was found the picture would remain unclear. And until it was clear Ben wouldn't rest easy. Danger lurked around Chloe. He felt it every time he was near her. He couldn't see it and didn't know what direction it was coming from, but he knew it was there and that if they weren't careful it would destroy Chloe and anyone who stood in the way.

Fortunately, Ben planned to be careful. Really careful. He might not know what role Chloe was going to play in his life, but he knew exactly what role he planned to play in hers. He was going to keep her safe. A little caution and a lot of prayer would go a long way toward that. Dinner and puppy choosing were extra.

Speaking of which, he had some trout to cook and a dog to walk.

And a very attractive woman to spend the evening with.

Despite his concerns, Ben couldn't help smiling as he got in his car and headed home.

Chapter Thirteen

Abel's soft whine commanded Chloe's attention and she glanced up from the file she was searching through. The puppy sat by the door, his head cocked to one side, his ears perked.

"You want to go out?"

Abel barked and scratched a paw against the door, his pint-size body vibrating with excitement.

"Sorry, buddy, you're going to have to wait. I took you out a half-hour ago and I don't plan to do the stairs again for a while."

Abel barked again. Chloe ignored him, choosing instead to stand and stretch tight, tense muscles. Her leg throbbed, her neck ached and she was sure she'd soon regret so many hours spent in one position, but right now all she felt was relief. She'd managed to search through sixteen files. All of them were cases that she'd been working on before the accident. Of those, four had caught and held her attention. Two were high-profile divorces, one involved tracing laundered funds and the last had required searching for evidence against a teacher who'd been accused of having a relationship with one of his students. In each case, Chloe'd been asked to retrieve information from the suspects' computers. Deleted e-mails, deleted files, things that most people assumed were gone could often still be found if one knew how to look. And Chloe definitely knew how to look.

She downed some cold coffee and limped back to her seat. Of the sixteen cases she'd been investigating, the ones that intrigued her were those she'd done the least amount of work on before the accident. Each of the four suspects had a lot to lose. A politician, a doctor, a respected business owner, a teacher with a wife and children. Any of them might have been desperate to keep his secrets hidden, but had one been desperate enough to commit murder? And if he had, what would cause him to keep coming after Chloe even after she'd dropped her investigation?

She didn't have answers to the questions, but at least she finally had questions. Until now, she'd been sliding closer and closer to believing she really was going crazy. Hopefully asking questions and seeking answers was the beginning of healing.

Abel barked again, jumping up against the door in what seemed like a desperate bid for escape.

"Am I that bad of company?"

A soft tap sounded on the wood and Abel tumbled backward, barking furiously and running for cover behind Chloe's legs.

"Some watchdog you are." Chloe scooped him up and strode toward the door. "Who's there?"

"Ben."

Ben? He wasn't supposed to be over until six. She glanced at the clock, realized that it was six and pulled open the door.

He looked as good as he had the night before, his sandy hair curling near his collar, his eyes blazing against his deeply tanned face. When he smiled, Chloe's heart melted into a puddle of yearning that she absolutely refused to acknowledge.

"Hi."

"Hi, yourself." He stepped into the living room, a cooler and brown paper bag in his arms, Cain nipping at the leash and tumbling along behind.

Ben glanced around the room, his gaze settling on the coffee table and the computer that sat there. Chloe had a notebook and pen lying next to it. A few crumbled sheets of paper were scattered on the table. One or two had dropped onto the floor. "Looks like you were working. Want to reschedule for another time?"

It would probably be for the best. Send Ben and his puppy on their way. Spend a few more hours doing research. Heat up a frozen meal and spend the rest of the evening alone. Those were safe and reasonable things to do. Unfortunately, Chloe didn't feel like being safe or reasonable. She felt like enjoying a couple of hours in the company of a man who demanded nothing more from her than conversation. "And miss out on a home-cooked meal? I don't think so."

"You don't usually do home cooked?"

"Only if heating things up in the microwave counts as home cooking."

Ben shook his head and smiled. "Not quite."

"I didn't think so. Opal says I'm culinary challenged. The fact is, I'm lazy. It seems like too much effort to cook a fancy meal for one."

"I'm with you on that. Cooking is much more fun when you're doing it for someone other than yourself." He stepped toward the kitchen, his tall, broad frame filling the room and stealing Chloe's breath.

She didn't understand it, didn't like it and was absolutely sure it could only mean trouble, but there was definitely something about Ben that drew her to him. His steadiness, his confidence, his faith, they were like blazing lights in what had become an ever-darkening world. When he was around, Chloe's anxiety and fear seemed to melt away; when he spoke, she could almost believe that everything was going to be okay.

It had been a long time since Chloe had felt that way around someone. Even before the accident she'd been self-reliant, depending on herself for the stability she craved. As much as she'd loved Adam, being with him had been more exciting than comforting, more stormy ocean than placid lake. They'd brought out the best in each other only when they weren't bringing out each others' worst. After he'd confessed to seeing another woman, Chloe finally acknowledged what she'd known all along—marrying him would send her right back into the chaotic life she'd worked so hard to escape.

"Are you okay?" Ben had moved back across the room and was standing in front of her, solid and warm. More real than nightmares or memories. More steady than Chloe's own rioting emotions.

"Fine. Just…" Confused? Scared? Guilty? All fit, but she wouldn't give them voice. "Sluggish. Sitting in front of the computer for too long does that to me."

He didn't believe her and she was sure he'd ask more questions, push for answers she wasn't sure she could give. Instead, he brushed her hair back from her face, hooking it behind her ears, his hands lingering on her shoulders, his thumbs resting against her collarbone. "I guess we'll have to do something about that."

To Chloe's horror an image flashed through her mind. Ben leaning close, his breath warm against her lips just before…

She shoved the thought away, her pulse accelerating, her cheeks heating as she stepped back. "What did you have in mind?"

"Nothing so horrible. Just a walk by the lake. I think the boys would enjoy it. I know I would."

A walk. She could do that. And she could do it without letting her mind wander back to very dangerous territory. "That sounds good. I've been cooped up inside most of the day. Besides quick trips outside for Abel, I've pretty much stayed put."

"Good. That's what Jake and I both want you to do."

"Did you two enjoy your fishing trip today?" Did you talk about me? Does Jake think I'm as crazy as the D.C. police seem to think I am? Those were the questions she wanted to ask, but didn't.

"It could have been better." Ben strode back into the kitchen, pulled open the drawer beneath Chloe's oven and grabbed a large frying pan.

"How so?"

"I could have caught a few edible fish." He pulled several plastic containers from the bag he'd carried in.

"You had to buy our dinner?"

"Worse." He opened the cooler and pulled out two large fish. "I had to trade for it."

"Trade?"

"Yeah. My babysitting services for Jake's fish."

"Babysitting for Jake's kids. Doesn't he have a baby and a toddler?" She was sure that was what Tiffany had said, but couldn't imagine Ben doing diaper duty.

"Yep. And unless Honor has been potty trained sometime in the past two days, they're both still in diapers." He pulled open a drawer, frowned, pulled open another one. "Knives?"

"To your right."

"Thanks. Here's the problem. I'm good at a few things. Cooking. Martial arts. Rock climbing. I'm even pretty decent at corralling teenagers. I'm not so good at others things. Like burping and changing babies, or playing baby doll with a two-year-old. I'm pretty confident I can handle one of the kids at a time, but double-duty might be beyond me."

"I'm sure you'll do just fine."

"I'm sure I'd do even better if I had another adult there with me."

"Very subtle, Ben."

"Subtlety is my middle name." He grinned, finished prepping the first fish and started on the second.

"And caution is mine. I might be willing to offer my help if I knew anything at all about kids, but I don't. Besides babysitting when I was a teenager, I haven't had much contact with the younger crowd."

"No little brothers or sisters in your life?"

"I was my mother's first and only mistake." The words slipped out and heat rose in Chloe's cheeks. Again.

"Sounds like your mother and mine were a lot alike."

"You said you had a sister."

"I do. My mother was too caught up in drugs and alcohol to keep her first mistake from repeating itself. Raven is younger than me. She and her husband live outside of town."

"I've always wanted a sister." Someone to share the aloneness with. Someone who would be the family connection Chloe had craved as a child and still sometimes yearned for.

"It was great. When she was little I actually did diaper duty, gave her baths, made sure she was fed."

"You were a lot older than her?"

"There's six years difference."

"That's…" Crazy. Sad. Horrifying.

"It is what it is. I took care of her the best I could until social services stepped in." He finished the second fish, opened up a shallow container and dipped both into a mixture of spices. "After that, we were separated. It took me years to find her again. And, actually, she was the one who found me.

Just showed up at the church one day. I've barely let her out of my sight since."

"That's a great story."

"It is." He grinned. "I never get tired of telling it. So, what do you say?"

"About?"

"Giving me a hand with Jake's kids."

"I doubt Jake would want me over at his place."

"Why wouldn't he?"

"I'm a walking danger zone."

"And his house is like Fort Knox. Locks. Alarms. You name it, he's got it."

"His wife—"

"You've met Tiffany. She's as laid-back as Jake is intense. She'll probably feel a lot more comfortable if there are two of us with the kids."

"She did seem pretty easygoing when I met her." But that didn't mean Chloe wanted to spend the evening watching her kids. Not when doing so meant she'd be spending another evening with Ben. Ben whose vivid gaze compelled her and whose laughter warmed the cold, hard knot of pain she'd been carrying around for months. Ben who could easily fill the empty place in her heart and who could just as easily break it.

"She is, but she's also a mama bear when it comes to her kids. I doubt she'll be able to enjoy her birthday dinner if she's worrying about whether or not I'll be able to handle Honor and Isaac on my own."

"Jake is taking her out for her birthday?"

"Yes. Does that make a difference?"

"Every woman deserves to be treated special on her birthday." Chloe's own birthdays were less than memorable. Her mother and grandmother hadn't wanted to acknowledge the infamous date of her birth. Most of her boyfriends had been too caught up in themselves to mark the day. Even Adam hadn't made much of it, his quick phone calls and hasty dinner arrangements making her feel more second-thought than special. Opal had sent cards and gifts, but she was the only one who'd ever cared enough to do so.

"Does that mean you'll help?" Ben laid the fish in the sizzling hot pain and a spicy aroma filled the air.

Chloe's stomach rumbled, reminding her that she hadn't eaten since breakfast and that her mind might be fuzzy from lack of food. Now was not a good time to make decisions. She knew it, but couldn't find the wherewithal to care. "I'll help if you get Jake and Tiffany's consent first."

"That goes without saying." He nodded toward the containers he'd set on the counter. "There's corn-bread batter in the yellow container. I'll get the oven preheated. If you oil a pan and pour the batter into it, we can get it started. I don't know about you, but I'm starving."

"I could definitely eat." A horse. A house. Anything large and filling.

Chloe followed Ben's instructions, then handed him the pan, her mouth watering as he slid it into the oven, a feeling of companionship and camaraderie washing over her. She and Adam had spent a lot of time together, but not all of it had been easy and comfortable. As a matter of fact, too much of that time had been spent arguing about his relationships with other women and Chloe's unwillingness to accept those friendships. She'd felt sure that innocent lunches and dinner would eventually turn into something less innocent. He'd insisted he loved her too much to be tempted by anyone else. In the end, Chloe's opinion regarding the matter had been proven accurate. That was cold comfort in the wake of all that had happened.

She ran her hand over already mussed hair and pulled plates

out of the cupboard, hoping to distract herself from thoughts of what had been. "Is there anything else I can do to help?"

"Grab the ice cream out of the bag and throw it in the freezer. I almost forgot about it."

"Forgot about ice cream? Is that even possible?"

"Chalk it up to last-minute changes in the menu and an ornery puppy who decided he didn't want to leave the house."

"Last-minute menu changes?"

"Opal called to ask me why I'd talked you into getting a puppy."

"I haven't spoken to her since yesterday afternoon. How could she possibly know about Abel?"

"The same way anyone in Lakeview knows anything. Rumor mill. Although I'm not sure if that's an accurate description since it was your landlady who called Opal with the information."

"I had a feeling I wouldn't get much privacy living in a house owned by Opal's friend." Chloe pulled forks, knives and spoons out of a drawer, grabbed napkins from the counter and finished setting the table. "So what did Opal's lecture about Abel have to do with last-minute menu plans?"

"I haven't figured that one out yet. One minute we were talking about dogs taking over Blooming Baskets and the next she was asking me what I planned to serve tonight." He grinned, flipping the fish and opening another plastic container. "I'd been planning to have fresh fruit for dessert, but Opal told me that wouldn't do. Apparently, you need chocolate and ice cream and lots of it."

"I guess I'll have to give her a call after you leave and tell her to stop meddling."

"Do you want her to stop meddling?" He opened the oven, peeked at the corn bread and closed it again, leaning a hip against the counter, his eyes meeting Chloe's and capturing her gaze.

"The truth? No. Every time Opal sticks her nose into my business, I realize how much she cares."

"I feel the same about my foster parents. Mom calls every Monday. Dad checks in by e-mail a couple times a week. It's good to know they're there even if their hints about marriage and children are getting old."

"They want you to get married again?"

"They want me to be happy. I think that's what all good parents want for their children." He pulled the bread out of the oven, turned off the burner and grabbed a plate. "Ready to eat?"

"It smells delicious."

"Hopefully it will be. Of course, if it's not, I'll just blame Jake for catching bad fish."

"You two are good friends."

"He moved here from D.C. a few years back. We've been like brothers ever since." He placed spice-crusted fish on her plate, spooned what looked like a three-bean salad from a container he pulled from the bag.

"He met Tiffany here?"

"Met her. Married her. Had a couple of kids."

"I'm surprised you haven't followed in his footsteps." The words slipped out and Chloe pressed her lips together. "Sorry, it's none of my business."

He shrugged, placed a plate in front of her. "I think a lot of people are surprised I haven't remarried, but what I had with Theresa was pretty special."

"What was she like?"

"Sweet. Soft-spoken. A little shy. Strong faith. Strong spirit. Really into homey things. Sewing. Cooking."

"She would have made a perfect pastor's wife."

"She would have, but that's not why I loved her." He sat down across from Chloe. "Unfortunately it's what just about every woman I've dated has been trying to be. I guess they all have the same idea about what it takes to be a pastor's wife."

"What's your idea?"

"My idea is that a pastor's wife should be whatever God calls her to be. Whether that means sewing, cooking, serving in church ministries, teaching. Computer forensics." He grinned, the humor in his eyes making the comment a joke rather than a promise. "We'd better eat before the puppies get restless. Do you mind if I ask the blessing?"

"Not at all."

Ben wrapped a hand around hers, his grip firm and strong as he offered a simple prayer of thanks.

This was what home should be. Not four walls and furniture, but companionship, friendship. Faith shared and expressed. The intimacy of the moment wrapped around Chloe's heart, holding it tight and promising something she shouldn't want, but did—more dinners, more quiet conversations, more Ben.

And that wasn't good at all.

As soon as Ben finished speaking, she tugged away from his hold, avoiding his deep blue gaze as she bit into the aromatic fish he'd prepared.

Ben's easy charm was nice, but there was no way she planned to fall for it. Her life was too complicated, her worries too real to waste energy and emotion on a relationship that was destined to fail the same way her other relationships had.

But what if it wasn't?

The question whispered through her mind, tempting her to believe in impossibilities, happily-ever-afters and a hundred dreams she'd buried with Adam and his betrayal.

But happily-ever-afters and dreams were for people who hadn't been deceived, people who still believed in love and all that it meant.

Chloe wasn't one of them.

Chapter Fourteen

They went for a walk after dinner, the two puppies tumbling along on leashes, the soft rustle of grass and the gentle lap of water against the shore filling the night. The waning moon cast a silvery glow across the dry grass, giving the world an ethereal beauty Chloe tried hard to appreciate. Tried. Despite Ben's presence, she didn't like being out after dark, the open space, the hulking trees and shadowy bushes taking on forms and faces that she was half convinced were real.

"Cold?"

She hadn't realized she was shivering until Ben spoke. At his words, she pulled her jacket closed, knowing it was fear and not the cold that had her shaking. "Maybe a little."

"Here." He shrugged off his jacket, draped it over her shoulders, the masculine outdoorsy scent of it surrounding Chloe.

"Now you're going to be cold."

"Not even close. My foster parents loved camping. They used to take us kids into the mountains every fall. That was cold. Compared to it, tonight is downright balmy." He wrapped a hand around her elbow, leading her along a sparsely covered patch of lawn, the rocks and soil treacherous under Chloe's unsteady gait.

"I've never been camping."

"Our church sponsors a youth camping trip every spring. You can sign up as chaperone and see what it's like."

"It sounds like fun, but spring is months away. Anything could happen before then."

"You think you'll move back to D.C.?"

"No, but I may not be able to stay here much longer."

"I know you're not asking for my opinion."

"But you'll give it anyway?"

He chuckled, the sound filling the night. "Something like that."

"Then I guess I'll ask. What's your opinion?"

"Trouble has a way of following us no matter how far we run from it. If we're going to have to face it anyway, we may as well face it with people who care about us."

"Maybe, but the trouble that's following me is dangerous. Not just to me, but to everyone around me. I couldn't live with myself if something happened to Opal because of me. I'd feel the same way if something happened to you, Tiffany or Jake."

"You're making our welfare your responsibility, but we can all take care of ourselves."

"That's what I thought about Adam and look what happened to him." An image filled her mind—fire, hot metal, Adam, blood seeping from his head and dripping onto the white shirt he wore.

"What happened to Adam had nothing to do with whether or not he could take care of himself. What Jackson did was unexpected. Something no one could have known to be prepared for. We're in a completely different situation now. We know there's potential danger and we're prepared for it."

"Forewarned is forearmed?"

"Exactly."

"It's not good enough, Ben. Until we find the person who's been stalking me, no one will be safe."

"Jake is working hard to find the answers we need." He turned her back toward the house. "I saw that you were working on your computer when I arrived. Dig anything up?"

"Not as much as I would have liked. I decided to look back over the cases I was working on before the accident. It's possible I've got information that I don't know I have. Something that a person might be willing to commit murder over to keep quiet."

"Maybe."

"But?"

"Someone has spent an awful lot of time trying to make it look like you're having a breakdown. I wonder why."

"Revenge?"

"That's the obvious reason, but usually acts of revenge are brutal and quick. This seems more like slow, malicious torture."

"I can't think of anyone who'd want to torture me. My clients and business acquaintances don't know me well enough to care. My friends have only been friends since I moved to D.C."

"How long ago was that?"

"Six years."

"Where were you before?"

"Chicago. I've got a few friends there that I still keep in touch with, but I can't imagine any of them wanting to harm me."

"Maybe not, but the way I see it, what's going on is really personal, more personal than just wanting to keep you out of an investigation. Maybe even more personal than wanting to pay you back for a perceived wrong. If that's true, someone you know is doing this to you."

"If someone in my life hated me that much, wouldn't I know it?"

"Not necessarily." They'd reached the porch and Ben gestured to the swing. "Want to sit for a minute?"

"If I sit, I might not be able to get back up. My leg's been giving me trouble today." Not to mention the fact that she'd had about all she could take of the darkness. Having Ben around might offer some sense of security, but a warning was crawling up her spine. Outside was not where she should be and the quicker she got back into the apartment the happier she'd be.

"Too bad, but it's probably for the best. I've got to get home. I've got a sermon to deliver in the morning. I'll walk you up to your apartment and then head out." He lifted Cain, who was racing back and forth across the porch, and pushed open the front door.

"What's your sermon about?"

"If I told you that, you'd have no reason to come hear it."

"Who said I was thinking about coming?"

"You probably weren't, but I bet you are now."

Chloe laughed. "As a matter of fact, I am."

"Good. Keep thinking about it and I'll be looking for you tomorrow." He laced his fingers through hers and led her up the stairs, waiting while she closed and locked the door.

She could hear his retreating footsteps as she collapsed into the easy chair. Hanging out with Ben had been fun, almost exhilarating, but it had done nothing to solve her problems. What it had done was give her something to think about. For the past few months she'd waffled between believing a member of The Strangers was after her and believing she was coming unhinged. It hadn't occurred to her that something completely different might be going on. Her injuries, her grief, her surgeries had consumed her life and left no room for much more than reaction to the circumstances she'd found herself in.

It was time to change that. To act instead of react. To start using her skills to find the answers she needed—who? Why?

She grabbed her laptop, pulled the comforter off her bed and settled back into the chair, flicking on the television and letting background noise fade as she began searching through her files once again. This time, though, she also reread e-mails from friends and co-workers, searching for something that would point her in the right direction and praying that she'd know it if she saw it.

Fire. Heat. The screaming sound of sirens. Her own frantic cries for help choking and gasping out as she reached for Adam's hand. Get out. We need to get out! The words shrieked through her mind, but she couldn't get the door open, couldn't find her way out of the smoke and flames. She banged her fist against the window and saw the shadow, leaning close, staring in at her, eyes glowing like the flames—red and filled with hate. She screamed, turning toward Adam, wanting desperately to wake him, to get them both out alive. But Adam wasn't there. Instead, she saw sandy hair, broad shoulders, a strong face covered with blood. Blue eyes wide and lifeless.

Ben.

Chloe screamed again, lunging up, fighting against the seat belt and her pain. No. Not a seat belt. A blanket. Not a car. An easy chair. Not the past. The present.

She took a deep, steadying breath and lifted Abel, who sat whining on the floor. He felt warm and solid, his furry body comforting as Chloe stood and paced across the room. Seeing Ben in the nightmare had made it that much more terrifying, the new twist on the old dream filling her with dread.

"I need this to be over. Not tomorrow. Not the next day.

Now. Before anyone else is hurt." The words were a prayer and a plea. One Chloe could only hope God heard and would answer. Anything else didn't bear thinking about.

She glanced at the clock. Four a.m. Too early to leave the house. Too late to try to get more sleep. She scratched the puppy under his chin and set him down on the floor. "How about a snack? Then we can do some more work on the computer."

Not that the hours she'd spent the previous night had revealed much. As far as she was concerned, she'd hit a dead end. She'd have to either find a way around it or take a different path.

"One that isn't as clearly connected to me. Maybe not a friend or a co-worker of mine. Maybe someone who…" What? Chloe shook her head, uncovered the plastic container of brownies Ben had left the previous night.

"I don't know who's after me, Abel, but I can tell you this— Ben's brownies are almost good enough to make me forget my worries for a while."

Almost, but not quite.

Chloe bit into the thick chocolate, poured a glass of milk, and sat down at her computer desk. Instead of logging on, she grabbed a pencil and piece of paper. Ben had given her a new possibility to consider. Were there others? Jackson was in jail, The Strangers weren't after her, she couldn't find any evidence that one of her friends or co-workers had an axe to grind with her. What else was there? Who else was there?

Adam's friends? His co-workers?

He'd been acting odd in the month before they broke up. After he'd confessed to seeing someone else, Chloe had chalked his behavior up to guilt and stress. Could something else have caused it?

She jotted a note down on the paper, wishing she could pick up the phone and call Ben, discuss the idea with him.

"Scratch that thought. I don't need to call Ben. I don't need to discuss my idea with him. I've got you to talk to, buddy." She bent down to stroke Abel's soft fur. "And a plate of brownies to devour."

But brownies were a poor substitute for human company and conversation, and Chloe figured she'd trade a brownie or two for someone willing to listen to her at this time of the morning.

She sighed, pacing across the floor, pulling back the curtains on the balcony door. The darkness beyond the window was complete, the moon already set, the stars hidden behind thick clouds. Soon it would be dawn, but until then, Chloe was alone, waiting for the darkness to disappear and for the bright light of day to pull her completely out of the nightmare.

Chapter Fifteen

It had been weeks since Chloe had been to church and she almost decided to skip it again, her throbbing head and aching leg protesting the hours spent in front of the computer. Only the thought of having to explain her absence to Opal got her in the shower, dressed and out the door. The church parking lot was nearly full when she arrived, the sanctuary buzzing with people as she moved down the aisle and found a seat near the back. Maybe if she was lucky, she'd go unnoticed, though based on the number of people who were looking her way, she doubted it.

"I thought that was your beat-up old Mustang in the parking lot. You should have called me. We could have ridden here together." Opal slid into the pew beside Chloe, hair bouncing around her square face, her dark gaze shrewd. "Everything go okay last night? You look a little pale."

"It was fine."

"Fine? You spent the evening with one of Lakeview's most

eligible bachelors and all you can manage to say is that it was fine?"

"The food was wonderful."

"And the company?"

"Wonderful, too."

"I knew it."

"Knew what?"

"That you and Ben would hit it off. Now, tell me why you're so pale."

"I didn't sleep well."

"Because?"

"My leg's been bothering me." That was as much of the truth as she was prepared to give.

"You've got an appointment with the doctor this week, right?"

"Yes."

"Well, make sure you tell him how much trouble you're having. I don't like the way you've been limping around."

"I fractured my femur and crushed my knee, Opal. The pain from that isn't going to go away."

"I know, but I still don't like it." She sighed, her flowery perfume nearly choking Chloe as she leaned close and patted her hand. "I'm glad you're here this morning. I didn't think any of my children would settle close to home. I'm glad one finally had the good sense to move back."

"Really? One of the girls is planning to move here?" Chloe couldn't help hoping that Opal's third daughter Anna was the one who would be returning. Five years older than Chloe, she'd been a good role model and friend when they were kids.

"I'm talking about you." Opal huffed the words, her disgust obvious. "That you didn't realize that wounds me deeply, Chloe."

"Wounds you deeply? I think we're heading for a guilt trip. Which means you want something from me."

Opal chuckled, her hand wrapping around Chloe's, the skin, once smooth and pale, now wrinkled and spotted with age. Still, her grip was firm, her eyes bright. "You know me too well, my dear. I do have a favor to ask."

"Do you need me to open the store for you tomorrow?"

"No, nothing like that. I've decided to go..." she glanced around, her broad, strong face flushing pink "...on the senior singles trip."

"Senior singles trip?"

"To Richmond for a few days of shopping and fun. Our Sunday school has been planning the trip for a while. I figure since I had to cut my visit with Elizabeth short when Jenna went into labor, I deserve a few days off."

"It sounds like fun."

"It will be, but I'll be gone Thursday through Sunday. Mary Alice is going to work full time those days. Between you, her and Laura we should be okay."

"So what do you need me to do?"

"Can you bring my mail in the house and check on Checkers?"

"Checkers does not need to be checked on. He can fend for himself just fine."

"Checkers is a sweet cat once you get to know him. He just needs a lot of love."

"And a pound of flesh." Chloe had been to Opal's house one time since her return to Lakeview and during the visit she'd been attacked by a very fat, very grumpy black-and-white cat.

"He barely touched you, Chloe. I'd think a young woman whose rearing I had a hand in would be too tough to complain about a tiny little scratch." Opal turned her attention to the pulpit and the choir that was filling the loft.

"It was more than a scratch, but I'll take care of Checkers anyway."

"Maybe I did raise you right after all." Opal smiled. "Just remember, Checkers is sweet, but he's finicky. He likes his dinner served at six o'clock on the dot. No sooner. No later."

Six o'clock in November meant being out past sundown. The thought filled Chloe with trepidation and she wiped a damp palm against her black skirt. "It might be better if I feed him in the afternoon. Maybe during my lunch break."

"The last time I went away Anna was in town. She put Checker's food in the bowl in the morning and he refused to touch it. I'd hate to think of him going hungry for four days."

Chloe sighed. "All right. I'll feed him at six. Was there something else you needed me to do?"

"I need to go shopping and I need a fashion expert to come with me."

"Fashion expert? For a trip to Richmond?"

"I've got a date Friday night." Opal's cheeks went pink again and Chloe couldn't help smiling.

"A date with Sam?"

"If it's any of your business, yes."

"Good for you, Opal."

"So you'll come shopping?"

"I'm not a fashion expert."

"You're the closest thing I've got. What do you say? It'll only be for a few hours tomorrow night."

"What time?"

"As soon as we close the store."

"Sounds good." It would sound better if they were going during the day, but Chloe didn't have the heart to say no.

"Wonderful. We'll have dinner, spend a few hours clothes shopping, and—" Before she could complete the thought the call to worship began and the before-church chatter ceased.

That worked for Chloe.

The noisy prattle of the sanctuary had done nothing to ease her pounding headache or offer her relief from the tension she'd been feeling all morning. She'd come hoping to find some small sense of peace. All she'd found were more worries. The thought of taking care of Checkers, of driving to Opal's house at night, filled her with a sick dread. Going shopping after dark didn't make her any happier. The fact that either bothered her only made Chloe even more conscious of just how much her life had changed in the past eleven months.

The music faded and Ben strode to the pulpit, his long legs and broad shoulders showcased to perfection in a dark suit and light blue shirt. His words were strong, but not dramatic as he welcomed the congregation, prayed, then stepped aside so that the music minister could lead the first song. Chloe knew her attention should be on the man leading the music, but instead it was drawn to Ben again and again. His smile seemed to encompass the room, his eyes even more vivid in the bright light that streamed in through tall windows.

He scanned the sanctuary, his gaze traveling the room. There was no way he could see Chloe in the midst of the crowd, but somehow he found her, his eyes meeting hers, his lips quirking in a half smile that made her treacherous heart dance a jig.

"Are you going to sing, or just stand there gawking at Ben?" Opal elbowed Chloe in the side, her quiet hiss forcing Chloe's attention away from the man who'd been taking up too many of her thoughts during the past few days.

"I wasn't gawking." She'd been looking. Maybe even staring. But she hadn't been gawking.

"Good to know. Now sing before someone notices that you're not. I don't want to spend the entire ride to Richmond answering questions about your disinterest in music."

"No one's noticing, Opal."

"Everyone's noticing. Now, sing."

Chloe managed to do as Opal suggested without glancing at Ben again. By the time he stood up to deliver the sermon, the tension and anxiety that had accompanied her through the long predawn hours had finally eased, the familiar hymns and sweet sounds of voices joining in praise accomplishing what no amount of alone-time could.

When Ben finally spoke, his words about faith in the midst of crisis spoke to her soul, the message echoing the quiet yearning that had brought her back to her Bible again and again over the past few days. She might not understand God's plan or His will, but she had to trust that He would work His best in her life.

The sermon ended and Chloe stood for the final hymn, the quick movement making her lightheaded. She grabbed the front of the pew, holding herself steady as she tried to blink the darkness from the edges of her vision.

"Are you okay? You've gone white as a sheet." Opal touched her arm, true concern etching lines around her eyes and mouth.

"Fine. I just stood up too quickly."

Opal's lips tightened and she shook her head. "A little dizzy? Sit down. Put your head between your knees."

"That won't be necessary. I'm completely recovered."

"Are you sure? Maybe I should drive you home."

"And then have to come pick me up for work tomorrow? I don't think so."

"Chloe—"

"Opal, I'm fine. I promise."

Opal looked like she wanted to argue, but raising four kids must have taught her when to fight and when to let go. "All right, but if you get out to your car and change your mind let me know."

"I will."

"I'll call you this evening to finalize plans for my trip to Richmond."

"To check up on me, you mean."

"That, too. Now, I'd better go see if I can find Sam so I can let him know I'm definitely going on the trip." She leaned over and kissed Chloe's cheek. "Be good, my dear. And be careful."

"I will be."

Opal merged into the crowd that was exiting the sanctuary while Chloe held back, waiting until the room emptied and just a few clusters of people remained. When she was sure her limping progress wouldn't block anyone's exit, she stepped out into the aisle and headed to door.

"Chloe, I was hoping I'd see you here." Brian McMath stepped up beside her, his slim, runner's frame dressed to perfection in a dark suit and staid tie.

"Brian. It's good to see you again." And would remain good as long as he didn't mention her scars again.

"I'm glad you feel that way. I've been thinking about the conversation we had the other day and I wanted to apologize if I came on too strong. I hope my interest in your scars and the medical treatment of them didn't make you uncomfortable." Coming from another doctor, the words might have sounded sincere. Coming from Brian McMath, they sounded phony and well-practiced.

"I appreciate your apology."

"Good. Then maybe you'll let me make things up to you. How about having lunch with me?" They stepped out of the sanctuary and headed toward the exit.

"I'm sorry, I can't."

"You have plans?"

"Yes." She planned to take Abel for a walk. Maybe take a nap.

"With Opal?"

Obviously, Brian wasn't going to give up. Chloe was about to tell him exactly what she had planned and why she wasn't going to disrupt those plans for him, when they stepped out into watery light and she saw Ben.

He looked great standing on the church steps, his hair curling around his collar, his relaxed confidence appealing. He must have sensed her gaze because he looked up, his half smile becoming a full-out grin as she approached.

"I thought I saw you sitting beside Opal. I'm glad you came." His hand was warm as he clasped it around hers, pulling her a step closer, his gaze settling on Brian. "I'm glad you're here, too, Brian. I hear things were hectic at the hospital this weekend. I thought maybe you'd be caught up in a case there."

"I don't believe in working on Sunday, pastor. I'm sure you know me well enough to know that."

"I'm sure I do." Ben smiled again, but Chloe had the distinct impression he didn't really care for the doctor or his comments.

Brian nodded, then turned to Chloe. "Since we're not going to be able to have lunch today, I'm going to take off. Maybe I'll see you at the quilting circle this Wednesday." He strode away before Chloe could comment and she wasn't sorry to see him leave.

"You're smiling. I guess that means you're glad to see him go."

"He's a little overwhelming."

"Good choice of words. So, maybe since you're not having lunch with Brian, you'd like to come over to my place and have lunch with me."

"Abel won't be happy if I leave him home alone much longer."

"You can bring him over."

"I don't want to put you out." She also didn't want to say no. No matter how much she knew she should.

"I've got beef stew and homemade rolls already made. More than enough for two people."

She really should refuse. Chloe knew it. But even as she was telling herself that she should stay away from Ben she was opening her mouth to agree. "Beef stew and rolls sound good. I can bring what's left of the brownies over for dessert."

"Sounds good. I'll meet you over at my place in fifteen minutes or so."

"See you then." Chloe limped down the steps and got in her car, sure that she was making a mistake. Allowing Ben into her life was dangerous for both of them. Chloe had already had her heart broken once, she had no intention of letting it happen again. But what bothered her more than thoughts of heartbreak was the dream—the image of Ben broken and lifeless in the front seat of a burning car.

Just thinking about it made her shudder. Sure Ben could take care of himself. Sure he was capable and strong, but Adam had been, too, and despite what Ben had said the previous night, Chloe couldn't help worrying.

She stepped out of the car and started up the porch steps, a flash of movement to the left catching her attention. She turned, her pulse leaping, her heart racing. She wasn't sure what she expected to see, but the small ball of fluff that was rushing toward her wasn't it. "Abel?"

She scooped the puppy up into her arms, fear burning a path down her throat and settling deep in her stomach. "How'd you get out here?"

She asked, but she really didn't want to know, didn't want to imagine someone opening her apartment door while she was gone, didn't want to think that someone might still be there. Instead, she stumbled back toward her car, locked herself inside, hesitating with her hand on the phone. She hadn't crated Abel before she'd left. Was it possible he'd snuck out the door while she was leaving? Slipped down the stairs and out the door without her notice?

Maybe.

Or maybe someone had broken into her apartment and inadvertently let him out. She could call the police. She could go see if her apartment door was open.

She could sit here all day trying to decide what to do.

She rubbed the puppy's fur, wishing she didn't have so much doubt in her ability to know real danger from imagined. She didn't want to call the police and look like a fool. She didn't want to not call if something was really going on. Abel growled a deep warning that made the hair on the back of Chloe's neck stand on end. She scanned the driveway, the yard, the trees. The porch.

She froze, watching in horror as the door she'd left closed slowly began to open.

Chapter Sixteen

Ben hadn't planned on inviting Chloe to lunch. Then again, he hadn't planned on seeing her at church. When he'd glanced around the sanctuary and caught sight of her, the jolt of awareness he'd felt was an unexpected surprise.

"I don't know what your plans are, Lord, but I sure would like to. Chloe's not the kind of woman I can be just friends with. If that's all You've got planned for us, I'm not sure I'm up for the task."

Cain barked, his feet slipping on tile as he raced through the kitchen and parked himself in front of the front door.

"Are they here?" Ben strode across the room and nudged Cain out of the way as a soft tap sounded on the wood. "Hi…"

The greeting died on his lips as he caught sight of Chloe, her face white, the few freckles that dusted the bridge of her nose standing out in sharp contrast.

He pulled her into the house, his hands skimming down thin arms and coming to rest on her waist. She was shaking, her breath coming in short, quick gasps. "Hey, are you okay?"

"Yes. No." A tear rolled down her cheek, and she swiped it away, the gesture abrupt and filled with irritation.

"What's wrong?"

"Everything." She sniffed back more tears, pacing across the room, her limp pronounced, her posture stiff.

"That covers a lot of bases, Chloe."

"It does, doesn't it?"

"What happened?" He urged her around to face him. Her eyes were deep emerald and filled with stark emotion. Anger. Frustration. Not the fear or sadness he'd expected to see.

"Just one more piece of evidence proving that I'm as unhinged as the D.C. police think."

"No one thinks you're unhinged."

"No, they just believe my imagination is working overtime. The worst part is, they're right."

"You've got a reason for saying that. Why don't you tell me?"

"Abel was outside when I got home from church. I hadn't left him out there."

Ben's hand tightened on Chloe's shoulder and he had to force his grip to ease. "Did you call Jake?"

"I was going to. I got in my car and grabbed the phone, but my downstairs neighbor came out before I made the call. I guess Abel was hanging out in the foyer. Connor thought he was a stray and put him outside. He was very apologetic."

She paused, a smile chasing away some of her irritation. "The fact that I was having a panic attack when he came outside sent him into fits of remorse. He wanted to call an ambulance, but I told him I'd be fine once I stopped hyperventilating."

She was making light of the situation, but Ben knew it had bothered her a lot more than she was saying. "I'm sure he'll get over the trauma eventually. Did you ever call Jake?"

"So he could come and tell me that Abel slipped out of the house while I was leaving?" She raked a hand through her hair and shook her head. "No way. I've been through that kind of embarrassment one too many times."

"I think it's better to be a little embarrassed than a lot dead." The words were harsher than he'd meant them and Chloe stiffened, the color that had slowly returned to her face gone again.

"Connor went up to the apartment with me. It was locked up tight. No sign that anyone had been there. Nothing out of the ordinary."

"That's how your apartment was when we found the photos on your digital camera and how it was when you overdosed on pain medication you've said you didn't take." His words were hard, ground out through gritted teeth and frustration. Chloe was a intelligent, strong woman. The fact that she seemed to want to believe that she was imagining things was something he couldn't understand.

"But this time nothing happened. No weird photos. No missing medicine."

"How do you know, Chloe? Did you check every container in your refrigerator? Make sure the furnace hadn't been tampered with? We need to call Jake and let him do what he does best—look for evidence."

"And when he finds nothing, I'll be right back where I started—struggling to figure out what's going on while everyone around me insists that nothing is."

"You'll never be back where you started." He smoothed the bangs out of her eyes, silky strands of hair catching on his rough palms. "You have people here who believe in you. That's not going to change."

"Won't it? What if this stuff goes on for a month? Two months? Don't you think Jake is going to get a little tired of running to my rescue when there's nothing to rescue me from?"

"There's something to rescue you from, Chloe. Just because we don't know what that is yet, doesn't mean it isn't real. Jake knows that. I know that. Neither of us are going to give up until we find the person responsible for everything that's happened to you."

She smiled, moving away from his touch, her hair sliding over his knuckles, the dark strands falling over her shoulders and covering the scars on her neck. What she'd been through couldn't be hidden, though. It lived in her eyes and her voice. "I think I know that, but I still don't want to go through the same thing I went through in D.C., feeling sure something terrible was going to happen only to have the police prove me wrong every time."

"They didn't prove you wrong. They just never proved you right. That's what we're going to do and the first step is letting Jake take a look at your apartment."

"He can look, but you're the one who's going to take responsibility if he decides it was a big waste of his time."

"Jake's philosophy is better safe than sorry. I feel the same." Ben picked up the phone and dialed Jake's home number, antsy to get things moving. No way did he believe Chloe had let Abel out of the apartment without realizing it. If she hadn't let the puppy out, someone else had. The sooner they discovered what that person had been doing in her apartment, the better Ben would feel.

"Reed here."

"Jake, it's Ben."

"What's up?"

"We've got a situation. I thought you might like to check it out."

"Tell me."

Ben gave Jake the details, knowing his friend would be as anxious to find out what was going on as he was.

"I'll be at your house in fifteen minutes. If Chloe gives me the key, I can go back to her apartment and check things out."

"Thanks."

"What did he say?" Chloe leaned against the wall, her posture deceptively relaxed, the anxiety she'd managed to harness showing only in her white-knuckled fists.

"He'll be here in fifteen minutes to get your keys. He wants to check things out."

"There won't be any evidence to lead him in the right direction. There never is."

"This time might be different."

"Or it might be the same as every other time." She smiled, but the frustration in her eyes was unmistakable. "I'm ready for the nightmare to be over, but no matter how hard I look, I can't see any ending to it."

"There's an ending to it. It may take time, but we'll find it." Ben pulled her forward, wrapping his arms around her waist. She leaned her head against his chest, her hair tickling his chin, a subtle floral scent drifting on the air. He wanted to inhale deeply, take it into his lungs and savor it. Memorize it so that in five years, ten, twenty, he'd remember standing in his house with Chloe, staring out over the parsonage yard, realizing...

What?

That it felt right, good, permanent. That there was going to be much more to their relationship than either of them expected or even wanted.

He shoved aside the thought, but didn't move away from Chloe. Partly because holding her did feel right, partly because she seemed to need his support.

Her hands rested on his waist, her body not stiff, but not

relaxed, either. As if she didn't want to allow herself to get too close. And maybe she didn't. She'd been through a lot with Adam. Keeping her distance might be the only way she felt she could keep her heart intact.

"You're right about it taking time to find the answers, Ben." She spoke quietly, lifting her head so that she could meet his gaze, her eyes the color of spring's promise, but filled with the starkness of winter. "That's exactly what I'm worried about. Time. I think it's running out."

He wished he could tell her she was wrong, but he felt the same way. Time wasn't on their side and the longer it took for them to track down Chloe's stalker, the more likely it was that that person would act again. Maybe next time with more serious results. "God is in control, not the person who's stalking you. It's His timing, His will that's going to be done. We can take comfort in that."

"Maybe so, but right now it seems like a cold comfort." She frowned, stepped out of his arms. "I've been a Christian since I was fifteen. I know God will work things out in His time and His way. I just wish I knew what that meant for my life."

"I think that's the hardest thing about faith, Chloe. Trusting the driver even when we can't clearly see the road He's taking us on."

"Oh, I can see the road all right. It's covered with ice and has a hundred-foot drop on either side."

Ben chuckled, smoothing his hands over Chloe's silky hair, framing her face with his palms. "If God's the driver, you don't have to worry about going over the edge."

"Maybe that's the problem. Maybe I've been doing most of the driving these past few years."

"If that's the case, you'd better take it slow and drive carefully."

"You're not going to tell me I should get out of the driver's seat?" She raised a dark eyebrow, the smile that curved her lips softening the sharp line of her jaw.

"I didn't think you'd want to hear me say something you already know."

"I do know it, but doing it isn't always as easy as it should be. I like plans. I like purpose. I like to know where I'm headed." She turned to stare out the window, her gaze fixed on some distant point. A thought. A memory. Something sad and ugly from the look in her eyes.

He wrapped an arm around her waist, tugging her back against his chest, wanting to offer comfort, but not sure that words could touch the hurt that Chloe tried so hard to hide. "There is a plan, you know. And a purpose. Whether you see it or not."

She nodded, her hair brushing against his chin, the silky strands reminding him of long-ago days, of femininity and softness, sweet smiles and gentle laughter. It had been a long time since he'd had any of those things in his life. Today, with Chloe in his arms and the gray-gold beauty of autumn outside the window, he missed them more than he had since the first days following Theresa's death.

That meant something and he couldn't ignore it. If there was one thing he'd learned from watching Theresa live, watching her die, it was that life was too short to waste time, to make excuses, to turn away from what God willed and wanted. His wife had embraced every challenge, every problem with open arms and an open heart. She hadn't let fear stop her, hadn't let her disease keep her from the things she felt called to do. Her example had set the course for much of Ben's life in the years since he'd buried her.

And it would set his course now.

If this was what God had planned for his life, if Chloe was, he wouldn't turn his back on it.

His arm tightened a fraction on her waist and he pulled her a little closer. One way or another, he had a feeling that with Chloe things were going to get a whole lot worse before they got better.

Chapter Seventeen

Jake arrived less than fifteen minutes after Ben called him, his face set in hard lines, his long legs eating up the ground as he paced Ben's living room. He didn't look happy and Chloe figured that could only mean bad news.

"I just got a call from a friend on the Arlington police force. He heard I was checking into your case and thought I might be interested in knowing that your fiancé had filed a crime report a few months before he was killed. Did you know that?"

"Yes. It didn't seem like a big deal at the time. Someone broke into his apartment, took a watch, a tie and cuff links. A few dollar bills he'd left lying on his dresser."

"It didn't seem like a big deal at the time, but now it does?"

"I was thinking about things last night. Ben had asked me if I'd felt stalked before the accident. The weeks leading up to it are blurry, but I don't recall anything strange happening. To me."

"But things were happening to Adam?" Jake pulled his notebook out, started writing. "What besides the break-in?"

"What are you thinking, Jake?" Ben lounged near the door, his shoulder against the wall, his thick hair mussed.

"I'm thinking there may be a connection between the break-in and the accident. I'm thinking that maybe Adam is that connection. That he was the intended victim, not Chloe."

"I wondered that, too, but why try to kill Adam by sabotaging my car?"

"Good question. I don't have an answer yet, but I plan to find one." Jake paced back across the room, paused in front of Chloe, his dark blue eyes staring into hers. "Do you have any ideas? Anything that didn't seem important at the time, but that seems like it might be connected now."

"Yes."

"You answered pretty quickly."

"Like I said, I was thinking about it last night. I planned to call you tomorrow."

"You should have called me this morning."

"What's done is done, Jake. Let's move on from here." Ben seemed completely at ease, but Chloe sensed a tension in him that belied his relaxed posture.

"Good point." Jake's sharp gaze was still on Chloe "So, tell me what you thought of last night."

"Not much, just some little things that didn't seem related when I looked at them separately. Once I started connecting the dots, they seemed to make a cohesive picture."

"Go ahead."

"A week or so before we broke up, Adam had his cell phone and home phone number changed. He said he was getting too many crank calls."

"Did you ask him what he meant?"

"Yes. He didn't give me a lot of details. Just said he was getting a lot of hang ups during the day and in the middle of the night. Once he had the number changed everything seemed fine."

She hesitated, then continued. "After I found out he'd been seeing someone else, I figured the calls had been from his girlfriend and put the issue out of my mind."

"Anything else?"

"Nothing definitive. Just a sense I had that something was wrong. In the months before we broke up, even in the weeks after, Adam didn't seem himself."

"He was seeing another woman and hiding it from you. Once you did find out, you broke up with him. I think that's a good reason to not be himself."

"That's what I thought, but Adam didn't believe in dwelling on things. Whether it was his mistake or someone else's, he was always quick to forgive and move on. Maybe I'm wrong, but when I think back, it seems like he was worried. Maybe even scared. And that wasn't like Adam at all."

"Looking backward at something doesn't often give us a clear picture." But as he spoke, Jake was scribbling in his notebook.

"Maybe not, but I've struggled to think of a reason someone would want to hurt me. If the stalker is after me because of The Strangers case, why the slow torture? Why not just do what Jackson did and get it over with quickly? If he's trying to keep me from discovering information hidden in one of the computers I was working on before the accident, he succeeded. I quit my job. Moved away. Why keep coming after me and risk being found out?

"You're making good points."

"They're Ben's not mine, but they make sense."

"They do and they're leading in the direction I've been thinking this case was going—if we're going to find your stalker we need to start looking at people who knew your fi-

ancé, who were close to him, who might have had something
to gain from his death and yours."

"Everyone loved Adam. I can't imagine someone wanting
to hurt him."

"Someone did hurt him. It's time to find out who. When
I get back to the office, I'm going to call and see if any evidence was collected from Adam's apartment after the break-
in, and I'm going to see if I can get copies of phone records
for his two old numbers. Maybe we'll find a pattern of calls,
match a number and name to it. You make a list of Adam's
friends and co-workers. And see if you can track down the
name of the woman he was seeing."

"His business partner might be able to tell me. James and
Adam went to high school together. They were like brothers."

"Then that's where you should start. I'm going to head over
to your apartment and do the preliminary walk-through. You
can meet me there in a half hour and we'll go through the
place together."

He stepped out the door and drove away, leaving Chloe
alone with Ben again. She wasn't sure how she felt about that.
In the moments before Jake had arrived, she'd stood with Ben's
arm wrapped around her waist, his breath ruffling her hair, the
comfort of his presence making her want to lean back against
his chest, accept his support. His strength.

She hadn't, but that was more a matter of timing than
willpower. If Jake hadn't arrived and broken the silence that
seemed filled with dreams and hopes, Chloe might have caved
in to temptation, allowed herself to lean on Ben for a just a
little while.

And that would have been a disaster. A little while with
Ben could never be enough.

"Did you love him?" Ben's question pulled Chloe from

her thoughts and she met his eyes, saw sympathy and concern in his gaze.

Had she loved Adam?

For a while she'd thought so, his attentiveness, humor and gregarious personality a perfect foil for her own more serious nature. Things had changed though, the excitement of new love fading. Or maybe the relationship hadn't changed as much as Chloe's perception of it had. She'd wanted to be first, not second, a necessity rather than an extra, a vital part of Adam's life rather than one more person to spend time with. She wanted so much more than what Adam wanted to give.

"I thought I did, but I don't think I knew what love really was."

"And you do now?"

"Now I know what it isn't."

"What's that?"

"Physical attraction, a sudden thrill of emotion when you see the person walk into the room." She shrugged. "In the end, I wanted more than that. Loyalty. Friendship. Shared goals and dreams. Maybe I wanted too much."

"I don't think you wanted any more than what you deserve." Ben was standing so close Chloe could see the flecks of silver in his eyes, could smell the woodsy fragrance that clung to him, feel the heat of his body warming the air around her.

She stepped back, swallowing past her suddenly dry throat. Everything she'd wanted from Adam, everything he couldn't give, she could see in Ben's eyes.

That wasn't good. At all.

She started toward the front door, wanting to put distance between them. "It must be time to go over to my house now."

"Why? Am I making you uncomfortable?"

"Not at all."

He grinned, a slow deliberate curving of his lips, his eyes

flashing with humor. "Could have fooled me. But you're right, we'd better get going. Grab your pup. I'll grab mine and we'll head out."

"You don't have to come."

"Is that the same as, 'I don't want you to come'?"

She wanted to say yes, but couldn't get the word past her lips. How could it be that in just over a week of knowing the man, he'd become such a big part of her life? She shook her head, lifting Abel and carrying him toward the door. "No. It's the same as 'You don't have to come.'"

He smiled, looped an arm through hers. "In that case, I think I'll tag along."

Ben's cell phone rang before they could walk out the door. "Give me a minute to get this. It might be an emergency."

He lifted the phone, frowning as he glanced at the caller ID. "It's Jake. He must have found something."

Chloe tensed, not sure what Jake was going to say, but pretty certain it wouldn't be good.

"Hello? Yeah, we're still at my place." He met Chloe's eyes, the heat of his gaze spearing through Chloe.

She paced across the room, her heart beating a hard, fast rhythm. She told herself it was from fear, that worry over what Jake had to say was causing her pulse to race, but she knew that was only part of the truth.

"I'll ask her. Chloe?"

She turned to face Ben again, steeling herself against the force of his gaze and for whatever he had to say. "Yes?"

"Whose photo was on your dresser?"

"No one's. I've got photographs hanging on my wall, but nothing on my dresser."

Ben relayed the information to Jake, listened for a moment, then nodded. "We'll be there in ten."

He hung up the phone and pulled open the door, gesturing for Chloe to step outside. "Jake found a photograph on your dresser. A picture of a man and woman. Both their heads have been cut out of the photo. You didn't see it when you got home this afternoon?"

"I didn't walk through the apartment. I just grabbed Abel's leash and the brownies and left. Since the door was locked, I assumed no one had been there."

"Someone was. Who has the key besides you?"

"My landlady. Opal. That's it."

"Who would have had access to it?"

"No one."

"Then whoever it was got in some other way. Let's get over to your place and see what Jake is thinking."

Chloe stepped outside, the cool overcast day doing nothing to reassure her as she hurried to her car and pulled open the door. Ben stopped her before she got in, his hand on her arm, his expression grim. "When we get to your place, Jake is going to ask a lot of questions. He comes off as gruff, but he means well."

"I get that about him."

"Good, because if you've got any idea who might be behind this, you need to tell him. No matter how unlikely you think it is. Any clue. Any detail you remember that might seem insignificant. He needs to know it all if he's going to be able to help you."

"If I had any idea who was behind what's been going on, I would have told the D.C. police." She shoved her bangs out of her eyes, disgusted to realize her hand was shaking. "But I'll answer his questions the best way I can. I'm as anxious as he is to get this all over with."

"It'll be over soon." Ben pulled her into a brief hug before he started toward his car. "I'll follow you to your place."

Chloe climbed into the Mustang and pulled out onto the

road, her stomach churning with nerves. When she was in D.C. she'd been desperate for someone to believe in her. Now she had two people standing beside her, doing everything they could to help her. Three if she counted Opal. That should have made her feel better. Instead, it increased her worry.

"But I'm not going to worry. I'm going to act. The answers are somewhere. I just have to find them." She muttered the words and Abel barked, as though agreeing.

She absently patted his head, her mind racing ahead. To the apartment. To the conversation she was about to have with Jake. To what needed to be done to find out who might have wanted to hurt Adam. Who was still trying to hurt Chloe.

"Lord, I'm going to need your help on this in a big way. The path I'm on is treacherous, but I know you can steer me to safety."

The prayer whispered through her mind as Chloe pulled up in front of the Victorian and stepped out of the car, waiting for Ben to do the same.

Chapter Eighteen

Jake was waiting in her apartment, a silver frame held in gloved hands. She knew the picture even before she got close enough to see it. The old-fashioned silver frame was one she'd bought from an antique dealer in Georgetown, the Victorian scrolling and fine details easily recognizable.

"I found this on your dresser. Is it yours?" As Ben had predicted, Jake's words were as gruff as ever, his gaze hard.

"Yes. It's our engagement picture. We had it taken a few weeks after Adam proposed. I couldn't make myself throw it away. I gave it to Adam's parents before I moved." She leaned close, blanching as she caught sight of the photograph.

Adam's face had been cut out, leaving a neat oval where his head had been. Chloe's image had fared even worse. It looked like someone had taken a razor blade and sliced through that side of the photo over and over again.

"Call them. See what they did with it."

It wasn't a request and Chloe didn't even consider arguing.

Her heart was pounding as she lifted the phone and dialed the familiar number.

"Hello?" The once vibrant voice of Karen Mitchell sounded weak and quiet, as if losing her only son had sapped some of her own life.

"Karen? It's Chloe."

"Chloe! How are you feeling, dear?"

"Fine. I just—"

"Then you're over your cold? I'm glad. You've been through so much this past year. Did the picture arrive in one piece?"

"Picture?" Chloe's hand tightened around the phone, her heart racing so fast she was sure she it would jump out of her chest.

"Your engagement photo. That is what you wanted me to send, isn't it?"

"Karen, I didn't ask you send the engagement picture. I didn't ask you to send anything."

"Dear, you called me last week and asked me to send it to you."

"No, I—"

Jake shook his head, a sharp, quick gesture that stalled the words in Chloe's throat. "Ask her where she sent it."

"Karen, listen, can you give me the address you sent the photo to?"

"So it didn't arrive? What a shame. I know how much the picture means to you."

"Do you have the address I gave you?"

"Of course. It's right in my address book." Papers rustled, Karen's words carrying over the sound and the throbbing pulse of Chloe's terror. "Here it is." She rattled off the address, a PO box that Chloe didn't recognize.

She wrote it down, her hand trembling, the letters and numbers wobbly and unclear. "Okay. Thanks."

"Is everything all right, dear? You don't seem yourself."

"Everything is fine. Listen, I was wondering if you still had Adam's laptop."

Jake raised an eyebrow at the question, but kept silent as she continued the conversation.

"Not his laptop. Jordyn said it belonged to the business. I do have his other computer, though. It's in the spare room with his other things. I haven't had the heart to go through everything."

"I understand. And I hate to even bring this up, but I'd really like to take a look at the computer. Can I send you the money to have it shipped here?"

Karen was silent for a moment. When she spoke, her voice was stronger than it had been. "Is something going on, Chloe?"

"I'm not sure. I'm hoping that Adam's computer might help me figure it out."

"I'll send it to you then. Shall I ship it to the same address?"

"No. Send it to this one." Chloe rattled off her address and phone number, then hung up, her pulse racing with anticipation and with fear.

"Asking for the computer was good thinking. If Adam was having trouble with someone, there may be evidence of that on his computer." Ben was holding Abel, his strong hand smoothing the puppy's long fur.

"That's what I'm hoping."

"What I'm hoping," Jake interrupted their conversation. "Is that our perpetrator's mistake will be to our benefit."

"Mistake?" In Chloe's estimation, her stalker had made far too few of those.

"The PO box. He had to have known how easily he could be traced through it."

"Maybe he didn't care." Ben sat on the couch, stretching his long legs, looking as if he belonged there.

"Or she." Jake leaned a shoulder against the wall, his brow creasing. "Someone was impersonating Chloe. It would be hard for a man to sound like a woman."

"A woman." Chloe rolled the words across her tongue, testing them out. "That would make sense."

"Hell hath no fury like a woman scorned." Jake muttered the words, his gaze on the photo. "And based on the way you've been carved out of this photo, I'm thinking someone definitely felt scorned."

"All we need to do is find out who." Chloe glanced at the photo again.

"Any ideas?"

"No, but the answer may lie in Adam's computers. Karen's going to send me his PC. I'll see if I can get James's permission to take a look at his laptop. E-mails. Old files. There may be a name there somewhere. If there is, I'll find it."

"Good. While you do that, I'll check into phone records and get information on our PO box owner."

"How long will that take?" Ben asked the question that was foremost in Chloe's mind.

"A few days, but getting the information is no guarantee we'll find our stalker. It's unlikely our perp is using a real name. In the long run, that won't matter. We're going to find our quarry. It's only a matter of time." Jake placed the framed photo in an evidence bag, sealed it closed. "I've already dusted for prints and checked to see if the locks on the balcony or front door were jimmied."

"Were they?" Chloe would rather think someone had jimmied her door than spend hours worrying that someone had her key.

"Not that I could see, but it wouldn't take much to open your front door. A credit card would probably do it."

"I thought that was only in the movies."

"No. It's a pretty simple thing to do once you know how. It's probably a good idea if you get new locks and bolts installed."

"I can call someone tomorrow."

"Or we can take care of it today." Ben stood and strode to the balcony door. "This one needs a bolt, too."

"I'm on the second floor."

"And your neighbors are gone more than they're home. It wouldn't be hard for someone to use a ladder to gain access to your apartment."

"Ben's right. It doesn't make sense to take chances. I'm going to get back to the office and run the prints I've found. Make a few phone calls. I'll be sending patrol cars down this way every hour or so until we get this case solved."

"I appreciate it."

"Just be careful and watch your back." Jake strode out the door and Ben started after him.

"I'm going to run to the hardware store and go home for some tools. Then I'll be back. Keep the door bolted until then."

"I've got tools."

"What kind?"

"What do you need?" Chloe hurried to her room and pulled a small toolbox from her closet, setting it on the bed and opening it.

"That looks pretty complete. I don't suppose you have spare locks in there."

"Spare locks aren't on the list of things a single woman needs to keep in her house."

"But pink hammers are?" He lifted the tool, smiling a little as he hefted the weight in his hand.

"Just because it's pink doesn't mean it's not functional."

"I'm sure it's functional. I'm just surprised."

"That it's functional? Or that I have a pink hammer?"

"That you'd choose something so frivolous. You told me the day we met that you weren't into frivolous things."

"The hammer isn't frivolous. It's functional and cute. And if you keep making fun of it, you might just end up with one for Christmas."

"We're going to exchange Christmas gifts?" He raised a brow, a smile hovering at the corner of his lips.

"Maybe. If I live that long." She meant it as a joke, but the words fell flat, the worry behind them seeping through. "Forget I said that."

"You know I can't." His hand cupped her jaw, his fingers caressing the tender flesh near her ear. "And you know I'm going to tell you everything will be okay. That Christmas will come and you'll be here to see it."

"I wish I were as confident of that as you are."

"I'll be confident for both of us." His gaze drifted from her eyes to her mouth, his fingers smoothing a trail from her jaw to her neck as he leaned toward her. "I shouldn't do this."

"No, you shouldn't."

"So tell me to stop."

She should, she really should. But she didn't. And as he leaned toward her, she leaned forward. Just a fraction of an inch, but it was enough. His lips brushed hers, the contact shivering through her.

She jerked back, nearly falling into the closet.

"Whoa!" Ben grabbed her arm, pulling her up before she landed in a heap on top of her shoes. "Careful."

"Sorry." Her cheeks were on fire, her heart skipping. This was definitely not good.

So why did she feel so happy about it?

"Don't apologize." Ben seemed completely unperturbed. "I'm not planning to."

He strode out of the room and out the front door, leaving Chloe alone with the two puppies. Curled up on the kitchen floor, neither bothered to rouse as she grabbed aspirin from the counter and swallowed two.

Ben had kissed her.

Or maybe she'd kissed Ben.

She wasn't sure which was more the truth and was pretty sure it didn't matter. After almost a year of saying that she would never, ever, ever get involved with another man, she'd just allowed herself to do exactly that.

"This isn't good, boys. It isn't good at all."

Neither of the puppies responded and Chloe dropped down into a chair, wincing as her leg protested the movement. "I think I need to go back to sleep and start this day all over again."

But she couldn't.

So the best thing she could do was get busy, take her mind off her terror and her confusing feelings for Ben.

Confusing?

Not hardly.

She knew exactly what she was feeling. That was the problem.

"Enough of this. I've got plenty to do besides mooning over a man."

She logged onto her computer, pulled up her address book and dialed James Kelly's home number. Adam's business partner and fellow private investigator, James had been the one who'd first contacted Chloe, bringing her in on an investigation he and Adam were working together. He'd been thrilled when she and Adam began dating, devastated when they'd broken up. In the months following Adam's death, shared grief had made Chloe's friendship with James even stronger.

Still, talking to him about Adam's betrayal, trying to get

information about the woman he'd been seeing, wasn't something Chloe had ever planned to do.

"Hello?"

"James? It's Chloe."

"Finally. My wife's been telling me not to call and check in on you, but I was getting close to ignoring her suggestion and giving you a ring."

"Were you really going to call to see how I was doing or were you going to call and ask me to take on a few cases?"

"Maybe a little of both."

Chloe smiled, imagining James's round face and balding head. A year older than his friend, James had always been more settled, more staid, maybe a little more boring than Adam. His generous spirit and calm nature had drawn others to him and had been the backbone of the private investigation service he'd co-owned with Adam. "Then I'll answer both. I'm doing fine. I don't freelance anymore."

"That's too bad. I haven't been able to find anyone as good as you."

"Or as reasonably priced?"

"That, too." There was a smile in his voice and Chloe felt some of the tension of the day easing.

"Keep looking. Eventually you will."

"If you'd agree to do a few simple jobs for me, I wouldn't have to go to all that effort."

"Few and simple? I doubt it."

James chuckled. "True. So, if you didn't call to tell me you were going back to work, what did you call about?"

"I have a favor to ask."

"Go ahead."

"Do you still have Adam's work laptop?"

"In my office. It hasn't been used since…he passed away."

"Do you mind if I take a look at it?"

"Take a look at it as in dig inside and see what you find?"

"Yes."

"Should I ask why?"

"It's complicated."

"I don't like the sound of that. Is everything okay?"

"It'll be better after I get the laptop." She hoped.

"I'll have Jordyn send it to you first thing tomorrow morning. Do we have your new address on file?"

"I gave it to Jordyn before I left."

"Then you can expect to get the laptop by the end of the week. And I'll be expecting to hear just exactly what you were searching for once you find it."

"It's a deal, James. Thanks a lot." She hesitated, not wanting to ask the next question no matter how much she knew it needed asking. "Listen, there's one more thing."

"What's that?"

"I've been wondering about the months before the accident. Adam didn't seem like himself in the weeks before it happened."

"You two had broken up. It was a pretty rough time for him."

"You know why we broke up, right?" She hadn't told him, but she was sure Adam had.

He was silent for a moment, then spoke quietly, his voice more subdued. "Yes. I was surprised and disappointed when Adam told me he was the cause. You two were the perfect match. I told him I couldn't understand why he'd mess that up."

Chloe ignored the last comment, not wanting to discuss her own disappointments, her own sense of failure. "You said you were surprised. You didn't know he was seeing someone?"

"Not until after the breakup. Even then he probably wouldn't have told me. If…"

"What?"

"I was being a little hard on you. I thought you'd just decided to call things off. He didn't want you taking the rap, so he told me what'd happened."

"Did he tell you who the other woman was?"

"No."

"Would you tell me if he had?"

"Chloe, Adam is gone. I don't have to keep his secrets anymore." The sadness in his voice was unmistakable and Chloe could feel her own grief welling up.

"Do you think there's anyone who does know?"

"You know how he was. A different lunch da—companion every day. Too many friends to count. He had more on his social calendar for a week than I usually have all month, but I doubt there was anyone who knew him better than we did. If neither us knew who she was. No one did." He sighed.

"You're right, but if you think of anything—or anyone—"

"I'll let you know." He sighed. "I've got to get going. My wife is waiting for me to take her to dinner. Jordyn will send you the laptop. Let me know if you need anything else. And if you decide to go back to freelancing, I want to be the first client on your list."

"I'll keep that in mind."

"He really did love you, Chloe. You know that don't you?"

"No." She swallowed back sadness and regret. "I don't, but thanks for saying it. I'll be in touch."

She hung up the phone before he could say more, unwilling to discuss what she mostly refused to even think about. Maybe he was right, maybe Adam had loved her in his own way. But in the end that hadn't been enough for either of them.

Chloe forced her sadness away, forced herself to brew a pot of coffee, to feed the puppies, to get her mind off the past and into the present. Ben would be back soon. They'd put new locks and bolts on the doors, but Chloe wasn't foolish enough to think that would keep her safe. Only one thing could do that—finding the person stalking her. In a couple days, she'd have both of Adam's computers. If there was information on them, some hint about what had been going on in the months before his death, she'd find it.

Chapter Nineteen

Monday morning came too early, the alarm sounding an insistent beep that pulled Chloe from restless sleep and into the new day. She groaned and yanked the covers over her head, wishing she could ignore the sound and go back to sleep.

Unfortunately, even if she'd been willing to face Opal's wrath—which she wasn't—she couldn't ignore Abel's muffled cries. Obviously he was as ready to be out of his bed as Chloe was to stay in hers.

"I'm coming."

She felt sluggish and off balance as she stumbled to the shower wishing she'd gotten into bed at a much earlier hour. Especially since she'd done absolutely nothing constructive during the hours she'd been awake. After she and Ben put bolts on the front and balcony doors, he'd left for home, rushing to get ready for the evening service. A service Chloe might have attended if she hadn't been worried about what might happen in her apartment during her absence.

And if she hadn't wanted to put some distance between herself and Ben.

Working together in the apartment had felt comfortable, their movements in sync, their conversations easy; Chloe had found herself thinking about spending time with him next week, next month, next year. That worried her almost as much as the kiss.

So, instead of enjoying fellowship and fun, she'd locked herself in the apartment and spent most of the night pacing the floor, checking the locks, listening for footfalls on the stairs, imagining the doorknob slowly turning.

"Good choice, Chloe." She scowled at her reflection in the mirror as she scraped still-wet hair into a ponytail. Her skin was pallid, the freckles on her nose and cheeks standing out in stark relief, the hollows under her cheeks shadowed. The day had barely begun and she was already tired and out of sorts. The worst part was, she'd left the container of brownies at Ben's house the previous day and couldn't find a drop of chocolate in the house.

"Opal better have some at the shop, Abel, or I'm going to leave you with her and go hunt some down." She lifted the puppy, attached his leash and started toward the front door.

As tired as she felt, she was glad to be going to work. At least when she was at Blooming Baskets she wouldn't be alone. Opal would be there, customers would drop by, Jenna would probably stop in for a few hours with the baby. There'd be plenty to keep Chloe's mind off her nightmares.

And off Ben.

And the kiss.

And the way her heart melted when she looked into his eyes.

"Stop it! He's a man. Just like any other man you know."

Liar.

Maybe. But she wasn't going to admit it. Nor would she spend any more time thinking about a man who seemed too good to be true and probably was.

"Too good to be true is always bad news, right, pup?"

Abel barked his agreement and Chloe stepped out of the apartment and started down the stairs. The house was quiet. The retired couple across the hall were probably still asleep, but downstairs soft music drifted from beneath the door that led to Connor's apartment. For a split second, Chloe considered knocking on his door and asking for an escort to her car, but she had mace in her pocket, a panic button on her key chain. An escort seemed like overkill, though it definitely would have gone a long way in making her want to walk out the door.

Outside, clouds boiled up from the horizon, the steel gray of the sky doing nothing to lift Chloe's mood. The silvery sheen of the lake, the gray-brown bark of the trees, the fall-brown grass, sapped the world of color and life, creating a place of silence. Of death.

"Forget going to Blooming Baskets and hoping for chocolate. I'm going to make sure I get some." She muttered the words as she put Abel in the back seat of the car and slammed the door shut.

Twenty minutes later, she strode into Blooming Baskets, a paper bag in one hand, Abel's leash and a drink carrier in the other. Coffee for Opal. Hot chocolate for herself.

Opal stepped out of the back room, a small white basket in her hands and a scowl on her face. "It's about time you got here. I was worried sick wondering what had happened to you."

"I'm not due in for five minutes."

"Chloe Davidson, every day for the past two weeks, you've been here at 7:45. It is now 7:55. You've aged me ten years for every minute. Do you realize how many years that makes me?"

"A hundred and sixty-four?" Chloe tried not to laugh as she set the bag on the front counter.

"Exactly."

"Sorry. I didn't realize you'd be worried."

"Didn't you? Just wait. One day you'll have kids. Then you'll know what it is to wait for someone to call and let you know they're okay."

"I don't think kids are in my future, Opal."

"You'd make a great mother."

"That won't be an issue since I'm not planning on getting married." She passed Opal the cup of coffee, telling herself that what she was saying was absolutely the truth. She was not interested in men. And she was not interested in Ben.

"You brought me coffee?"

"Consider it a peace offering. I really am sorry I worried you, but every once in a while a girl's just got to have chocolate."

"Is that what you've got in the bag?"

"Yep. Two chocolate cake doughnuts. Each."

"Are they glazed?"

"Are there any other kind"

"Not in my mind." Opal smiled, pulled a doughnut out of the bag and handed it to Chloe.

"Eat. You're looking pale again."

"I didn't sleep well last night."

"Probably the puppy keeping you awake."

"Probably. What's on the schedule for today?"

"Plenty. Four baskets for the missionary luncheon at Grace Christian. Prep for the Costello wedding shower this Saturday. Two arrangements for the hospital. One that needs to be delivered to a retirement village outside of town. Two to private residents."

"Are you delivering or am I?"

"I am. It'll take me less time."

"Because you're a lead foot."

"Because I know where I'm going. Besides, you do look exhausted. It's probably for the best that you not spend the day driving around. And I think we'll skip tonight, too. I can't drag you out shopping when you're so exhausted."

"You weren't going to be dragging me, Opal. I was happy to go with you."

"Be that as it may, you're not going to go. Betsy Reynolds has decided to go to Richmond, too. She called me last night and was begging me to go shopping with her. I'll just call and tell her I can do it after all."

"So I'm being replaced," Chloe teased, biting into the rich chocolate doughnut, happy to be out of the apartment and away from her worries for a while. She had made plenty of mistakes in her life, but coming to Lakeview wasn't one of them. Maybe she hadn't quite gotten the hang of floral design, but at least she had some measure of stability in her life again. She also had Opal and that was worth its weight in gold.

"Not yet, but if you keep talking instead of working, I just might have to." Opal's amused words were enough to get Chloe moving, and she lifted Abel and brought him to the back room.

It didn't take long to ease into the flow of the day. By noon, Opal was out in the van making her deliveries and Chloe was cleaning up petals and stems from the work area in the back of the shop. She tried to work quickly, but the sluggish feeling she'd woken with hadn't left despite hot chocolate, two cups of coffee and a sugar-laden doughnut.

Doughnuts. She'd managed to eat both of hers.

The bell over the front door rang and she stepped out into the front of the shop, pasting a smile on her face and hoping she looked more lively than she felt.

"Hi, can I help…?" The question died on her lips as she caught sight of Ben, his jaw shadowed by a beard, his eyes blazing brilliant blue, a smile curving his lips. Dark jeans. A soft flannel shirt layered over a black T-shirt that hugged well-defined muscles. He looked good, really good.

Chloe resisted the urge to smooth the strands of hair that had fallen from her ponytail and were straggling around her face. "Ben, what are you doing here?"

"I was driving by and thought I'd stop in to see how you were doing."

"Driving by?"

"Driving by on my way here to see how you're doing."

Laughter bubbled up and spilled out, filling the room and chasing away the anxiety that had plagued Chloe all morning. "Thanks."

"For what?" He stepped closer, reaching for her hand and tugging her out from behind the display case, his gaze taking in her black pants and pink shirt, her scraggly hair and makeup-free face.

"For stopping in to see how I was doing. And for making me laugh."

"You're welcome." He did what she hadn't, reaching out and smoothing strands of hair from her cheeks, his fingers blazing trails of warmth that made her heart race.

She stepped back, her face heating, her mind shouting that if she didn't watch it she'd be in big trouble. That she was already in big trouble.

"So how are you doing?"

"I'm doing great."

"Liar."

"I'm doing okay."

"Try again."

"I feel lousy. Happy now?"

"Not even close." He ran a hand over his jaw. "I won't be happy until we find the person who's after you."

"If we find the person." Before he finishes what he started.

She didn't say the rest, but it was what she'd been thinking during the darkest hours of the night and what she was still thinking in the cold gray light of the November day.

"We'll find him. Jake's heading in the right direction with the investigation. I feel strongly about that. So does he."

"You spoke to him today?"

"I stopped by his office before I came here."

"I wish you hadn't."

"Because you think I'm getting too involved?" He crossed his arms over his chest, his stance relaxed, but alert, his gaze just a little hard.

"Because I don't want you involved at all." At least her head didn't. Her heart was another matter entirely.

"Funny, I don't think that's the truth, either."

"The truth is simple. Getting involved with me is dangerous. Anyone in his right mind would see that and go running in the other direction." Chloe shoved her bangs out of her eyes, grabbed a small white basket from behind the counter, then stalked across the room to pull white and pink roses from the cooler.

"I'm not just anyone. And I'm not running." The hint of steel in his voice surprised Chloe and she met his eyes, saw the hard determination there.

"Ben—"

"Maybe you're used to people abandoning you when things get tough, but that's not my style. Whatever happens in the next days, weeks or months, I plan to be part of it."

"Why? We've known each other a week—"

"Ten days." He grinned, but the steel was still there.

"My point is, you don't have a commitment to me. There's

no reason for you to get more involved in my problems then you already are."

"Whether or not I have a commitment to you has nothing to do with it."

"It has everything to do with it." She placed a square of floral foam in the bottom of the basket and jabbed a rose into it. "We barely know each other and you're letting yourself get caught up in my mess. You could be off doing a hundred other things that would be a lot less dangerous to your health."

"And yet here I am." He grabbed her hand before she could mash another rose into the arrangement. "Don't you think there's a reason for that, Chloe? A reason God brought us into each other's lives at exactly this time?"

"I stopped thinking I understood God's ways months ago." She slid her hand away from his, using less force to place the next flower.

"You don't have to understand, you just have to trust."

She looked up and into the vibrant blue depths of his eyes, felt herself drawn into them and into his certainty. "Trust isn't easy for me."

"It's not easy for anyone when things get tough. We doubt. We question. In the end, we either choose to believe God is still working His will through our lives or we end up turning away from our faith. I don't think you're the kind to turn away."

"You're right. I'm not." But there had been times before she'd come to Lakeview that she'd wondered if she might, if maybe everything she'd believed, everything she'd trusted in was a lie.

She pulled baby's breath from the cooler, shoving a few stems in between the roses.

"Then have faith that God put me into your life for a reason and stop worrying so much about what that might mean."

Ben pulled baby's breath from the pile she'd set on the counter and pressed the stem into the foam, his knuckles brushing against hers, the simple act of working together sealing the connection that shouldn't be between them, but was.

"You're wrong, Ben. I do have to worry about what that might mean."

"Because you're afraid of what might happen to anyone who gets close to you?"

"Because I've lived what might happen to anyone who gets close to me and I don't want to live it again."

"You're not going to."

"You can't know that."

"No, I can't." His knuckles brushed against hers again, but this time he turned his hand and captured her fingers, his thumb caressing the tender flesh on the underside of her wrist. "But I do know this—there's nothing in the world that can keep God's will and plan from being worked out and His plan is always for our best. Whatever happens, it'll be okay."

He tugged her forward so that she was leaning over the glass display case, just inches from Ben and the strength he offered. For a moment she was sure he would kiss her again. She thought about moving forward, thought about pulling back, hadn't quite decided between the two when he brushed a hand over her hair.

A pink petal fluttered down and settled in the floral arrangement she was designing.

"Were you fighting with roses when I got here?"

"I was fighting with Abel who was fighting with pink hydrangea. Opal will not be pleased."

"I bet not. Will she be back soon?"

"Probably within the hour."

"And you're here alone until then?"

"Yes."

"I'm not sure that's such a good idea."

"Good idea or not, it is what it is." Chloe shoved more baby's breath into the sea of white and pink roses and frowned. "This isn't exactly going the way I planned."

"What'd you plan?"

"Something that looked a lot better."

He eyed the floral arrangement and Chloe expected him to say what most people would—it looks great. Instead, he pulled a few roses from the middle of the basket, spaced them closer to the edge of the foam. "Maybe a little more of the filler would help."

"A pastor, a chef and a floral designer. Is there anything you can't do?"

"I can't leave you alone here by yourself."

"Sure you can. Just walk out the door."

"Not until Opal gets here. So, what do you say we finish this and order a pizza? I don't know about you, but I'm ready for lunch."

"Ben—"

"It's just lunch."

"It's just you babysitting me."

"It doesn't feel anything at all like babysitting to me." The words were warm and filled with promise.

"I don't think this is a good idea."

"Good idea or not, it is what it is." He smiled, his eyes flashing with amusement.

And suddenly having him around didn't seem like such a bad thing. Despite her worry, despite her fear, for just a while, Chloe decided to believe what Ben had said—that God had put him in her life for a reason, that a divine plan was being worked out and that in the end everything would be okay.

Chapter Twenty

There were two messages on Chloe's machine when she got home. The first from Karen telling her that Adam's hard drive was on the way. The second was from Adam's former receptionist, Jordyn Winslow. She'd mailed the laptop and wanted to know if Chloe needed anything else.

Chloe glanced at the clock as she stripped off her jacket. Jordyn had her ear to the ground when it came to matters that involved anything to do with Adam and James's business or their personal lives. She prided herself on knowing their schedules during work and away from it. If there was anyone besides James who might have an idea of who Adam had been seeing, it was Jordyn.

It was just past five when Chloe picked up the phone, almost hoping that the receptionist had left for the day. It would be much easier to leave a message than to ask what needed asking in person.

Her hopes were dashed when Jordyn's chipper voice filled the line.

"Kelly and Hill Investigative Services. Can I help you?" The greeting was the same, but different. Adam's name no longer a part of it. Grief speared Chloe's heart, making her mute for a moment too long.

"Hello? Can I help you?" Jordyn's tone had lost some of its peppiness.

"Jordyn, it's Chloe."

"Hi, Chloe. It's good to hear from you. James said you're settling in down there. Is it as peaceful as you were hoping?"

"Yes. The lake is beautiful and the area is much quieter than D.C."

"I bet. Personally, I'm not sure I could do what you've done. Move out to the country. Too many years of suburban life have spoiled me. I like the convenience of having everything close by. I don't know how you're keeping your sanity." Was the comment about sanity a subtle jab? Chloe could never be sure with Jordyn. They'd known each other for the three years Chloe had been freelancing for the company, but they'd never been friends.

"Rural life isn't for everyone, but it's definitely for me."

"To each her own, I suppose. Though I'm not sure what the point of giving up a lucrative business to become a florist was. You'd done well for yourself, Chloe. It's a shame to waste all those years of work." Jordyn's words were patronizing, but Chloe didn't let them bother her. A fixture at Adam and James's office since they'd partnered as private investigators ten years before, Jordyn had an opinion about most things and wasn't afraid to share them.

"Like you said, to each her own. My decision might not make sense to you, but I haven't regretted it." Chloe set fresh water and food down for Abel and limped to the balcony, unbolting the French doors and stepping out in the crisp evening air.

"Yes, well, we'll see how you feel in a month. Did you get my message?"

"Yes, thanks for sending the laptop out."

"James said you needed it ASAP. I wasn't sure there was quite as much hurry as he made it out to be, but humored him anyway. You know how men can be."

Not really, but she didn't plan to admit that to Jordyn whose blond-haired beauty attracted more men than Chloe had ever been able to keep track of. "They're interesting, that's for sure."

"Interesting? Frustrating is more the word I was thinking. Anyway, the laptop is on the way. You should receive it by the end of the week. James didn't say what you needed it for."

Chloe decided the nonquestion needed no response, and she ignored it. "I appreciate you getting it out so quickly, Jordyn. I know how busy you are."

"Not as busy anymore. Adam kept things hopping around here. Without him, things just aren't the same."

"Adam did love his job." Go ahead, bring it up. Ask her before you chicken out. "Jordyn, you asked if I needed anything else, and I was wondering…"

If she knew who Adam had cheated with? If she'd watched him leave for lunch with his girlfriend and silently applauded Chloe's downfall.

"What?"

"Adam was seeing someone besides me. I wondered if you knew who it was." There, it was out, and a lot less painful to say than she'd thought it would be.

"I'd heard rumors that's why the two of you broke up, but I didn't want to believe it was true. Adam seemed like such a loyal type of guy."

"Yeah, he did. I guess you don't know who he was seeing?"

"I'm afraid not."

"All right. Thanks anyway."

"No problem. Do me a favor and call me when the laptop arrives, okay? I've got it insured and want to make sure it gets there in one piece."

"Sure."

"Great. I'll talk to you soon, then." The phone line went dead, and Chloe set the receiver down. James didn't know who Adam had been seeing. Jordyn didn't. Chloe certainly didn't.

But the computers might. One e-mail, that's all it would take. One note that spoke of more than friendship. Deleted or not, they'd be there, buried in the computer, waiting to be found.

Chloe just wasn't sure she was ready to find the information. A nameless, faceless woman was much easier to deal with than a real identity. A name. Maybe a face. Maybe the knowledge that it was someone Chloe knew, had maybe even liked.

Not that it mattered now. Adam was gone, his betrayal minuscule in comparison to his death. All they'd shared—laughter, joy, tears and pain—fading to bittersweet memory.

Hot tears filled Chloe's eyes and she blinked them back, rubbing at the band of scars on her hand, the cool air from the still-opened French doors bathing her heated face. She wanted so badly to go back to the night of the accident, rewind the clock, change the outcome. But the past couldn't be changed. All she could do was move forward into the unknown.

As if he sensed her distress, Abel whined, rolling over on his back and begging for attention. She knelt down and scratched him under the chin. "You're a good puppy. Even if you did destroy the hydrangea and chew the leg of Opal's desk."

His tail thumped the floor, his tongue lolled out, the sight comical and cute. If she'd had her cameras she'd have taken a picture, but Jake hadn't returned them and had made no mention of how long they'd be in his custody. Instead, she straightened, limping into the kitchen and eyeing the contents of her refrigerator. There wasn't much. Some fruit. A bag of baby carrots. A nearly empty half-gallon of milk. Apple juice. Why hadn't she stopped at the store on the way home and picked up groceries?

She dug into the cupboard, found a box of Pop-Tarts, and ripped open the wrapper. They weren't chocolate, but they were better than nothing.

Abel barked, tumbling toward the door, just as a soft rap sounded against the wood.

"Who is it?"

"It's Mrs. Anderson, dear. I've got a package for you."

"A package?" Chloe pulled open the door and smiled at her neighbor, a spry woman of eighty-nine who spent her days volunteering at the community center and her evenings enjoying the company of her husband of sixty years.

"Yes. Charles said it was on the front porch when he came home. I guess it couldn't fit in your mailbox." She held out what looked like a wrapped shoe box. "He thought it best to bring it inside. No sense leaving it outside for thieves to get."

"Thank you for bringing it over, Mrs. Anderson. And please tell your husband I appreciate him bringing it inside."

"It was no problem at all, dear. Now, I've got to run. It's senior night at the movie theater and Charles and I are going to meet some friends there."

"Have fun."

"You, too."

Chloe waited until the elderly woman was back inside her apartment, then closed the door and bolted it. The package was light and wrapped in brown packing paper, her name and address printed in broad, firm letters on one side. She turned the package over, saw no sign of a return address, nothing to indicate where it had come from.

A warning shivered along her spine, the box like a coiled

serpent ready to strike. Anything could be inside. Pictures. Letters. Poison. Body parts.

"Okay. You're really losing it, Chloe. Knock it off before you convince yourself there are explosives inside and call the bomb squad to rescue you."

She set the box on the kitchen table, took a steak knife and slit through tape and paper. There was more paper beneath, bright yellow wrapping paper that she made quick work of. The white box inside looked innocuous enough, but there was no card or note. There also weren't any blood stains or awful odors, but that didn't mean there wasn't something awful inside.

Finally, Chloe couldn't put off the inevitable any longer. She braced herself and lifted the lid, nearly laughing out loud when she saw what was inside. A brown and green turtle was shoved into the small space, one golden eye staring up at her.

She pulled it out, smiling as she saw the dog tag hanging from a string around its neck. Speedy Too.

Ben.

How he'd managed to find a floppy stuffed turtle, Chloe didn't know. Why he'd taken the time to buy it and send it to her was something she wasn't sure she wanted to know. Everything else aside—all the danger, all the fear, all the nightmares—she wasn't ready to get involved in a relationship. She wasn't sure she'd ever be ready for that.

But if she were, someone like Ben would be perfect....

Don't even go there, Chloe. Don't even think about it. Ben is a charming guy with a congregation of single women standing in line hoping to get his attention. Let them. You're not interested.

Aren't you?

She ran her hand over the turtle's shell, imagining Ben buying it and the dog tag, wrapping them in the box, going to the post office. He'd gone through a lot of trouble and that wasn't something many people had done for her in the past.

She grabbed the phone, found Ben's number and dialed.

"Hello?" His voice rumbled across the line, comfortably familiar and much too welcome.

"Hi, Ben. It's Chloe."

"Hey. Everything okay?" His voice deepened, warmed, pulled her in.

"Fine." She smoothed her hand over the turtle again, her throat tight for reasons she refused to name. "I got a package in the mail today."

"Did you?"

"No return address. No note. At first I thought it might be an unpleasant surprise."

"More mutilated pictures?"

"I was thinking something explosive. I got pretty close to calling the bomb squad."

"That would have made interesting news for the gossip mill."

"Fortunately, it didn't come to that."

"No?"

"It seems someone has a thing for turtles. Speedy ones."

"You don't say."

"I do. And I also say that that someone shouldn't have gone to so much trouble."

"Who said it was any trouble? Maybe that someone happened to be shopping for a birthday present for his niece and saw the turtle and thought of you."

"And just happened to find a pet tag with the perfect name written on it?"

"Something like that." He laughed, the sound rumbling across the phone line.

"You could have just brought it over. It would have saved you the effort and the cost of postage."

"And have you give me a hundred reasons why you couldn't accept it?"

"I wouldn't have given you a hundred reasons."

"Sure you would have. And then I would have felt obligated to list a hundred reasons why you could accept it. That seemed like a lot more effort than putting it in the box and mailing it."

Chloe smiled, setting Speedy Too down on the counter and crossing to the balcony. The night was clear, the stars bright in the indigo sky. "You're probably right. I would have argued, but in the end you would have convinced me. Speedy Too is the most thoughtful gift I've ever received."

"Then I'm glad I followed my gut and bought it."

"Ben, I'm not sure what you want from me, but—"

"I don't want anything from you, but friendship."

"A kiss is a little more than friendship."

"Let's chalk that up to a momentary lapse of judgment and forget it happened."

"I don't think that's possible."

"And I think I'm flattered."

Chloe's cheeks heated, and she was glad Ben wasn't there to see it. "You know what I mean. A kiss changes everything. It takes nothing and makes it into something."

"What's between us could never be nothing. Kiss or no kiss."

"That's just the thing. I don't want there to be something between us."

"There already is." He sighed, and she could picture him standing in his kitchen, maybe a cup of coffee in his hands, his hair falling across his forehead.

"I—"

"Let's be friends for a while, Chloe. We can worry about what comes next later."

"Nothing is going to come next."

"You just keep telling yourself that."

"I will. And now I've really got to go. Abel needs some attention."

Chloe could hear Ben's laughter as she hung up the phone and she couldn't stop her answering smile. He was right. There was something between them. From the moment she'd met him she'd felt the connection, a living thing that seemed to be growing with every moment they spent together.

Friendship.

She liked the sound of that.

The silence of the night wrapped around her, the bright stars and crescent moon hanging over the dark lake, the distant mountains rising up to touch the sky. God's creation. His design. Ready for His purpose. His will. Whatever that might be.

Maybe one day Chloe would know. For now, she could barely see the beauty for the shadows. She shuddered, stepping back into the apartment and closing the door against the darkness.

Abel tumbled near her feet as she sat down in front of her laptop and pulled up work files. Maybe she'd missed something in her previous searches. Maybe there was something there still waiting to be discovered.

She could only pray that if there was, she'd find it soon because no matter how confident Ben and Jake were, Chloe had a feeling that all her fears were about to come true and that the nightmare she'd been running from for months would soon overtake her.

Chapter Twenty-One

Three nights and eighteen hours of searching computer files revealed no secrets that seemed worth killing to keep hidden. Jake's investigation seemed to be turning up just as few leads. When he stopped by the shop Thursday to tell her there'd been no fingerprints on the frame or photo and that a man they'd identified as the owner of the PO box had gone to ground and couldn't be located, Chloe was ready to lock up the shop and go home.

If it hadn't been just a little past nine in the morning, she might have.

The day seemed to stretch on for an eternity, and by the time she was ready to close Blooming Baskets for the evening, Chloe wanted nothing more than a hot bath to sooth her aching leg and a warm bed to hide in. That's exactly what she planned to have. After she did the exercises the orthopedic specialist had recommended during Chloe's appointment the previous day and after she fed Opal's demon cat and checked her mail.

Unfortunately, doing the last meant making the fifteen-minute drive to Opal's house in the dark, getting out of the Mustang in the dark, walking into a dark house in the dark.

"I've got to stop this kind of negative thinking, Abel. Dark, dark, dark, dark. Obsessing on it is only making me more nervous. I need to refocus my thoughts. Try to look at the bright side of things." Chloe stopped at the head of Opal's driveway, reaching out her window to pull mail out of the box, then following the winding path toward the ranch-style house her friend owned. Built in the seventies, the house wasn't nearly as fancy as some of its neighbors, but the three-acre lakefront lot was a premium and Opal loved it.

Chloe loved it, too. Her fondest childhood memories centered around Opal and her family, their house, the lake and the small cottage next door where Chloe had spent seven summers of her life.

She pulled up in front of the house and turned off the engine, the headlights dying and leaving the area shadowed and foreboding.

As fond as her memories of the place were, Chloe wasn't sure she wanted to get out of the car and go into the house. It looked different at night, the windows gaping wounds that bled darkness, the front door an ebony slash against the pale siding. Abandoned. Lonely. The kind of place where bad things might happen and probably would.

"But it's just a house, right? There's no one lurking in the shadows, waiting for me to get out of the car."

Abel snored in response, his head resting on his paws as he snoozed on the back seat. "You know you're supposed to be a companion, a watchdog, a fierce defender of your human, don't you?"

Abel opened one eye and closed it again.

"Obviously, I'm on my own on this one. Which is okay,

because I can handle it." She took a deep breath, pulled Opal's keys from her purse and started to open the car door. Head-lights shone in the rearview mirror, the unexpected bright-ness nearly blinding Chloe. She jumped, jamming her car keys back into the ignition, fear squeezing the breath from her lungs. No one should be coming down the driveway while Opal was away. She needed to put the car in reverse and drive away while she still could, but the oncoming car blocked her retreat, the blue spruce that lined the driveway prevented her from pulling around it.

She was trapped.

No. Not trapped. All she had to do was use her cell phone and call for help. Of course, by the time help arrived it might be too late. She'd be lying dead on the pavement.

Get out of the car. Go in the house. Call for help.

She grabbed her purse, Opal's keys still in her hand, and jumped from the car, racing toward the house, headlights pin-ning her against the gray-black night.

An easy target to see.

An easy one to take out with a gun.

Or to ram with a car.

There were a million ways Chloe could be killed here in the dark in front of Opal's house, but not if she could get in-side the house first.

A door slammed, someone shouted, but Chloe's focus was on the door and safety. She shoved the keys into the lock, opened the door, jerked it closed again.

The doorbell rang before she could even turn the lock, the sound so jarring Chloe stumbled forward, knocking into the door, her cell phone tumbling from her hand. She landed hard on her knees, her pulse echoing hollowly in her ears as the doorbell chimed again and the door swung open.

A dark figure loomed in the threshold, then crouched beside

her, the scent of pine and man enveloping Chloe as he leaned close. "You run pretty fast for a woman with one bad leg."

Ben.

She didn't know whether to hug him or hit him and settled for accepting the hand he offered and allowing herself to be pulled to her feet. "I wasn't expecting company."

"Neither was I. Are you okay?"

"Besides my wounded pride, I'm fine. I need to go out and get Abel, though. He might not be doing as well out alone in a strange place."

"He's fine. I grabbed him and put him back in your car before he could get too far."

"Thanks. Should I ask why you're here?"

"Opal called me this morning and asked me to stop by to feed her cat. Apparently he likes to be fed at six o'clock on the dot."

"Not a minute sooner."

"Or later."

"It sounds like she told you the exact same thing she told me."

"That her cat is finicky and refuses to eat if the food is put in his bowl at any other time of the day and that when Opal's daughter took care of Checkers he didn't eat the entire time, because she fed him in the morning."

"Verbatim." Chloe raked a hand through her hair and shook her head. Amused. Irritated. Happy that Ben was there with her, but not sure she was happy to be feeling that way.

"You know she's matchmaking, right?" Ben flicked on the light, spreading a warm glow through the small living room and illuminating his tan face and sandy hair, his vivid eyes, the hard angle of his jaw and the soft curve of his lips.

"Yeah, and I cannot believe that the same woman who told

her kids to keep their noses out of other people's business is sticking hers into ours."

"She probably figured she was killing two birds with one stone. She gets us together for a few minutes and makes sure you're safe."

"You're probably right. What happened Sunday really shook her. I think she was hoping I'd be safer here than I'd been in D.C."

"You will be soon."

"I hope you're right, but to be honest, I'm not so sure. I've been researching my old case files for the past three nights and I can't find anything even remotely suspicious."

"Have you heard from Jake?"

"Yeah, he's coming up empty, too. The biggest lead he has is the PO box, but the owner has disappeared."

"How about the phone records?"

"Jake hasn't mentioned them, probably for fear of embarrassing me. No doubt there were thousands of calls, most of them from women."

"That's Adam's embarrassment, not yours."

"Is it? Because it doesn't feel that way." She moved through the house, not wanting to continue the conversation.

The living room opened into a modern kitchen, the white cupboards, tile floor and granite counters much different than the dark wood and linoleum of past years. Despite the changes, the room had the same homey feel as it had when Chloe was a girl, the taupe walls, white wainscoting, and deep blue chair rail inviting all who visited to stay awhile.

Checkers, however, wasn't as welcoming.

He stood in one corner of the room, guarding two porcelain bowls, his tubby black-and-white body stiff with irritation.

"All right, cat. We can do this the hard way, or the easy way."

"I take it you've had run-ins with him before?" Ben moved into the kitchen, his hand wrapping around her arm as he moved between her and the cat.

"Yes. At our very first meeting. The one and only time I've been here since I've been back in Lakeview."

"Bite or scratch?"

"Scratch."

"Then he doesn't completely despise you. Last time I was here, he nearly chewed through my thumb."

"Then I guess you'd better keep your distance. Your congregation won't be happy with me if you show up Sunday with a digit missing."

"Are you kidding me? I consider this a personal challenge. Do you know where Opal keeps the cat food?"

"In the cupboard under the sink."

"Okay. So, here's the plan. I'll distract him. You grab the food and pour it into the bowl."

Chloe pulled a plastic container filled with cat food out from under the cupboard and turned toward Checkers.

He hissed, his tail fluffing, his golden eyes glittering.

"Is there a plan B?"

"I'm afraid not." Ben smiled and grabbed a dish towel that hung from the refrigerator door handle. "Ready?"

"As I'll ever be."

He stepped forward, trailing the towel on the floor in front of the cat. "Come on, kitty, out of the way."

Checkers leaped past him, yowling wildly as he raced from the room.

"I thought maybe he'd play, but I guess scare tactics work just as well."

"He'll be back." Chloe poured the food and refilled the water dish. "But our mission is accomplished."

"With no casualties." Ben took the food container from her hand and returned it. "We make a good team."

They did. That was the problem. They seemed to complement each other almost too much, fitting into each other's lives with almost frightening ease, as if they'd known each other years rather than days. If the circumstances had been different, if Chloe were different, her heart would probably flutter with anticipation every time she saw him, her mind jumping forward weeks and months and imagining the relationship lasting far into the future.

Who was she kidding? Her mind already did.

"Hey." His hands framed her face, forcing her to look up and into his eyes before they smoothed back into the loose strands of her hair. "Whatever you're worrying about, don't."

"I'm not worrying." She spoke lightly and leaned away from his touch, but he didn't release his hold, his hands dropping to her shoulders, his thumbs caressing the skin over her collarbones.

"You are worrying. Maybe about the case. Maybe about us."

Us. He spoke the word with confidence. As if they weren't just a team, but a couple. "Ben—"

"But you don't need to worry, Chloe. Between you, me and Jake, we'll find the person who's after you." He paused. "As for us, we're friends. There's nothing to worry about there."

Friends? He'd claimed that twice now and she hadn't believed him either time. As much as she didn't want it, the truth was in her mind, in her heart. What was between them now might be friendship, but it was something more, too. "You keep saying we're friends, Ben, but I get the feeling you might be interested in something more."

His eyes blazed into hers. Then, as if he'd banked whatever fire was inside, they cooled. "What I'm interested in is entirely up to you. Come on, we need to finish up here. I've got a business meeting at the church in half an hour. And you need to get home and rest up for tomorrow night when we tackle the Reed kids together."

The end to the conversation was purposeful and Chloe didn't see any reason to try to continue it. What would she say? What could she say? If things were up to her, she'd...

What?

Be content with friendship?

Try for something more?

She didn't know. Couldn't know until after all the other problems in her life were solved. If they were ever solved. And right now, she wasn't sure they would be.

Chapter Twenty-Two

Friday night came much more quickly than Chloe was happy with. It wasn't that she didn't want to babysit for Tiffany and Jake's kids, it was simply that she hadn't done any babysitting in years. The closest she'd been to a child under five was at church, and even then she hadn't been hands-on, preferring to stay away from nursery duty in favor of working with teens.

The tiny infant Tiffany placed in her arms was nothing like the teenagers Chloe had worked with. As a matter of fact, he looked way too delicate for her peace of mind. She glanced at the clock over the Reeds' fireplace mantel. Six-oh-five.

Ben had better hurry up. There was no way she wanted to be left alone with two kids under the age of three.

"Did Ben say how long he'd be?" Jake's voice was gruff.

"Actually, he promised to be here before you left. I'm sure he'll be here soon." She hoped. He'd left as soon as they'd finished feeding Checkers, handing her scribbled directions to Jake's house and telling Chloe there was an emergency he had to deal with before meeting her there.

That was forty minutes ago.

Not that she was counting.

"Maybe we should stick around until he gets here." Tiffany touched her son's downy cheek, smiling a little as the baby turned toward her hand.

"We've got reservations, hon. If we're late, we might not get a table."

"Then we'll make new reservations for another night."

"Not on your birthday." He met Chloe's eyes. "Will it be a problem if we leave?"

"No, go ahead. I wouldn't want you to lose your table."

"Isaac's already been fed. Just lay him down in his bassinet and he should drop right off to sleep." Tiffany smoothed a hand over her son's dark hair, the softness in her face, the love in her eyes so obvious it almost hurt to look at.

Chloe glanced down at the baby's smooth skin and deep blue eyes. He looked like his father. The little redheaded girl standing close to Jake, a pint-size version of her mother. "Will I need to feed him again before you get back?"

"Nope. We should be home before his next feeding. Right, honey?"

"Three hours tops." Jake speared Chloe with a look that left no doubt about what he was thinking. "You have done this before haven't you?"

"I used to babysit all the time."

"Infants?"

"Yes."

"Toddlers?"

"Yes."

"Then you know how quickly a kid Honor's age can get into trouble."

"I do." She just hoped she was still up to the task of keeping them out of it.

"She needs to be watched at all times. Don't—"

"Honey." Tiffany placed a hand on Jake's arms. "You just said you didn't want to be late. Shouldn't we be going?"

"Right. We won't be far. Just at the clubhouse. If anything happens call me on my cell."

"I will."

Tiffany leaned down to kiss her daughter. "Be good for Ms. Chloe." She straightened and turned back to Chloe. "She can stay up for another half hour. Then she needs to get in bed. Though she might not be as easy to get settled as Isaac."

"I'll do my best. I'm sure everything will be fine."

"It better be." Jake grumbled the words as he leaned over to kiss his daughter, waiting until his wife opened the front door and stepped outside before he speared Chloe with a dark look. "An off-duty friend of mine is going to be here in five minutes. He'll be doing stakeout until Ben shows up. If anything happens, just flick the lights. He'll come in and help until we get back."

"That isn't—" The hard look in his eyes kept her from finishing the thought. "Okay. Great. Have fun."

"You, too." He stepped outside and shut the door, leaving Chloe with a sleepy infant, a bouncy toddler and absolutely no idea what she was going to do with either.

Ben's cell phone rang as he pulled up in front of Jake's house. Forty minutes late. He grimaced, grabbing the phone as he stepped out of the car. "Ben Avery."

"You done with that emergency, yet?" Jake's voice was gritty and soft. Obviously, he'd snuck away from his wife to make the call.

"I just pulled up in front of your house."

"Martin's still there?"

Ben glanced at the small blue pickup parked on the street in front of the house and waved at the off-duty deputy. "Yeah. He's here."

"Good. Do me a favor and tell him he's free to go home, but if he mentions a word of this to my wife, he's fired."

Ben laughed, striding toward the vehicle. "You didn't tell her?"

"And have her lecture me all night about my lack of faith in humankind? I don't think so."

"She's right. You don't have much faith in people."

"Sure I do. It just depends on the people." He paused. "I've got to get back to the table before Tiffany catches on to what I'm doing. Take care of my kids."

"You know I will."

"See you."

Ben sent Martin home and strode toward the restored Queen Ann that Jake and Tiffany lived in. Hopefully, Chloe hadn't had it too hard while he was MIA.

He knocked on the door, bracing himself for utter chaos.

"Who's there?" Chloe's voice sounded through the door, muted, but firm and calm. Maybe things inside the house weren't quite as bad as he'd expected.

"Ben."

"And I should let you in why?"

"Because you can't manage without me?"

"Try again."

"Because I realize the error of my ways and want to apologize?"

"Still not working."

"Because I've got half a dozen chocolate chip cookies in my hand?"

"That'll work." She swung the door open, stepping back to let him in. The brightly lit foyer with its colorful quilts hanging from the hall was as familiar as Ben's own home.

Chloe was familiar, too. Like an old friend he'd reconnected with rather than someone he'd only recently met. Tonight, she'd left her black hair hanging loose, the bangs falling into her eyes and hiding her expression as they so often did.

"You said you had cookies?"

"Right here." He handed her the bag that Ella had packed for him, smiling when Chloe dug in, pulling out a cookie and biting into it.

"Delicious. So good I think I'll have another." She pulled a second from the bag. "You weren't baking cookies while I was babysitting, were you?"

"I don't think that would get me too many points with you or the Reeds." He shrugged out of his jacket, dropped it onto the couch. "I had a big problem to deal with. It took a little longer than I expected."

"A little longer? You said you'd be here before Jake and Tiffany left."

"I tried, but I got held up."

"Is everything okay?"

"I'm happy to report that Mammoth is doing fine."

"Mammoth?" Chloe moved through the foyer and into the kitchen. Ben followed, noting the subtle hitch to her stride and the gingerly way she moved as she bent to pick a stuffed bear from the floor. "Should I ask?"

"He's a pig. His owner lives a few miles outside of town. She collects animals that no one else wants."

"And Mammoth is one of them?"

"Yes. And he lives up to his name. He's huge. When he gets out of his pen, he isn't always easy to corral again."

"Did you manage it?"

"Yeah, but my clothes didn't survive to tell the story. I had to go home and change. How about you? It looks like you managed to settle the troops."

"Nearly. Honor isn't quite asleep yet."

"Maybe I should go peek in on her."

"I don't think you're going to have to." Chloe cocked her head and smiled. "I think I hear the pitter-patter of little feet."

Seconds later, Honor appeared, her chubby cheeks rosy, her smile wide as she raced toward him.

He swooped down to grab her, tickling her belly as he lifted her into his arms. "Hey, little bit, aren't you supposed to be in bed?"

She giggled and wriggled in his arms as he started back toward the hall and the stairs that led to her room. "Want to come?"

Chloe shook her head, a half smile softening her face as she watched. "I think I'll let you settle her down this time."

It didn't take long to tuck Honor back in bed. Convincing her to stay there took a few more minutes. By the time Ben made it back downstairs, Chloe was seated in a chair, a cup of coffee in her hand. "Want some?"

"I think I will. And a couple of those cookies if you saved me any."

"I might have. Sit down. I'll get you the bag and some coffee." She started to rise, but Ben pressed her back down into her seat, not liking the pale cast to her skin or the dark circles beneath her eyes. "I'll get it."

He'd been hoping there'd be swift resolution to Chloe's troubles, that Jake's investigation would quickly lead to a suspect and an arrest. Unfortunately, evidence was elusive, the leads going nowhere.

He had a feeling that the answers they needed were right at their fingertips. More precisely, at Chloe's fingertips. Her investigative skills would lead them to the person they were seeking. It was just a matter of time.

"You're quiet."

Chloe's words pulled him from his thoughts and he carried his coffee and the cookies to the table, taking a seat opposite her. "Just thinking."

"About?"

"You."

Her cheeks heated, the subtle color making her eyes seem even more green, her skin even more silky. "I'm not sure that's a good idea."

"I'm not sure there's anything either of us can do about it." Whether Chloe liked it or not, they'd been brought together for a reason and Ben had every intention of seeing things through to the end. No matter what that might be. "Have you received the laptop and hard drive you were waiting for?"

"Not yet. I'm hoping they'll both be there when I get home. I'm anxious to get started. I think if there are any clues to what's going on, they'll be on one of Adam's computers."

"I was thinking the same."

"If we're right, the case could be solved in days. If we're wrong…" She fiddled with her coffee cup, her long fingers and sturdy hands more capable looking than graceful.

"What?"

"I don't know. That's the scary part. What will happen if we're wrong and I don't find something? What direction can we go except back where we were? Jackson and The Strangers or me going insane."

"The second isn't even a possibility. The first is doubtful."

"And everything else is a mystery?"

"For now, but hopefully not for much longer."

"Hopefully not." She stood and stretched, her slim figure encased in her work uniform of black slacks and a fitted pink sweater, her hair a dark waterfall that slid across her cheek as she leaned over the sink and rinsed her coffee cup.

Ben imagined her doing that in the morning, bright sunlight reflecting off her blue-black hair, her eyes still dark from sleep.

And decided it might be best to force his mind in another direction. "Were the kiddos good for you?"

"Isaac's been asleep the whole time. Honor is a little firecracker, but we had fun."

"You like kids?"

"I guess I do." She leaned against the counter. "I hadn't thought about it much before tonight."

"Too busy?"

"Too sure I'd never have them."

"Adam didn't want kids?"

"He did. I just couldn't imagine ever being a mother. Mine was lousy at it. I figured I probably would be, too."

"And now?"

"I still think I'd be lousy at it, but at least I know I like kids." She grinned and snagged the cookie bag from Ben's hand. "You've had three. The last one is mine."

"I fought a pig for those cookies."

"And I wrangled a two-year-old into bed."

"Good point. The cookie is all yours."

"Thanks. Of course, I planned on eating it anyway." She pulled the cookie from the bag. "I'd better go check on Isaac and Honor."

He caught her hand before she could walk way, feeling the delicate bones beneath her skin, the subtleness of her flesh. "Just so you know. I think you're wrong."

"About?"

"Being a mother. Personally, I think you'd make a great one."

She stared at him for just a moment, her eyes wide. Then her lips curved in a half smile. "Opal was saying the same thing to me a few days ago."

"Yeah?"

"Yeah. And I told her the same thing I'm going to tell you. Whether or not I'll be a good mother isn't an issue since I don't plan to ever get married."

"That's a shame." He stood, lifted a lock of her hair, let it slide through his fingers. "Because I think you'd make a good wife, too."

Her cheeks turned cherry red and she backed away. "I suppose I should say I'm glad you think so."

"But you're not going to?"

"Good guess. Now, I really do need to check on the kids." She hurried away and this time Ben let her go.

He probably shouldn't have mentioned Chloe having kids or getting married. Probably shouldn't have, but he didn't regret it. She was a woman who understood the value of family and relationships, and no matter how hard he tried, he couldn't imagine her living her life alone. What that meant as far as he was concerned, he didn't know.

Or maybe he did.

Maybe he just wasn't ready to accept it.

Eventually, though, he'd have to face the facts. His life had changed since he'd met Chloe, and unless he missed his guess, it was going to continue to change. God's plan was being worked out, the tide of events that had brought Chloe into his life was leading them ever closer to a conclusion that hadn't yet been made clear.

Time.

That's all they needed.

Ben could only pray they'd get it.

Chapter Twenty-Three

Ben insisted on following Chloe home and, no matter her misgiving about their relationship, Chloe was happy for his company as she hurried across the yard. The new moon steeped the night in blackness and the silence seemed filled with danger, every soft sound amplified, every shadow sinister. She tried to ignore the fear that coursed through her as she stepped into the house and up the stairs, but it was like a living thing, wrapping around her lungs and stealing her breath.

If Ben noticed her anxiety, he didn't comment, just followed her up the stairs to her apartment. A package sat next to her door, and Chloe recognized it immediately. "Adam's hard drive. I was hoping it would come today."

She started to lift it, but Ben took it from her hands. "I'll get this. You get the door. It'll be easier that way."

"Thanks." She pushed the door open and flicked on the light, Abel's happy yips greeting her. "I'm coming, little guy—"

Ben pulled her to a stop before she could cross the room.

"Why don't you wait here? I'll get the pup. He's in your room?"

"Yes. In his crate."

"Wait here." He didn't give her time to argue, and she didn't bother asking why he was walking through the small living room, pulling open the coat closet door, then stepping into the bathroom, ignoring Abel's unhappy cries.

She didn't have to ask. She knew why.

He was checking things out, making sure there wasn't anything or anyone unexpected waiting behind a closed door.

Just the thought of someone lurking behind the shower curtain or in a closet made her skin crawl. She stayed put as Ben stepped into her room and released Abel who bounded out to dance around her feet.

She lifted him and stepped across the living room and into her bedroom, watching as Ben pulled open the closet door. "I guess it's a good thing I've got a small place. It cuts down on the number of places someone can hide."

"I'm not too worried about someone hiding here, but it's always better to be sure."

He moved back out into the living room, pushed the curtains away from the balcony doors. They were still bolted shut against the darkness outside.

"It looks like everything is just as it should be."

He lifted the hard drive from the floor where it he'd set it. "Where do you want this?"

"Over next to my computer, but I'll do it once I take the packaging off."

"Tell you what. While you do that, I'll bring Abel out."

"That's not necessary, Ben."

"Actually, it is." There was a hint of a smile in his eyes, but Chloe had no doubt he that he intended to do exactly what he suggested whether she protested or not.

He pulled the house keys from her hand, grabbed the leash

that was hanging from the knob and pushed open the door. "I'll be back in a few."

The door closed, the lock slid home, Chloe shook her head.

"Infuriating, exasperating man."

Strong, dependable man.

Attractive, loyal, intelligent man.

"You are not going to spend the next fifteen minutes listing all Ben's attributes. Do something constructive instead."

She tore the packaging from the hard drive, pulled the machine from the box. She'd helped Adam choose his PC more than a year ago when he'd upgraded from an outdated slower model. They'd purposely chosen a system that was compatible with Chloe's, thinking they'd be merging their lives. Now Adam was gone, but maybe some of who he'd been was left behind, easy to find in his e-mail accounts or perhaps hidden deep in the bowels of the hard drive. Whatever was there, Chloe would find it and she prayed that when she did, the shadowy stranger who haunted her dreams would be pulled into the light, that the nightmare she was living would be over.

But even that wouldn't bring Adam back.

Tears burned her eyes, but she ignored them, forcing herself to move instead, to focus her attention on the hard drive, on connecting it to her own system, typing in the password she'd created out of random letters and numbers. She only meant to make sure everything was working, but each keystroke brought her closer to solving the mystery and she was drawn deeper and deeper into the investigation.

Adam's e-mail account had been canceled a few months after his death. It didn't matter. The computer system hadn't been cleaned and anything that had been there was still there, begging to be found. She started typing, the sound of the front door opening and closing barely registering as she began her search.

★ ★ ★

"Coffee?" Ben's voice pulled her from the trail she'd been following and Chloe struggled to make sense of his question.

"What?"

"Want a cup of coffee? I've just brewed a pot."

Groggy and fuzzy-headed, Chloe stood, wincing as stiff muscles protested. "Maybe I will have some."

"Are you making any progress?"

"I've retrieved e-mails from the months before the accident and printed them out so I can read them more carefully. Right now, I'm not seeing anything unusual."

"What would be unusual?"

"Maybe if I knew it I'd find it." She accepted the cup Ben held out for her, rubbing a hand against the crick in her neck. "Computer forensics is a lot like searching for needles in haystacks. Lots and lots of stuff you don't want to find and only one thing you're really looking for."

"You love it, though."

She took a sip of coffee and met his eyes. "I do."

"But you're not doing it anymore. Why?"

"The accident made me reassess my life. I decided to move back to a place I loved and try something new for a living." Something that didn't remind her of the past and all its horrors.

"Maybe."

"Maybe what?"

"Maybe that's what you're telling yourself, but I'm not sure it's the truth." He stared at her through hooded eyes, his expression hidden.

"Then what do you think the truth is?"

"I think you're doing penance. Denying yourself a job you love because you think Adam's death is your fault."

"I don't need to be psychoanalyzed, Ben."

"That's good, because I don't know the first thing about

doing it." He placed his coffee cup in the sink, shrugged on the jacket he must have taken off when he came back inside. "What I do know is that God has a purpose and plan for each of us. When we're living that, we find contentment and reason. When we're denying it, we can never be satisfied with what we accomplish."

"Are you saying you think I'm supposed to work with computers, not flowers?"

"I'm saying I've watched you do both and it's obvious to me which one you should be doing. I'm just not sure why it's not obvious to you. It's late. I'm going to head out." He pulled open the door and stepped out into the hall. "You know, you've got a skill not many people possess, Chloe. A tenacity and drive that allows you to search for answers relentlessly. It's a gift. One you're wasting in Opal's shop."

"It's not a gift. It's a job. One I've chosen not to do anymore."

"Too bad. There are a lot of people you could help, a lot of good you could do. Lock the door. I'll see you tomorrow at six." He strode away, and Chloe closed the door, shoving the bolt into place.

"He's wrong, Abel." She picked up the puppy, rubbed his head. "Just because I mutilated one flower arrangement doesn't mean I'm not cut out to be a florist. And just because I spent a few minutes—" she glanced at the clock "—an hour and a half in front of the computer without budging doesn't mean that's what I should spend my life doing."

Did it?

When she'd left D.C. she'd been running. From the nightmare, from her terror and memories. From her guilt. She'd thought leaving her old life behind would free her from those things. And maybe, as Ben had suggested, she'd thought denying herself the career she'd loved would serve as payment for the fact that she'd survived while Adam perished.

Penance.

It wasn't something she'd ever thought about, wasn't something she'd consciously sought to give, but maybe Ben was right. Maybe she was punishing herself, denying herself the career she'd worked so hard for, the skill she'd spent years honing because she couldn't bear the thought that her life stretched out before her while Adam's had been cut short.

Maybe.

But that wasn't the only reason she'd left her old life behind. When Ben had spoken of God's purpose and plan, the words had dug talons into her soul that closed tight and weren't letting go. Before the accident, she hadn't wondered what God thought of her career, her marriage plans, her day-to-day activities. She'd prayed, gone to church, tried to live her life with integrity. She just wasn't sure she'd lived it with purpose.

When she'd left D.C., that's what she'd been looking for. A chance to step back, take a clearer look at where she'd been, where she was going and how those things fit into God's will and plan. Slowly, it seemed she was finding the answers here in this quiet rural town with its tight-knit community and beautiful landscape. The longer she stayed in Lakeview the more she felt the truth. There was a correct path to take, a clear direction He had set for her. All she had to do was trust that it was for the best, that wherever it led, He'd be there.

And that was the hard part.

Faith. Believing in what couldn't be seen, trusting in something that could only sometimes be felt. Hoping in a future that sometimes seemed uncertain. "But I want to believe, Lord. I want to trust. I want to have faith that wherever You lead, I can go. That whatever happens, You're in control of it, working it out for the best. For my best."

A sense of peace filled her as she placed Abel on the floor and poured herself another cup of coffee. She might not know what the future would bring, she might not even know what tomorrow would bring, but she knew that it was all in God's hands. For now, that would have to be enough.

"Come on, Abel. We've got more files to discover."

A killer to uncover.

A job to do. A new life to create. One that might have more to do with computers than flowers. More to do with faith than work. More to do with trust than doubt.

More to do with God than self.

And that, Chloe thought, was going to be the biggest change of all.

Chapter Twenty-Four

She found it at just past three in the morning. A deleted e-mail that chased fatigue from her body and brought her straight up in her seat, her heart thrumming with excitement. She printed it out, scanned the content one more time. Just three lines. Innocuous out of context, but in light of what had happened, a red flag.

You'll regret what you've done. Maybe not today or tomorrow, but eventually. Once you see the error of your ways, we'll talk. J.

J.?

Chloe could think of at least five of Adam's friends who had that name. Probably more. The message had been e-mailed from a free online account and contained no clue as to who the sender was. Chloe printed out the contents of Adam's address book, searching for the e-mail address and finding it. There was no contact information and no name listed. Chloe would have to give Jake the address and see if he could have the user information released from the e-mail provider.

An hour later, she was still at the computer, but hadn't found any more e-mails from the same account. That seemed odd. Of course, everything seemed odd in the wee hours of the morning. Finally, she gave up, crawling into bed and staring up at the ceiling, praying for sleep that didn't want to come. When it did, Chloe's dreams were filled with troubling images. Not the nightmare. More a mishmash of faces and voices, identities and words that were just out of reach.

She woke more tired than when she'd gone to bed, grabbed a quick cup of coffee, then called Jake. He took down the e-mail address and promised to look into it immediately, but even that didn't seem fast enough. Like the images in her dreams, the answers they needed to find the stalker were just out of reach.

She glanced at the clock. Nine o'clock was early for anyone to be in Adam's old office, but she dialed the number anyway. James and Jordyn were both in for a few hours on Saturday. Hopefully, one of them would get back to her.

To her surprise, Jordyn answered the phone, her upbeat tone a little too bright after so few hours of sleep. "Kelly and Hill Investigations, how can I help you?"

"Jordyn, it's Chloe."

"You're calling early."

"I'm doing some research and need to get more information from you."

"Well, you're lucky you reached me. James is testifying on Monday. We're working on his testimony. Otherwise I wouldn't be in for several more hours."

"I'm glad things worked out."

"So, what do you need?"

"You've got a list of company contacts, right?"

"Yes, but that information is confidential."

"I don't need the whole list. I've got an e-mail address and I thought it might belong to one of Adam's clients. I was hoping you could check the list and see if the address matches anyone on the list."

"I don't know, Chloe. I'm not sure I'm allowed to do that. Why don't you give me the address and I'll check with James?"

"That's fine." Chloe rattled it off. "Can you please tell James this is really important?"

"I'll tell him, but I can't promise we'll be back to you with this before Monday."

"That's all right." Though it seemed like a long time to wait when she was so close to finding the information she'd been seeking.

"Good. By the way, did you get Adam's laptop, yet?"

"No, but hopefully it will come in today and I'll find some more e-mails from the address I just gave you."

"Good luck with that. Adam wasn't much for keeping old e-mails. He was always losing communications from clients and then having me call to have them resend the information. It used to drive me to distraction."

"Deleted e-mails are no problem, Jordyn. The information is still in the computer's memory, it's just hidden."

"Yes, well, you're the expert in those things. Not me. Good luck on your search and I'll get back to you once I speak to James."

Chloe hung up the phone and paced across the room. She had a lead, but nowhere to run with it. She'd have to wait until the laptop arrived, wait until Jordyn got back to her, wait until Jake was able to get the contact information from the e-mail account.

Wait.

"But I'm not so good at waiting, pup." She grabbed the

leash from the door. "Let's take a quick walk. Then maybe we should get out for a while. Run to the pet store. Get some groceries. Hopefully, when we get back I'll have some more ideas about tracing the person who's using that address."

A few hours of shopping hadn't given Chloe any clearer insight into the problem. It had filled her cupboards, though, and when the phone rang at a little past noon, she was putting together a grilled cheese sandwich and a salad.

"Hello?"

"Chloe, it's Ben."

Chloe's heart leaped at his voice. "Hi. What's up?"

"Cain. He's racing around the house like a sugar-hyped kid. I thought maybe it was time for that playdate."

"I don't know."

"You're busy?"

"Having lunch."

"Maybe I could join you."

"You're inviting yourself for lunch?"

"It's easier than waiting for an invitation."

Chloe laughed. "I'm not a fancy cook. Grilled cheese and salad."

"I'll bring dessert. See you in ten."

He made it in seven, the cool, crisp scent of autumn drifting into the apartment as he strode through the door, a brown paper bag in one hand, Cain dancing around his feet. "You look tired."

"Is that the way you greet every woman you have lunch with or am I just special?"

"You're definitely special." He smiled, but there was a hint of truth in his words and in the somber gaze he swept over her. "How long did you stay up last night?"

"Long enough to find what I was looking for." She grabbed

the printed e-mail and handed it to Ben. "Tell me what you think while I grill the sandwiches."

He read it quickly, his expression darkening. "Did you call Jake?"

"First thing this morning. He's going to try and get the e-mail provider to release the account holder's contact information."

"Which may or may not be useful."

"True, but I'm hoping I'll find a few more e-mails on Adam's laptop. Maybe contact information in his address book. That will definitely be useful."

"And that'll be here when?"

"Probably today or Monday. I'm hoping for today."

"Me, too. The sooner we get this solved, the better I'll feel." He frowned, staring down at the e-mail as if he could find the sender's identity hidden in the message. "This could be about anything business or personal."

"And it might not have anything to do with the accident or the break-in or the phone calls Adam received, but look at the date on it. That's just a couple of days after Adam and I broke up. I think that's significant."

"It's a start, anyway."

"Yeah. Hopefully of something big." Chloe placed grilled cheese sandwiches on a platter, salad in a bowl and set both on the table. "I'm ready for all this to be over."

"Have you decided what you're going to do when it is?"

"I can't think past today. When everything is settled, I'll plan for more."

Ben nodded, not asking the questions Chloe could see in his eyes. "We'd better eat and get these dogs outside. Cain needs to run off some energy."

The walk was pleasant, though Chloe was sure Ben was as

distracted as she was, conversation that had always seemed to flow so easily when she was with him, felt stilted and strange.

"Is something wrong?" She asked the question as they moved back up the stairs to her apartment. "You're quiet today."

He met her gaze, his eyes the vivid blue of the sky in spring. "I'm worried. We've got bits and pieces of the puzzle, but not enough to see the picture clearly. Whoever is after you must realize how close we're getting."

"I don't think he cares."

"Which worries me even more." He raked a hand through his hair and frowned. "Maybe you should leave town for a while."

"Where would I go? My friends are all in D.C. I haven't heard from my mother or grandmother in years."

"Anywhere where you can stay hidden until this is over. My parents. One of my foster siblings. They'd be willing to take you in."

"But I'm not willing to go. I've been running for almost a year. I won't run anymore." She meant it. Despite the fear, despite the nightmare, she couldn't keep running. Not if she ever wanted to have the life she dreamed of, the peace she longed for.

The muscle in Ben's jaw tightened, but he nodded. "I can understand that. I even respect it. But I don't like it."

"I'll be careful, Ben. I'm not planning to make myself any more vulnerable than I already am." She hesitated, then wrapped her arms around his waist, hugging him close for just a moment before she stepped away.

"What was that for?"

"For caring. There haven't been that many people in my life who have."

"I care, Chloe." He leaned forward, brushed his lips against hers. "And when you're ready, maybe we'll discuss just how much. I've got to go. We've got a prayer meeting at the church. Then I've got to run to the hospital to visit a sick friend. How about I come by and pick you up and we go to Opal's together?"

"Sure."

He smiled. "I think this is the first time I've offered to help that you haven't argued. We're making progress. I'll see you."

The apartment was silent in the wake of his departure, Chloe's heart beating just a little faster than normal. She pressed a finger against her lips, sure she could still feel his warmth there.

She'd come to Lakeview hoping to find peace and safety, but it seemed she'd found a lot more—community, friendship, contentment. Ben. Faith, first budding, then blooming, filling her heart, telling her that no matter what happened, everything would be okay.

Chapter Twenty-Five

The mail carrier knocked on her door at three, the short quick rap against the wood startling Chloe from the half-sleep she'd fallen into.

Excitement, anticipation and fear coursed through her as she tore open the box and set the laptop up on her kitchen table.

As Jordyn had said, most of Adam's e-mails had been deleted. Chloe checked the address book, found it empty, and frowned. Adam might have deleted e-mails, but would he have deleted the contents of his address book?

She didn't think so.

But someone else might have. Someone who had something to hide. James? Jordyn? Had one of them been embezzling funds? Or doing something else illegal that Adam had uncovered? If so, why sabotage Chloe's car? Why come after her?

She didn't have the answers, but Chloe hoped she'd find them. Prayed she'd find them.

First, she grabbed the phone, called Jake again, this time leaving a message on his voice mail. She knew her thoughts were rambling and unclear, her words unfocused, but her mind was already racing forward, following paths and trails through the computer files, hurrying toward the key to everything that had happened.

She searched for two hours, printing out copies of deleted e-mails, scanning through them, coming up blank time and time again.

"It's in here. I know it is." She stood and stretched, her thigh screaming in protest, her muscles cramped from too many hours spent in front of the computer, frustration thrumming through her. Whatever was imbedded in the computer was going to have to remain there for another hour or so. She had Checkers to feed, Opal's mail to check.

The thought of calling Ben and asking him to do both by himself flitted through her mind, but she pushed it aside. An hour away from the computer would do her good, clear her mind. So would talking to Ben. Maybe he could come in afterward, read through the files she'd already printed, see if anything struck him as off.

"Good excuse for inviting him over, Chloe." She mumbled the words, then lifted Abel. "Sorry, guy. You're going to have to stay home this time. But I'll take you out for a little while now to make up for it." She grabbed her purse and keys and headed outside.

Evening had come, painting the sky deep purple, the trees and grass gray. Chloe shivered from the chill and from the fear that she could never quite leave behind. She wouldn't let it beat her though, wouldn't go back inside and lock herself into the apartment, hide her head under the pillows.

But maybe she should have.

As she moved down the steps and out into the yard, Abel barked, darting toward a shadow that was separating from the trees. A woman. Above average height. Blond hair. Very familiar.

And suddenly very frightening, the wild look in her blue eyes telling Chloe all she needed to know about Adam's receptionist.

She forced down fear and panic, took a step back toward the house. "Jordyn. What are you doing here?"

"I'm sure you already know."

"You got the information from James and brought it for me?" Chloe took another step back as she spoke, moving away from the tree line and toward the house, her hand sliding toward her pocket and the pepper spray she carried there.

"Don't play stupid, Chloe. It's an insult to Adam and his taste in women." She pulled something from her pocket and pointed it at Chloe. The tiny gun looked more like a toy than a weapon. "And while you're at it, stop trying to get back to your apartment. That older couple who's always coming and going might not look so cute with bullets in their heads."

Chloe blanched at the words, but did as Jordyn commanded, stopping short, her heart hammering a frantic rhythm. One swift movement and she'd have the pepper spray in her hand, but first she needed to be close enough to use it.

The panic button!

Her hand slid over the zipper of her purse. Why had she put the keys in it when she'd locked the door?

"Drop the purse, Chloe. Now."

Die now or stay alive and hope for escape?

There was no choice, and Chloe dropped the purse.

Jordyn smiled, the cold wildness in her eyes making Chloe shiver. "That's better. Now, keep your hand out of your pocket. I'm sure you're still carrying around pepper spray. You would have been smart to get something a little more deadly." She waved the gun. "It's too late now, though, isn't it?"

"What's going on, Jordyn?"

"What do you think is going on? I've come for a visit to see how you're holding up. Losing Adam must have been so devastating for you. Of course, since he was never really yours, I guess you can't complain."

"What do you want?"

"Revenge."

"For what?"

"For what you did to Adam, of course. What he and I had was special. You ruined it. Then you killed him."

"I didn't kill him."

"Of course you did." She spit the words out, moving a step closer.

Come on. Keep coming.

Just a few steps closer and Chloe would take a chance and go for the pepper spray.

"If you hadn't brought that information to the FBI, Adam would still be alive."

"Then it wasn't you who sabotaged my car?" Keep her talking. Keep her moving forward.

"Maybe you really are stupid. Matthew Jackson wanted you dead. It would have made me very happy for you to end up that way. But I didn't do anything to your car. I have more subtle ways of getting rid of people who stand in my way." She smiled, her teeth flashing white in the fading light. "Take the pepper spray out of your pocket. Throw it into the trees."

Chloe hesitated.

"Now, Chloe, or those sweet old people will be vulture food."

Chloe did as she was told, her muscles tight and ready for action. If only she knew what action to take.

"By the way, I wanted to tell you when we chatted just how much I love your place. Very cute. Very quaint. Very you. Now, come on. We have to go before the newest man in your life shows up and makes me go to more effort than I already have."

"Go where?"

"To finish what I started in D.C. I thought dissolving those pills in that bit of orange juice you had in your fridge would take care of things, but you managed to survive. Too bad. Overdosing wouldn't have been such a bad way to die."

"Look, Jordyn—"

"You look, Chloe. I played second fiddle to you for years, knowing that eventually Adam would come back to me. He did. Just as he was supposed to. Then you ruined everything. I'm sure guilt is eating you alive. It's time to put an end to your misery. And mine."

"Whatever you're planning won't work. I already told the police that I thought you or James might be responsible for everything that's been happening."

"But you're crazy, Chloe. Everyone in D.C. knows it. Since Adam's death, it's obvious the trauma was too much for you to deal with. All those night terrors in the hospital, your insistence that someone was after you. It was only a matter of time before you cracked."

"Things are different here."

"Are they? You think that because you've got some good-looking pastor hanging around and a sheriff who seems to be taking you seriously that no one will believe it when your suicide note is found? I've got news for you, Chloe, people believe whatever is easiest. Get in the car."

"There'll be an investigation, Jordyn, and you'll be one of the top suspects."

"I doubt it, but even if I am, they won't be able to prove anything. They'll have your suicide note, but no body. No evidence to link the two of us together. Nothing that a prosecutor would be willing to bring to trial, anyway. Do you know how many killers are free because there's simply no evidence to link them to the crime? Now get in the car. We've got places to go."

No way. Gun or no gun, Chloe wasn't getting in the car, she pivoted, the sharp movement sending pain shooting up her thigh. Her leg collapsed out from under her and she stumbled, tried to right herself. Something slammed into her head, stars burst in front of her eyes and she was falling into darkness and into the nightmare.

Chloe wasn't answering the door and she hadn't answered her phone. It was possible she was in the apartment, caught up in the investigation and oblivious to the world. Ben had seen her in action, watched her fingers fly across the keyboard. Doing so had been a surprise and revelation, had told him a lot more than Chloe's words just how much she needed to be back at her work.

Maybe she was working now, bent over the computer, intent, focused. Maybe. But he didn't think so. What he thought was that Chloe was gone. The fact that her car was still parked in the driveway could only mean one thing—trouble.

He dialed Jake's number as he strode back outside, praying that he was wrong, knowing that he was right and hoping that he and Jake would be able to find Chloe in time.

Chloe woke to icy terror and throbbing pain, water filling her nose and throat. The urge to gasp for breath, to suck in liquid in hopes of finding air nearly overwhelmed her. Darkness beneath, darkness above, something tied to her legs and pulling her down. She fought against it, pushing upward, out of the water, gasping for air, sucking in huge heaving breaths, the sickening pain in her head worsening with the movement.

She blinked, trying to clear her vision, caught a glimpse of wood, an oar. Saw Jordyn staring down at her, watching through glassy eyes.

"You just won't die will you?" She lifted the oar, swinging hard.

Chloe ducked back under the water, the weight on her legs dragging her down farther than she expected. She tried to keep her buoyancy, but sank deep, the darkness of the water profound, her lungs screaming in protest.

More fighting, more struggling, until finally she broke the surface of the water again. The boat was farther away now, the quiet slap of the oar hitting the water the only sound Chloe could hear. It was near dark, the hazy purple of dusk deepening to blue-black, the crisp day turning frigid with night. Chloe shivered, sank back under the water again, choking. Gasping. Sliding into darkness. She flailed, the cold and the weight on her legs sapping her energy, stealing her strength. She struggled back up again, tried to swim toward shore and sank again.

If you want to live, you'd better stop panicking and think, Chloe.

The thought pierced through her terror. Think or die. It was as simple as that.

She let herself sink into the water, reaching down to feel whatever it was that was dragging her down. Thick rope wrapped her ankles together, pulled taut by something. What? A weight? An anchor? She pulled hard on the rope, yanking the object up until she was holding what felt like a cinder block. Then she pushed to the surface again, just managing to suck in a breath of air before she sank beneath the water again. Her vision swam, her stomach heaved and she almost lost her grip on the weight and on consciousness. She bit the inside of her cheek, the pain clearing her head as she struggled back out of the water again.

Where was the shore? Where was safety?

In the dim light the shore looked too far away, the house in the distance tiny and insubstantial. To the left, the lake stretched as far as Chloe could see. To the right, trees shot up at the shoreline, distant and unreachable. Still, if her legs were free, she could swim to safety easily enough.

If.

Jake hopped out of his car and strode toward Ben, his stride long and stiff, his face grim. "Any sign of her?"

"No, but I found her puppy hiding under her car."

"Not good." The sympathy and worry in Jake's gaze was obvious. "When was the last time you spoke to her?"

"Around noon." Ben ran a hand over his jaw, forcing himself to think clearly, to stay focused. "I've already walked the perimeter of the house twice. The earth's too dry to hold prints."

"Did you talk to her neighbors?"

"I tried. They weren't home." Ben surveyed the area, urgency pounding through him, demanding action. "Something's happened to her."

"I've called in all my off-duty officers. We'll work a grid from here to the lake and the road. If she's here, we'll find her."

"And if she's not?"

"We'll contact media, get her picture out there. Pray that somebody's seen her."

"I've been doing that. Now I want to act."

"Understood, but we go traipsing around without a plan and we'll waste time, maybe destroy evidence." Jake's phone rang and he answered, his jaw tight, his words terse. "Reed, here. Yeah. I'll check it out. Thanks."

"What's up?"

"Guy a half a mile from here was walking his dog and found a boat washed up in the reeds near his house. He said there's some stuff inside of it. A purse. Flowers. It seemed strange so he called it in."

"Let's go."

"Maybe I should take this one myself."

"Maybe not. Let's go." Ben strode toward the cruiser, fear a hard knot in his chest. Chloe was somewhere nearby. He felt that as surely as he felt that she was in danger. They had to find her. Soon.

They took the cruiser, racing the half mile to a long tree-lined driveway and a two-story home that looked out over the lake. The man who met them seemed shaken as he led them down to the water. There was no dock, just thick weed-choked grass and slick rocks. A boat bobbed in the water, white lilies on its water-logged bottom, a purse lying on its side the contents spilling out.

"When did you first notice this?" Jake spoke as he moved toward the boat.

"Just a few minutes ago. I saw it when I let the dog out. It wasn't here when I got home an hour ago."

"And did you see anyone out here? Hear anything?"

"Nothing. It's just been a regular day." The man ran a hand over sparse hair. "I might not have thought that much about the boat, but the flowers and purse worried me."

"They worry me, too. I'm glad you called." Jake pulled on gloves, grabbed the bow of the boat and dragged it up over the rocks and onto shore. "There's a paper here. Looks like a note." He picked it up, holding it gingerly, his face hardening as he read. "We've got a problem."

"We already had one."

"It's just gotten worse." He gestured Ben over, holding the

note out for him to see. The words were smudged but easy to read.

"A suicide note."

"Chloe's suicide note."

"Written by someone else." Ben shoved the boat back toward the water.

"We need to get other transportation. That boat could contain evidence."

"We don't have time to find another boat." Ben gritted his teeth and stared his friend down. He was going out on the lake, with or without Jake. With or without his approval.

Finally, Jake nodded. "Let's go."

A few minutes of swimming with the cinder block in her arm convinced Chloe that she'd be better off expending her energy in another way. First she tried feeling for the ends of the rope, hoping she might be able to untie it, but each time she stopped paddling with her free arm, she dipped under the water.

"That's not going to work, Chloe. Come up with something else." She spoke out loud, the words sputtering and gasping into air and water, her teeth chattering. "Lord, if there's some way out of this, I hope you'll show me quickly because I don't know how much longer I can do this."

But there didn't seem to be a way out, just one painful stroke after another toward a way-too-distant shore. Chloe's head throbbed with each movement, her body telling her to quit while her mind screamed for her to keep going. She slipped under the water, choking and gagging as she surfaced again, the rope wrapping around her wrist and sliding over her skin.

Sliding over her skin.

The thought worked its way past her pain and fatigue, and

she reached down, tried to shove the rope past her jeans. It moved. Not much, but enough to give her hope. One handed wasn't going to work though. She'd have to let go of the cinder block. Use both hands to shove the rope down. Once she did that, she'd be pulled back down toward the bottom of the lake. If she failed, she didn't know if she'd be able to fight her way back up again.

Unfortunately, her choices were limited and so was her time.

"Lord, I trust you. Whatever happens, I know you're with me." With that, she let go of the cement block, grabbed the rope that was wrapped around her legs and started to push it down as she sank deeper into the water. The rope pulled tight, so tight she couldn't get her fingers between it and her legs. Panic speared through her, but she forced it back, trying again, feeling fingernails bend and skin tear as she finally made room between rope and denim. Pull. Tug. Push. Yank. Muscles quivering. Head pounding. Fear like she'd only ever known once before. The nightmare, but different. Not fire and hot metal. Water and burning lungs. Blackness outside and inside. Alone.

But not alone.

God had not abandoned her. Would not abandon her.

The rope moved, inching down toward her ankles, scraping past her jeans. She yanked the fabric up with one hand, shoving the rope down, feeling it give. Then she was free, floating up toward the surface, her lungs ready to explode, the desperate need for oxygen making her want to gasp and breathe and hope for the best.

She broke the surface of the lake, coughing and gasping, her body trembling with fatigue and with cold. She had to swim, but her movements were clumsy, her efforts weak.

She wasn't going to give up, though. She wasn't going to

quit. She was going to get out of the lake and she was going to make sure Jordyn was arrested for her crimes.

Her energy and attention were focused on the goal—a distant light that she was sure must be home. What she wasn't sure about was whether or not she was actually getting any closer to it.

Suddenly the light disappeared, a dark shape appearing in front of Chloe. For a moment, her muddled thoughts conjured a monster rising up from the depth of the lake. Then the truth of what she was seeing registered—a boat.

Jordyn. She was sure it was the same boat. Sure that Jordyn would lean over the edge, raise the oar, slam it down into the water. Or worse. Take out the gun and shoot her.

She turned, trying to swim away, her arms flailing, her muscles giving out. She sank. Surfaced. Sank again.

"Chloe!" The shout carried over the splash and gasp of her frantic attempt to escape.

An arm hooked around her waist and she was pulled back against a hard chest. "Stop struggling, Chloe. I've got you."

Ben.

His voice rumbled in her ear, his body warming her, but doing nothing to ease the shivers that racked her body.

"Are you okay?"

She nodded, but her teeth were chattering too hard to get the words out.

"Here she comes, Jake."

Before Chloe knew what was happening, she was out of Ben's arms and in a boat, a leather jacket draped around her shoulders, Jake Reed flashing a light in her face. "You hurt anywhere?"

"My head." The words rasped out as Ben pulled himself into the boat. "Jordyn hit me with something. Maybe her gun."

"Jordyn Winslow? That's one of the names you gave me earlier."

"Yes, Adam's receptionist." She was still shivering, her muscles so tight with cold she wasn't sure she'd ever be warm again.

Ben pulled her toward him, rubbed her arms briskly, the heat he generated speeding through her body. "Better?"

"Yes." But not because she was warmer. Because he was there, warm, solid, steady.

He ran a hand over the back of her head, probing the tender flesh there. "You're bleeding. Can you call for an ambulance, Jake?"

"There's no—"

"There's no sense arguing. You're going to the hospital."

"I'm not much for hospitals. My experiences there haven't been pleasant."

"Maybe not in the past, but this time will be different. This time I'll be with you." Ben's words were a warm caress against her ear and Chloe relaxed back into his arms, allowing herself to believe what she hadn't in a very long time—that she was safe and that everything was going to be all right.

Chapter Twenty-Six

"Fifteen stitches does not make me an invalid, Opal." Chloe smiled as she spoke, accepting the bowl of chicken noodle soup Opal handed her.

"Fifteen stitches and a concussion. The doctor said you should take it easy."

"And I have been."

"How does starting back up in computer forensics constitute resting?"

"I haven't done any work. I've just been contacting old clients and letting them know I will be."

"Yes, well, I still have to decide if I forgive you for that. You were doing so well at Blooming Baskets."

Chloe would have laughed if she wasn't sure it would send pain shooting through her head. "Opal, I have as much artistic vision as a rock and you know it."

"Okay, so flowers weren't the perfect fit for you."

"But computers are."

"Apparently so. And you know that I'm happy if you are. If

computers are what you're meant to do, far be it from me to try to keep you from them." Opal leaned forward and kissed her cheek. "Now, I've really got to get home. Checkers is still angry about not being fed on time Saturday night."

"Maybe if you explained that I was fighting for my life and kind of distracted, he'll forgive me."

"Doubtful. Call me if you need something."

"I will." Chloe started to rise, but froze when Opal sent a searing look in her direction.

"Do not get up from there. At all."

Before Chloe could respond, a soft knock sounded on the door. "Good. Now I really can leave." Opal hurried to the door and pulled it open. "You're late."

"Two minutes. And I had good reason." Ben stepped into the room, a white paper bag in his hand. "Apple pie and ice cream from Becky's."

"I suppose that's acceptable. I'll be back in an hour or so. Thanks for taking over for me."

"Opal, please tell me you didn't ask Ben to come baby-sit me."

"I did not ask him to babysit you. I asked him to lend a hand. I'll see you in a bit." She walked out the door before Chloe could tell her exactly what she thought of her meddling ways.

"Feeling better?" Ben sat on the couch beside her, his gaze taking in everything about her appearance.

Unfortunately, that included scraggly hair, pale skin, swollen hands and, of course, plenty of stitches.

"Now that Jordyn is in custody, I feel better than I have in almost a year. I still can't believe she went home and was acting like nothing happened. I was sure she'd take off and go into hiding."

"From what Jake says, she'd convinced herself that no one

would suspect her. In her mind, she'd committed the perfect crime."

"Except I didn't die."

"Thank the Lord for that." Ben ran a hand over his jaw, his eyes shadowed. "I was sure we'd lost you when I saw that suicide note."

"I guess I'm tougher than you think."

"I've always thought you were tough. I was just afraid whoever had you was tougher."

"Jordyn did pack a pretty mean punch." Chloe fingered the bandage at the back of her head. "She really was crazy, Ben. I found e-mails in Adam's laptop—"

"What were you doing working when you're supposed to be resting?"

"I just took a quick peek."

"How long of a quick peek?"

"A couple of hours."

"That's what I thought." Ben chuckled, his hand resting on her shoulder, his finger warm against her neck. "So, what did you find?"

"That Jordyn thought she and Adam were going to be together forever. She's been in love with him for years."

"Was she the other woman?"

"I think so. From what I gathered, they went out a few times years ago. Then seemed to reconnect for a while, during the months before Adam died. She proclaimed her love for him over and over again in her e-mails."

"And scared him away?"

"Knowing Adam, yes." She shrugged. "The most recent e-mails, the ones she sent right before he died, were mostly hateful rantings. She threatened me a few times. Told him that if he got back together with me, we'd both be sorry."

"Did you show Jake?"

"Yeah, he's already come by for the e-mails and taken the laptop in as evidence. He mentioned something that surprised me."

"What's that?"

"He thinks there might be a connection between Jordyn and Matthew Jackson. I was freelancing for James when I worked on The Strangers case. There's a good possibility Jordyn somehow made contact with one of the group's members, maybe hoping she'd find someone who wanted to get me out of the way. There's no proof that's what happened, but it makes sense."

"If he's right that might have been enough to send her over the edge. If she thought she'd get rid of you, but it backfired and Adam was killed—"

"She would have gone a little crazy. Guilt can be a terrible thing."

"I'm not sure she was capable of guilt, but she did corner the market on hate."

"I wish…" Chloe's voice trailed off and she shook her head, not sure what she wished, what she wanted.

"That you could have known?"

"Yes, but even that wouldn't have saved Adam."

Ben pulled her into his arms, his hands smoothing down her back and resting at her waist. "No, it wouldn't have, but you can't spend your life thinking about that, Chloe."

"I know." She blinked hard, trying to force back tears. They refused to be stopped and slid down her cheeks, dripping onto Ben's shirt.

He brushed away the moisture, his palm warm against her skin. "Are you crying for Adam?"

"He never even had a chance."

"But you do. A chance at life. At friendship. At love. Adam wouldn't want you to pass that up."

At love?

Chloe looked up into his eyes, felt herself pulled in again. Into his confidence. His strength. Into all the things she'd wanted for so long, but was sure she'd never have.

"You're right. He wouldn't. And I don't want to pass those things up, either."

His lips curved, the slow, easy smile tugging at Chloe's heart. "That makes two of us."

He leaned forward, kissing her with passion and with promise, chasing the nightmare away and replacing it with a dream of the future spent with a man who shared her faith, her goals, her heart. A man put into her life by God. A gift that Chloe would always be thankful for.

Epilogue

The dark night pressed in around her, the sound of laughter and music a backdrop to the wild beating of her heart. Chloe shoved a box of floral decorations out of the way and reached for her suitcase and the small bag of clothes sitting beside it, the heady aroma of hyacinth drifting on the air and filling her with longing and with joy. This was it, then. A new beginning. A new dream. A new life.

She was ready for it.

"Need a hand?" The words were warm and filled with humor, the dark figure that stepped from the shadows stealing her breath.

"Maybe more than one. I thought I'd put the suitcase into your car, but Tiffany and Opal helped me pack and I'm not sure I can handle it while I'm wearing heels."

"Then let me handle it for you." Ben's arms slipped around her waist, pulling her backward. She turned, staring up into his face, wanting to memorize this moment, the way she felt standing in his arms.

He smiled, caressing her shoulder, his fingers gliding over her skin, trailing heat with every touch. "Have I told you how beautiful you look today?"

"A hundred times."

"Then this will be a hundred and one. You're beautiful, Chloe. So beautiful you take my breath away." He trailed kisses up her neck, his hand cupping the back of her head, his body warm against hers.

"I was just thinking the same about you."

"That I'm beautiful?" His laughter rumbled near her ear.

"That you take my breath away." Chloe sank into his embrace, her love for Ben strong and sure and undeniable. "And that if we keep this up we may not make our flight."

"I'm not sure that would be such a bad thing."

"Me, neither." She tilted her head as his lips caressed the sensitive flesh beneath her jaw.

"So maybe we should go to my place and forget the airport." His eyes gleamed in the moonlight, dark and filled with promise.

"There you are." Opal bustled across the parking lot, salt and pepper curls bouncing with each step. "I thought you were changing into your traveling suit and coming right back to the reception."

"I got sidetracked."

"So I see, but if you two plan on making that flight to Thailand, you'd better get moving."

Ben met Chloe's gaze, the joy, the hope that she felt reflected in his eyes. "I'll get the suitcase into the car."

"I'll get changed."

"And I'll have everybody ready and waiting to say goodbye and throw rose petals. Five minutes. And don't make me come looking for you again."

Chloe smiled, following Opal back into the church and

closing herself into Ben's office, her husband's office. She'd lived through so much heartache, so many tears, but those were in the past. Today was for new beginnings, fresh starts. Laughter. Joy. Peace.

A soft knock sounded at the door, and Chloe opened it, her heart skipping a beat as she caught sight of Ben. He'd changed into jeans and a polo shirt, his sandy hair falling over his forehead, his eyes gleaming brilliant blue. "Ready?"

"Absolutely."

"Then let's get started on the rest of our lives." He wrapped an arm around her waist, led her into the reception hall. His foster parents were there, standing beside the door with a dozen or more of his foster siblings. His sister Raven and her husband, Shane, were there, too. Opal. Sam. Tiffany and Jake. Hawke and Miranda.

So many people, so much happiness.

Chloe's heart welled with it, her eyes filling as white rose petals fell like gentle spring rain, washing over her, washing through her as Ben swept her into his arms and carried her into the future.

★ ★ ★ ★ ★

IF YOU ENJOYED THIS BOOK
WE THINK YOU WILL ALSO LOVE

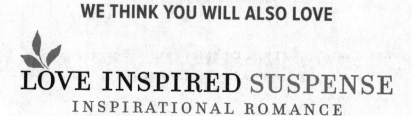

LOVE INSPIRED SUSPENSE
INSPIRATIONAL ROMANCE

Courage. Danger. Faith.

Find strength and determination in stories
of faith and love in the face of danger.

6 NEW BOOKS AVAILABLE EVERY MONTH!

Determined to find her father's true killer when she's finally exonerated and freed after seventeen years in prison, Kinsley Garrett puts herself right into a murderer's crosshairs. But with help from her neighbor police chief Marcus Bayne, can she survive long enough to expose the truth?

Read on for a sneak preview of
Evidence of Innocence *by Shirlee McCoy,*
available May 2021 from Love Inspired Suspense.

Marcus followed Kinsley, stopping short when he heard fabric rustling. He glanced around, looking for signs that they weren't alone. Kinsley's yard was well kept. A couple of fruit trees. A small garden plot. Shrubs to the left that separated her property from the neighbor's.

Was that where the sound had come from?

"What's wrong?" she asked, heading back in his direction.

He heard the soft click of a gun safety being removed and knew what was about to happen.

He shouted for Kinsley to get down and threw himself in her direction as the first shot exploded. He landed on top of her, covering her body with his as a bullet slammed into the ground nearby.

He pulled his firearm, aiming toward the shrubs. "Police! Put your weapon down!"

There was a flurry of movement and then silence.

"Chief! Is everything okay?" Charlotte Daniels ran around the side of the house, firearm drawn. "I was running patrol past the house and saw the fire, and then I heard gunfire."

"Someone shot at Kinsley. Stay here. I'm going to find out who it was."

He didn't wait for her response.

The perp already had a head start. Marcus was going to make certain he didn't get more of one. Kinsley had been attacked twice in one night. Her house had been set on fire while she was in it.

Was Randy Warren trying to silence her?

Marcus needed to find him.

He needed to stop him.

And he needed to make certain Randy wouldn't have a chance to come after Kinsley again.

Don't miss
Evidence of Innocence *by Shirlee McCoy*
available May 2021 wherever
Love Inspired Suspense books and ebooks are sold.

LoveInspired.com

LOVE INSPIRED
INSPIRATIONAL ROMANCE

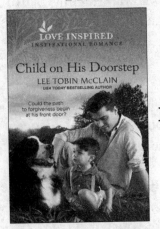

Save $1.00
on the purchase of ANY Love Inspired or Love Inspired Suspense book.

Available wherever books are sold, including most bookstores, supermarkets, drugstores and discount stores.

Save $1.00

on the purchase of any Love Inspired or Love Inspired Suspense book.

Coupon valid until August 31, 2021.
Redeemable at participating outlets in the U.S. and Canada only.
Limit one coupon per customer.

52616916

5 65373 00076 2 (8100)0 12478

LICOUP0820TRADE